*To Jake,*
*The bravest boy I know.*
*Love, Mom*

# JODI
# PICOULT

*Perfect Match*

HODDER

First published in Great Britain in 2005 by Hodder and Stoughton
An Hachette UK company
First published in America in 2002 by Atria
A division of Simon & Schuster, Inc.

This paperback edition published in 2013

4

A CIP catalogue record for this title is available from the British Library

ISBN 978 1 444 75458 2

Typeset in Berkeley Book by Palimpsest Book Production Limited,
Falkirk, Stirlingshire

Printed and bound by
CPI Group (UK) Ltd, Croydon CR0 4YY

Hodder and Stoughton policy is to use papers that are natural, renewable and
recyclable products and made from wood grown in sustainable forests.
The logging and manufacturing processes are expected to conform to
the environmental regulations of the country of origin.

Hodder and Stoughton Ltd
A division of Hodder Headline PLC
338 Euston Road
London NW1 3BH

www.hodder.co.uk

# ACKNOWLEDGMENTS

I'm often asked how much of my books come from my own life, and given the nature of the issues I cover the answer is, thankfully, not much. *Perfect Match* was particularly difficult, however, because I would sit at the breakfast table with my children and take away their conversations to put into the mouth of young Nathaniel Frost. So I'd like to thank Kyle, Jake, and Samantha – not only for their jokes and their stories, but because they gave me the soul of my main character, a mother who would do anything for someone she loves. Thanks to my psychiatric research staff, Burl Daviss, Doug Fagen, Tia Horner, and Jan Scheiner; to my medical experts, David Toub and Elizabeth Bengtson; to Kathy Hemenway for an insight into social work; to Katie Desmond for all things Catholic; to Diana Watson for sharing kindergarten war stories; to Chris Keating and George Waldron for early legal information; to Syndy Morris for transcribing so fast; and to Olivia and Matt Licciardi, for the Holy Goats and the oxygen query. Also, thanks to Elizabeth Martin and her brother, who found my ending; and to Laura Gross, Jane Picoult, Steve Ives, and JoAnn Mapson for reading the early draft and loving it enough to help me make it better. Judith Curr and Karen Mender make me feel like a supernova among a constellation of Atria authors. Having Emily Bestler and Sarah Branham as my angels in the editorial department at Atria makes me the luckiest author alive; and Camille McDuffie and Laura Mullen – my fairy godmothers of publicity – deserve wands and crowns so everyone will know how much magic they can weave. I need to thank my husband, Tim van Leer, who is not only a ready source of information about guns, stars, and stonework but who also spoils me with coffee and salads and smooths the world so that I am free to do what I love to do. And finally, I'd like to thank three people who have become such strong research contributors that it's hard to imagine writing anything without their input: Detective-Lieutenant Frank Moran, who made me think like a detective; Lisa Schiermeier, who not only taught me DNA but also mentioned, in passing, the wonderful medical twist that made my head start humming; and Jennifer Sternick, the district attorney who talked into a tape recorder for four straight days, and without whom *Perfect Match* would simply not have been possible.

# Prologue

When the monster finally came through the door, he was wearing a mask.

She stared and stared at him, amazed that no one else could see through the disguise. He was the neighbor next door, watering his forsythia. He was the stranger who smiled across an elevator. He was the kind man who took a toddler's hand to help him cross the street. *Can't you see?* she wanted to scream. *Don't you know?*

Beneath her, the chair was unforgiving. Her hands were folded as neatly as a schoolgirl's, her shoulders were squared; but her heart was all out of rhythm, a jellyfish writhing in her chest. When had breathing become something she had to consciously remember to do?

Bailiffs flanked him, guiding him past the prosecutor's table, in front of the judge, toward the spot where the defense attorney was sitting. From the corner came the sibilant hum of a TV camera. It was a familiar scene, but she realized she had never seen it from this angle. *Change your point of view, and the perspective is completely different.*

The truth sat in her lap, heavy as a child. She was going to do this.

That knowledge, which should have stopped her short, instead coursed through her limbs like brandy. For the first time in weeks, she didn't feel as if she were sleepwalking on the ocean floor, her lungs fiery, holding on to the breath she'd taken before she went under – a breath that would have been bigger, more deliberate, had she known what was coming. In this horrible place, watching this horrible man, she suddenly felt normal again. And with this feeling came the most wonderfully normal thoughts: that she hadn't wiped down the kitchen table after breakfast; that the library book which had gone missing was behind the dirty clothes hamper; that her car was fifteen hundred miles overdue to have the oil changed. That in the next two seconds, the bailiffs escorting him would step back to give him privacy to speak to his attorney.

In her purse, her fingers slipped over the smooth leather cover of her checkbook, her sunglasses, a lipstick, the furry nut of a Life Saver, lost from its package. She found what she was looking for and grabbed it, surprised to see that it fit with the same familiar comfort as her husband's hand.

One step, two, three, that was all it took to come close enough to the monster to smell his fear, to see the black edge of his coat against the white collar of his shirt. Black and white, that was what it came down to.

For a second she wondered why no one had stopped her. Why no one had realized that this moment was inevitable; that she was going to come in here and do just this. Even now, the people who knew her the best hadn't grabbed for her as she rose from her seat.

That was when she realized she was wearing a disguise, just like the monster. It was so clever, so *authentic;* nobody really knew what she had turned into. But now she could feel it cracking into pieces. *Let the whole world see,* she thought, as the mask fell away. And she knew as she pressed the gun to the defendant's head, she knew as she shot him four times in quick succession, that at this moment she would not have recognized herself.

# I

When we are struck at without a reason, we should strike back again very hard; I am sure we should – so hard as to teach the person who struck us never to do it again.

– Charlotte Brontë, *Jane Eyre*

*We're in the woods, just the two of us. I have on my best sneakers, the ones with rainbow laces and the place on the back that Mason chewed through when he was just a puppy. Her steps are bigger than mine, but it's a game – I try to jump into the hole her shoes leave behind. I'm a frog; I'm a kangaroo; I'm magic.*

*When I walk, it sounds like cereal getting poured for breakfast. Crunch. 'My legs hurt,' I tell her.*

*'It's just a little bit longer.'*

*'I don't want to walk,' I say, and I sit right there, because if I don't move she won't either.*

*She leans down and points, but the trees are like the legs of tall people I can't see around. 'Do you see it yet?' she asks me.*

*I shake my head. Even if I could see it, I would have told her I couldn't.*

*She picks me up and puts me on her shoulders. 'The pond,' she says. 'Can you see the pond?'*

*From up here, I can. It is a piece of sky, lying on the ground. When Heaven breaks, who fixes it?*

# I

I have always been best at closings.

Without any significant forethought, I can walk into a courtroom, face a jury, and deliver a speech that leaves them burning for justice. Loose ends drive me crazy; I have to tidy things up to the point where I can put them behind me and move on to the next case. My boss tells anyone who'll listen that he prefers to hire prosecutors who were waiters and waitresses in former lives – that is, used to juggling a load. But I worked in the gift-wrapping department of Filene's to put myself through law school, and it shows.

This morning, I've got a closing on a rape trial and a competency hearing. In the afternoon, I have to meet with a DNA scientist about a bloodstain inside a wrecked car, which revealed brain matter belonging to neither the drunk driver accused of negligent homicide nor the female passenger who was killed. All of this is running through my mind when Caleb sticks his head into the bathroom. The reflection of his face rises like a moon in the mirror. 'How's Nathaniel?'

I turn off the water and wrap a towel around myself. 'Sleeping,' I say.

Caleb's been out in his shed, loading his truck. He does stonework – brick paths, fireplaces, granite steps, stone walls. He smells of winter, a scent that comes to Maine at the same time local apples come to harvest. His flannel shirt is streaked with the dust that coats bags of concrete. 'How is his fever?' Caleb asks, washing his hands in the sink.

'He's fine,' I answer, although I haven't checked on my son; haven't even seen him yet this morning.

I am hoping that if I wish hard enough, this will be true. Nathaniel wasn't really that sick last night, and he wasn't running a temperature above 99 degrees. He didn't seem himself, but that alone wouldn't keep me from sending him to school – especially on a day when I'm due in court. Every working mother has been caught between this Scylla and Charybdis. I can't give a hundred percent at home because of my work; I can't give a hundred percent at work because of my home; and I live in fear of the moments, like these, when the two collide.

'I'd stay home, but I can't miss this meeting. Fred's got the clients coming to review the plans, and we're all supposed to put in a good showing.' Caleb looks at his watch and groans. 'In fact, I was late ten minutes ago.' His day starts early and ends early, like most subcontractors. It means that I bear the brunt of getting Nathaniel to school, while Caleb is in charge of the pickup. He moves around me, gathering his wallet and his baseball cap. 'You won't send him to school if he's sick . . .'

'Of course not,' I say, but heat creeps beneath the neck of my blouse. Two Tylenol will buy me time; I could be finished with the rape case before getting a call from Miss Lydia to come get my son. I think this, and in the next second, hate myself for it.

'Nina.' Caleb puts his big hands on my shoulders. I fell in love with Caleb because of those hands, which can touch me as if I am a soap bubble certain to burst, yet are powerful enough to hold me together when I am in danger of falling to pieces.

I slide my own hands up to cover Caleb's. 'He'll be fine,' I insist, the power of positive thinking. I give him my prosecutor's smile, crafted to convince. 'We'll be fine.'

Caleb takes a while to let himself believe this. He is a smart man, but he's methodical and careful. He will finish one project with exquisite finesse before moving on to the next, and he makes decisions the same way. I've spent seven years hoping that lying next to him each night will cause some of his deliberation to rub off, as if a lifetime together might soften both our extremes.

'I'll get Nathaniel at four-thirty,' Caleb says, a line that, in the language of parenting, means what *I love you* once did.

I feel his lips brush the top of my head as I work the clasp on the back of my skirt. 'I'll be home by six.' *I love you, too.*

He walks toward the door, and when I look up I am struck by pieces of him – the breadth of his shoulders, the tilt of his grin, the way his toes turn in in his big construction boots. Caleb sees me watching. 'Nina,' he says, and that smile, it tips even more. 'You're late too.'

The clock on the nightstand says 7:41. I have nineteen minutes to rouse and feed my son, stuff him into his clothes and his car seat, and make the drive across Biddeford to his school with enough time to get myself to the superior court in Alfred by 9:00.

My son sleeps hard, a cyclone in his sheets. His blond hair is too long; he needed a haircut a week ago. I sit on the edge of the bed. What's two seconds more, when you get to watch a miracle?

I wasn't supposed to get pregnant five years ago. I wasn't supposed to get pregnant, ever, thanks to a butcher of an OB who removed an ovarian cyst when I was twenty-two. When I had been weak and vomiting for weeks, I went to see an internist, certain I was dying from some dread parasite, or that my body was rejecting its own organs. But the blood test said there was nothing wrong. Instead, there was something so impossibly right that for months afterward, I kept the lab results taped to the inside of the medicine cabinet of the bathroom: the burden of proof.

Nathaniel looks younger when he's asleep, with one hand curled under his cheek and the other wrapped tight around a stuffed frog. There are nights I watch him, marveling at the fact that five years ago I did not know this person who has since transformed me. Five years ago I would not have been able to tell you that the whites of a child's eyes are clearer than fresh snow; that a little boy's neck is the sweetest curve on his body. I would never have considered knotting a dish towel into a pirate's bandanna and stalking the dog for his buried treasure, or experimenting on a rainy Sunday to see how many seconds it takes to explode a marshmallow in the microwave. The face I give to the world is not the one I save for Nathaniel: After years of seeing the world in absolutes, he has taught me how to pick out all the shades of possibility.

I could lie and tell you that I never would have gone to law school or become a prosecutor if I'd expected to have children. It's a demanding job, one you take home, one you cannot fit around soccer games and nursery school Christmas pageants. The truth is, I have always loved what I do; it's how I define myself: *Hello, I'm Nina Frost, assistant district attorney.* But I also am Nathaniel's mother, and I wouldn't trade that label for the world. There is no majority share; I am split down the middle, fifty-fifty. However, unlike most parents, who lie awake at night worrying about the horrors that could befall a child, I have the chance to do something about them. I'm a white knight, one of fifty lawyers responsible for cleaning up the state of Maine before Nathaniel makes his way through it.

Now, I touch his forehead – *cool* – and smile. With a finger I trace the slight bow of his cheek, the seam of his lips. Asleep, he bats my hand away, buries his fists under the covers. 'Hey,' I whisper into his ear. 'We need to get moving.' When he doesn't stir, I pull the covers down – and the thick ammonia scent of urine rises from the mattress.

*Not today.* But I smile, just like the doctor said to when accidents happen for Nathaniel, my five-year-old who's been toilet trained for three years. When his eyes open – Caleb's eyes, sparkling and brown and so engaging that people used to stop me on the street to play with my baby in his stroller – I see that moment of fear when he thinks he's going to be punished. 'Nathaniel,' I sigh, 'these things happen.' I help him off the bed and start to peel his damp pajamas from his skin, only to have him fight me in earnest.

One wild punch lands on my temple, driving me back. 'For God's sake, Nathaniel!' I snap. But it's not his fault that I'm late; it's not his fault that he's wet the bed. I take a deep breath and work the fabric over his ankles and feet. 'Let's just get you cleaned off, okay?' I say more gently, and he defeatedly slides his hand into mine.

My son tends to be unusually sunny. He finds music in the stifled sounds of traffic, speaks the language of toads. He never walks when he can scramble; he sees the world with the reverence of a poet. So this boy, the one eyeing me warily over the lip of the tub, is not one I recognize. 'I'm not mad at you.' Nathaniel ducks his head, embarrassed. 'Everyone has accidents. Remember when I ran over your bike last year, with the car? You were upset – but you knew I didn't mean to do it. Right?' I might as well be talking to one of Caleb's granite blocks. 'Fine, give me the silent treatment.' But even this backfires; I cannot tease him into a response. 'Ah, I know what will make you feel better . . . you can wear your Disney World sweatshirt. That's two days in a row.'

If he had the option, Nathaniel would wear it *every* day. In his room, I overturn the contents of every drawer, only to find the sweatshirt tangled in the pile of soiled sheets. Spying it, he pulls it free and starts to tug it over his head. 'Hang on,' I say, taking it away. 'I know I promised, but it's got pee all over it, Nathaniel. You can't go to school in this. It has to be washed first.' Nathaniel's lower lip begins to tremble, and suddenly I – the skilled arbitrator – am reduced to a plea bargain. 'Honey, I swear, I'll wash this tonight. You can wear it for the rest of the week. And all of next week, too. But right now, I need your help. I need us to eat fast, so that we can leave on time. All right?'

Ten minutes later, we have reached agreement, thanks to my complete capitulation. Nathaniel is wearing the damn Disney World sweatshirt, which has been hand-rinsed, hastily spun through the dryer, and sprayed with a pet deodorizer. Maybe Miss Lydia will have allergies; maybe no one will notice the stain above Mickey's wide smile. I hold up two cereal boxes. 'Which one?' Nathaniel shrugs, and by now I'm convinced his silence has less to do with shame than getting a rise out of me. Incidentally, it's working.

I set him down at the counter with a bowl of Honey Nut Cheerios while I pack his lunch. 'Noodles,' I announce with flair, trying to boost him out of his blue funk. 'And . . . ooh! A drumstick from dinner last night! Three Oreos . . . and celery sticks, so that Miss Lydia doesn't yell at Mommy again about nutrition pyramids. There.' I zip up the insulated pack and put it into Nathaniel's backpack, grab a banana for my own breakfast, then check the clock on the microwave. I give Nathaniel two more Tylenol to take – it won't hurt him this once, and Caleb will never know. 'Okay,' I say. 'We have to go.'

Nathaniel slowly puts on his sneakers and holds out each small foot to me to have the laces tied. He can zip up his own fleece jacket; shimmy into his own backpack. It is enormous on those thin shoulders; sometimes from behind he reminds me of Atlas, carrying the weight of the world.

Driving, I slide in Nathaniel's favorite cassette – the Beatles' *White Album,* of all things – but not even 'Rocky Raccoon' can snap him out of this mood. Clearly, he's gotten up on the wrong side of the bed – the *wet* side, I think, sighing. A tiny voice inside me says I should just be grateful that in approximately fifteen minutes it will be someone else's problem.

In the rearview mirror, I watch Nathaniel play with the dangling strap of his backpack, pleating it into halves and thirds. We come to the stop sign at the bottom of the hill. 'Nathaniel,' I whisper, just loud enough to be heard over the hum of the engine. When he glances up, I cross my eyes and stick out my tongue.

Slowly, slow as his father, he smiles at me.

On the dashboard, I see that it is 7:56. Four minutes ahead of schedule.

We are doing even better than I thought.

★     ★     ★

The way Caleb Frost sees it, you build a wall to keep something unwanted out . . . or to hold something precious in. He considers this often when he builds, fitting sparkling granite and craggy limestone into niches, a three-dimensional puzzle drawn thick and straight across the edge of a lawn. He likes to think of the families inside these baileys he constructs: insulated, safe, protected. Of course, this is ridiculous. His stone walls are knee-high, not castle-worthy. They have large gaps in them for driveways and paths and grape arbors. And yet every time he drives past a property he's shaped with his own heavy hands, he pictures the parents sitting down to dinner with their children, harmony wrapping the table like mosquito netting, as if literal foundations might lay the pattern for emotional ones.

He stands at the edge of the Warren property with Fred, their contractor, as they all wait for Caleb to put on a show. Right now, the land is thick with birches and maples, some tagged to show the potential location of the house and the septic system. Mr. and Mrs. Warren stand so close they are touching. She is pregnant; her belly brushes her husband's hip.

'Well,' Caleb begins. His job is to convince these people that they need a stone wall surrounding their property, instead of the six-foot fence they are also considering. But words are not his specialty; that's for Nina. Beside him, Fred clears his throat, prompting.

Caleb cannot sweet-talk this couple; he can only see what lies ahead for them: a white Colonial, with a screened porch. A Labrador, leaping to catch monarch butterflies in his mouth. A row of bulbs that will, next year, be tulips. A little girl riding a tricycle, with streamers flying from the handlebars down the length of the drive, until she reaches the barrier Caleb has crafted – the limit, she has been told, of where she is safe.

He imagines himself bent over this spot, creating something solid in a space where there had been nothing before. He imagines this family, three of them by then, tucked within these walls. 'Mrs. Warren,' Caleb asks with a smile, the right words finally coming. 'When are you due?'

In one corner of the playground, Lettie Wiggs is crying. She does this all the time, pretends that Danny socked her when the truth is she just wants to see if she can get Miss Lydia to come running from whatever it is Miss Lydia's doing. Danny knows it too, and Miss Lydia, and everyone, except for Lettie, who cries and cries as if it's going to get her somewhere.

He walks past her. Walks past Danny, too, who isn't Danny anymore, but a pirate, clinging to a barrel after a shipwreck. 'Hey, Nathaniel,' says Brianna. 'Check this out.' She is crouched behind the shed that holds soccer balls as soft as ripe melons, and the ride-on bulldozer that you can only ride on for five minutes before it's someone else's turn. A silver spider has stretched a web from the wood to the fence behind it, zagged like a shoelace. At one spot a knot the size of a dime is tangled in the silk.

'That's a fly.' Cole pushes his glasses up on his nose. 'The spider, she wrapped it up for her dinner.'

'That's so gross,' Brianna says, but she leans closer.

Nathaniel stands with his hands in his pockets. He thinks about the fly, how it stepped onto the web and got stuck, like the time Nathaniel walked into a snowdrift last winter and lost his boot in the muck at the bottom. He wonders if the fly was just as scared as Nathaniel had been of coming in barefoot through the snow, of what his mother would say. Probably the fly had just figured it was going to take a rest. Probably it had stopped for a second to see how the sun looked like a rainbow through that web, and the spider grabbed him before he could get away.

'Bet she eats the head first,' Cole says.

Nathaniel imagines the wings of the fly, pinned to its back as it is turned and wrapped tight. He lifts his hand and slashes it through the web; walks away.

Brianna is fuming. 'Hey!' she yells. And then, *'Miss Lydia!'*

But Nathaniel doesn't listen. He looks up, surveying the top beam of the swings and the jungle gym with the slide that's as shiny as the blade of a knife. The jungle gym is taller by a few inches. Settling his hands on the rungs of the wooden ladder, he begins to climb.

Miss Lydia doesn't see him. His sneakers send down a rain of tiny pebbles and dirt, but he balances. Up here, he is taller than his father, even. He thinks that maybe the cloud behind him has an angel fast asleep in its center.

Nathaniel closes his eyes and jumps, his arms glued to his sides like that fly's. He doesn't try to break his fall, just hits hard, because it hurts less than everything else.

'Best croissants,' Peter Eberhardt says, as if we have been in the middle of a conversation, although I've only just walked up to stand beside him at the coffee machine.

'The Left Bank,' I answer. We might as well be in the middle of a conversation, come to think of it. Except this one has been ongoing for years.

'A little closer to home?'

This I have to think about. 'Mamie's.' It's a diner in Springvale. 'Worst haircut?'

Peter laughs. 'Me, in my middle school yearbook.'

'I was thinking of it as a verb, not a noun.'

'Oh, well, then. Wherever Angeline gets her perm.' He holds out the coffee and fills my cup for me, but I'm laughing so hard some of it spills on the floor. Angeline is the clerk of the South District Court, and her coiffure resembles something between a muskrat curled on her head and a plate of buttered bowtie noodles.

This is our game, Peter and me. It began when we were both assistant DAs in the West District, splitting our time between Springvale and York. In Maine, defendants can come to court and plead innocent, guilty, or request to meet with the prosecutor. Peter and I would sit across from each other at a desk, trading court complaints like aces in a poker game.

*You do this traffic ticket, I'm sick of them. Okay, but that means
you get this trespassing charge.* I see Peter far less now that we
are both trying felonies in the superior court, but he is still the
person I'm closest to in the office. 'Best quote of the day?'

It is only ten-thirty; the best may be to come. But I put on
my prosecutor's face and look solemnly at Peter, and give him
an instant replay of my closing in the rape case. 'In fact, ladies
and gentlemen, there is only one act that would be more criminally reprehensible, more *violating,* than what this man did –
and that would be to set him free to do it again.'

Peter whistles through the space in his front teeth. 'Ooh,
you *are* the drama queen.'

'That's why they pay me the big bucks.' I stir creamer into
my coffee, watch it clot like blood on the surface. It reminds
me of the brain matter case. 'How goes the domestic abuse
trial?'

'Don't take this the wrong way, but I am so freaking sick
of victims. They're so . . .'

'Needy?' I say dryly.

'Yes!' Peter sighs. 'Wouldn't it be nice to just get through a
case without having to deal with all their baggage?'

'Ah, but then you might as well be a defense attorney.' I
take a gulp of the coffee, leave the cup on the counter, three-
quarters full. 'See, if you ask me, I'd rather get through a case
without *them.*'

Peter laughs. 'Poor Nina. You've got your competency hearing
next, don't you?'

'So?'

'So, whenever you have to face Fisher Carrington you
look . . . well, like I did in that middle school yearbook. On the
verge of being scalped.'

As prosecutors, we have a tenuous relationship with the local
defense attorneys. Most of them we hold a grudging respect
for; after all, they are just doing their jobs. But Carrington is
a different breed. Harvard-educated, silver-haired, stately – he
is everyone's father; he is the distinguished elder gentleman

offering advice to live by. He is the sort of man juries want to believe, just on general principle. It has happened to all of us at one time or another: We put up a mountain of hard evidence against his Newman-blue eyes and knowing smile, and the defendant walks.

Needless to say, we all hate Fisher Carrington.

Having to face him at a competency hearing is like getting to Hell and finding out that the only food available is raw liver – insult added to injury.

Legally, competency is defined as being able to communicate in a way that the fact finder can understand. For example, a dog may be able to sniff out drug evidence but can't testify. For children at the center of sexual abuse cases – ones where the abuser hasn't confessed – the only way to get a conviction is to get the kid to testify. But before that happens, the judge has to determine that the witness can communicate, knows the difference between the truth and a lie . . . and understands that in court you have to tell the truth. Which means that when I am trying a sexual abuse case with a young child, I routinely file a motion for a competency hearing.

So: Imagine you are five years old and have been brave enough to confess to your mother that your daddy rapes you every night, although he's said he'll kill you for telling. Now imagine that, as a practice run, you have to go to a courtroom that seems as big as a football stadium. You have to answer questions a prosecutor asks you. And then you have to answer questions fired at you by a stranger, a lawyer who makes you so confused that you cry and ask him to stop. And because every defendant has the right to face his accuser, you have to do all this while your daddy is staring you down just six feet away.

Two things can happen here. Either you are found incompetent to stand trial, which means the judge throws out the case, and you don't have to go to court again . . . although you have nightmares for weeks afterward about that lawyer asking you horrible questions, and the look on your father's face, and most likely, the abuse continues. Or, you are found competent, and you get to repeat this little scene all over again . . . this time, with dozens of people watching.

I may be a prosecutor, but I'm also the first to tell that if you cannot communicate in a certain way, you cannot get justice in the American legal system. I have tried hundreds of sexual abuse cases, seen hundreds of children on that stand. I have been one of the lawyers who tugs and pulls at them, until they reluctantly let go of the make-believe world they've dreamed to block out the truth. All this, in the name of a conviction. But you cannot convince me that a competency hearing itself doesn't traumatize a child. You cannot convince me that even if I win that hearing, somehow, the child doesn't.

As defense attorneys go, Fisher Carrington is quite respectful. He doesn't reduce children to jelly on their high stools in the witness box; he doesn't try to disorient them. He acts like a grandfather who will give them lollipops if they tell the truth. In all but one case we both tried, he managed to have the child declared incompetent to stand trial, and the perp walked out free. In the other case, I convicted his client.

The defendant spent three years in jail.

The victim spent seven years in therapy.

I look up at Peter. 'Best-case scenario,' I challenge.

'Huh?'

'Yeah,' I say softly. 'That's my point.'

When Rachel was five, her parents got a divorce – the kind that involved bitter mudslinging, hidden bank accounts, and cans of paint splashed on the driveway at midnight. A week later, Rachel told her mother that her daddy used to stick his finger inside her vagina.

She has told me that one time, she was wearing a Little Mermaid nightgown and eating Froot Loops at the kitchen table. The second time, she was wearing a pink Cinderella nightgown and watching a *Franklin* video in her parents' bedroom. Rachel's mother, Miriam, has verified that her daughter had a Little Mermaid nightgown, and a Cinderella nightgown, the summer she was three years old. She remembers borrowing the Franklin video from her sister-in-law. Back then, she and her husband were still living together. Back then, there were times she left her husband alone with their little girl.

There are a lot of people who'd wonder how on earth a five-year-old can remember what happened to her when she was three. God, Nathaniel can't even tell me what he did *yesterday*. But then, they have not heard Rachel tell the same story over and over. They have not talked to psychiatrists, who say that a traumatic event might stick like a thorn in the throat of a child. They do not see, as I do, that since her father has moved out, Rachel has blossomed. And even without all that – how can I overlook the word of any child? What if the one I choose to discount is one who has been truly hurt?

Today, Rachel sits on my swivel chair in my office, twirling in circles. Her braids reach the tops of her shoulders, and her legs are as skinny as matchsticks. This is not the optimal place to hold a quiet interview, but then again, my office never is. There are cops running in and out, and the secretary I share with the other district attorneys chooses this moment, of course, to put a file on my desk. 'Is it going to take long?' Miriam asks, her eyes never veering from her daughter.

'I hope not,' I tell her, and then greet Rachel's grandmother, who will be in the gallery for emotional support during the hearing. Because she is a witness herself, Miriam isn't allowed to be there. Yet another catch-22: The child on the stand, in most cases, doesn't even have the security of a mother close by.

'Is this really necessary?' Miriam asks for the hundredth time.

'Yes.' I say it flatly, staring her in the eye. 'Your ex-husband has rejected our offer of a plea. That means Rachel's testimony is the only thing I've got to prove it even happened.' Kneeling in front of Rachel, I stop the motion of the swivel chair. 'You know what?' I confess. 'Some-times, when my door's closed, I spin around too.'

Rachel folds her arms around a stuffed animal. 'Do you get dizzy?'

'No. I pretend I'm flying.'

The door opens. Patrick, my oldest friend, sticks his head inside. He's wearing full dress blues, instead of his usual detective's street clothes. 'Hey, Nina – did you hear that the post office had to recall its series of Famous Defense Attorney stamps? People didn't know which side to spit on.'

'Detective Ducharme,' I say pointedly. 'I'm a little busy now.'

He blushes; it sets off his eyes. As kids, I used to tease him about those. I convinced him once, when we were about Rachel's age, that his were blue because there was no brain in his skull, just empty space and clouds. 'Sorry – I didn't realize.' He has captivated all the women in the room just like that; if he wanted to, he could suggest they do jumping jacks and they'd probably begin calisthenics right away. What makes Patrick Patrick is that he doesn't want to; he never has.

'Ms. Frost,' he says formally, 'are we still on for our meeting this afternoon?'

Our meeting is a long-standing weekly luncheon date at a hole-in-the-wall bar and grill in Sanford.

'We are.' I'm dying to know why Patrick's dressed to the nines; what's brought him to the superior court – as a detective in Biddeford, his stomping grounds are more often the district courthouse. But all this will have to wait. I hear the door close behind Patrick as I turn back to Rachel. 'I see you brought a friend with you today. You know, I think you're the first kid who's ever brought in a hippo to show to Judge McAvoy.'

'Her name is Louisa.'

'I like that. I like your hairdo, too.'

'I got to have pancakes this morning,' Rachel says.

That earns a nod of approval for Miriam; it's crucial that Rachel's eaten a good breakfast. 'It's ten o'clock. We'd better go.'

There are tears in Miriam's eyes as she bends down to Rachel's height. 'This is the part where Mommy has to wait outside,' she says, and she's trying hard not to cry, but it's there in her voice, in the way the sounds are too round, overstuffed with pain.

When Nathaniel was two and broke his arm, I stood in the ER as the bones were set and put in their cast. He was brave – so brave, not crying out, not once – but his free hand held onto mine so tightly that his fingernails left little half-moons in my palm. The whole time I was thinking that I would gladly break my arm, my heart, myself, if it meant my son wouldn't have to hurt like this.

Rachel is one of the easier ones; she is nervous but not a wreck. Miriam is doing the right thing. I will make this as painless as possible for both of them.

'Mommy,' Rachel says, the reality hitting like a tropical storm. Her hippo falls to the floor and there is no other way to describe it: She tries to crawl inside her mother's skin.

I walk out of my office and close my door, because I have a job to do.

'Mr. Carrington,' the judge asks, 'why are we putting a five-year-old on the stand here? Isn't there any way to resolve this case?'

Fisher crosses his legs and frowns a little. He has this down to an art. 'Your Honor, the last thing I want is for this case to proceed.'

*I'll bet,* I think.

'But my client cannot accept the state's offer. From the first day he set foot in my office, he's denied these events. Moreover, the state has no physical evidence and no witnesses. . . . All Ms. Frost has, in fact, is a child with a mother who's hell-bent on destroying her estranged husband.'

'We don't care if he goes to jail at this point, Your Honor,' I interrupt. 'We just want him to give up custody and visitation.'

'My client is Rachel's biological father. He understands that the child may have been poisoned against him, but he isn't willing to give up his parental rights to a daughter he loves and cherishes.'

*Yadda yadda yadda.* I'm not even listening. I don't have to; Fisher grandstanded to me on the phone when he called to reject my last plea bargain. 'All right,' Judge McAvoy sighs. 'Let's get her up there.'

The court is empty, except for me, Rachel, her grandmother, the judge, Fisher, and the defendant. Rachel sits by her grandmother, twirling her stuffed hippopotamus's tail. I lead her to the witness box, but when she sits down, she cannot see over the railing.

Judge McAvoy turns to his clerk. 'Roger, why don't you run into my chambers and see if there's a stool for Miss Rachel.'

It takes a few more minutes of adjustments. 'Hi, Rachel. How are you?' I begin.

'I'm okay,' she says, in the smallest voice.

'May I approach the witness, Your Honor?' Closer up, I won't be as intimidating. I keep smiling so hard my jaw begins to hurt. 'Can you tell me your whole name, Rachel?'

'Rachel Elizabeth Marx.'

'How old are you?'

'Five.' She holds up the fingers to show me proof.

'Did you have a party on your birthday?'

'Yes.' Rachel hesitates, then adds, 'A princess one.'

'I bet it was fun. Did you get any presents?'

'Uh-huh. I got the Swimming Barbie. She does the backstroke.'

'Who do you live with, Rachel?'

'My mommy,' she says, but her eyes slide toward the defense table.

'Does anybody else live with you?'

'Not anymore.' A whisper.

'Did you used to live with someone else?'

'Yes,' Rachel nods. 'My daddy.'

'Do you go to school, Rachel?'

'I'm in Mrs. Montgomery's class.'

'Do you have rules there?'

'Yes. Don't hit and raise your hand to talk and don't climb up the slide.'

'What happens if you don't follow the rules in school?'

'My teacher gets mad.'

'Do you understand the difference between telling the truth and telling a lie?'

'The truth is when you tell what happened, and a lie is when you make something up.'

'That's right. And the rule in court, where we are right now, is that you have to tell the truth when we ask you questions. You can't make anything up. Do you understand?'

'Yes.'

'If you lie to your mom, what happens?'

'She gets mad at me.'

'Can you promise that everything you say today is going to be the truth?'

'Uh-huh.'

I breathe deeply. First hurdle, cleared. 'Rachel, the man over there with the silver hair, his name is Mr. Carrington. He's got some questions for you too. Do you think you can talk to him?'

'Okay,' Rachel says, but she's getting nervous now. This was the part I couldn't tell her about; the part where I didn't have all the answers.

Fisher stands up, oozing security. 'Hi there, Rachel.'

She narrows her eyes. I *love* this kid. 'Hi.'

'What's your bear's name?'

'She's a *hippo*.' Rachel says this with the disdain that only a child can pull off, when an adult stares right at the bucket on her head and cannot see that it is a space helmet.

'Do you know who's sitting with me at that table over there?'

'My daddy.'

'Have you seen your daddy lately?'

'No.'

'But you remember when you and your daddy and your

mommy all lived together in the same house?' Fisher's hands are in his pockets. His voice is as soft as flannel.

'Uh-huh.'

'Did your mommy and daddy fight a lot in the brown house?'

'Yes.'

'And after that, your daddy moved out?'

Rachel nods, then remembers what I've told her about having to say your answer out loud. 'Yes,' she murmurs.

'After your daddy moved out, then you told somebody that something happened to you . . . something about your daddy, right?'

'Uh-huh.'

'You told somebody that Daddy touched your pee-pee?'

'*Yes.*'

'Who did you tell?'

'Mommy.'

'What did Mommy do when you told her?'

'She cried.'

'Do you remember how old you were when Daddy touched your pee-pee?'

Rachel chews on her lip. 'It was back when I was a baby.'

'Were you going to school, then?'

'I don't know.'

'Do you remember if it was hot or cold outside?'

'I, um, I don't know.'

'Do you remember whether it was dark outside, or light?'

Rachel starts rocking on the stool, shaking her head.

'Was Mommy home?'

'I don't know,' she whispers, and my heart plummets. This is the point where we will lose her.

'You said you were watching *Franklin*. Was that on TV, or was it a video?'

By now, Rachel isn't even making eye contact with Fisher, or with any of us. 'I don't know.'

'That's all right, Rachel,' Fisher says calmly. 'It's hard to remember, sometimes.'

At the prosecutor's table, I roll my eyes.

'Rachel, did you talk to your mommy before you came to court this morning?'

At last: Something she knows. Rachel lifts her head and smiles, proud. 'Yes!'

'Is this morning the first time you talked to Mommy about coming to court?'

'Nope.'

'Have you met Nina before today?'

'Uh-huh.'

Fisher smiles. 'How many times have you talked to her?'

'A whole bunch.'

'A bunch. Did she tell you what to say when you got up into this little box?'

'Yes.'

'And did she tell you that you needed to say that Daddy touched you?'

'Yes.'

'Did Mommy tell you that you needed to say that Daddy touched you?'

Rachel nods, the tips of her braids dancing. 'Uh-huh.'

I begin to close my file on this case; I already know where Fisher's going; what he has done. 'Rachel,' he says, 'did your mommy tell you what would happen today if you came in here and said that Daddy touched your pee-pee?'

'Yes. She said she would be proud of me, for being such a good girl.'

'Thank you, Rachel,' Fisher says, and sits down.

Ten minutes later, Fisher and I stand in front of the judge in chambers. 'I'm not suggesting, Ms. Frost, that you put words in that child's head,' the judge says. 'I am suggesting, however, that she believes she is doing what you and her mother want her to do.'

'Your Honor,' I begin.

'Ms. Frost, the child's loyalties to her mother are much stronger than her loyalty to a witness oath. Under those circumstances, any conviction the state might secure could be overturned anyway.' He looks at me, not without sympathy. 'Maybe six months from now, things will be different, Nina.' The judge clears his throat. 'I'm finding the witness not competent to stand trial. Does the state have another motion in regard to this case?'

I can feel Fisher's eyes on me, sympathetic instead of victorious, and this makes me fume. 'I need to talk to the mother and child, but I believe the state will be filing a motion to dismiss without prejudice.' It means that as Rachel grows older, we can recall the charge and try again. Of course, Rachel might not be brave enough for that. Or her mother might just want her to get on with life, instead of reliving the past. The judge knows this, and I know this, and there is nothing either of us can do about it. It's simply the way the system works.

Fisher Carrington and I walk out of chambers. 'Thank you, counselor,' he says, and I don't answer. We veer off in different directions, magnets repelled.

This is why I'm angry: 1) I lost. 2) I was supposed to be on Rachel's side, but I turned out to be the bad guy. After all, I am the one who made her undergo a competency hearing, and it was all for nothing.

But none of this shows in my face as I lean down to talk to Rachel, who is waiting in my office. 'You were so brave today. I know you told the truth and I'm proud of you, and your mom's proud of you. And the good news is, you did such a great job, you don't have to do it again.' I make sure I look her in the eye as I say this, so it slips inside, praise she can carry in her pockets. 'I need to talk to your mom, now, Rachel. Can you wait outside with your grandma?'

Miriam falls apart before Rachel has closed the door behind herself. 'What *happened* in there?'

'The judge found Rachel not competent.' I recount the testimony she didn't hear. 'It means we can't prosecute your ex-husband.'

'How am I supposed to protect her, then?'

I fold my hands on my desk, gripping the edge tight. 'I know you have a lawyer representing you in your divorce, Mrs. Marx. And I'd be happy to call him for you. There's still a social services investigation going on, and maybe they can do something to curtail or supervise the visitations . . . but the fact is, we can't put on a criminal prosecution right now. Maybe when Rachel gets older.'

'By the time she's older,' Miriam whispers, 'he will have done it to her a thousand more times.'

There is nothing I can say to this, because it is most likely true.

Miriam collapses in front of me. I have seen it dozens of times, strong mothers who simply go to pieces, like a starched sheet that melts at a breath of steam. She rocks back and forth, her arms crossed so tight at her waist that it doubles her over. 'Mrs. Marx, . . . if there's anything I can do for you . . .'

'What would you do if you were me?'

Her voice rises like a snake, tugs me forward. 'You did not hear this from me,' I say quietly. 'But I would take Rachel, and I would run.'

Minutes later, from my window, I see Miriam Marx searching through her purse. For her car keys, I think. And quite possibly, for her resolve.

There are many things Patrick loves about Nina, but one of the best things about her is the way she enters a room. *Stage presence*, that's what his mother used to call it when Nina barreled into the Ducharme kitchen, helped herself to an Oreo from the cookie jar, and then paused, as if to give everyone else a chance to catch up to her. All Patrick knows is that his back can be to the door, and when Nina comes in, he can feel it – a tickle of energy on the nape of his neck, a snap to attention as every eye in the place turns toward her.

Today, he is sitting at the empty bar. Tequila Mockingbird is a cop hangout, which means it doesn't really get busy until dinnertime. In fact, there have been times that Patrick has wondered whether the establishment opens early simply to accommodate himself and Nina for their standing Monday lunches. He checks his watch, but he knows he is early – he *always* is. Patrick doesn't want to miss the moment she walks in, the way her face turns unerringly to his, like the needle of a compass at true north.

Stuyvesant, the bartender, flips over a tarot card from a deck. From the looks of it, he's playing solitaire. Patrick shakes his head. 'That's not what they're for, you know.'

'Well, I don't know what the hell else to do with 'em.' He is sorting them by suit: wands, cups, swords, and pentacles. 'They got left behind in the ladies' room.' The bartender stubs out his cigarette and follows the line of Patrick's gaze toward the door. 'Jesus,' he says. 'When are you going to tell her?'

'Tell her what?'

But Stuyvesant just shakes his head and pushes the pile of cards toward Patrick. 'Here. You need these more than I do.'

'What's that supposed to mean?' Patrick asks, but at that moment Nina walks in. The air in the room hums like a field full of crickets, and Patrick feels something light as helium filling him, until before he knows it he has gotten up from his seat.

'Always a gentleman,' Nina says, tossing her big black purse beneath the bar.

'And an officer, too.' Patrick smiles at her. 'Go figure.'

She isn't the girl who used to live next door, hasn't been for years. Back then she had freckles and jeans with holes at the knees and a ponytail yanked so tight it made her eyes pull at the corners. Now, she wears pantyhose and tailored suits; she has had the same short-bob hairstyle for five years. But when Patrick gets close enough, she still smells like childhood to him.

Nina glances at his uniform as Stuyvesant slides a cup of coffee in front of her. 'Did you run out of clean laundry?'

'No, I had to spend the morning at an elementary school

talking about Halloween safety. The chief insisted I wear a costume, too.' He hands her two sugars for her coffee before she asks. 'How was your hearing?'

'The witness wasn't found competent.' She says this without betraying a single emotion on her face, but Patrick knows her well enough to realize how much it's killing her. Nina stirs her coffee, then smiles up at him. 'Anyway, I have a case for you. My two o'clock meeting, actually.'

Patrick leans his head on his hand. When he went off to the military, Nina was at law school. She'd been his best friend then, too. Every other day that he was serving on the USS *John F. Kennedy* in the Persian Gulf, he received a letter from her, and through it, the vicarious life he might have had. He learned the names of the most detested professors at U of Maine. He discovered how terrifying it was to take the bar exam. He read about falling in love, when Nina met Caleb Frost, walking down a brick path he'd just laid in front of the library. *Where is this going to take me?* she had asked. And Caleb's answer: *Where do you want it to?*

By the time Patrick's enlistment was up, Nina had gotten married. Patrick considered settling down in places that rolled off the tongue: Shawnee, Pocatello, Hickory. He went so far as to rent a U-Haul truck and drive exactly one thousand miles from New York City to Riley, Kansas. But in the end, it turned out that he'd learned too well from Nina's letters, and he moved back to Biddeford, simply because he could not stay away.

'And then,' Nina says, 'a pig leaped into the butter dish and ruined the whole dinner party.'

'No shit?' Patrick laughs, caught. 'What did the hostess do?'

'You're not listening, Patrick, goddammit.'

'Sure I am. But Jesus, Nina. Brain matter on the passenger seat visor that doesn't belong to anyone in the car? Might as well be a pig in the butter dish you're talking about.' Patrick shakes his head. 'Who leaves his cerebral cortex behind in someone else's rig?'

'You tell me. You're the detective.'

'Okay. My best guess? The car's been reconditioned. Your defendant bought it used, never knowing that the previous owner drove to a secluded rest stop and blew his brains out in the front seat. It got cleaned up well enough for resale value . . . but not for the indomitable Maine State Lab.'

Nina stirs her coffee, then reaches across to Patrick's plate to take a French fry. 'That's not impossible,' she admits. 'I'll have to trace the car.'

'I can get you the name of a guy we used as an informant once – he ran a reconditioning business before he started dealing.'

'Get me the whole file. Leave it in my mailbox at home.'

Patrick shakes his head. 'I can't. That's a federal offense.'

'You're kidding,' Nina laughs. 'It's not like you're leaving a bomb.' But Patrick doesn't even smile; for him the world is a place of rules. 'Fine, then. Leave it outside the front door.' She glances down as her beeper sounds, pulls it from the waistband of her skirt. 'Oh, damn.'

'Problem?'

'Nathaniel's preschool.' She takes her cell phone from her black bag and dials a number. 'Hi, it's Nina Frost. Yes. Of course. No, I understand.' She hangs up, then dials again. 'Peter, it's me. Listen, I just got a call from Nathaniel's school. I have to go pick him up, and Caleb's at a job site. I've got two motions to suppress on DUIs; can you cover for me? Plead the cases, I don't care, I just want to get rid of them. Yeah. Thanks.'

'What's the matter with Nathaniel?' Patrick asks as she slips the phone back into her bag. 'Is he sick?'

Nina looks away from him; she almost seems embarrassed. 'No, they specifically said he wasn't. We got off to a rocky start today; I'm betting he just needs to sit on the porch with me and regroup.'

Patrick has spent plenty of hours on the porch with Nathaniel and Nina. Their favorite game in the fall is to bet Hershey's kisses on which leaf will drop from a given tree first. Nina plays to win, just like she does with everything else in her life, but then she claims she is too stuffed to reap the bounty and she donates all her chocolate to Nathaniel. When Nina is with her son, she seems – well, brighter, more colorful – and softer. When they are laughing with their heads bent close, Patrick sometimes sees her not as the attorney she is now but as the little girl who was once his partner in crime.

'I could go get him for you,' Patrick suggests.

'Yeah, you just can't leave him in my mailbox.' Nina grins and grabs the other half of Patrick's sandwich from his plate. 'Thanks, but Miss Lydia made a personal request to see me, and believe me, you don't want to get on that woman's bad side.' Nina takes a bite, then hands the rest to Patrick. 'I'll call you later.' She hurries out of the bar before Patrick can say good-bye.

He watches her go. Sometimes he wonders if she ever slows down, if she's moving so fast through her own life that she cannot even realize the physics of the trajectory she's taken: Bend the curve of time, and even yesterday looks unfamiliar. The truth is, Nina will forget to call him. And Patrick will phone her instead and ask if Nathaniel is all right. She'll apologize and say she meant to get back to him all along. And Patrick . . . well, Patrick will forgive her, just like he always does.

'Acting out,' I repeat, looking Miss Lydia in the eye. 'Did Nathaniel tell Danny again that I'd put him in jail if he didn't share the dinosaurs?'

'No, this time it's aggressive behavior. Nathaniel's been ruining other children's work – knocking down block structures, and at one point he scribbled over a little girl's drawing.'

I offer my most winning smile. 'Nathaniel wasn't quite himself this morning. Maybe it's some kind of virus.'

Miss Lydia frowned. 'I don't think so, Mrs. Frost. There are other incidents . . . he was climbing the swing set today, and jumping off the top –'

'Kids do that kind of thing all the time!'

'Nina,' Miss Lydia says gently, Miss Lydia who in four years has never used my first name, 'was Nathaniel speaking before he came to school this morning?'

'Well, of course he –' I begin, and then I stop. The bed-wetting, the rushed breakfast, the black mood – there is much I remember about Nathaniel that morning, but the only voice I hear in my mind is my own.

I would know my son's voice anywhere. Pitched and bubbled; I used to wish I could bottle it, like the Sea Witch who stole from the Little Mermaid. His mistakes – *hossipal* and *pisghetti* and *apple spider* – were speed bumps that might keep him from growing up too soon; correct them and he'd reach that destination long before I was ready. As it is, things are already changing too quickly. Nathaniel no longer mixes up his pronouns; he has mastered dipthongs – although I sorely miss hearing him say *brudder* like a Bowery cop. Just about the only hiccup in speech I can still lay claim to is Nathaniel's absolute inability to pronounce the letters *L* and *R*.

In my memory, we are sitting at the kitchen table. Pancakes – shaped like ghosts, with chocolate chip eyes – are stacked high in front of us, along with bacon and orange juice. A big breakfast is the way we bribe Nathaniel on the Sundays that Caleb and I feel guilty enough to go to Mass. The sun hits the lip of my glass and a rainbow spills onto my plate. 'What's the opposite of left,' I ask.

Without missing a beat, Nathaniel says, 'White.'

Caleb flips a pancake. As a kid, he lisped. Listening to Nathaniel brings abject pain, and the belief that his son will be teased mercilessly, too. He thinks we should correct Nathaniel, and asked Miss Lydia if Nathaniel's pronunciations could be fixed by a speech pathologist. He thinks a child going into kindergarten next year should have the eloquence of Laurence Olivier. 'Then what's the opposite of white?' Caleb asks.

'*Bwack.*'

'*Rrrright,*' Caleb stresses. 'Try it. *Rrrright.*'

'*Wwwwhite.*'

'Just leave it, Caleb,' I say.

But he can't. 'Nathaniel,' he presses, 'the opposite of *left* is *right*. And the opposite of *right* is . . . ?'

Nathaniel thinks about this for a moment. *'Ewase,'* he answers.

'God help him,' Caleb mutters, turning back to the stove.

Me, I just wink at Nathaniel. 'Maybe He will,' I say.

In the parking lot of the nursery school, I kneel down so that Nathaniel and I are face-to-face. 'Honey, tell me what's wrong.'

Nathaniel's collar is twisted; his hands are stained red with fingerpaint. He stares at me with wide, dark eyes and doesn't say a thing.

All the words he isn't speaking rise in my throat, thick as bile. 'Honey,' I repeat. 'Nathaniel?'

*We just think he needs to be at home,* Miss Lydia had said. *Maybe you can spend this afternoon with him.* 'Is that what you need?' I ask out loud, my hands sliding from his shoulders to the soft moon of his face. 'Some quality time?' Smiling hard, I fold him into a hug. He is heavy and warm and fits into my arms seamlessly, although at several other points in Nathaniel's life – his infancy, his toddlerhood – I have been certain that we matched equally as well.

'Does your throat hurt?' Shake.

'Does anything hurt?' Another shake.

'Did something upset you at school? Did someone say something that hurt your feelings? Can you tell me what happened?'

Three questions, too many for him to process, much less answer. But that doesn't keep me from hoping that Nathaniel is going to respond.

Can tonsils become so swollen they impede speech? Can strep come on like lightning? Doesn't meningitis affect the neck first?

Nathaniel parts his lips – here, he's going to tell me now – but his mouth is a hollow, silent cavern.

'That's okay,' I say, although it isn't, not by a long shot.

*   *   *

Caleb arrives at the pediatrician's office while we are waiting to be seen. Nathaniel sits near the Brio train set, pushing it in circles. I'm glaring daggers at the receptionist, who doesn't seem to understand that this is an *emergency*, that my son is not acting like my son, that this isn't a goddamned *common cold*, and that we should have been seen a half hour ago.

Caleb immediately goes to Nathaniel, curling his big body into a play space meant for children. 'Hey, Buddy. You're not feeling so great, huh?'

Nathaniel shrugs, but doesn't speak. He hasn't spoken now in God knows how many hours?

'Does something hurt, Nathaniel?' Caleb says, and that's about all I can take.

'Don't you think I've already asked him?' I explode.

'I don't know, Nina. I haven't been here.'

'Well, he isn't talking, Caleb. He isn't responding to me.' The full implications of this – the sad truth that my son's illness isn't chicken pox or bronchitis or any of a thousand other things I could understand – make it hard to stand upright. It's the strange things, like this, that always turn out to be awful: a wart that won't go away, which metastasizes into cancer; a dull headache that turns out to be a brain tumor. 'I'm not even sure if he's hearing what I say to him, now. For all I know it's some . . . some virus that's attacking his vocal cords.'

'Virus.' There is a pause. 'He was feeling sick yesterday and you shoved him off to school this morning, regardless –'

'This is *my* fault?'

Caleb just looks at me, hard. 'You've been awfully busy lately, that's all I'm saying.'

'So I'm supposed to apologize for the fact that my job isn't something I can do on my own clock, like yours? Well, excuse me. I'll ask if the victims would be kind enough to get raped and beaten at a more convenient time.'

'No, you'll just hope that your own son has the good sense to get sick when you're not scheduled in court.'

It takes me a moment to respond, I'm that angry. 'That is so –'

'It's true, Nina. How can everyone else's kid be a priority over your own?'

'Nathaniel?'

The soft voice of the pediatric nurse practitioner lands like an ax between us. She has a look on her face I cannot quite read, and I'm not sure if she's going to ask about Nathaniel's silence, or his parents' lack of it.

It feels like he's swallowed stones, like his neck is full of pebbles that shift and grind every time he tries to make a sound. Nathaniel lies on the examination table while Dr. Ortiz gently rubs jelly under his chin, then rolls over his throat a fat wand that tickles. On the computer screen she's wheeled into the room, salt and pepper blotches rise to the surface, pictures that look nothing like him at all.

When he crooks his pinky finger, he can reach a crack in the leather on the table. Inside it's foam, a cloud that can be torn apart.

'Nathaniel,' Dr. Ortiz says, 'can you try to speak for me?'

His mother and father are looking at him so hard. It reminds him of one time at the zoo, when Nathaniel had stood in front of a reptile cage for twenty whole minutes thinking that if he waited long enough, the snake would come out of its hiding place. At that moment he'd wanted to see the rattlesnake more than he'd ever wanted *anything*, but it had stayed hidden. Nathaniel sometimes wonders if it was even in there at all.

Now, he purses his mouth. He feels the back of his throat open like a rose. The sound rises from his belly, tumbling over the stones that choke him. Nothing makes its way to his lips.

Dr. Ortiz leans closer. 'You can do it, Nathaniel,' she urges. 'Just try.'

But he *is* trying. He is trying so hard it's splitting him in two. There is a word caught like driftwood behind his tongue, and he wants so badly to say it to his parents: *Stop.*

'There's nothing extraordinary on the ultrasound,' Dr. Ortiz says. 'No polyps or swelling of the vocal cords, nothing physical that might be keeping Nathaniel from speaking.' She looks at us with her clear gray eyes. 'Has Nathaniel had any other medical problems lately?'

Caleb looks at me, and I turn away. So I gave Nathaniel Tylenol, so I'd prayed for him to be all right because I had such a busy morning coming. So what? Ask nine out of ten mothers; they all would have done what I did . . . and that last one would have thought hard about it before discounting the idea.

'He came home from church yesterday with a stomachache,' Caleb says. 'And he's still having accidents at night.'

But that's not a medical problem. That's about monsters hiding under the bed, and bogeymen peering in the windows. It has nothing to do with a sudden loss of speech. In the corner, where he is playing with blocks, I watch Nathaniel blush – and suddenly I'm angry with Caleb for even bringing it up.

Dr. Ortiz takes off her glasses and rubs them on her shirt. 'Sometimes what looks like a physical illness isn't,' she says slowly. 'Sometimes these things can be about getting attention.'

She doesn't know my son, not nearly as well as I do. As if a five-year-old might even be capable of such Machiavellian plotting.

'He may not even be consciously aware of the behavior,' the doctor continues, reading my mind.

'What can we do?' Caleb asks, at the same moment I say, 'Maybe we should talk to a specialist.'

The doctor responds to me, first. 'That's exactly what I was going to suggest. Let me make a call and see if Dr. Robichaud can see you this afternoon.'

Yes, this is what we need: an ENT who is trained in this sort of illness; an ENT who will be able to lay hands on Nathaniel and feel an impossibly small *something* that can be fixed. 'Which hospital is Dr. Robichaud affiliated with?' I ask.

'He's up in Portland,' the pediatrician says. 'He's a psychiatrist.'

★          ★          ★

July. The town pool. A hundred and two degrees in Maine, a record.

'What if I sink?' Nathaniel asked me. I stood in the shallow end, watching him stare at the water like it was quicksand.

'Do you really think I'd let you get hurt?'

He seemed to consider this. 'No.'

'All right then.' I held out my arms.

'Mom? What if this was a pit of lava?'

'I wouldn't be wearing a bathing suit, for one.'

'What if I get in there and my arms and legs forget what to do?'

'They won't.'

'They *could.*'

'Not likely.'

'One time is all it takes,' Nathaniel said gravely, and I realized he'd been listening to me practice my closings in the shower.

An idea. I rounded my mouth, raised my arms, and sank to the bottom of the pool. The water hummed in my ears, the world went slow. I counted to five and then the blue shimmied, an explosion just in front of me. Suddenly Nathaniel was underwater and swimming, his eyes full of stars and his mouth and nose blowing bubbles. I caught him tight and broke the surface. 'You saved me,' I said.

Nathaniel put his hands on either side of my face. 'I had to,' he said. 'So you could save me back.'

The first thing he does is draw a picture of a frog that is eating the moon. Dr. Robichaud doesn't have a black crayon, though, so Nathaniel has to make the night sky blue. He colors so hard the crayon breaks in his hand, and then wonders if someone is going to yell at him.

No one does.

Dr. Robichaud told him he could do anything he wanted, while everyone sat around and watched him play. Everyone: his mom and dad, and this new doctor, who has hair so white-yellow that he can see her scalp underneath, beating like a heart. The room has a gingerbread-style dollhouse, a rocking horse for kids younger than Nathaniel, a beanbag chair shaped like a baseball mitt. There are crayons and paints and puppets and dolls. When Nathaniel moves from one activity to another, he notices Dr. Robichaud writing on a clipboard, and he wonders if she is drawing too; if she has the missing black crayon.

Every now and then she asks him questions, which he couldn't answer even if he wanted to. *Do you like frogs, Nathaniel?* And: *That chair is comfortable, don't you think?* Most of the questions are stupid ones that grown-ups ask, even though they don't really want to listen to the answers. Only once has Dr. Robichaud said something that Nathaniel wishes he could respond to. He pushed the button on a chunky plastic tape recorder and the sound that came out was familiar: Halloween and tears all rolled together. 'Those are whales singing,' Dr. Robichaud said. 'Have you ever heard them before?'

*Yes,* Nathaniel wanted to say, *but I thought it was just me, crying on the inside.*

The doctor starts to talk to his parents, big words that slide in his ear and then turn tail and run away like rabbits. Bored, Nathaniel looks under the table again for the black crayon. He smoothes the corners of his picture. Then he notices the doll in the corner.

It's a boy doll, he sees that the minute he turns it over. Nathaniel doesn't like dolls; he doesn't play with them. But he is tugged toward this toy, lying twisted on the floor. He picks it up and fixes the arms and the legs, so that it doesn't look like it's hurt anymore.

Then he glances down and sees the blue crayon, broken, still curled in his hand.

How clichéd is this: The psychiatrist brings up Freud. Somatoform disorder is the DSM-IV term for what Sigmund called hysteria – young women whose reaction to trauma manifested itself into valid physical ailments without any etiological physical cause. Basically, Dr. Robichaud says, the mind can make the body ill. It doesn't happen as often as it did in Freud's day, because there are so many more acceptable outlets for emotional trauma. But every now and then it still happens, most often in children who don't possess the right vocabulary to explain what's upsetting them.

I glance over at Caleb, wondering if he's buying any of this. The truth is, I just want to get Nathaniel home. I want to call an expert witness I once used, an ENT in New York City, and ask him for a referral to a specialist in the Boston area who can look at my son.

Nathaniel was fine yesterday. I am not a psychiatrist, but even I know that a nervous breakdown doesn't happen overnight.

'Emotional trauma,' Caleb says softly. 'Like what?'

Dr. Robichaud says something, but the sound is drowned out. My gaze has gone to Nathaniel, who is sitting in the corner of the playroom. In his lap, he holds a doll facedown. With his other hand, he is grinding a crayon between the cheeks of its buttocks. And his face, oh his face – it's as blank as a sheet.

I have seen this a thousand times. I have been in the offices of a hundred psychiatrists. I have sat in the corner like a fly on the wall as a child shows what he cannot tell, as a child gives me the proof I need to go prosecute a case.

Suddenly I am on the floor beside Nathaniel, my hands on his shoulders, my eyes locked with his. A moment later, he is in my arms. We rock back and forth in a vacuum, neither of us able to find words to say what we know is true.

Past the school playground, on the other side of the hill, in the forest – that's where the witch lives.

We all know about her. We believe. We haven't seen her, but that's a good thing, because the ones who see her are the ones who get taken away.

Ashleigh says the feeling you get when the wind climbs the back of your neck and you can't stop shivering; that's the witch coming too close. She wears a flannel jacket that turns her invisible. She sounds like leaves falling down.

Willie was in our class. He had eyes sunk so far in his head they sometimes disappeared, and he smelled like oranges. He was allowed to wear his Teva sandals even after it got cold out, and his feet would get muddy and blue, and my mother would shake her head and say, 'See?' and I did – I saw, and I wished I could do it too. The thing was, one day Willie was sitting next to me at snack, dunking his graham crackers into his milk until they all became a slushy mountain at the bottom . . . and the next day, he was gone. He was gone, and he never came back.

At the hiding spot under the slide, Ashleigh tells us that the witch has taken him. 'She says your name, and after that, you can't help it, you'll do anything she says. You'll go anywhere she wants.'

Lettie starts to cry. 'She'll eat him. She'll eat Willie.'

'Too late,' Ashleigh says, and in her hand is a white, white bone.

It looks too small to come from Willie. It looks too small to come from anything that ever walked. But I know better than anyone what it is: I found it, digging under the dandelions near the fence. I was the one who gave it to Ashleigh.

'She's got Danny right now,' Ashleigh says.

Miss Lydia told us during circle time that Danny was sick. We'd put his face up on the Who's Here board, flipped over to the sad side. After recess, we were all going to make him a card. 'Danny's sick,' I tell Ashleigh, but she just looks at me like I'm the dumbest person ever. 'Did you think they would tell us the truth?' she says.

So when Miss Lydia isn't watching, we slip under the fence where the dogs and the rabbits sometimes get in – Ashleigh and Peter and Brianna and me, the bravest. We will save Danny. We will get him before the witch does.

But Miss Lydia finds us first. She makes us go inside and sit in Time Out and says we should never, never, ever leave the playground. Don't we know we could get hurt?

Brianna looks at me. Of course we know; it's why we left in the first place.

Peter starts to cry, and tells her about the witch, and what Ashleigh said. Miss Lydia's eyebrows come together like a fat black caterpillar. 'Is this true?'

'Peter's a liar. He made the whole thing up,' Ashleigh says, and she doesn't even blink.

That's how I know that the witch has already gotten to her.

# 2

Just so you know: if this ever happens to you, you will not be ready. You will walk down a street and wonder how people can behave as if the whole world has not been tipped on its axis. You will comb your mind for signs and signals, certain that one moment – *aha!* – will trip you like a twisted root. You will bang your fist so hard against the stall door in the public bathroom that your wrist will bruise; you'll start to cry when the man at the tollbooth tells you to have a nice day. You will ask yourself *How come;* you will ask yourself *What if.*

Caleb and I drive home with an elephant sitting between us. At least this is how it seems: this huge bulk driving us to our separate sides, impossible to ignore, and yet we both pretend we cannot see it. In the backseat, Nathaniel sleeps, holding a half-eaten lollipop given to him by Dr. Robichaud.

I am having trouble breathing. It is that elephant, again, sitting so close to me with one elbow crushing my chest. 'He has to tell us who,' I say finally, the words breaking free like a river. 'He has to.'

'He *can't.*'

That is the issue, in a nutshell. Nathaniel is not able to speak, even if he wants to. He doesn't know how to read or write yet. Until he can communicate, there is no one to blame. Until he can communicate, this is not a case; this is just a heartache.

'Maybe the psychiatrist is wrong,' Caleb says.

I turn in my seat. 'You don't believe Nathaniel?'

'What I believe is that he hasn't *said* anything yet.' He glances in the rearview mirror. 'I don't want to keep talking about this, in front of him.'

'Do you think that'll make it go away?'

Caleb doesn't respond, and there is my answer. 'The next exit's ours,' I say stiffly, because Caleb is still driving in the left lane.

'I know where I'm going, Nina.' He brings the car to the right, signals at the exit sign. But a minute later, he misses the turnoff.

'You just –' The accusation dies as I see his face, striped by grief. I don't think he even knows he's crying. 'Oh, Caleb.' I reach out to touch him, but that goddamned elephant is in the way. Caleb throws the car into park and gets out, walking along the road's shoulder, drawing huge breaths that make his chest swell.

A moment later, he returns. 'I'll turn around and go back,' he announces – to me? To Nathaniel? To himself?

I nod. And think, *If only it were that easy.*

Nathaniel bites down hard on his back teeth so that the hum of the road goes right through him. He isn't asleep, but he is pretending to be, which is almost as good. His parents are talking, the words so soft at the corners that he can't quite hear. Maybe he will never sleep again. Maybe he will just be like a dolphin, and stay half-asleep.

Miss Lydia taught them about dolphins last year, after they'd turned the classroom into an ocean of blue crepe paper and glitter-glue starfish. So Nathaniel knows these things: that dolphins shut an eye and half their brain, sleeping on one side, while the other side watches out for danger. He knows that mommy dolphins swim for their resting babies, pulling them along in an underwater current, as if they are attached by invisible threads. He knows that the plastic rings which rope six-packs of Coke can hurt dolphins, make them wash up weak onshore. And that even though they breathe air, they'll die there.

Nathaniel also knows that if he could, he would roll down the window and jump out, so far that he'd cross the highway barrier and the tall fence to plummet along the rocky cliff, landing in the ocean below. He'd have sleek silver skin and a smile curved permanently on his mouth. He'd have a special body part – like a heart, but different – filled with oil and called a melon, just like the thing you eat in the summertime. Except this would be in the front of his head and would help him find his way even in the blackest ocean, on the blackest night.

Nathaniel imagines swimming off the coast of Maine toward the other end of the world, where it already feels like summer. He squinches his eyes as tight as he can, concentrates on making a joyful noise, of navigating by those notes, of hearing them bounce back to him.

Although Martin Toscher, MD, is considered an authority in his field, he would gladly trade his laurels to completely eliminate his area of expertise. Examining one child for evidence of sexual abuse is more than enough; the fact that he's logged hundreds of cases in Maine is phenomenally disturbing.

The subject of the examination lies on the OR table, anesthetized. It would be his suggestion, given the traumatic nature of the exam, but before he had even proposed it to the parents, the mother asked if it could be done that way. Now, Martin walks through the procedure, speaking aloud as he works so that his findings can be recorded. 'The glans penis appears normal, Tanner 0.' He repositions the child. 'Looking at the anal verge . . . there are multiple obvious healing abrasions, about one to one and a half centimeters up, that are approximately one centimeter in diameter, on average.'

He takes an anal speculum from the table nearby. Chances are if there are additional mucosal tears higher up in the bowel wall, they'd know – the child would be physically ill by now. But he lubricates the instrument and gently inserts it, attaches the light source, and cleans out the rectum with a long cotton swab. Well, thank God for that, Martin thinks. 'The bowel is clean to eight centimeters.'

He strips off his gloves and mask, washes up, and leaves the nurses to fuss over the child in recovery. It's a light anesthesia, it will wear off quickly. The moment he walks out of the operating room, he is approached by the parents.

'How is he?' asks the father.

'Nathaniel's doing well,' Martin replies, the words everyone wants to hear. 'He may be a little drowsy this afternoon, but that's perfectly normal.'

The mother pushes past all these platitudes. 'Were there any findings?'

'There did seem to be evidence consistent with an assault,' the doctor says gently. 'Some rectal abrasions that are healing. It's hard to say when they were incurred, but they're certainly not fresh. Maybe a week or so's gone by.'

'Is the evidence consistent with penetration?' Nina Frost demands.

Martin nods. 'It's not from falling down on a bicycle, for example.'

'Can we see him?' This from the boy's father.

'Soon. The nurses will page you when he's awake in recovery.'

He starts to leave, but Mrs. Frost stops him with a hand on his arm. 'Can you tell if it was penile penetration? Digital? Or some foreign object?'

Parents ask whether their children still feel the pain from the assault. If the scar is something that will affect them later on. If they will remember, in the long term, what happened to them. But these questions, well, they make him feel as if he is being cross-examined.

'There's no way to know that level of detail,' the doctor says. 'All we can say at this point is, yes, something happened.'

She turns away and stumbles against the wall. Wilts. Within seconds she is a small, keening ball on the floor, her husband's arms wrapped around her for support. As Martin heads back to the operating suite, he realizes it's the first time that day he has seen her act like a mother.

It's foolish, I know, but I've lived my life believing in superstitions. Not throwing spilled salt over my shoulder or wishing on eyelashes or wearing lucky shoes to trials – instead, I've considered my own good luck directly correlated to the misfortunes of others. Starting out as a lawyer, I begged for the sexual assaults and molestations, the horrors no one wants to face. I told myself that if I faced the problems of strangers on a daily basis, it would magically keep me from having to face my own.

Visiting violence repeatedly, you become inured to atrocity. You can look at blood without blinking, you can say the word *rape* and not wince. It turns out, though, that this shield is a plastic one. That all defenses break down when the nightmare happens in your own bed.

On the floor of his bedroom, Nathaniel is playing quietly, still groggy from the anesthesia. He guides Matchbox cars around a track. They zoom to a certain spot, a booster, and suddenly shoot with great speed up a ramp through the jaws of a python. If the car is just the tiniest bit too slow, the snake snaps its mouth shut. Nathaniel's car passes through with flying colors every time.

My ears are filled with all the things Nathaniel is not saying: *What's for dinner; can I play on the computer; did you see how fast that car went?* His hands close around the Matchbox like the claw of a giant; in this make-believe world he is the one calling the shots.

The python's jaws ratchet shut, so loud in this silence that it makes me jump. And then I feel it, the softest jelly-roll along my leg, the bumping up my spine. Nathaniel is holding the Matchbox car, running it up the avenue of my arm. He parks in the hollow of my collarbone, then touches one finger to the tears on my cheek.

Nathaniel puts the car onto the track and climbs into my lap. His breath is hot and wet on my collar as he burrows close. This makes me feel sick – that he should choose me to keep him safe, when I have already failed miserably. We stay like this for a long time, until evening comes and stars fall onto his carpet, until Caleb's voice climbs the stairs, searching for us. Over the penance of Nathaniel's head I watch the car on its track, spinning in circles, driven by its own momentum.

*          *          *

Shortly after seven o'clock, I lose Nathaniel. He isn't in any of his favorite haunts: his bedroom, the playroom, on the jungle gym outside. I had thought Caleb was with him; Caleb thought he was with me. 'Nathaniel!' I yell, panicked, but he can't answer me – he couldn't answer me even if he felt like giving away his hiding place. A thousand scenes of horror sprint through my mind: Nathaniel being kidnapped from the backyard, unable to scream for help; Nathaniel falling down our well and sobbing in silence; Nathaniel lying hurt and unconscious on the ground. 'Nathaniel!' I cry again, louder this time.

'You take the upstairs,' Caleb says, and I hear the worry in his voice, too. Before I can answer he heads for the laundry room; there is a sound of the dryer door opening and then closing again.

Nathaniel is not hiding under our bed, or in his closet. He isn't curled underneath cobwebs in the stairwell that leads to the attic. He isn't in his toy chest or behind the big wing chair in the sewing room. He isn't beneath the computer table or behind the bathroom door.

You'd think I've run a mile, I'm panting that hard. I lean against the wall outside the bathroom and listen to Caleb slam cabinets and drawers in the kitchen. *Think like Nathaniel,* I tell myself. Where would I be if I were five?

I would be climbing rainbows. I would be lifting rocks to find crickets sleeping underneath; I would be sorting the gravel in the driveway by weight and color. But these are all the things Nathaniel used to do, things that fill the mind of a child before he has to grow up. Overnight.

There is a thin drip coming from the bathroom. The sink; Nathaniel routinely leaves it on when he brushes his teeth. I suddenly want to see that trickle of water, because it will be the most normal thing I've witnessed all day. But inside, the sink is dry as a bone. I turn to the source of the noise, pull back the brightly patterned shower curtain.

And scream.

*               *               *

The only thing he can hear underwater is his heart. Is it like this for dolphins, too? Nathaniel wonders, or can they hear sounds the rest of us can't – coral blooming, fish breathing, sharks thinking. His eyes are wide open, and through the wet the ceiling is runny. Bubbles tickle his nostrils, and the fish drawn onto the shower curtain make it real.

But suddenly his mother is there, here in the ocean where she shouldn't be, and her face is as wide as the sky coming closer. Nathaniel forgets to hold his breath as she yanks him out of the water by his shirt. He coughs, he sneezes sea. He hears her crying, and that reminds him that he has to come back to this world, after all.

Oh, my God, he isn't breathing – he isn't breathing – and then Nathaniel takes a great gulp of air. He is twice his weight in his soaked clothes, but I wrestle him out of the tub so that he lies dripping on the bathmat. Caleb's feet pound up the stairs. 'Did you find him?'

'Nathaniel,' I say as close to his face as I can, 'what were you doing?'

His golden hair is matted to his scalp, his eyes are huge. His lips twist, reaching for a word that doesn't come.

Can five-year-olds be suicidal? What other reason can there be for finding my son, fully dressed, submerged in a tub full of water?

Caleb crowds into the bathroom. He takes one look at Nathaniel, dripping, and the draining tub. 'What the *hell?*'

'Let's get you out of these clothes,' I say, as if I find Nathaniel in this situation on a daily basis. My hands go to the buttons of his flannel shirt, but he twists away from me, curls into a ball.

Caleb looks at me. 'Buddy,' he tries, 'you're gonna get sick if you stay like this.'

When Caleb gathers him onto his lap, Nathaniel goes completely boneless. He's wide-awake, he's looking right at me, yet I would swear that he isn't here at all.

Caleb's hands begin to unbutton Nathaniel's shirt. But instead, I grab a towel and wrap it around him. I hold it close at Nathaniel's neck and lean forward, so that my words fall onto his upturned face. 'Who did this to you?' I demand. 'Tell me, honey. Tell me so that I can make it better.'

'Nina.'

'Tell me. If you don't tell me, I can't do anything about it.' My voice hitches at the middle like a rusting train. My face is as wet as Nathaniel's.

He's trying; oh, he's trying. His cheeks are red with the effort. He opens his mouth, pours forth a strangled knot of air.

I nod at him, encouraging. 'You can do this, Nathaniel. Come on.'

The muscles in his throat tighten. He sounds like he is drowning again.

'Did someone touch you, Nathaniel?'

'Jesus!' Caleb wrenches Nathaniel away from me. 'Leave him alone, Nina!'

'But he was going to say something.' I get to my feet, jockeying to face Nathaniel again. 'Weren't you, baby?'

Caleb hefts Nathaniel higher in his arms. He walks out of the bathroom without saying another word, cradling our son close to his chest. He leaves me standing in a puddle, to clean up the mess that's been left behind.

Ironically, in Maine's Bureau of Children, Youth and Family Services, an investigation into child abuse is not an investigation at all. By the time a caseworker can officially open a case, he or she will already have psychiatric or physical evidence of abuse in the child, as well as the name of a suspected perpetrator. There will be no guesswork involved – all the research will have been completed by that point. It is the role of the BCYF caseworker to simply go along for the ride, so that if by some miracle it reaches the trial stage, everything has been done the way the government likes.

Monica LaFlamme has worked in the Child Abuse Action Network of the BCYF for three years now, and she is tired of coming in during the second act. She looks out the window of her office, a squat gray cube like every other government office in the complex, to a deserted playground. It is a metal swing set resting on a concrete slab. Leave it to the BCYF to have the one play structure left in the region that doesn't meet updated safety standards.

She yawns, pinches her finger and thumb to the bridge of her nose. Monica is exhausted. Not just from staying up for Letterman last night, but in general, as if the gray walls and commercial carpet in her office have somehow seeped into her through osmosis. She is tired of filling out reports on cases that go nowhere. She is tired of seeing forty-year-old eyes in the faces of ten-year-old children. What she needs is a vacation to the Caribbean, where there is so much color exploding – blue surf, white sand, scarlet flowers – that it renders her blind to her daily work.

When the phone rings, Monica jumps in her chair. 'This is Monica LaFlamme,' she says, crisply opening the manila folder on her desk, as if the person on the other end of the line has seen her daydreaming.

'Yes, hello. This is Dr. Christine Robichaud. I'm a psychiatrist up at Maine Medical Center.' A hesitation, and that is all Monica needed to know what is coming next. 'I need to report a possible case of sexual abuse against a five-year-old male.'

She takes notes as Dr. Robichaud describes behaviors she's seen over and over. She scrawls the name of the patient, the names of his parents. Something nicks the corner of her mind, but she pushes it aside to concentrate on what the psychiatrist is saying.

'Are there any police reports you can fax me?' Monica asks.

'The police haven't been involved. The boy hasn't identified the abuser yet.'

At that, Monica puts down her pen. 'Doctor, you know I

can't open an investigation until there's someone to investigate.'

'It's only a matter of time. Nathaniel is experiencing a somatoform disorder, which basically renders him mute without any physical cause. It's my belief that within a few weeks or so, he'll be able to tell us who did this to him.'

'What are the parents saying?'

The psychiatrist pauses. 'This is all new behavior.'

Monica taps her pen on her desk. In her experience, when the parents claim to be completely surprised by the speech or actions of a child who has been abused, it often ends up that one parent or both is the abuser.

Dr. Robichaud is well aware of this, too. 'I thought that you might want to get in at the ground level, Ms. LaFlamme. I referred the Frosts to a pediatrician trained in child sexual abuse cases, for a detailed medical examination of their son. He should be faxing you a report.'

Monica takes down the information; hangs up the phone. Then she looks over what she's written, in preparation for beginning yet another case that will most likely fizzle before a conviction is secured.

*Frost*, she thinks, rewriting the name. Surely it must be someone else.

We lay in the dark, not touching, a foot of space between us.

'Miss Lydia?' I whisper, and feel Caleb shake his head. 'Who, then? Who's alone with him, other than the two of us?'

Caleb is so quiet I think he's fallen asleep. 'Patrick watched him for a whole weekend when we went to your cousin's wedding last month.'

I come up on an elbow. 'You've got to be kidding. Patrick's a police officer. And I've known him since he was six.'

'He doesn't have a girlfriend –'

'He's only been divorced for six months!'

'All I'm saying,' Caleb rolls over, 'is you may not know him as well as you think.'

I shake my head. 'Patrick *loves* Nathaniel.'

Caleb just looks at me. His response is clear, although he never speaks it aloud: *Maybe too much.*

The next morning Caleb leaves while the moon is still hanging crooked on its peg in the sky. We have discussed this plan, trading our time like chips in a poker game: Caleb will finish his wall, then be home by midday. The implication is that I can go to the office when he returns, but I won't. My work, it will have to wait. This all happened to Nathaniel when I wasn't present to bear witness; I cannot risk letting him out of my sight again.

It's a noble cause to champion – protecting my child. But this morning I am having trouble understanding lionesses that guard their cubs, and relating more to the hamster that devours her offspring. For one thing, my son hasn't seemed to notice that I want to be his hero. For another, I'm not so sure I want to be one, either. Not if it means sticking up for a boy who fights me at every turn.

God, he has every right to hate me for being so selfish now.

Yet patience has never been my strong point. I solve problems; I seek reprisal. And even though I know it is not a matter of will for Nathaniel, I am angry that his silence is protecting the person who should be held accountable.

Today Nathaniel is falling apart at the seams. He insists on wearing his Superman pajamas, although it is nearly noon. Worse, he had an accident in his bed last night, so he stinks of urine. It took Caleb over an hour to get him out of his wet clothes yesterday; it took me two hours to realize I don't have the emotional or physical strength to fight him this morning. Instead, I've moved on to another battle.

Nathaniel sits like a stone gargoyle on his stool, his lips pressed together, resisting my attempts to get some food into him. He has not eaten since breakfast the previous day. I have held up everything from maraschino cherries to a gingerroot, the whole contents of the refrigerator from A to Z and back again. 'Nathaniel.' I let a lemon roll off the counter. 'Do you want spaghetti? Chicken fingers? I'll make you whatever you want. Just pick.'

But he only shakes his head.

If he does not eat, it isn't the end of the world. No, that was *yesterday*. But there is a part of me that believes if I can do this – fill my son – it will keep him from hurting inside. There's a part of me that remembers the first job of a mother is to feed her child; and if I can succeed at this one small thing, maybe it will mean I have not completely failed him.

'Tuna? Ice cream? Pizza?'

He begins to turn slowly on the stool. At first it is a mistake – a slip of his foot that sets him spinning. Then he does it deliberately. He hears me ask a question and he very purpose-fully ignores me.

'Nathaniel.'

Twirl.

Something snaps. I am angry at myself, at the world, but because it is easier, I lash out at him. 'Nathaniel! I am *speaking* to you!'

He meets my gaze. Then lazily pivots away from me.

'You will listen to me, *now!*'

Into this charming domestic scene walks Patrick. I hear his voice before he finds us in the kitchen. 'Armageddon must be coming,' he calls out, 'because I can't think of any other reason that would keep you away from work two days straight, when –' As he turns the corner, he sees my face and slows down, moving with the same care he'd use to enter a crime scene. 'Nina,' he asks evenly, 'are you all right?'

Everything Caleb said about Patrick last night hits me, and I burst into tears. Not Patrick, too; I couldn't stand for more than one pillar of my world to crumble. I just cannot believe that Patrick might have done this to my son. Here's proof: Nathaniel hasn't run screaming from him.

Patrick's arms come around me and I swear, if not for that, I would sink onto the floor. I hear my voice; it's uncontrollable, a verbal twitch. 'I'm fine. I'm a hundred percent,' I say, but my conviction shakes like an aspen leaf.

How do you find the words to explain that the life you woke up in yesterday is not the one you woke up in today? How do you describe atrocities that aren't supposed to exist? As a prosecutor, I have buffeted myself with legalese – *penetration, molestation, victimization* – yet not a single one of these terms is as raw and as true as the sentence *Someone raped my son.*

Patrick's eyes go from Nathaniel to me and back again. Is he thinking that I've had a breakdown? That stress has snapped me in half? 'Hey, Weed,' he says, his old nickname for Nathaniel, who grew by leaps and bounds as an infant. 'You wanna come upstairs with me and get dressed, while your mom, um, wipes down the counter?'

'No,' I say, at the same moment that Nathaniel bolts from the room.

'Nina,' Patrick tries again. 'Did something happen at Nathaniel's school?'

'Did something happen at Nathaniel's school,' Nina repeats, the words rolling like marbles on her tongue. *'Did something happen.* Well, that's the $64,000 question, now, isn't it?'

He stares at her. If he looks hard enough, he will find the truth; he always has been able to. At age eleven, he knew that Nina had kissed her first boy, although she had been too embarrassed to tell Patrick; he knew that she'd been accepted to an out-of-state college long before she'd gotten the nerve worked up to confess that she was leaving Biddeford.

'Someone hurt him, Patrick,' Nina whispers, breaking before his eyes. 'Someone, and I . . . I don't know who.'

A shiver rumbles through his chest. 'Nathaniel?'

Patrick has told parents that their teens have died in a drunken car crash. He has supported widows at the graveside of their suicidal husbands. He has listened to the stories of women who've lived through rape. The only way to get through it is to step back, to pretend you are not part of this civilization, whose members cause such grief to each other. But this . . . oh, with this . . . there is no distance.

Patrick feels his heart grow too large in his chest. He sits with Nina on the floor of her kitchen as she tells him the details of a story he never wanted to hear. *I could walk back through that door,* he thinks, *and start over. I could turn back time.*

'He can't speak,' Nina says. 'And I don't know how to make him.'

Patrick pulls her back at arm's length. 'You *do* know how. You make people talk to you all the time.'

When she raises her face, he sees what he's given her. You cannot be doomed, after all, as long as you can still see the faint outline of hope on the opposite shore.

The day after his son goes mute for reasons that Caleb does not want to believe, he walks outside the front door and realizes his home is falling apart. Not in the literal sense, of course – he's too careful for that. But if you look closely, you notice that the things which should have been taken care of ages ago – the stone path in front of the house, the crest at the top of the chimney, the brick kneewall meant to circle the perimeter of their land – all of these projects had been abandoned for another commissioned by a paying customer. He puts his coffee mug down on the edge of the porch and walks down the steps, trying to look objectively at each site.

The front path, well, it would take an expert to realize how uneven the stones are; that's not a priority. The chimney is a pure embarrassment; it's chipped along the whole left side. But getting to the roof this late in the afternoon doesn't make any sense, plus, it helps to have an assistant when you're working that high up. Which means that Caleb turns first to the knee-wall, a foot-wide hollow brick embellishment at the perimeter of the road.

The bricks are stacked at the spot where he'd left off nearly a year ago. He got them from commercial contractors who knew he'd been looking for used bricks, and they come from all over New England – demolished factories and wrecked hospital wards, crumbling colonial homes and abandoned schoolhouses. Caleb likes their marks and scars. He fancies that maybe in the porous red clay there might be some old ghosts or angels; he'd be all right with either walking the edge of his land.

Thank goodness, he's already dug below the frost line. Crushed stone rests six inches deep. Caleb hauls a bag of Redi-Mix into his arms and pours it into the wheelbarrow he uses for mixing. Chop and drag, set a rhythm as the water blends with the sand and concrete. He can feel it taking over as soon as he lays the first course of bricks, wiggles them into the cement until they seat – when he puts his whole body into his work like this, his mind goes wide and white.

It is his art, and it is his addiction. He moves along the edge of the footing, placing with grace. This wall will not be solid; there will be two smooth facings, crowned with a decorative concrete cap. You'll never know that on the inside, the mortar is rough and ugly, smeared. Caleb doesn't have to be careful on the spots that no one sees.

He reaches for a brick and his fingers brush over something smaller, smoother. A plastic soldier – the green army man variety. The last time he'd been working on this, Nathaniel had come with him. While Caleb dug the trench and filled it with stone, his son had hidden a battalion in the fort made of tumbled bricks.

Nathaniel was three. 'I'm gonna take you down,' he had said, pointing the soldier at Mason, the golden retriever.

'Where did you hear *that?*' Caleb asked, laughing.

'I hearded it,' Nathaniel said sagely, 'way back when I was a baby.'

*That long ago,* Caleb had thought.

Now, he holds the plastic soldier in his hand. A flashlight trips along the driveway, and for the first time Caleb realizes that it is past sunset; that somehow, in his work, he's missed the end of the day. 'What are you doing?' Nina asks.

'What does it look like I'm doing?'

'Now?'

He turns, hiding the toy soldier in his fist. 'Why not?'

'But it's . . . it's . . .' She shakes her head. 'I'm putting Nathaniel to bed.'

'Do you need my help?'

He realizes after the words escape that she will take it the wrong way. *Do you* want *help*, he should have said. Predictably, Nina bristles. 'I think after five years I can probably figure it out all by myself,' she says, and heads back toward the house, her flashlight leaping like a cricket.

Caleb hesitates, unsure whether he should follow her. In the end, he chooses not to. Instead he squints beneath the pinpricks of stars and puts the green soldier into the hollow made by the two sides of the wall. He sets bricks on either side, following the course. When this wall is finished, no one will know that this army man sleeps inside. No one but Caleb, that is, who will look at it a thousand times a day and know that at least one flawless memory of his son was saved.

Nathaniel lies in bed thinking about the time he took a baby chick home from school. Well, it wasn't a chick exactly . . . it was an egg that Miss Lydia had put in the trash, as if they were all too dumb to count that there were now three eggs instead of four in the incubator. The other eggs, though, had turned into little yellow cotton balls that cheeped. So that day before his father picked him up, Nathaniel went into Miss Lydia's office and slipped the egg out of the garbage can, into the sleeve of his shirt.

He'd slept with it under his pillow, sure if it had a little more time it would turn into a chick like the others had. But all it had come to were nightmares – of his father making an omelet in the morning, cracking the shell, and a live baby chick falling into the sizzling pan. His father had found the egg beside his bed three days later; it had tumbled to the floor. He hadn't cleaned the mess up in time: Nathaniel could still remember the silvered dead eye, the knotted gray body, the thing that might have been a wing.

Nathaniel used to think the Creature he'd seen that morning – it wasn't a chick, that was for sure – was the scariest something that could ever exist. Even now, from time to time when he blinks, it is there on the backs of his eyelids. He has stopped eating eggs, because he is afraid of what might be inside. An item that looks perfectly normal on the surface might only be disguised.

Nathaniel stares up at his ceiling. There are even scarier things; he knows that now.

The door to his bedroom opens wider, and someone steps in. Nathaniel is still thinking of the Creature, and the Other, and he can't see around the bright hall light. He feels something sink onto the bed, curl around him, as if Nathaniel is the dead thing now and needs to grow a shell to hide inside.

'It's okay,' his father's voice says at his ear. 'It's only me.' His arms come around tight, keep him from trembling. Nathaniel closes his eyes, and for the first time since he's gone to bed that night, he doesn't see the chick at all.

The moment before we step into Dr. Robichaud's office the next day, I have a sudden surge of hope. What if she looks at Nathaniel and decides she has misinterpreted his behavior? What if she apologizes, stamps our son's record with red letters, MISTAKEN? But when we walk inside, there's a new person joining us, and it is all I need to blow my fairy-tale ending sky high. In a place as small as York County, I couldn't prosecute child molestation cases and not know Monica LaFlamme. I don't have anything against her, specifically, just her agency. In our office we change the acronym of BCYF to suit us: TGDSW – Those God Damn Social Workers; or RTSM – Red Tape Society of Maine. The last case I'd worked with Monica had involved a boy diagnosed with oppositional defiance disorder – a condition, ultimately, that prevented us from prosecuting his abuser.

She gets up, her hands extended, as if she is my best friend. 'Nina . . . I am so, so sorry to hear about this.'

My eyes are flint; my heart is hard as a diamond. I do not fall for this touchy-feely bullshit in my profession; I'm sure as hell not going to fall for it in my personal life. 'What can you do for me, Monica?' I ask bluntly.

The psychiatrist, I can tell, is shocked. Probably she's never heard anyone talk back to the BCYF before. Probably she thinks she ought to put me on Prozac.

'Oh, Nina. I wish I could do more.'

'You always do,' I say, and that's the point when Caleb interrupts.

'I'm sorry, we haven't been introduced,' he mumbles, squeezing my arm in warning. He shakes hands with Monica and says hello to Dr. Robichaud, ushering Nathaniel inside to play.

'Ms. LaFlamme is the caseworker assigned to Nathaniel,' the psychiatrist explains. 'I thought it might be helpful for you to meet her; have her answer some of your questions.'

'Here's one,' I start. 'How do I go about getting BCYF *uninvolved?*'

Dr. Robichaud looks nervously at Caleb, then at me. 'Legally –'

'Thank you, but legally, I pretty much know the routine. See, that was a trick question. The answer is that the BCYF is already uninvolved. They *never* get involved.' I'm babbling, I can't help it. Seeing Monica here is too strange, like work and home have tunneled through the same wormhole in time. 'I give you a name and tell you what he did . . . and *then* you can go do your job?'

'Well,' Monica says, her voice as smooth as caramel. I have always hated caramel. 'It's true, Nina, that a victim has to give an ID before we –'

A victim. She has reduced Nathaniel to any of a hundred cases I have prosecuted over the years. To any of a hundred lousy outcomes. That is why, I realize, seeing Monica LaFlamme in

Dr. Robichaud's office has turned me inside out. It means Nathaniel has already been given a number and a file in a system that I know is bound to fail him.

*'This is my son,'* I say through clenched teeth. 'I don't care what procedure calls for. I don't care if you don't have an ID; if you don't get one for months or years. Take the whole population of Maine, then, and rule them out one by one. But *start,* Monica. Jesus Christ. *Start.'*

By the time I finish speaking, the others are staring at me as if I've grown another head. I glance at Nathaniel – playing with blocks, although none of these good people convened on his behalf are watching, for God's sake – and walk out the door.

Dr. Robichaud catches up to me in the parking lot. Her heels click on the pavement, and I smell a cigarette being lit. 'Want one?'

'Don't smoke. But thanks.'

We are leaning against a car that isn't mine. A black Camaro festooned with fuzzy dice. The door is unlocked. If I get in and drive away, can I steal that person's life, too?

'You sound a little . . . frazzled,' Dr. Robichaud says.

I have to laugh at that. 'Is Understatement 101 a course in med school?'

'Of course. It's the prereq for Lying Through One's Teeth.' Dr. Robichaud takes a final drag and crushes out her cigarette beneath her pump. 'I know it's the last thing you want to hear, but in Nathaniel's case, time isn't your enemy.'

She doesn't know that. She hadn't even met Nathaniel a week ago. She doesn't look at him every morning and remember, in sharp counterpoint, the little boy who used to ask so many questions – why birds on electrical wires don't get electrocuted, why fire is blue in the center, who invented dental floss – that I once, stupidly, wished for peace and quiet.

'He'll come back to you, Nina,' Dr. Robichaud says quietly.

I squint into the sun. 'At what price?'

She doesn't have an answer for that. 'Nathaniel's mind is protecting him now. He isn't in pain. He isn't thinking about

what happened nearly as much as you are.' Hesitating, she
extends an olive branch. 'I could refer you to an adult psychiatrist, who might be able to prescribe something.'

'I don't want any drugs.'

'Maybe you'd like someone to talk to, then.'

'Yes,' I say, turning to face her. 'My son.'

I look at the book once more to check. Then I pat my lap with
one hand, and snap my fingers. 'Dog,' I say, and as if I've cued
it, our retriever comes running.

Nathaniel's lips curve as I shove the dog away. 'No, Mason.
Not now.' He turns in a circle beneath the wrought-iron table,
settles on my feet. A cool October wind sends leaves para-
chuting our way – crimson and ocher and gold. They catch in
Nathaniel's hair, bookmark themselves in the pages of the sign
language manual.

Slowly, Nathaniel's hands creep out from beneath his thighs.
He points to himself, then extends his arms, palms upright.
Curling his fingers in, he draws his hands close. *I want*. He
pats his lap, tries to snap his fingers.

'You want the dog?' I say. 'You want Mason?'

Nathaniel's face goes several shades sunnier. He nods, his
mouth gaping wide in a grin. This is his first whole sentence
in nearly a week.

At the sound of his name, the dog lifts his shaggy head and
pokes his nose into Nathaniel's belly. 'Well, you asked for it!'
I laugh. By the time Nathaniel has managed to push Mason
away, his cheeks are flushed with pride. We have not learned
much – the signs for *want*, and *more*, and *drink*, and *dog*. But
we have made a start.

I reach for Nathaniel's tiny hand, one I have fashioned into
all the letters of the American Sign Language alphabet this
afternoon . . . although soft, small fingers don't stay tangled
that well in knots. Folding down his middle and fourth fingers
so that all the others are still extended, I help him make the
combined *I, L, Y* that signifies *I love you*.

Suddenly Mason leaps up, nearly crashing over the table, and bounds to the gate to greet Caleb. 'What's going on?' he asks, one glance taking in the thick manual, the rigid set of Nathaniel's hand.

'*We*,' I say, pointedly moving my index finger from shoulder to shoulder, 'are *working.*' I make two fists – S handshapes – and tap one on the other, to simulate hard labor.

'*We*,' Caleb announces, grabbing the book from the table to tuck it under his arm, 'are not *deaf.*'

Caleb is not in favor of Nathaniel learning American Sign Language. He thinks if we give Nathaniel such a tool, he might never have the incentive to speak again. I think that Caleb hasn't spent enough time trying to divine what his son wants to eat for breakfast. 'Watch this,' I urge, and nod at Nathaniel, trying to get him to do his sentence again. 'He's so smart, Caleb.'

'I know he is. It's not him I'm worried about.' He grabs my elbow. 'Can I talk to you alone for a minute?'

We move inside and close the slider, so that Nathaniel cannot hear. 'How many words do you think you have to teach him before you can start using *this* language to ask him who did it?' Caleb says.

Bright spots of color rise to my cheeks. Have I been that transparent? 'All I want, all Dr. Robichaud wants, is to give Nathaniel a chance to communicate. Because being like *this* is frustrating him. Today I taught him to say "I want the dog." Maybe you'd like to explain to me how that's going to lead to a conviction. Maybe you'd like to explain to your son why you're so dead set on taking away the only method he has to express himself.'

Caleb spreads his splayed hands like an umpire. It is the sign for *don't*, although I am sure he does not know this. 'I can't fight with you, Nina. You're too good at it.' He opens the door and kneels down in front of Nathaniel. 'You know, it's an awfully nice day to be sitting here, studying. You could play on the swings, if you want –'

*Play: two Y handshapes, caught at the pinkies to shake.* '– or build a road in your sandbox . . .'

*Build: U handshapes, stacking one on top of the other over and over.*

'. . . and you don't have to say anything, Nathaniel, if you're not ready. Not even with words that you make with your hands.' Caleb smiles at Nathaniel. 'Okay?' When Nathaniel nods, Caleb picks him up, swinging him high over his head to sit on his shoulders. 'What do you say we go pick the crab apples in the woods?' he asks. 'I'll be your ladder.'

Just before he breaks the edge of our property, Nathaniel twists on his father's shoulders. It's hard to see from this distance, but it seems that he's holding up a hand. To wave? I start to wave back, and then realize that his fingers are making that *I, L, Y* combination, then reconfiguring into what looks like a peace sign.

It may not be technically right, but I can understand Nathaniel, loud and clear.

*I love you, too.*

Myrna Oliphant, the secretary shared by all five assistant district attorneys in Alfred, is a woman nearly as wide as she is high. Her sensible shoes squeak when she walks, she smells of Brylcreem, and she can allegedly type an astounding hundred words a minute, although no one has ever actually seen her do it. Peter and I always joke that we see more of Myrna's back than her front, since she seems to have a sixth sense about disappearing the moment any of us need her.

So when I walk into my office eight days after Nathaniel stops speaking, and she comes right up to me, I know everything's wrong. 'Nina,' she says, tsking. 'Nina.' She puts her hand to her throat – there are real tears in her eyes. 'If there's anything . . .'

'Thank you,' I say, humbled. It does not surprise me that she knows what has happened; I told Peter and I'm sure he filled everyone else in on the relevant details. The only sick days I've ever used have been when Nathaniel had strep or chicken pox; in a way my absence from work now has been no different, except that this illness is more insidious. 'But you know, right now, I just need to get things taken care of here, so that I can go back home.'

'Yes, yes.' Myrna clears her throat, going professional. 'Your messages, of course, Peter's been taking care of. And Wallace is expecting you.' She heads back to her desk, but hesitates a moment, remembering. 'I put a note up at the church,' she says, and that's when I remember she, too, is a member of the congregation at St. Anne's. There is a small roped square on the News and Notes bulletin board, where people can request that a Hail Mary or Our Father be said for family members or friends in need. Myrna smiles at me. 'Maybe God's listening to those prayers even now.'

'Maybe.' I do not say what I'm thinking: *And where was God when it happened?*

My office is just the way I left it. I sit gingerly in my swivel chair, push the papers around on my desk, scan my phone messages. It is good to come back to a place that looks, and is, exactly the way I've remembered it in my mind.

A knock. Peter comes in, then shuts the door behind him. 'I don't know what to say,' he admits.

'Then don't say anything. Just come in and sit down.'

Peter sprawls in the chair on the other side of my desk. 'Are you sure, Nina? I mean, is it possible that the psychiatrist is jumping to conclusions?'

'I saw the same behaviors she did. And I jumped to the same conclusions.' I look up at him. 'A specialist found physical proof of penetration, Peter.'

'Oh, Jesus.' Peter clasps his hands between his knees, at a loss. 'What can I do for you, Nina?'

'You've been doing it. Thanks.' I smile at him. 'Whose brain matter was it, in the car?'

Peter's eyes are soft on my face. 'Who the hell cares? You shouldn't be thinking about that. You shouldn't even be *here.*'

I am torn between confiding in him, and ruining his good impression of me. 'But Peter,' I admit quietly, 'it's *easier*.'

There is a long moment of silence. And then: 'Best year,' Peter dares.

I grab the lifeline. That's simple – I was promoted, and had Nathaniel, within months of each other. '1996. Best victim?'

'Polly Purebred, from the Underdog cartoon.' Peter glances up as our boss, Wally Moffett, comes into my office. 'Hey, chief,' he says to Wally, and then to me, 'Best friend?' Peter gets up, heads for the door. 'The answer is *me*. Whatever, whenever. Remember that.'

'Good man,' Wally says, as Peter leaves. Wally is the standard-issue district attorney: lean as a shark, with a full head of hair and a mouthful of capped movie-star teeth that could win him reelection all by themselves. He's also an excellent lawyer; he can cut to the heart before you realize the first incision has even been made. 'Needless to say, this job is here when you're ready,' Wally begins, 'but I'll personally bar the door if you plan on coming back anytime soon.'

'Thanks, Wally.'

'I'm sorry as hell, Nina.'

'Yeah.' I glance down at my blotter. There's a calendar underneath it. No pictures of Nathaniel are on my desk – a long habit I kept from District Court, when the scum of the earth would come in to plead their cases in my office. I didn't want them to know I had a family. I didn't want that to come back and haunt me.

'Can I . . . can I try the case?'

The question is so small, it takes a moment to realize I've asked it. The pity in Wally's eyes makes me drop my own gaze to my lap. 'You know you can't, Nina. Not that I'd rather have anyone else lock this sick fuck up. But no one in our office can do it. It's a conflict of interest.'

I nod, but I still can't speak. I wanted that, I wanted it so badly.

'I've already called the district attorney's office in Portland. There's a guy up there who's good.' Wally smiles crookedly.

'Almost as good as you are, even. I told them what was going on, and that we might need to borrow Tom LaCroix.'

There are tears in my eyes when I thank Wallace. For him to have gone out on a limb like this – before we even have a perp to prosecute – is extraordinary.

'We take care of our own,' Wally assures me. 'Whoever did this is going to pay.'

It is a line I've used myself, to appease frantic parents. But I know, even as I say it, that there will be an equal cost extracted from their child. Still, because it is my job, and because I usually have no case without a testifying witness, I tell the parents I'd do anything to get that monster into jail. I tell the parents that in their shoes I'd do whatever it takes, including putting their children on the stand.

But now I'm the parent, and it is my child, and that changes everything.

One Saturday I took Nathaniel to my office, so that I could finish up some work. It was a ghost town – the Xerox machines sleeping like beasts, the computers blinking blind, the telephones quiet. Nathaniel occupied himself with the paper shredder while I reviewed files. 'How come you named me Nathaniel?' he asked, out of the blue.

I checked off the name of a witness on a pad. 'It means "Gift from God." '

The jaws of the paper shredder ground together. Nathaniel turned to me. 'Did I come wrapped and everything?'

'You weren't quite that kind of a gift.' As I watched, he turned off the shredder and began to play with the collection of toys I kept in the corner for children who had the misfortune of being brought to my office. 'What name would you rather have?'

When I was pregnant, Caleb would end each day by saying good night to his baby with a different name: Vladimir, Grizelda, Cuthbert. *Keep this up,* I had told him, *and this baby's going to arrive with an identity crisis.*

Nathaniel shrugged. 'Maybe I could be Batman.'

'Batman Frost,' I repeated, completely serious. 'It's got a nice ring to it.'

'There are four Dylans in my school – Dylan S. and Dylan M. and Dylan D. and Dylan T. – but there isn't another Batman.'

'Which is an important consideration.' All of a sudden I felt Nathaniel crawling under the hollow of my desk, a warm weight on my feet. 'What are you doing?'

'Batman needs a cave, Mom, *duh.*'

'Ah. Right.' I folded my legs underneath me to give Nathaniel more room, and scrutinized a police report. Nathaniel's hand stretched up to grab a stapler, an impromptu walkie-talkie.

The case was a rape, and the victim had been found comatose in the bathtub. Unfortunately, the perp had been smart enough to run the water, thereby obliterating nearly any forensic evidence we might have gotten. I turned the page in the file and stared at gruesome police photos of the crime scene, the sunken eggplant face of the woman who had been assaulted.

'Mom?'

Immediately I whipped the photo facedown. This was precisely why I did not mix my work life and my home life. 'Hmm?'

'Do you always catch the bad guys?'

I thought of the victim's mother, who could not stop crying long enough to give a statement to the police. 'Not always,' I answered.

'Most of the time?'

'Well,' I said. 'At least half.'

Nathaniel considered this for a moment. 'I guess that's good enough to be a superhero,' he said, and that was when I realized this had been an interview for the position of Robin. But I didn't have time to be a cartoon sidekick.

'Nathaniel,' I sighed. 'You know why I came in here.' Specifically, to get ready for Monday's opening arguments. To go over my strategy and my witness list.

I looked at Nathaniel's waiting face. Then again, maybe

justice was best served from a Batcave. An oxymoron chased through my mind: *I am going to get nothing done today. I am doing everything I want to.* 'Holy Guacamole, Batman,' I said, kicking off my shoes and crawling underneath my desk. Had I ever known that the interior wall was made of cheap pine, and not mahogany? 'Robin reporting for duty, but only if I get to drive the Batmobile.'

'You can't be Robin for real.'

'I thought that was the point.'

Nathaniel stared at me with great pity, as if someone like me really ought to have learned the rules of the game this far along in life. Our shoulders bumped in the confines of my desk. 'We can work together and everything, but your name has to be Mom.'

'Why?'

He rolled his eyes. 'Because,' Nathaniel told me. 'It's who you are.'

'Nathaniel!' I call out, blushing a little. It's not a sin, is it, to have no control over one's child? 'I'm sorry, Father,' I say, holding the door wide to let him inside. 'He's been . . . shy lately with visitors. Yesterday, when the UPS man came, it took me an hour to find where he was hiding.'

Father Szyszynski smiles at me. 'I told myself I should have called first, instead of dropping in unannounced.'

'Oh, no. No. It's wonderful that you came.' This is a lie. I have no idea what to do with a priest in my house. Do I serve cookies? Beer? Do I apologize for all the Sundays I don't make it to Mass? Do I confess to lying in the first place?

'Well, it's part of the job,' Father Szyszynski says, tapping his collar. 'The only thing I have to do on Friday afternoons is eavesdrop on the ladies' auxiliary meeting.'

'Is that considered a perk?'

'More like a cross to bear,' the priest says, and smiles. He sits down on the couch in the living room. Father Szyszynski is wearing high-tech running sneakers. He does local half-marathons;

his times are posted on the News and Notes boards, next to the index cards that request prayers for the needy. There is even a photo of him there, lean and fit, without his collar, crossing a finish line – in it, he looks nothing like a priest; just a man. He's in his fifties, but he appears to be ten years younger. Once, I heard him say that he'd tried to make a pact with Satan for eternal youth, but he couldn't find the devil's extension in the diocese phone book.

I wonder which nosy gossip in the church rumor mill told the priest about us. 'The Sunday school class misses Nathaniel,' he tells me. He's being politically correct. If he wanted to be more accurate, he'd say that the Sunday school class misses Nathaniel more than half the Sundays of the year, since we don't make it regularly to Mass. Still, I know that Nathaniel likes coloring pictures in the basement during the service. And he especially likes afterward, when Father Szyszynski reads to the kids from a great, old illustrated children's Bible while the rest of the congregation is upstairs having coffee. He gets right down onto the floor in their circle, and according to Nathaniel, acts out floods and plagues and prophecies.

'I know what you're thinking,' Father Szyszynski says.

'Do you.'

He nods. 'That in the year 2001 it's archaic to assume the Church is such a large part of your life it could offer you comfort at a time like this. But it can, Nina. God wants you to turn to Him.'

I stare right at the priest. 'These days I'm not too high on God,' I say bluntly.

'I know. It doesn't make much sense, sometimes, God's will.' Father Szyszynski shrugs. 'There have been times I've doubted Him myself.'

'You've obviously gotten over it.' I wipe the corner of my eyes; why am I crying? 'I'm not even really a Catholic.'

'Sure you are. You keep coming back, don't you?'

But that's guilt, not faith.

'Things happen for a reason, Nina.'

'Oh, yeah? Then do me a favor and ask God what reason there could possibly be for letting a child get hurt like this.'

'*You* ask Him,' the priest says. 'And when you're talking, you might want to remember you have something in common – He watched His son suffer, too.'

He hands me a picture book – *David and Goliath,* watered down for a five-year-old. 'If Nathaniel ever comes out,' he pitches his voice extra loud, 'you tell him that Father Glen left a present.' That's what they call him, all the kids at St. Anne's, since they can't pronounce his last name. *Heck,* the priest has said, *after a few tall ones, I can't pronounce it myself.* 'Nathaniel particularly enjoyed this story when I read it last year. He wanted to know if we could all make slingshots.' Father Szyszynski stands up, leads the way to the door. 'If you want to talk, Nina, you know where to find me. You take care.'

He starts down the path, the stone steps that Caleb placed with his own hands. As I watch him go I clutch the book to my chest. I think of the weak defeating giants.

Nathaniel is playing with a boat, sinking it, then watching it bob to the surface again. I suppose I should be grateful that he's in this tub at all. But he has been better, today. He has been talking with his hands. And he agreed to this bath, on the condition that he take off his own clothes. Of course I let him, struggling not to run to his aid when he couldn't work a button through a hole. I try to remember what Dr. Robichaud told us about power: Nathaniel was made helpless; he needs to feel like he's gaining control of himself again.

I sit on the lip of the tub, watching his back rise and fall with his breathing. The soap shimmers like a fish near the drain. 'Need help?' I ask, lifting one hand up with the other, a sign. Nathaniel shakes his head vigorously. He picks up the bar of Ivory and runs it over his shoulder, his chest, his belly. He hesitates, then plunges it between his legs.

A thin white film covers him, making him otherworldly, an angel. Nathaniel lifts his face to mine, hands me the soap to put back. For a moment, our fingers touch – in our new language, these are our lips . . . does that make this a kiss?

I let the soap drop with a splash, then circle my pursed mouth with a finger. I move my index fingers back and forth, touching and retreating. I point to Nathaniel.

*Who hurt you?*

But my son doesn't know these signs. Instead, he flings his hands out to the sides, proud to show off his new word. *Done.* He rises like a sea nymph, water sluicing down the sides of his beautiful body. As I towel off each limb and pull pajamas over Nathaniel, I silently ask myself if I am the only person who has touched him at this place, at that one, until every inch of him is covered again.

In the middle of the night Caleb hears a hitch in his wife's breathing. 'Nina?' he whispers, but she doesn't answer. He rolls onto his side, curls her closer. She's awake, he can feel it coming from her pores. 'Are you all right?' he asks.

She turns to him, her eyes flat in the dark. 'Are *you?*'

He pulls her into his arms and buries his face in the side of her neck. Breathing her calms Caleb; she is his own oxygen. His lips trace her skin, hold over her collarbone. He tilts his head so that he can hear her heart.

He is looking for a place to lose himself.

So his hand moves from the valley of her waist to the rise of a hip, slips beneath the thin strip of her panty. Nina draws in her breath. She is feeling it too, then. She needs to get away from here, from this.

Caleb slides lower and rocks his palm against her. Nina grabs tighter at his hair, almost to the point of pain. *'Caleb.'*

He is hard now, heavy and pressed into the mattress. 'I know,' he murmurs, and he goes to slide a finger inside.

She is dry as a bone.

Nina yanks at his hair, and this time he rolls off her, which is what she's wanted all along. 'What is the matter with you!' she cries. 'I don't want to do this. I can't, now.'

She throws back the covers and pads out of the bedroom into the dark.

Caleb looks down, sees the small drop of semen he's left on the sheets. He gets out of bed and covers it up, so that he will not have to look at it. Then he follows Nina, searching her out by sheer instinct. For long moments, he stands in the doorway of his son's bedroom, watching her watch Nathaniel.

Caleb does not accompany us to the psychiatrist's office for our next appointment. He says he has a meeting he cannot reschedule, but I think this is only an excuse. After last night, we have been dancing around each other. Plus, Dr. Robichaud is working on signing now, until Nathaniel gets his voice back, and Caleb disagrees with that tactic. He thinks that when Nathaniel is ready to tell us who hurt him, he will, and until then, we are only pushing.

I wish I had his patience, but I cannot sit here and watch Nathaniel struggle. I can't stop thinking that for every single moment Nathaniel is silent, there is someone else in this world who should have been rendered speechless, stopped in his tracks.

Today, we have worked our way through practical signs for food – cereal, milk, pizza, ice cream, breakfast. The terms in the ASL book are grouped like that – in units that go together. There is a picture of the word, the written letters, and then a sketch of a person making the sign. Nathaniel gets to pick what we study. He has jumped from the seasons, to things to eat, and is now flipping the pages again.

'Where he'll stop nobody knows . . .' Dr. Robichaud jokes.

The book falls open to a page with a family on it. 'Oh, that's a good one,' I say, trying the sign at the top – the F hand-shapes making a circle away from oneself.

Nathaniel points to the child. 'Like this, Nathaniel,' Dr. Robichaud says. 'Boy.' She mimics touching the bill of a base-ball cap. Like many of the signs I've learned, this one is a perfect match to the real thing.

'Mother,' the psychiatrist continues, helping Nathaniel hold out his hand, touch the thumb to the side of his chin, and wiggle the fingers.

'Father.' The same sign, but the thumb touches the side of the forehead. 'You do it,' Dr. Robichaud says.

*Do it.*

All those thin black lines on the page have tangled together, a fat snake that's coming toward him, grabbing him by the neck. Nathaniel can't breathe. He can't see. He hears Dr. Robichaud's voice all around him, *father father father.*

Nathaniel lifts his hand, puts a thumb to his forehead. He wiggles the fingers of his hand. This sign looks like he's making fun of someone.

Except it isn't funny at all.

'Look at that,' the psychiatrist says, 'he's better than we are, already.' She moves on to the next sign, *baby.* 'That's good, Nathaniel,' Dr. Robichaud says after a moment. 'Try this one.'

But Nathaniel doesn't. His hand is jammed tight to the side of his head, his thumb digging into his temple. 'Honey, you're going to hurt yourself,' I tell him. I reach for his hand and he jumps back. He will not stop signing this word.

Dr. Robichaud gently closes the ASL book. 'Nathaniel, do you have something you want to say?'

He nods, his hand still fanning out from the side of his head. All the air leaves my body. 'He wants Caleb –'

Dr. Robichaud interrupts. 'Don't speak for him, Nina.'

'You can't think that he –'

'Nathaniel, has your daddy ever taken you somewhere, just the two of you?' the psychiatrist asks.

Nathaniel seems confused by the question. He nods slowly.

'Has he ever helped you get dressed?' Another nod. 'Has he ever hugged you, in your bed?'

I am frozen in my seat. My lips feel stiff when I speak. 'It's not what you're thinking. He just wants to know why Caleb isn't here. He misses his father. He wouldn't have needed a sign if it was . . . if it was . . .' I can't even say it. 'He could have pointed, a thousand times over,' I whisper.

'He might have been afraid of the consequences of such a direct identification,' Dr. Robichaud explains. 'A label like this gives him an extra layer of psychological protection. Nathaniel,' she continues gently. 'Do you know who hurt you?'

He points to the ASL book. And signs *father* again.

Be careful what you wish for. After all these days, Nathaniel has given a name, and it is the one I would never have expected to hear. It is the one that renders me as immobile as a stone, the very material Caleb prefers to work with.

I listen to Dr. Robichaud make the call to BCYF; I hear her tell Monica there is a suspect, but I am a hundred miles away. I'm watching with the objectivity of someone who knows what will happen next. A detective will be put on the case; Caleb will be called in for questioning. Wally Moffett will contact the Portland DA's office. Caleb will either confess and be convicted on the strength of that statement; or else Nathaniel will have to accuse him in open court.

This nightmare is only just beginning.

He could not have done it. I know this as well as I know anything about Caleb after so many years. I can still see him walking the halls at midnight, holding an infant Nathaniel by his feet, the only position in which our colicky baby would stop screaming. I can see him sitting next to me at Nathaniel's graduation from the two-day class in preschool, how he'd cried without shame. He is a good, strong, solid man; the kind of man you would trust with your life, or your child's.

But if I believe that Caleb is innocent, it means I don't believe Nathaniel.

Small memories prick at my mind. Caleb, suggesting that Patrick might be the one to blame. Why bring up his name, if not to take the heat off himself? Or Caleb telling Nathaniel he didn't have to learn sign language if he didn't want to. Anything, to keep the child from confessing the truth.

I have met convicted child molesters before. They don't wear badges or brands or tattoos announcing their vice. It's hidden under a soft, grandfatherly smile; it's tucked in the pocket of a button-down shirt. They look like the rest of us, and that's what makes it so frightening – to know that these beasts move among us, and we are none the wiser.

They have girlfriends and wives who have loved them, unaware.

I used to wonder how mothers wouldn't have some inkling that this was going on in their homes. There had to have been a moment where they made a conscious decision to turn away before they saw something they didn't want to. No wife, I used to think, could sleep next to a man and not know what was playing through the loop of his mind.

'Nina.' Monica LaFlamme touches my shoulder. When did she even arrive? I feel like I'm coming awake from a coma; I shake myself into consciousness and look for Nathaniel right away. He's playing in the psychiatrist's office, still, with a Brio train set.

When the social worker looks at me, I know that this is what she's suspected all along. And I cannot blame her. In her shoes, I would have thought the same thing. In fact, in the past, I have.

My voice is old, stripped. 'Have the police been called?'

Monica nods. 'If there's anything I can do for you . . .'

There is somewhere I need to go, and I cannot have Nathaniel with me. It hurts to have to ask, but I have lost my barometer for trust. 'Yes,' I ask. 'Will you watch my son?'

I find him at the third job site, making a stone wall. Caleb's face lights up as he recognizes my car. He watches me get out, and then he waits, expecting Nathaniel. It's enough to propel me forward, so that by the time I reach him I am nearly at a dead run, and I slap him as hard as I can across the face.

'Nina!' Caleb catches my wrists and holds me away from him. 'What the hell!'

'You bastard. How could you, Caleb? How *could* you?'

He pushes me away, rubbing his fingers against his cheek. My hand rises on it, a bright print. Good. 'I don't know what you're talking about,' Caleb says. 'Slow down.'

'Slow down?' I spit out. 'I'll make it really simple: Nathaniel told us. He told us what you did to him.'

'I didn't do anything to him.'

For a long moment, I don't say a word, just stare. 'Nathaniel said I . . . I . . . ,' Caleb falters. 'That's ridiculous.'

It is what they all say, the guilty ones, and it makes me unravel. 'Don't you dare tell me that you love him.'

'Of course I do!' Caleb shakes his head, as if to clear it. 'I don't know what he said. I don't know why he said it. But Nina, Jesus Christ. Jesus *Christ.*'

When I don't respond, every year we've spent together unspools, until we are both standing knee deep in a litter of memories that don't matter. Caleb's eyes are wide and wet. 'Nina, please. Think about what you're saying.'

I look down at my hands, one fist gripping the other tightly. It is the sign for *in*. In trouble. In love. In case. 'What I think is that kids don't make this up. That Nathaniel didn't make this up.' I raise my gaze to his. 'Don't come home tonight,' I say, and I walk back to my car with great precision, as if my heart has not gone to pieces inside me.

Caleb watches the taillights of Nina's car disappear down the road. The dust that's kicked up in her wake settles, and the scene still looks like it did a minute ago. But Caleb knows things are completely different now; that there is no going back.

He will do anything for his son. Always has, always will.

Caleb looks down at the wall he's been crafting. Three feet, and it took him the better part of the day. While his son was in a psychiatrist's office, turning the world inside out, Caleb has been lifting stone, fitting it side by side. Once when he'd been dating Nina he'd shown her how to set together rocks with proportions that did not seem to meet. *All you need is one edge in common,* he'd told her.

Case in point, this jagged piece of quartz, kitty-corner to a fat, low block of sandstone. Now, he lifts the piece of sandstone and hurls it into the road, where it breaks into pieces. He raises the quartz and sends it spinning into the woods behind him. He demolishes the wall, all this work, piece by careful piece. Then he sinks into the pile of rubble and presses his dusty hands to his eyes, crying for what cannot be put back together.

I have one more place to go. In the clerk's office of the East District Court, I move like an automaton. Tears keep coming, no matter how I try to will them away. This is not a professional demeanor, but I couldn't care less. This is not a professional matter, it's a personal one.

'Where do you keep the protective order forms for juveniles?' I ask the clerk, a woman who is new to the court, and whose name I have forgotten.

She looks at me as if she's afraid to answer. Then she points to a bin. She fills it out for me, as I feed her the answers in a voice that I can't place.

Judge Bartlett receives me in chambers. 'Nina.' He knows me, they all do. 'What can I do for you?'

I hold the form out for him and lift my chin. *Breathe, speak, focus.* 'I am filing this on behalf of my son, Your Honor. I'd prefer not to do it in open court.'

The judge's eyes hold mine for a long second, then he takes the paper from my hands. 'Tell me,' he says gently.

'There is physical evidence of sexual abuse.' I am careful not to say Nathaniel's name. That, I cannot bear yet. 'And today, he identified the abuser as his father.' *His father,* not *my husband.*

'And you?' Judge Bartlett asks. 'Are you all right?'

I shake my head, my lips pressed tight together. I grasp my hands so tightly that I lose feeling in the fingers. But I don't say a word.

'If there's anything I can do,' the judge murmurs. But there is nothing he can do, or anyone else, no matter how many times the offer is extended. Everything has already been *done*. And that is the problem.

The judge scrawls the craggy landscape of his signature across the bottom of the form. 'You know this is only temporary. We'll have to have a hearing in twenty days.'

'That's twenty days I have to figure this out.'

He nods. 'I'm sorry, Nina.'

So am I. For not seeing what was under my nose. For not knowing how to protect a child in the world, but only in the legal system. For every choice I've made that has brought me to this moment. And, yes, for the restraining order that burns a hole in my pocket the entire drive back to my son.

These are the rules at home:
  Make your bed in the morning. Brush your teeth twice a day. Don't pull the dog's ears. Finish your vegetables, even if they're not as good as the spaghetti.

These are the rules at school:
  Don't climb up the outside of the slide. Don't walk in front of the swings while a friend is swinging. Raise your hand in Circle if you have something to say. Everybody gets to play a game, if they want to. Put on a smock if you're going to paint.

I know other rules, too:
  Buckle your seat belt.
  Never speak to a stranger.
  Don't tell, or you'll burn in Hell.

# 3

Life, it turns out, goes on. There is no cosmic rule that grants you immunity from the details just because you have come face-to-face with a catastrophe. The garbage cans still overflow, the bills arrive in the mail, telemarketers interrupt dinner.

Nathaniel comes into the bathroom just as I put the cap back on the tube of Preparation H. I read once that rubbing it into the skin around the eyes makes the swelling go down, the red fade. I turn to him with a smile so bright he backs away. 'Hey, sweetie. Did you brush your teeth?' He nods, and I take his hand. 'Let's read a book, then.'

Nathaniel scrambles onto his bed like any other five-year-old – it is a jungle, and he is a monkey. Dr. Robichaud has said that the children bounce back fast, faster even than their parents do. I hold onto this excuse as I open the book – one about a pirate blind in one eye who cannot see that the parrot on his shoulder is actually a poodle. I make it through the first three pages, and then Nathaniel stops me, his hand splayed across the bright painted pictures. His index finger waggles, and then he holds that hand up to his forehead again, making a sign I wish I could never see again.

*Where's Daddy?*

I take the book and set it on the nightstand. 'Nathaniel, he's not coming home tonight.' *He's not coming home* any *night*, I think.

He frowns at me. He doesn't know how to ask *why* yet, but that is what's caught in his head. Is he thinking that he's responsible for Caleb's exile? Has he been told there will be some kind of retribution, for confessing?

Holding his hands between mine – to keep him from inter-rupting – I try to make this as easy as I can. 'Right now, Daddy can't be here.'

Nathaniel tugs his arms free, curls his fingers up and in. *I want.*

God, I want, too. Nathaniel, angry, turns away from me. 'What Daddy did,' I say brokenly, 'was wrong.'

At that, Nathaniel bolts upright. He shakes his head vehemently.

This, I've seen before. If a parent is the one sexually abusing a child, the child is often told that it's a measure of love. But Nathaniel keeps shaking his head, so hard that his hair flies from side to side. 'Stop. Nathaniel, please stop.' When he does, he looks at me with the strangest expression, as if he does not understand me at all.

It is why I say the words out loud. I need to hear the truth. I need confirmation from my son. 'Did Daddy hurt you?' I whisper, the leading question Dr. Robichaud would not ask, would not let *me* ask.

Nathaniel bursts into tears and hides under his covers. He will not come out, not even when I say I'm sorry.

Everything in the motel room is the color of wet moss – the frayed rug, the bowl of the sink, the bilious bedspread. Caleb turns on the heat and the radio. He takes off his shoes and sets them neatly beside the door.

This is not a home; this is barely a residence. Caleb wonders about the other people staying at these efficiency cabins here in Saco. Are they all in limbo like him?

He cannot imagine sleeping here one night. And yet he knows he will live here a lifetime, if that is what it takes to help his son. He would give anything, for Nathaniel. Even, appar-ently, himself.

Caleb sits on the edge of the bed. He picks up the phone, then realizes he has no one to call. But he holds the receiver to his ear for a few moments, until the operator gets on and reminds him that no matter what, on the other end, someone is listening.

There is nothing for it: Patrick can't start his day without a chocolate croissant. The other cops rib him about it constantly – *Too upscale for doughnuts, are you, Ducharme?* He brushes it off, willing to suffer some teasing as long as the police secretary who orders the daily tray of baked goods includes his personal favorite. But that morning, when he walks into the cafeteria to grab his snack and fill his coffee cup, Patrick's croissant is missing.

'Aw, come on,' he says to the beat cop standing next to him. 'Are you guys being assholes? Did you hide it in the ladies' room again?'

'We didn't touch it, Lieutenant, swear.'

Sighing, Patrick walks out of the cafeteria to the desk where Mona is checking her e-mail. 'Where's my croissant?'

She shrugs. 'I placed the same order as always. Don't ask me.'

Patrick begins to walk through the police station, scanning the desks of the other detectives and the room where the street officers relax during their breaks. He passes the chief in the hall. 'Patrick, you got a second?'

'Not right now.'

'I have a case for you.'

'Can you leave it on my desk?'

The chief smirks. 'Wish you were half as single-minded about your police work as you are about your damn doughnuts.'

'Croissants,' Patrick calls to his retreating back. 'There's a difference.'

In the booking room, seated next to the bored desk sergeant, he finds the perp: a kid who looks like he was playing cop in his dad's uniform. Brown hair, bright eyes, chocolate on his chin. 'Who the hell are you?' Patrick demands.

'Officer Orleans.'

The desk sergeant folds his hands over his ample stomach. 'And the detective who's about to rip your head off, here, is Lieutenant Ducharme.'

'Why's he eating my breakfast, Frank?'

The older cop shrugs. 'Because he's only been here a day –'

'Six hours!' the kid proudly corrects.

Frank rolls his eyes. 'He don't know better.'

'*You* do.'

'Yeah, but if I told him so I wouldn't have gotten to see all this excitement.'

The rookie holds out the remaining bite of the croissant, his peace offering. 'I, uh, I'm sorry, Lieutenant.'

Patrick shakes his head. He considers going to the fridge and raiding the lunch the kid's mom has probably packed him. 'Don't let it happen again.'

Hell of a way to start a day; he counts on the combination of caffeine in the chocolate and his coffee to get him jump-started. By ten o'clock, no doubt, he'll have a monster headache. Patrick stalks back to his desk and plays his voice mail – three messages; the only one he really cares about is Nina's. 'Call me,' it says – that's all, no name, nothing. He picks up the phone, then notices the file that the chief has left on his desk.

Patrick opens the manila folder, reads the report from BCYF. The telephone receiver falls to the desk, where it lies buzzing long after he has run out of his office.

'All right,' Patrick says evenly. 'I'm going to get right on this. I'll go and talk to Caleb the minute I leave here.'

It's about all I can take, the incredible level calm of his voice. I drive my hands through my hair. 'For God's sake, Patrick. Will you just stop being such a . . . such a *cop?*'

'You want me to tell you that I feel like beating him unconscious for doing this to Nathaniel? That then I'd beat him up all over again for what he's done to you?'

The fury in his voice takes me by surprise. I tilt my head,

playing his anger over in my mind. 'Yes,' I answer softly. 'I do want you to tell me that.' He rests his hand on the back of my head. It feels like a prayer. 'I don't know what to do.'

Patrick's fingers cup my skull, separate the strands of my hair. I give myself up to this; imagine that he's unraveling my thoughts. 'That's why you've got me,' he says.

Nathaniel balks when I tell him where we're going. But if I stay inside for another minute, I am going to lose my mind.

Light falls through the stained-glass ceiling panels of St. Anne's, washing Nathaniel and me in a rainbow. At this hour, on a weekday, the church is as quiet as a secret. I walk with great care, trying not to make any more of a sound than is absolutely necessary. Nathaniel drags his feet, scuffing his sneakers along the mosaic floor.

'Stop that,' I whisper, and immediately wish I hadn't. My words reverberate against the stone arches and the polished pews and come running back to me. Trays of white votives glow; how many of these have been lit for my son?

'I'll only be a minute,' I tell Nathaniel, settling him in one of the pews with a handful of Matchbox cars. The polished wood makes a perfect racetrack – to prove this, I send a hot rod speeding to the other end. Then I walk toward the confessionals before I change my mind.

The booth is tight and overheated. A grate slides open against my shoulder; although I cannot see him, I can smell the starch Father Szyszynski uses on his clerical shirts.

There is a comfort to confession, if only because it follows rules that are never broken. And no matter how long it's been, you remember, as if there is a collective Catholic subconscious. You speak, the priest answers. You begin with the littlest sins, stacking them like a tower of alphabet blocks, and the priest gives you a prayer to knock them all down, so that you can start over.

'Bless me, Father, for I have sinned. It has been four months since my last confession.'

If he's shocked, he does a good job of hiding it.

'I . . . I don't know why I'm here.' Silence. 'I found out something, recently, that is tearing me apart.'

'Go on.'

'My son . . . he's been hurt.'

'Yes, I know. I've been praying for him.'

'I think . . . it seems . . . it's my husband who did this to him.' On the small folding chair, I am doubled over. Sharp pains move through me, and I welcome them – by now, I had thought myself incapable of feeling anything.

There is such a long silence I wonder if the priest has heard me. Then: 'And what is *your* sin?'

'My . . . what?'

'You can't confess for your husband.'

Anger bubbles up like tar, burning my throat. 'I didn't intend to.'

'Then what *did* you want to confess today?'

I have come to simply speak the words aloud to someone whose job is to listen. But instead I say, 'I didn't keep my son safe. I didn't see it at all.'

'Innocence isn't a sin.'

'How about ignorance?' I stare at the latticework between us. 'How about being naïve enough to think that I actually *knew* the man I fell in love with? How about wanting to make him suffer the way Nathaniel's suffering?'

Father Szyszynski lets this statement stand. 'Maybe he is.'

My breath catches. 'I love him,' I say thickly. 'I love him just as much as I hate him.'

'You need to forgive yourself for not being aware of what was happening. For wanting to strike back.'

'I don't know if I can.'

'Well, then.' A pause. 'Can you forgive *him?*'

I look at the shadow that is the priest's face. 'I am not that godly,' I say, and exit the confessional before he can stop me.

What's the point; I am already living my penance.

★          ★          ★

He doesn't want to be here.

The church, it sounds the way it does inside his head – a whooshing that's louder than all the words that aren't being spoken. Nathaniel looks at the little room his mother has gone into. He pushes a car down the pew. He can hear his heart.

He sets the rest of the Matchbox cars into their parking spots and inches his way out of the pew. With his hands burrowed under his shirt like a small animal, Nathaniel tiptoes down the main aisle of the church.

At the altar he kneels down on the steps to pray. He'd learned a prayer in Sunday school, one he was supposed to do at night that he usually forgot. But he remembers that you can pray for anything. It's like a birthday candle wish, except it goes straight to God.

He prays that the next time he tries to say something with his hands, everyone will understand. He prays that he will get his daddy back.

Nathaniel notices a marble statue beside him – a woman, holding Baby Jesus on her lap. He forgets her name, but she's all over the place here – on paintings and wall hangings and more stone sculptures. In every one, there's a mother with a child.

He wonders if once there was a daddy standing on that pedestal, in that painting, portrayed with the rest of the holy family. He wonders if everyone's father gets taken away.

Patrick knocks on the door of the cabin that the manager of Coz-E-Cottages has pointed out. When it swings open, Caleb stands on the other side, red-eyed and unshaven. 'Look,' Patrick says right away, 'this is incredibly awkward.'

Caleb looks at the police shield in Patrick's hand. 'Something tells me it's a little more awkward for me than for you.'

This is the man who has lived with Nina for seven years. Slept beside her, made a baby with her. This is the man who has had the life Patrick wanted. He had thought that he'd come to terms with the way things had worked out. Nina was happy,

Patrick wanted her to be happy, and if that meant that he himself was out of the picture, so be it. But that equation only worked when the man Nina chose was worthy. When the man Nina chose didn't make her cry.

Patrick has always believed Caleb to be a good father, and it stuns him a little, now, to realize how badly he wants Caleb to be the perp. If he is, it immediately discredits Caleb. If he is, there is proof that Nina picked the wrong guy.

Patrick feels his fingers curve into fists, but he tamps down on the urge to inflict pain. In the long run, that's not going to help either Nina or Nathaniel.

'Did you put her up to this?' Caleb says tightly.

'You did this all by yourself,' Patrick answers. 'Are you willing to come down to the station?'

Caleb grabs a jacket from the bed. 'Let's go right now,' he says.

At the threshold of the door, he reaches out and touches Patrick's shoulder. Instinct makes Patrick tense; reason forces him to relax. He turns and looks coolly at Caleb. 'I didn't do it,' Caleb says quietly. 'Nina and Nathaniel, they're the other half of me. Who would be stupid enough to throw that away?'

Patrick does not let his eyes betray him. But he thinks, for the first time, that perhaps Caleb is telling the truth.

Another man might not have felt comfortable with the relationship between his own wife and Patrick Ducharme. Although Caleb had never doubted Nina's fidelity – or even her feelings for him – Patrick wore his tattered heart on his sleeve. Caleb had spent enough dinners watching Patrick's eyes follow his wife around the kitchen; he'd seen Patrick spin Nathaniel in the air and tuck the boy's giggles into his pockets when he thought no one was looking. But Caleb did not mind, really. After all, Nina and Nathaniel were his. If he felt anything for Patrick, it was pity, because he wasn't as lucky as Caleb.

Early on, Caleb had been jealous of Nina's close friendship with Patrick. But she was a woman with a number of male friends. And it quickly became clear that Patrick was too much a part of Nina's past: Asking her to remove him from her life would have been a mistake, like separating Siamese twins who grew out from a shared heart.

He is thinking of Nina, now, as he sits at the scarred table in the investigation room of the police station with Patrick and Monica LaFlamme. He is remembering, specifically, the way Nina categorically denied any suggestion that Patrick might have been the one to hurt Nathaniel – yet just a few days later, had seemingly accused Caleb without a second thought.

Caleb shivers. Once, Patrick had said that they keep the interrogation rooms ten degrees cooler than the rest of the station, to make suspects physically uncomfortable. 'Am I under arrest?' he asks.

'We're just talking.' Patrick doesn't meet Caleb's eye. 'Old friends.'

Old friends, oh yes. Like Hitler and Churchill.

Caleb doesn't want to be sitting here, defending himself. He wants to talk to his boy. He wants to know if Nina finished reading him the pirate book. He wants to know if Nathaniel wet his bed again.

'We might as well get started.' Patrick turns on a tape recorder.

Caleb suddenly realizes his best source of information is sitting three feet away. 'You saw Nathaniel,' he murmurs. 'How is he?'

Patrick glances up, surprised. He's used to being the one who asks the questions.

'Was he okay, when you were there? Did he look like he'd been crying?'

'He was . . . he was all right, given the circumstances,' Patrick says. 'Now –'

'Sometimes, if he's not eating, you can distract him by talking about something he likes. Soccer, or frogs, like that. And while you talk you just keep putting food on his fork. Tell Nina.'

'Let's talk about Nathaniel.'

'What do you think I'm doing? Has he said anything yet? Verbally, I mean. Not with his hands?'

'Why?' Patrick asks guardedly. 'Are you worried he might have more to tell us?'

'Worried? I wouldn't care if the only word he could say was my name. I wouldn't care if it meant I'd be locked up for life. I just want to hear it for myself.'

'His accusation?'

'No,' Caleb says. 'His voice.'

I have run out of places to go. The bank, the post office, an ice cream for Nathaniel. A local park, the pet store. Since leaving the church, I have dragged us from building to building, running errands that don't need to be done, all so that I won't have to go back to my own home.

'Let's visit Patrick,' I announce, swinging into the parking lot of the Biddeford police station at the last minute. He'll hate me for this – checking up on his investigation – but above all, he'll understand. In the backseat of the car, Nathaniel slumps to the side, letting me know what he thinks of this idea.

'Five minutes,' I promise.

The American flag cracks sharply in the cold wind as Nathaniel and I walk up the path toward the front door. *Justice for all.* When we are about twenty feet away, the door opens. Patrick steps out first, shielding his eyes against the sun. Directly behind him are Monica LaFlamme and Caleb.

Nathaniel sucks in his breath, then wrenches free of me. At the same moment, Caleb sees him and goes down on one knee. His arms catch Nathaniel tight, hold him close. Nathaniel looks up at me with a wide smile, and in that awful moment I realize he thinks I have planned this for him, a wonderful surprise.

Patrick and I stand a distance away, bookends, bracketing this story as it happens.

He comes to his senses first. 'Nathaniel,' Patrick says quietly, firmly, and he goes to pull my son away. But Nathaniel is having none of that. He wraps his arms around Caleb's neck, he tries to burrow inside his coat.

Over our son's head, Caleb's eyes meet mine. He stands up, taking Nathaniel with him.

I force myself to look away. To think of the hundreds of children I've met – the ones who are bruised and filthy and starving and neglected – who scream as they are removed from their homes, and beg to stay with an abusive mother or father.

'Buddy,' Caleb says quietly, forcing Nathaniel to look at him. 'You know I'd like nothing better than to spend some time with you right now. But . . . I have something to do.'

Nathaniel shakes his head, his face crumpling.

'I'm gonna see you just as soon as I can.' Caleb walks toward me, bouncing Nathaniel in his arms; peels him off his own body and settles him into my embrace. By now, Nathaniel is crying so hard that the silent sobs choke him. His rib cage shudders under my palm like a dragon coming to life.

As Caleb heads toward his truck, Nathaniel lifts his gaze. His eyes are slitted and nearly black. He raises his fist and hits me on the shoulder. Then he does it again, and again, a tantrum waged against me.

'Nathaniel!' Patrick says sharply.

But it doesn't hurt. Not nearly as much as the rest.

'You have to expect some regression,' Dr. Robichaud says quietly, as we both watch Nathaniel lie listlessly on his stomach on the carpet of the playroom. 'His family is coming apart; in his mind, he's responsible for it.'

'He ran to his father,' I say. 'You should have seen it.'

'Nina, you know better than most people that doesn't prove Caleb's innocent. Kids in that situation believe they've got a special bond with the parent. Nathaniel running to him – that's textbook behavior.'

Or maybe, I let myself think, Caleb did nothing wrong. But I push the doubt away, because I am on Nathaniel's side now. 'So what do I do?'

'Absolutely nothing. You keep being the mother you always have been. The more Nathaniel understands that parts of his life are going to remain the same, the more quickly he'll overcome the changes.'

I bite my lip. It is in Nathaniel's best interests to admit to my own faults, but that's never easy to do. 'That may not be the best idea. I work a sixty-hour week. I wasn't exactly the hands-on parent. Caleb was.' Too late, I realize these were not the right words to use. 'I mean . . . well, you know what I mean.'

Nathaniel has rolled onto his side. Unlike the other times we've been in Dr. Robichaud's office, nothing has engaged his attention today. The crayons sit untouched, the blocks are neatly stacked in the corner, the puppet theater is a ghost town.

The psychiatrist takes off her glasses and wipes them on her sweater. 'You know, as a woman of science, I've always believed that we have the power to shape our own lives. But there's a big part of me that also thinks things happen for a reason, Nina.' Dr. Robichaud glances toward Nathaniel, who has gotten to his feet now, and is finally moving toward the table. 'Maybe he's not the only one who's starting over.'

Nathaniel wants to disappear. It can't be that hard; it happens every day to all sorts of things. The rain puddle outside the school is gone by the time the sun is in the middle of the sky. His blue toothbrush vanishes and is replaced by a red one. The cat next door goes out one night and never comes back. When he thinks about all this, it makes him cry. So he tries to dream of good things – X-Men and Christmas and maraschino cherries – but he can't even make pictures of them in his head. He tries to imagine his birthday party, next May, and all he can see is black.

He wishes he could close his eyes and fall asleep forever, just stay in that place where dreams feel so real. Suddenly he has a thought: Maybe *this* is the nightmare. Maybe he'll wake up and everything will be the way it is supposed to be.

From the corner of his eye Nathaniel sees that fat stupid

book with all the hands in it. If it wasn't for that book, if he'd never learned how to talk with his fingers, if he'd stayed quiet, this wouldn't have happened. Drawn upright, he walks to the table where it rests.

It's a loose-leaf, the kind of binder with three big teeth. Nathaniel knows how to open one; they have them at home. When the jaw is wide he takes out the first page, the one with a happy smiling man using his hand to say hello. The next page shows a dog, and a cat, and the signs for them. Nathaniel throws both on the floor.

He starts ripping out big chunks of paper, scattering them all around his feet like snow. He stomps on the pages with pictures of food. He tears in half the ones that show a family. He watches himself do this on the magic wall, a mirror on this side but glass out there. And then he looks down, and sees something.

This picture, it's the one he's been looking for all along.

He grabs the piece of paper so hard it wrinkles in his fist. He runs to the door that leads into Dr. Robichaud's office, where his mother is waiting. He does it just the way the black-and-white man on the page does. Pinching together his thumb and his forefinger, Nathaniel drags them across his neck, as if he is cutting his own throat.

He wants to kill himself.

'No, Nathaniel,' I say, shaking my head. 'No, baby, no.' Tears are running down his cheeks, and he holds fast to my shirt. When I reach for him he fights me, smooths a paper over my knee. He jabs his finger at one of the sketches.

'Slowly,' Dr. Robichaud instructs, and Nathaniel turns to her. He draws a line across his windpipe again. He taps together his forefingers. Then he points to himself.

I look down at the paper, at the one sign I do not recognize. Like the other groupings in the ASL book, this one has a heading. RELIGIOUS SYMBOLS. And the motion of Nathaniel's hands has not been suicidal. He has been tracing an imaginary clerical collar; this is the sign for *priest*.

*Priest. Hurt. Me.*

Tumblers click in my mind: Nathaniel mesmerized by the word *father* – although he has always called Caleb *daddy*. The children's book Father Szyszynski brought, which disappeared before we even had a chance to read it at bedtime, and still has not turned up. The fight Nathaniel put up this morning when I told him we were going to church.

And I remember one more thing: a few weeks ago, one Sunday when we'd mustered the effort to go to Mass. That night, when Nathaniel was getting undressed, I noticed he was wearing underwear that wasn't his. Cheap little Spiderman briefs, instead of the $7.99 miniature boxers I bought at GapKids so that Nathaniel could match his dad. *Where are yours?* I had asked.

And his answer: *At church.*

I assumed he'd had an accident at Sunday school and had received this spare pair from his teacher, who rummaged through the Goodwill bin. I made a mental note to thank Miss Fiore for taking care of it. But I had a wash to do and a child to bathe and a pair of motions to write, and I never did get a chance to speak to the teacher.

Now, I take my son's shaking hands, and I kiss the finger-tips. Now, I have all the time in the world. 'Nathaniel,' I say, 'I'm listening.'


An hour later, in my own home, Monica carries her mug to the sink. 'Is it all right with you if I tell your husband?'

'Of course. I would have told him myself, but . . .' My voice trails off.

'That's my job,' she finishes, saving me from speaking the truth: Now that I have forgiven Caleb, I do not know if he will forgive me.

I busy myself with the dishes – rinsing our mugs, squeezing dry the tea bags and putting them into the trash. I have specif-ically tried to focus on Nathaniel since leaving Dr. Robichaud's office – not only because it is the right thing to do, but because I am a terrible coward at heart. What will Caleb say, do?

Monica's hand touches my forearm. 'You were protecting Nathaniel.'

I look directly at her. No wonder there is a need for social workers; the relationships between people knot so easily, there needs to be a person skilled at working free the threads. Sometimes, though, the only way to extricate a tangle is to cut it out and start fresh.

She reads my mind. 'Nina. In your shoes, he would have reached the same conclusions.'

A knock on the door captures our attention. Patrick lets himself in, nods to Monica. 'I'm just on my way out,' she explains. 'If you want to reach me later, I'll be in my office.'

This is directed to both Patrick and me. Patrick will need her, presumably, to be kept abreast of the case. I will need her, presumably, for moral support. As soon as the door closes behind Monica, Patrick steps forward. 'Nathaniel?'

'He's in his room. He's okay.' A sob hops the length of my throat. 'Oh, my God, Patrick. I should have known. What did I do? What did I *do?*'

'You did what you had to,' he says simply.

I nod, trying to believe him. But Patrick knows it isn't working. 'Hey.' He leads me to one of the stools in the kitchen, sits me down. 'Remember when we were kids, and we used to play *Clue?*'

I wipe my nose with my sleeve. 'No.'

'That's because I always trounced you. You'd pick Mr. Mustard every time, no matter what the evidence said.'

'I must have let you win.'

'Good. Because if you've done it before, Nina, it's not going to be that hard to do it again.' He puts his hands on my shoulders. 'Give over. I know this game, Nina, and I'm good at it. If you let me do what I have to, without messing yourself up in the process, we can't lose.' Suddenly he takes a step away from me, stuffs his hands into his pockets. 'And you've got other things to work on, now.'

'Other things?'

Patrick turns, meets my eye. 'Caleb?'

It's like that old contest: Who will blink first? This time, I can't bear it; I am the one to look away. 'Then go lock him up, Patrick. It's Father Szyszynski. I know it, and you know it. How many priests have been convicted of doing just this – *shit!*' I wince, my own mistake hammering back. 'I talked to Father Szyszynski about Nathaniel during confession.'

'You *what?* What were you thinking?'

'That he was my *priest.*' Then I glance up. 'Wait. He thinks it's Caleb. That's what I thought, then. That's good, right? He doesn't know that he's the suspect.'

'What's important is whether Nathaniel knows it.'

'Isn't that crystal clear?'

'Unfortunately, it's not. Apparently, there's more than one way to interpret the word *father*. And by the same logic, there's a whole country full of priests out there.' He looks at me soberly. 'You're the prosecutor. You know this case can't afford another mistake.'

'God, Patrick, he's only five. He signed *priest*. Szyszynski is the only priest he even knows, the only priest who has any contact with him on a regular basis. Go ahead and ask Nathaniel if that's who he meant.'

'That's not going to stand up in court, Nina.'

Suddenly I realize that Patrick has not come only for Nathaniel; he has also come for me. To remind me that while I'm being a mother, I still have to think like a prosecutor now. We cannot name the accuser for Nathaniel; he has to do it himself. Otherwise, there is no chance of a conviction.

My mouth is dry. 'He isn't ready to talk yet.'

Patrick holds out his hand to me. 'Then let's just see what he can tell us today.'

Nathaniel is on the top bunk, sorting his daddy's old collection of baseball cards into piles. He likes the feel of their frayed edges, and the way they smell gray. His dad says to be careful, that one day these could pay for college, but Nathaniel couldn't care less.

Right now he likes touching them, staring at all the funny faces, and thinking that his dad used to do the same thing.

There's a knock, and his mom comes in with Patrick. Without hesitation, Patrick climbs up the ladder – all six-feet-two inches of him squashing into the small space between ceiling and mattress. It makes Nathaniel smile a little. 'Hey, Weed.' Patrick thumps the bed with a fist. 'This is comfy. Gotta get me one of these.' He sits up, pretends to crack his head on the ceiling. 'What do you think? Should I ask your mom to buy me a bed like this too?'

Nathaniel shakes his head and hands Patrick a card. 'Is this for me?' Patrick asks, then reads the name and smiles broadly. 'Mike Schmidt, rookie. I'm sure your dad will be thrilled you've been so generous.' He tucks it into his pocket and takes out a pad and pen at the same time. 'Nathaniel, you think it would be all right if I asked you some questions?'

Well. He is tired of questions. He is tired, period. But Patrick climbed all the way up here. Nathaniel jerks his head, *yes*.

Patrick touches the boy's knee, slowly, so slowly that it doesn't even make Nathaniel jump, although these days everything does. 'Will you tell me the truth, Weed?' he asks softly.

Slower this time, Nathaniel nods.

'Did your daddy hurt you?'

Nathaniel looks at Patrick, then at his mother, and emphatically shakes his head. He feels something open up in his chest, making it easier to breathe.

'Did somebody else hurt you?'

*Yes*.

'Do you know who it was?'

*Yes*.

Patrick's gaze is locked with Nathaniel's. He won't let him turn away, no matter how badly Nathaniel wants to. 'Was it a boy or a girl?'

Nathaniel is trying to remember – how is it said again? He looks at his mother, but Patrick shakes his head, and he knows that, now, it is all up to him. Tentatively, his hand comes up to his head. He touches his brow, as if there is a baseball cap there. 'Boy,' he hears his mother translate.

'Was it a grown-up, or a kid?'

Nathaniel blinks at him. He cannot sign those words.

'Well, was he big like me, or little like you?'

Nathaniel's hand hovers between his own body, and Patrick's. Then falls, deliberately, in the middle.

That makes Patrick grin. 'Okay, it was a medium guy, and it was someone you know?'

*Yes.*

'Can you tell me who?'

Nathaniel feels his whole face tighten, muscles bunching. He squeezes his eyes shut. *Please please please*, he thinks. *Let me.* 'Patrick,' his mother says, and she takes a step forward, but Patrick holds out a hand and she stops.

'Nathaniel, if I brought you a bunch of pictures' – he points to the baseball cards –'like these . . . do you think you could show me who this person was?'

Nathaniel's hands flutter over the piles, bumblebees choosing a place to light. He looks from one card to the other. He cannot read, he cannot speak, but he knows that Rollie Fingers had a handlebar moustache, Al Hrabosky looked like a grizzly bear. Once something sticks in his head, it stays there; it's just a matter of getting it back out again.

Nathaniel looks up at Patrick; and he nods. This, this he can do.


Monica has been in accommodations far worse than the efficiency suite where she finds Caleb Frost, but this is almost more jarring, and she thinks it is because she has seen the sort of home where he is supposed to be. The minute Caleb recognizes her face through the keyhole of the door, he throws it open. 'What's the matter with Nathaniel?' he asks, true fear washing over his features.

'Nothing. Nothing at all. He's made another disclosure. A new ID.'

'I don't understand.'

'It means you're no longer a suspect, Mr. Frost,' Monica says quietly.

Questions rise in him like a bonfire. 'Who,' Caleb manages, the word tasting of ash.

'I think you should go home and speak to your wife about it,' she answers, then turns briskly and walks away, her purse tucked primly beneath her arm.

'Wait,' Caleb calls out. He takes a deep breath. 'Is . . . is Nina okay with that?'

Monica smiles, lets the light reach her eyes. 'Who do you think asked me to come?'

Peter agrees to meet me at the district court, where I'm going to have the restraining order vacated. The process takes all of ten minutes, a rubber stamp, with the judge asking only one question: *How is Nathaniel?*

By the time I come into the lobby, Peter is racing through the front door. He immediately comes toward me, concern drawing down the corners of his mouth. 'I got here as soon as I could,' he says breathlessly. His eyes dart to Nathaniel, holding my hand.

He thinks I need him to twist the letter of the law for me, squeeze blood from the stone heart of a judge, do something to stack the scales of justice in my favor. Suddenly I am embarrassed by the reason I called him.

'What is it?' Peter demands. 'Anything, Nina.'

I slip my hands in my coat pockets. 'I really just wanted to get a cup of coffee,' I admit. 'I wanted to feel, for five minutes, like everything was back the way it used to be.'

Peter's gaze is a spotlight; it sees down to my soul. 'I can do that too,' he says, and loops his arm through mine.

Although there are no seats left at the bar at Tequila Mockingbird by the time Patrick arrives, the bartender takes one look at him and hints strongly to a visiting businessman that he take his drink to a booth in the back. Patrick wraps his black mood around him like a parka, hops onto the vacant stool, and signals to Stuyvesant. The bartender comes over pouring his usual, Glenfiddich. But he hands Patrick the bottle, and keeps the glass of scotch behind the bar. 'Just in case someone else here wants a shot,' Stuyv explains.

Patrick looks at the bottle, at the bartender. He tosses his car keys on the counter, a fair trade, and takes a long swig of the liquor.

By now, Nina has been to the court and back. Maybe Caleb has made it home in time for dinner. Maybe they've gotten Nathaniel to bed early, and are even now lying in the dark next to each other.

Patrick picks up his bottle again. He has been in their bedroom before. Big king-size bed. If he was married to her, they'd sleep on a narrow cot, that's how close to her he would be.

He'd been married himself for three years, because he believed that if you wanted to get rid of a hole, you filled it. He had not realized at the time that there were all sorts of fillers that took up space, but had no substance. That made you feel just as empty.

Patrick pitches forward as a blond woman hits him hard on the shoulder. 'You pervert!'

'What the *hell?*'

She narrows her eyes. They are green, and caked with too much mascara. 'Did you just touch my ass?'

'No.'

Suddenly, she grins, insinuating herself between Patrick and the elderly man on his right. 'Well, damn. How many times will I have to walk by before you do?'

Sliding her drink beside Patrick's bottle, she holds out her hand. Manicured. He hates manicured hands. 'I'm Xenia. And you are?'

'Really not interested.' Patrick smiles tightly, turns back to the bar.

'My mom didn't raise a quitter,' Xenia says. 'What do you do for a living?'

'I'm a funeral director.'

'No, really.'

Patrick sighs. 'I'm on the vice squad.'

'No, *really.*'

He faces her again. 'Really. I'm a police officer.'

Her eyes widen. 'Does that mean I'm busted?'

'Depends. Did you break any laws?'

Xenia's gaze travels the length of his body. 'Not yet.' Dipping a finger in her drink – something pink and frothy – she touches her shirt, and then his. 'Wanna go to my place and get out of these wet clothes?'

He blushes, then tries to pretend it didn't happen. 'Don't think so.'

She props her chin on her fist. 'Guess you better just buy me a drink.'

He starts to turn her down again, then hesitates. 'All right. What are you having?'

'An Orgasm.'

'Of course,' Patrick says, hiding a smile. It would be so easy – to go home with this girl, waste a condom and a few hours' sleep, get the itch out of his blood. Chances are, he could fuck her without ever telling her his name. And in return, for just a few hours, he would feel like someone wanted him. He would be, for a night, someone's first choice.

Except this particular someone would not be *his* first choice.

Xenia trails her nails along the nape of Patrick's neck. 'I'm just going to carve our initials in the door of the ladies' room,' she murmurs, backing away.

'You don't know my initials.'

'I'll make them up.' She gives a little wave, then disappears into the crowd.

Patrick calls over Stuyvesant and pays for Xenia's second drink. He leaves it sweating on a cocktail napkin for her. Then he walks out of Tequila Mockingbird stone sober, facing the fact that Nina has ruined him for anyone else.

Nathaniel lies on the lower bunk while I read him a book before bedtime. Suddenly, he jackknifes upright and fairly flies across the room, to the doorway where Caleb stands. 'You're home,' I say, the obvious, but he doesn't hear. He is lost in this moment.

Seeing them together, I want to kick myself again. How could I ever have believed that Caleb was at fault?

The room is suddenly too small to hold all three of us. I back out of it, closing the door behind me. Downstairs, I wash the silverware that sits on the drying rack, already clean. I pick Nathaniel's toys up from the floor. I sit down on the living room couch; then, restless, stand up and arrange the cushions.

'He's asleep.'

Caleb's voice cuts to the quick. I turn, my arms crossed over my chest. Does that look too defensive? I settle them at my sides, instead. 'I'm . . . I'm glad you're home.'

'Are you?'

His face gives nothing away. Coming out of the shadows, Caleb walks toward me. He stops two feet away, but there might as well be a universe between us.

I know every line of his face. The one that was carved the first year of our marriage, by laughing so often. The one that was born of worries the year he left the contracting company to go into business for himself. The one that developed from focusing hard on Nathaniel as he took his first steps, said his first word. My throat closes tight as a vise, and all the apologies sit bitter in my stomach. We had been naïve enough to believe that we were invincible; that we could run blind through the hairpin turns of life at treacherous speeds and never crash. 'Oh, Caleb,' I say finally, through the tears, 'these things, they weren't supposed to happen to *us*.'

Then he is crying too, and we cling to each other, fitting our pain into each other's hollows and breaks. 'He did this. He did this to our baby.'

Caleb holds my face in his hands. 'We're going to get through it. We're going to make Nathaniel get better.' But his sentences turn up at the ends, like small animals begging. 'There are three of us in this, Nina,' he whispers. 'And we're all in it together.'

'Together,' I repeat, and press my open mouth against his neck. 'Caleb, I'm so sorry.'

'Shh.'

'I am, no, I am –'

He cuts me off with a kiss. The action arrests me; it is not what I have been expecting. But then I grab him by the collar of his shirt and kiss him back. I kiss him from the bottom of my soul, I kiss him until he can taste the copper edge of sorrow. *Together.*

We undress each other with brutality, ripping fabric and popping buttons that roll under the couch like secrets. This is the anger overflowing: anger that this has happened to our son, that we cannot turn back time. For the first time in days I can get rid of the rage; I pour it into Caleb, only to realize that he is doing the same to me. We scratch, we bite, but then Caleb lays me down with the softest touch. Our eyes lock when he moves inside me; neither one of us would dare to blink. My body remembers: This is what it is to be filled by love, instead of despair.

The last case I worked on with Monica LaFlamme had not been a success. She sent me a report, stating that a Mrs. Grady had called her. Apparently, while drying her seven-year-old off after a bath, Eli grabbed the Mickey Mouse towel and began to simulate sexual thrusting, then named his stepfather as the perp. The child was taken to Maine Medical Center, but there were no physical findings. Oh, and Eli suffered from something called oppositional defiance disorder.

We met at my office, in the room we use to assess children for competency exams. On the other side of a one-way mirror was a small table, tiny chairs, a few toys, and a rainbow painted on the wall. Monica and I watched Eli run around like a hellion, literally climbing the curtains. 'Well,' I said. 'This should be fun.'

In the adjoining room, Mrs. Grady ordered her son to stop. 'You need to calm down, Eli,' she said. But that just made him scream more, run more.

I turned to Monica. 'What's oppositional defiance disorder, anyway?'

The social worker shrugged. 'My guess?' she said, gesturing toward Eli. '*That*. He does the opposite of what you ask him to do.'

I gaped at her. 'It's a real psychiatric diagnosis? I mean, it's not just the definition of being seven years old?'

'Go figure.'

'What about forensic evidence?' I unrolled a grocery bag, and pulled out a neatly folded towel. Mickey's face leered up at me. The big ears, the sideways grin – it was creepy on its own merits, I thought.

'The mother washed it after the bath that night.'

'Of course she did.'

Monica sighed as I handed the towel to her. 'Mrs. Grady's intent on going to trial.'

'It's not her decision.' But I smiled as Eli's mother took a spot beside me and the police officer who was investigating the case. I gave her my spiel, about seeing what information Ms. LaFlamme could get out of Eli, for the record.

We watched through the mirror as Monica asked Eli to sit down.

'No,' he said, and started running laps.

'I need you to come sit down in this chair. Can you do that, please?'

Eli picked up the chair and threw it in the corner. With supreme patience, Monica retrieved it and set it down beside her own. 'Eli, I need you to come sit in this chair for a little while, and then we'll go get Mommy.'

'I want my mommy now. I don't want to be here.' But then he sat down.

Monica pointed to the rainbow. 'Can you tell me what color this is, Eli?'

'Red.'

'That's very good! How about this color?' She touched her finger to the yellow stripe.

Eli rolled his eyes in her direction. 'Red,' he said.

'Is that red, or is it a different color than the other stripe?'

'I want my mommy,' Eli shouted. 'I don't want to talk to you. You are a big fat fart.'

'All right,' Monica said evenly. 'Do you want to go get your mommy?'

'No, I don't want my mommy.'

After about five more minutes, Monica terminated the interview. She raised her brows at me through the glass and shrugged. Mrs. Grady leaned forward immediately. 'What happens next? Do we set a date for court?'

At that, I took a deep breath. 'I'm not sure what happened to your son,' I said diplomatically. 'Probably, there was some abuse involved; his behavior seems to indicate that. And I think you would be wise to assess your husband's involvement with Eli. However, we can't prosecute this case criminally.'

'But . . . but you just said it. There was *abuse*. What more does there have to be?'

'You saw Eli now. There's no way he's going to be able to come into a courtroom and sit down on a chair and answer questions.'

'If you spend more time with him –'

'Mrs. Grady, it's not just me. He's going to have to answer questions posed by the defense attorney and the judge, and there's going to be a jury a few feet away staring at him, too. You understand better than anyone does what Eli's behavioral issues are, because you see them on a daily basis. But unfortunately, the legal system doesn't work for people who can't respond within its framework.'

The woman's face was white as a sheet. 'Well . . . what do

you do, then, with cases like this? How do you protect children like Eli?'

I turned to the one-way mirror, where Eli was breaking crayons in half. 'We can't,' I admitted.

I bolt upright in bed, my heart racing. A dream. It has only been a dream. My heart is pounding, sweat covers me like a veil, but my house is still.

Caleb lies on his side, facing me, breathing deeply. There are silver tracks crossing his face; he has been crying in his sleep. I touch my finger to a tear, bring it to my mouth. 'I know,' I whisper, and then lie awake for the rest of the night.

I doze off as the sun comes up, and wake to the first frost of the winter. It comes early in Maine, and it changes the landscape. Hoary and barbed, the world is a place that might shatter the moment you step into it.

Caleb and Nathaniel are nowhere to be found; the house is so quiet it throbs around me as I dress and make my way downstairs. The cold sneaks in through the crack beneath the door and wraps itself around my ankles while I drink a cup of coffee and stare at the note on the table. WE'RE IN THE BARN.

When I find them, they are mixing mortar. Well, Caleb is. Nathaniel crouches on the floor of the workshop, using bits of brick to outline the dog sleeping on the cement slab floor. 'Hey,' Caleb grins, glancing up. 'We're building a brick wall today.'

'So I see. Has Nathaniel got a hat and gloves? It's too cold out for –'

'I've got them right here.' Caleb jerks his chin to the left; there are the blue fleece accessories.

'Well. I have to go out for a little while.'

'So go.' Caleb drags the hoe through the cement, mixing it.

But I don't want to. I'm not needed here; I know that. For years, I've been the main breadwinner; the odd wheel out. Lately, though, I've gotten used to my own house. Lately, I haven't much wanted to leave.

'Maybe I –'

Whatever I'm about to say is interrupted as Caleb leans down and yells right into Nathaniel's face. *'No!'* Nathaniel quails, but not before Caleb grabs his arm and pulls him away.

'Caleb –'

'You don't touch the antifreeze,' Caleb yells at Nathaniel. 'How many times do I have to tell you that? It's *poison*. It can hurt you *badly.*' He picks up the bottle of Prestone he's been mixing into the mortar to keep it from freezing in this temperature, and then covers the mess Nathaniel's made with a cloth. A stain, alien green, seeps through and spreads. The dog laps at the sweet spill, until Caleb shoves it away. 'Get out of there, Mason.'

In the corner, Nathaniel's on the verge of tears. 'Come here,' I say, opening up my arms. He flies into them, and I kiss the top of his head. 'Why don't you go get a toy from your room to play with while Daddy's working?'

Nathaniel runs off to the house with Mason at his heels, both of them smart enough to know a reprieve when it comes up and grabs them. Caleb shakes his head in disbelief. 'Just undermine me, Nina, you go right ahead.'

'I'm not undermining you. I'm . . . well, look at him, Caleb, you scared him to death. He wasn't doing it on purpose.'

'It doesn't matter. He was told and he didn't listen.'

'Don't you think he's been through enough lately?'

Caleb wipes his hands on a towel. 'Yes, I do. So how's he going to take it when the dog he loves drops dead, because he broke the rules and did something he was expressly told not to do?' He caps the Prestone, sets it high on a shelf. 'I want him to feel like a normal kid again. And if Nathaniel had done this three weeks ago, you can bet I would have punished him.'

This logic I can't even follow. Biting down on my response, I turn and walk out. I am still angry with Caleb by the time I reach the police department and find Patrick asleep at his desk.

I slam the door of his office, and he nearly falls out of his chair. Then he winces, holds his hand to his head. 'I'm just glad to see that you public servants are really earning all my tax dollars,' I say sourly. 'Where's the digital lineup?'

'I'm working on it,' Patrick responds.

'Oh, yeah, I can see that you're really exerting yourself.'

He stands up and frowns at me. 'Who peed in your coffee?'

'I'm sorry. Just some domestic bliss spilling over. No doubt I'll find my manners by the time you find probable cause to lock up Szyszynski.'

Patrick looks me right in the eye. 'How's Caleb?'

'Fine.'

'Doesn't sound like things are fine . . .'

'Patrick. I'm here because I need to know that something's going on. Anything. Please. Show me.'

He nods and takes my arm. We move through corridors I have never navigated at the Biddeford Police Department, and finally wind up in a back room not much bigger than a closet. The lights are off, a green screen hums on a computer, and the boy who sits in front of the keyboard has acne and a fistful of Munchos. 'Dude,' he says to Patrick.

I turn to Patrick, too. 'You're kidding.'

'Nina, this is Emilio. Emilio helps us with digital imaging. He's a computer whiz.'

He leans over Emilio and hits a button on the keyboard. Ten photos appear on the screen, one of them Father Szyszynski's.

I lean forward, look close. There is nothing in the priest's eyes or his easy smile that would make me believe he is capable of such an abomination. Half of the people in the photos are dressed in the vestments of priests; the other half are wearing the standard issue jumpsuit of the local jail. Patrick shrugs. 'The only picture I could find of Szyszynski was in his clerical collar. So I have to make the convicts look like priests, too. That way there won't be any cause for question later on, after Nathaniel makes his ID.'

He says it like it is going to happen. For that, I adore him. As we watch, Emilio superimposes a collar over a picture of a ham-faced thug. 'Got a minute?' Patrick asks me, and when I nod, he leads me out of the little makeshift office, through a side door, and into a courtyard.

There is a picnic table, a basketball hoop, and around this, a high chain link fence. 'All right,' I say immediately. 'What's wrong?'

'Nothing's wrong.'

'If nothing was wrong, you would have been able to talk to me in front of your teenage hacker.'

Patrick sits down on the bench of the picnic table. 'It's about the lineup.'

'I *knew* it.'

'Will you just stop?' Patrick waits until I sit down, then looks right into me. Those eyes, they've got a history with mine. They were the first things I saw when I came to, after being hit in the skull with a baseball thrown by Patrick at Little League. They were the fortification I needed at sixteen to ride the chairlift at Sugarloaf, although I am terrified of heights. For almost my whole life, they've told me I'm doing all right, during moments when it was not in my own power to answer. 'You need to understand something, Nina,' Patrick says. 'Even if Nathaniel points right to Szyszynski's picture . . . it's a weak disclosure. Surveying a lineup isn't something a five-year-old can really understand. It could be he picks the only familiar face; it could be he points to anyone, just to get us to leave him alone.'

'Don't you think I know that?'

'You understand what it takes to secure a conviction. We can't lead him into making an ID just because you want this case to move faster. All I'm saying is that Nathaniel might be able to talk a week from now. Maybe even tomorrow. Eventually, he's going to be able to say the name of the perp, and that's going to be a much stronger accusation.'

Leaning forward, I bury my hands in my hair. 'And then what am I supposed to do? Let him testify?'

'That's the way it works.'

'Not when my child's the victim,' I snap.

Patrick touches my arm. 'Nina, without Nathaniel's testimony against Szyszynski, you have no case.' He shakes his head, certain I haven't really thought this through.

But I have never been more sure of anything in my life. I will do what it takes to keep my son from being a witness. '-You're right,' I tell Patrick. 'And that's why I'm counting on you to get the priest to confess.'

Before I realize it, I've driven to St. Anne's. I pull into the parking lot and get out of my car, avoiding the front walk to tiptoe, instead, around to the back of the building. The rectory is here, attached to the main body of the church. My sneakers leave prints in the frost, the trail of an invisible man.

If I climb onto the ridge of a drainage well, I can see into the window. This is Father Szyszynski's personal apartment, the living room. A cup of tea sits, the bag still draining, on a side table. A book – Tom Clancy – is cracked open on the couch. All around are gifts he's received from parishioners: a handmade afghan, a wooden Bible stand, a framed drawing by a child. All of these people believed him, too; I have not been the only sucker.

What I am waiting for, exactly, I don't know. But as I stand there I remember the day before Nathaniel had stopped speaking, the last time we had all gone to Mass. There had been a reception for the two clergymen who'd come to visit, a banner hung from the serving table wishing them a safe journey home. I remember that the flavored coffee that morning was hazelnut. That there were no powdered sugar doughnuts left, though Nathaniel had wanted one. I remember talking to a couple I had not seen in several months, and noticing that the other children were following Father Szyszynski downstairs for his weekly storytime. 'Go, Nathaniel,' I'd said. He had been hiding behind me, clinging to my legs. I fairly pushed him into joining the others.

I pushed him into it.

I stand here on the drainage ditch for over an hour, until the priest comes into his living room. He sits down on the couch and picks up his tea and he reads. He doesn't know I'm watching him. He doesn't realize that I can slide into his life, just as surreptitiously as he has slid into mine.

As Patrick has promised, there are ten photos – each the size of a baseball card, each with a different 'priest' portrayed on the front. Caleb examines one. 'The San Diego Pedophiles,' he murmurs. 'All that's missing are the stats.'

Nathaniel and I come into the room, holding hands. 'Well,' I say brightly. 'Look who's here.'

Patrick gets to his feet. 'Hiya, Weed. Remember when I talked to you the other day?' Nathaniel nods. 'Will you talk to me today, too?'

He is already curious about the photos; I can feel it in the way he's tugging toward the couch. Patrick pats the cushion beside him, and Nathaniel immediately climbs up. Caleb and I sit on either side of them, in two overstuffed chairs. *How formal we look*, I think.

'I brought some pictures for you, just like I said I would.' Patrick takes the rest from the manila envelope and arranges them on the coffee table, as if he is going to play solitaire. He looks at me, and then at Caleb – a silent warning that now this is his show. 'You remember telling me that someone hurt you, Weed?'

*Yes.*

'And you said you knew who it was?'

Another nod, this one longer in coming.

'I want to show you some pictures, and if one of these people is the one who hurt you, I want you to point to it. But if the person who hurt you *isn't* in one of the pictures, you just shake your head no, so I know he's not there.'

Patrick has phrased this perfectly – an open, legally valid invitation to make a disclosure; a question that does not lead Nathaniel to believe there's a right answer.

Even though there is.

We all watch Nathaniel's eyes, dark and boundless, moving from one face to another. He is sitting on his hands. His feet don't quite reach the floor.

'Do you understand what I need you to do, Nathaniel?' Patrick asks.

Nathaniel nods. One hand creeps out from beneath a thigh. I want him to be able to do this, oh, I want it so badly it aches, so that this case will be set into motion. And just as badly, for the same reasons, I want Nathaniel to fail.

His hand floats over each card in succession, a dragonfly hovering over a stream. It lights, but doesn't settle. His finger brushes Szyszynski's face, moves on. With my eyes, I try to will him back. 'Patrick,' I blurt out. 'Ask him if he recognizes anyone.'

Patrick smiles tightly. Through his teeth, he says, 'Nina, you *know* I can't do that.' Then, to Nathaniel: 'What do you think, Weed? Do you see the person who hurt you?'

Nathaniel's finger dips like a metronome, traces the edge of Szyszynski's card. He hesitates there, then begins to move the other cards. We all wait, wondering what he is trying to tell us. But he slides one photo up, and another, until he has two columns. He connects them with a diagonal. All this deliberation, and it turns out he is only making the letter N.

'He touched the card. The right one,' I insist. 'That ID's good enough.'

'It's not.' Patrick shakes his head.

'Nathaniel, try again.' I reach over and mess the pictures up. 'Show me which one.'

Nathaniel, angry that I've ruined his work, shoves at the cards so that half of them fly off the table. He buries his face on his bent knees and refuses to look at me.

'That was useful,' Patrick mutters.

'I didn't see you doing anything to help!'

'Nathaniel.' Caleb reaches across me to touch our son's leg. 'You did great. Don't listen to your mother.'

'That's *lovely*, Caleb.'

'I didn't mean it like that and you know it.'

My cheeks are burning. 'Oh, really?'

Ill at ease, Patrick begins to stuff the pictures back into the envelope. 'I think we ought to talk about this somewhere else,' Caleb says pointedly.

Nathaniel's hands come up to cover his ears. He burrows sideways, between the sofa pillows and Patrick's leg. 'Now look what you've done to him,' I say.

The mad in the room is all the colors of fire, and it presses down on him, so that Nathaniel has to make himself small enough to fit in the cracks of the cushions. There is something hard in Patrick's pocket where he's pressed up tight to it. His pants smell like maple syrup and November.

His mother, she's crying again, and his dad is yelling at her. Nathaniel can remember when just waking up in the morning used to make them happy. Now, it seems that no matter what he does, it's wrong.

He knows this is true: What happened happened because of him. And now that he's dirty and different, his own parents do not know what to do with him.

He wishes he could make them smile again. He wishes he had the answers. He knows they are there, but they're dammed up in his throat, behind the Thing He Is Not Supposed to Tell.

His mother throws up her hands and walks toward the fireplace, her back to everyone. She's pretending no one can see, but she's crying hard now. His father and Patrick are trying hard not to look at each other, their eyes bouncing like a Superball off everything in the tiny room.

When his voice returns, it reminds Nathaniel of the time his mother's car would not start last winter. She turned the key and the engine groaned, whining and whining before it kicked to life. Nathaniel feels that same thing now, in his belly. That kindling, that croak, the tiniest bubble rising up his windpipe. It chokes him; it makes his chest swell. The name that gets shoved out is feeble, thin as gruel, not nearly the thick and porous block that has absorbed all his words these past weeks. In fact, now that it sits on his tongue, bitter pill, it is hard to believe something this tiny has filled all the space inside him.

Nathaniel worries no one will hear him, since so many angry words are flying like kites in the room. So he comes up on his knees, presses himself along Patrick's side, cups his hand to the big man's ear. And he speaks, he speaks.

Patrick feels the warm weight of Nathaniel on his left side. And no wonder; Patrick himself is ducking from the comments Caleb and Nina are winging at each other; Nathaniel has to be faring just as poorly. He slides an arm around the child. 'It's okay, Weed,' he murmurs.

But then he feels Nathaniel's fingers brush the hair at his nape. A sound slips into his ear. It's not much more than a puff of breath, but Patrick has been waiting. He squeezes Nathaniel once more, because of what he's done. Then he turns to interrupt Caleb and Nina. 'Who the hell,' Patrick asks, 'is Father Glen?'

The logical time to search the church is during Mass, when Father Szyszynski – a.k.a. Father Glen, to the children like Nathaniel who cannot pronounce his last name – is otherwise occupied. Patrick cannot remember the last time he went on a hunt for evidence wearing a coat and tie, but he wants to blend in with the crowd. He smiles at strangers while they all file into the church before nine A.M.; and when they turn into the main nave of the church he walks in the opposite direction, down a staircase.

Patrick doesn't have a warrant, but then this is a public space, and he does not need one. Still, he moves quietly through the hallway, reluctant to draw attention to himself. He passes a classroom where small children sit wriggling like fish at even smaller tables and chairs. If he were a priest, where would he stash the Goodwill box?

Nina has told him about the Sunday when Nathaniel came home with a different pair of underwear on beneath his clothes. It might not mean anything. But then again, it might. And Patrick's job is to overturn all the stones so that when he goes to back Szyszynski into a corner, he has all the ammunition he needs to do it.

The Goodwill box is not next to the water fountain or the restrooms. It's not in Szyszynski's office, a richly paneled vestibule stacked with wall-to-wall religious texts. He tries a couple of locked doors in the hallway, rattling them to see if they'll give way.

'Can I help you?'

The Sunday school teacher, a woman who has the look of a mother about her, stands a few feet behind Patrick. 'Oh, I'm sorry,' he says. 'I didn't mean to interrupt your class.'

He tries to summon all his charm, but this is a woman who is probably used to white lies, to hands caught in the cookie jar. Patrick continues, thinking on his feet. 'Actually, my two-year-old just soaked through his jeans during Father Szyszynski's sermon . . . and I hear there's a Goodwill box somewhere around here?'

The teacher smiles in sympathy. 'Water into wine gets them every time,' she says. She leads Patrick into the classroom, where fifteen tiny faces turn to assess him, and hands him a big blue Rubbermaid box. 'I have no idea what's inside, but good luck.'

Minutes later Patrick is hidden in the boiler room, the first place he finds where he won't readily be disturbed. He is knee deep in old clothing. There are dresses that must be a good thirty years old, shoes with worn soles, toddler's snow pants. He counts seven pairs of underwear – three of which are pink, with little Barbie faces on them. Lining the remaining four up on the floor, he takes a cell phone from his pocket and dials Nina.

'What do they look like?' he says when she answers. 'The underwear.'

'What's that humming? Where are you?'

'In the boiler room of St. Anne's,' Patrick whispers.

'Today? *Now?* You're kidding.'

Impatient, Patrick pokes at the briefs with one gloved finger. 'Okay, I've got a pair with robots, one with trucks, and two that are plain white with blue trim. Does anything sound familiar?'

'No. These were boxers. They had baseball mitts on them.'

How she remembers this, he can't imagine. Patrick couldn't even tell you what pair of shorts he has on today. 'There's nothing here that matches, Nina.'

'It's got to be there.'

'If he kept them, which we don't know he did, they could very well be in his private quarters. Hidden.'

'Like a trophy,' Nina says, and the sadness in her voice makes Patrick ache.

'If they're there, we'll get them with a warrant,' he promises. He doesn't say what he is thinking: that the underwear alone will not really prove anything. There are a thousand ways to explain away that kind of evidence; he has most likely heard them all.

'Have you talked to –'

'Not yet.'

'You'll call me, won't you? After?'

'What do you think?' Patrick says, and hangs up. He bends down to fork all the spilled clothing back into the bin, and notices something bright in an alcove behind the boiler. Working his big body into a pretzel, he stretches out a hand but cannot grab it. Patrick looks around the custodial closet, finds a fireplace poker, and slides it behind the bulk of the boiler to the small hollow. He snags a corner of it – paper, maybe? – and manages to drag it within his arm's reach.

Baseball mitts. One hundred percent cotton. Gap, size – S.

He pulls a brown paper bag from his pocket. With his gloved fingers, he turns the underwear over in his hand. On the left rear, slightly off center, there is a stiff stain.

In the custodial closet, directly beneath the altar where Father Szyszynski is at that moment reading Scripture aloud, Patrick bows his head and prays that in a situation as unfortunate as this one, there might be a shred of pure luck.

Caleb feels Nathaniel's giggle like a tiny earthquake, shuddering up from the rib cage. He presses his ear down more firmly against his son's chest. Nathaniel is lying on the floor; Caleb is lying on him, his ear tipped close to the boy's mouth. 'Say it again,' Caleb demands.

Nathaniel's voice is still thready, syllables hanging together by a string. His throat needs to learn how to hold a word again, cradle it muscle by muscle, heft it onto the tongue. Right now, this is all new to him. Right now, it is still a chore.

But Caleb can't help himself. He squeezes Nathaniel's hand as the sound flounders out, spiky and tentative. *'Daddy.'*

Caleb grins, so proud he could split in two. Beneath his ear, he hears the wonder in his son's lungs. 'One more time,' Caleb begs, and he settles in to listen.

A memory: I am searching all over the house for my car keys, because I am already late to drop Nathaniel at school and go to work. Nathaniel is dressed in his coat and boots, waiting for me. 'Think!' I say aloud, and then turn to Nathaniel. 'Have you seen my keys?'

'They're under there,' he answers.

'Under where?'

A giggle erupts from deep inside him. 'I made you say *underwear.*'

When I laugh along with him, I forget what I've been looking for.

Two hours later, Patrick enters St. Anne's again. This time, it is empty. Candles flicker, casting shadows; dust motes dance in the slices of light thrown by the stained-glass windows. Patrick immediately heads downstairs to Father Szyszynski's office.

The door is wide open, the priest sits at his desk. For a moment, Patrick enjoys the feeling of voyeurism. Then he knocks, twice, firmly.

Glen Szyszynski glances up, smiling. 'Can I help you?'

*Let's hope so,* Patrick thinks, and he walks inside.

Patrick pushes a Miranda form across the investigation room table toward Father Szyszynski. 'It's just a standard practice, Father. You're not in custody, and you're not under arrest . . . but you're willing to answer questions, and the law says I need to tell you you've got rights before I ask you a single thing.'

Without hesitation, the priest signs the list of rights Patrick has just read aloud.

'I'm happy to do anything that helps Nathaniel.'

Szyszynski had immediately volunteered to help with the investigation. He agreed to give a blood sample when Patrick said they needed to rule out anyone who'd been around Nathaniel. At the hospital, watching the phlebotomist, Patrick had wondered if the sickness in this man's veins was measurable, as much a part of the fluid as the hemoglobin, the plasma.

Now, Patrick leans back in his chair and stares at the priest. He has faced a thousand criminals, all of whom proclaim their innocence or pretend to have no idea what he is talking about. Most of the time he is able to acknowledge their barbarity with the cool detachment of a law enforcement professional. But today, this slight man sitting across from him – well, it is all Patrick can do to not beat the priest bloody just for speaking Nathaniel's name.

'How long have you known the Frosts, Father?' Patrick asks.

'Oh, I've known them since I first came to the parish. I had been sick for a while, and was given a new congregation. The Frosts moved to Bid-deford a month after I became a priest here.' He smiles. 'I baptized Nathaniel.'

'Do they come to church regularly?'

Father Szyszynski's gaze slides to his lap. 'Not as regularly as I'd like,' he admits. 'But you didn't hear it from me.'

'Have you taught Nathaniel in Sunday school?'

'I don't teach it; a parent does. Janet Fiore. While the service is going on upstairs.' The priest shrugs. 'I love children, though, and I like to connect with the little ones –'

*I bet you do,* Patrick thinks.

'– so after the service, when the congregation is enjoying fellowship and coffee, I take the children downstairs and read a story to them.' He grins sheepishly. 'I'm afraid I'm a bit of a frustrated actor.'

No surprise there, either. 'Where are the parents, while you're reading?'

'Enjoying a few moments to themselves upstairs, for the most part.'

'Does anyone else read to the children with you, or are you alone?'

'Just me. The Sunday school teachers usually finish cleaning the room, and then go up for coffee. The storytime only lasts about fifteen minutes.'

'Do the children ever leave the room?'

'Only to go to the bathroom, right down the hall.'

Patrick considers this. He does not know how Szyszynski managed to get Nathaniel by himself, when all the other children were allegedly present, too. Maybe he gave them the book to look over for themselves, and followed Nathaniel into the bathroom. 'Father,' Patrick says, 'have you heard how Nathaniel was hurt?'

There is a hesitation, and then the priest nods. 'Yes. Unfortunately, I have.'

Patrick locks his eyes on Szyszynski's. 'Did you know that there's physical evidence Nathaniel was anally penetrated?' He is looking for the slightest pinking of the man's cheeks; a telltale hitch of his breathing. He is looking for surprise, for backpedaling, for the beginnings of panic.

But Father Szyszynski just shakes his head. 'God help him.'

'Did you know, Father, that Nathaniel has told us *you* were the one that hurt him?'

Finally, the shock that Patrick has expected. 'I . . . I . . . of course I haven't hurt him. I would never do that.'

Patrick remains silent. He wants Szyszynski to think about all the priests around the globe who've been found guilty of this offense. He wants Szyszynski to realize that he's walked himself right onto the gallows of his own execution. 'Huh,' Patrick says. 'Funny, then. Because I talked to him just the other night, and he specifically told me that it was Father Glen. That's what the kids call you, isn't it, Father? Those kids you . . . love?'

Szyszynski shakes his head repeatedly. 'I didn't. I don't know what to say. The boy must be confused.'

'Well, Father, that's why you're here today. I need to know if you can think of any reason why Nathaniel might say you hurt him, if you didn't.'

'The child's been through so much –'

'Did you ever insert anything in his anus?'

'No!'

'Did you ever see anyone insert anything in his anus?'

The priest draws in his breath. 'Absolutely not.'

'Then why do you imagine Nathaniel would say what he did? Can you think of anything that might have made him think it happened, even though it didn't?' Patrick leans forward. 'Maybe a time you were alone with him, something occurred between you two that might have put this idea into his head?'

'I was never alone with him. There were fourteen other children around.'

Patrick rocks his chair back on its rear legs. 'Did you know that I found a pair of Nathaniel's underwear behind the boiler of the custodial closet? The laboratory says there's semen on it.'

Father Szyszynski's eyes widen. 'Semen? *Whose?*'

'Was it yours, Father?' Patrick asks quietly.

'*No.*'

A flat denial. Patrick has expected nothing less than this. 'Well, I hope for your sake you're right, Father, because we're going to be able to tell from DNA testing on your blood whether that's true.'

Szyszynski's face is pale and drawn; his hands are trembling. 'I'd like to leave now.'

Patrick shakes his head. 'I'm sorry, Father,' he says. 'But I'm placing you under arrest.'

Thomas LaCroix has never met Nina Frost, although he's heard about her. He remembers when she got a conviction for a rape that occurred in a bathtub, although all the evidence had been washed away. He has been a district attorney too long to doubt his own abilities – last year, he even locked away a priest in Portland for this same crime – but he also knows that these sorts of cases are extremely difficult to win. However, he wants to put on a good act. It has nothing to do with Nina Frost or her son – he'd just like York County's prosecutors to know how they do things up in Portland.

She answers the phone on the first ring. 'It's about time,' she says, when he introduces himself. 'I really need to discuss something with you.'

'Absolutely. We can talk tomorrow at the courthouse, before the arraignment,' Thomas begins. 'I just wanted to call before –'

'Why did they pick you?'

'I beg your pardon?'

'What makes you the best attorney Wally could find to prosecute?'

Thomas draws in his breath. 'I've been in Portland for fifteen years. And I've tried a thousand cases like this.'

'So you're just phoning in a performance, now.'

'I didn't say that,' Thomas insists, but he is thinking: *She must be a wonder on cross-examination.* 'I understand that you're nervous about tomorrow, Nina. But the arraignment, well, you know exactly what it's going to entail. Let's just get through it, and then we can sit down and strategize about your son's case.'

'Yes.' Then, dryly: 'Do you need directions?'

Another dig – this is her territory, her life; he is an outsider on both counts. 'Look, I can imagine what you're going through. I have three children of my own.'

'I used to think I could imagine it too. I thought that's what made me good at what I did. I was wrong on both counts.'

She falls silent, all the fire having burned out of her. 'Nina,' Thomas vows, 'I will do everything in my power to prosecute this case the way you would.'

'No,' she replies quietly. 'Do it better.'

'I didn't get a confession,' Patrick admits, striding past Nina into her kitchen. He just wants his failure immediately set out there, like a carcass to be picked apart. There's nothing she can say to berate him he hasn't already said to himself.

'You . . .' Nina stares at him, then sinks onto a stool. 'Oh, Patrick, no.'

Anguish pushes on his shoulders, makes him sit down too. 'I tried, Nina. But he wouldn't cave in. Not even when I told him about the semen, and Nathaniel's disclosure.'

'So!' Caleb's voice interrupts firmly, brightly. 'You finished with your ice cream, buddy?' He throws a warning like a knife between his wife and Patrick; tilts his head meaningfully toward Nathaniel. Patrick has not even noticed the boy sitting at the table, having a bedtime snack. He took one look at Nina, and forgot there might be anyone else in the room.

'Weed,' he says. 'You're up late.'

'It's not bedtime yet.'

Patrick has forgotten about Nathaniel's voice. Still rough, it sounds better suited to a grizzled cowboy than a small child, but it is a symphony all the same. Nathaniel hops off his seat to run to Patrick, extends a skinny arm. 'Wanna feel my muscle?'

Caleb laughs. 'Nathaniel was watching the Ironman competition on ESPN.'

Patrick squeezes the tiny biceps. 'Gosh, you could deck me with an arm like that,' he says soberly, then turns toward Nina. 'He's strong. Have you seen how *strong* this guy is?'

He is trying to convince her of a different sort of strength, and she knows it. Nina crosses her arms. 'He could be Hercules, Patrick, and he'd still be my little boy.'

'Mom,' Nathaniel wails.

Over his head, Nina mouths, 'Did you arrest him?'

Caleb puts his hands on Nathaniel's shoulders, steering him back toward his bowl of melting ice cream. 'Look, you two need to talk – and clearly, here isn't the best place to do it. Why don't you just go out? You can fill me in after Nathaniel's gone to sleep.'

'But don't you want to –'

'Nina,' Caleb sighs, 'you're going to understand what Patrick says, and I'm going to need to have it explained. You might as well be the translator.' He watches Nathaniel take the last bite of ice cream into his mouth. 'Come on, buddy. Let's see if that guy from Romania popped a vein in his neck yet.'

At the threshold of the kitchen door, Nathaniel lets go of his father's hand. He runs toward Nina, catching her at the knees, a near tackle. 'Bye, Mom,' he says, smiling, his dimples deep. 'Sweep tight.'

It's an uncanny malapropism, Patrick thinks. If Nina could, she'd whisk away this whole mess for Nathaniel. He watches her kiss her son good night. As Nathaniel hurries back toward Caleb, she ducks her head and blinks, until the tears aren't quite as bright in her eyes. 'So,' she says, 'let's go.'

In an effort to improve the revenues on slow Sunday nights, Tequila Mockingbird has established the Jimmy Buffet Key Largo Karaoke Night, an all-you-can-eat burgerfest paired with singing. When Patrick and I walk into the bar, our senses are assaulted: A string of lights in the shape of palm trees adorn the bar; a crepe-paper parrot hangs from the ceiling; a girl with too much makeup and too little skirt is butchering 'The Wind Beneath My Wings.' Stuyvesant sees us come in and grins. 'You two never come in on a Sunday.'

Patrick looks at some poor waitress, shivering in a bikini as she serves a table. 'And now we know why.'

Stuyv sets two napkins down in front of us. 'The first margarita is on the house,' he offers.

'Thanks, but we need something a little less . . .'

'Festive,' I finish.

Stuyvesant shrugs. 'Suit yourself.'

After he turns away to get our drinks and burgers, I feel Patrick's eyes on me. He is ready to talk, but I'm not, not just yet. Once the words are hanging there in the open air, there is no taking back what is going to happen.

I look at the singer, clutching the mike like a magic wand. She has absolutely no voice to speak of, but here she is, belting out her off-key rendition of a song that's crappy to begin with. 'What makes people do things like that?' I say absently.

'What makes people do any of the things they do?' Patrick lifts his drink, bares his teeth after he takes a sip. There is a smattering of applause as the woman gets down from the makeshift stage, probably because she's done. 'I hear that karaoke's some kind of self-discovery deal. Like yoga, you know? You go up there and you muster the courage to do something you never in a million years thought you could do, and when it's over, you're a better person because of it.'

'Yeah, and the rest of the audience needs Excedrin. Give me hot coals to walk over, any day. Oh, *that's* right, I've already done that.' To my embarrassment, tears come to my eyes; to hide this, I take a great gulp of my whiskey. 'Do you know when I talked to him, he told me to think about forgiveness? Can you believe he had the nerve to say that to me, Patrick?'

'He wouldn't admit anything,' Patrick answers softly. 'He looked at me like he didn't have a clue what I was talking about. Like when I told him about the underwear, and the semen stain, it was a shock.'

'Patrick,' I say, lifting my gaze to his, 'what am I going to do?'

'If Nathaniel testifies –'

'No.'

'Nina . . .'

I shake my head. 'I'm not going to be the one who does that to him.'

'Then wait a while, until he's stronger.'

'He is *never* going to be strong enough for that. Am I supposed to wait until his mind has managed to erase it . . . and then make him sit on a witness stand and bring it all back again? Tell me, Patrick, how is that in Nathaniel's best interests?'

Patrick is quiet for a moment. He knows this system like I do; he knows I'm right. 'Maybe once the semen comes back as a match, the priest's lawyer can talk to him and work out some kind of deal.'

'A deal,' I repeat. 'Nathaniel's childhood is being traded for a deal.'

Without saying a word, Patrick lifts my whiskey glass and hands it to me. I take a tentative sip. Then a larger one, even though my throat bursts into flame. 'This . . . is horrible,' I wheeze, coughing.

'Then why did you order it?'

'Because *you* always do. And I don't feel like being myself tonight.'

Patrick grins. 'Maybe you should just have your usual white wine, then, and go up and sing for us.'

As if he has cued it, the woman who assists the karaoke machine man approaches us, holding out a binder. Her bleached hair hangs into her face, and she is wearing pantyhose with her tropical sarong miniskirt. 'Hons,' she says to us. 'You want to do a duet?'

Patrick shakes his head. 'I don't think so.'

'Oh, come on. There are some cute songs here for couples like you. 'Summer Nights,' remember that one from *Grease?* Or how about that one Aaron Neville and Linda Ronstadt do?'

I am not here; this is not happening. A woman is not pressuring me into singing karaoke when I have come to discuss putting my son's rapist in jail. 'Go away,' I say succinctly.

She glances down at my hamburger, untouched. 'Maybe

you can get a side of manners with that,' she says, and twitches back to the stage.

When she's gone, the weight of Patrick's eyes rests heavy on me. 'What?' I demand.

'Nothing.'

'Clearly, there's something.'

He takes a deep breath, lets it out. 'You may not ever forgive Szyszynski, Nina, but you won't be able to move past this . . . to help *Nathaniel* move past this . . . until you stop cursing him.'

I drain the rest of my liquor. 'I will curse him, Patrick, until the day he dies.'

A new singer fills in the space that has fallen between the two of us. A heavyweight woman with hair that touches her ass, she sways her considerable hips as the riff begins playing on the karaoke machine.

*It only takes a minute . . .*
*For your life to move on past . . .*

'What is she doing up there?' I murmur.

'Yeah . . . she's actually *good*.'

We both look away from the stage, and our eyes meet. 'Nina,' Patrick says, 'you're not the only one hurting. When I see you like this . . . well, it kills me.' He looks down at his drink, stirs it once. 'I wish –'

'I wish too. But I could wish till the world stops turning, and it wouldn't change a thing, Patrick.'

*History was once today . . .*
*Before the moment got away. . . .*
*Nice guys, baby, always finish last.*

Patrick laces his fingers with mine on the table. He looks at me, hard, as if he is going to be quizzed on the details of my face. Then, with what seems to be a great effort, he turns away.

'The truth is there shouldn't be any justice for motherfuckers like him. People like that, they ought to be shot.'

Clasped together, our hands look like a heart. Patrick squeezes, I squeeze back. It is all the communication we need, this pulse between us, my reply.

The most pressing issue the next morning involves what we are supposed to do with Nathaniel. It hasn't occurred to either Caleb or myself before this; only when the courthouse looms into view do I realize that Nathaniel cannot be at this arraignment . . . and cannot be left alone. In the hallway, he stands between us, holding both of our hands – a living bridge.

'I could sit with him in the lobby,' Caleb volunteers, but I immediately reject that solution. Caleb looks down at Nathaniel. 'Don't you have a secretary who could watch him for a while?'

'This isn't my district,' I point out. 'And I'm not leaving him with someone I don't know.'

Of course not, never again. Although, as it turns out, it is not the strangers we have to be wary of.

We are leaning hard against this impasse when a guardian angel arrives. Nathaniel sees her first, and tears down the hallway. 'Monica!' he shrieks, and she lifts him into the air, swinging him around.

'That is the most fabulous word I've ever heard,' Monica laughs.

Nathaniel beams. 'I can talk now.'

'That's what Dr. Robichaud told me. She said she can't get a word in edgewise anymore when you come to her office.' She switches Nathaniel onto her other hip and turns to us. 'How are you holding up?'

As if there is an answer to that question, today.

'Well,' Monica says, as if we've responded. 'We're just going to head down to the playroom near the family court. Sound good, Nathaniel?' She raises her brows. 'Or do you have alternate plans for him?'

'No . . . not at all,' I murmur.

'That's what I figured. Child care this morning . . . it probably wasn't your top priority.'

Caleb touches Nathaniel's golden hair. 'Be good,' he says, and kisses his cheek.

'He's always good.' Monica sets him on his feet, and begins to lead him away. 'Nina, you know where to find us when you're done.'

I watch them walk for a moment. Two weeks ago I could not stand Monica LaFlamme; now I am indebted to her. 'Monica,' I call out, and she turns. 'Why don't you have children?'

Shrugging, she smiles faintly. 'To date, no one's asked me.'

Our eyes meet, and that is all it takes to erase the history between us. 'Their loss,' I say, and I smile.

Thomas LaCroix is two inches shorter than I am, and going bald. It makes no difference whatsoever, of course, but I find myself shooting glances at Wally during this meeting, wondering why he could not find the most perfect specimen of a prosecutor, one polished on the outside as well as the inside, so that no jury could possibly find fault.

'We're turning this entirely over to Tom,' my boss says. 'You know we support you and Caleb, we're a hundred percent behind you . . . but we don't want there to be any problems on appeal. And if we're in the courtroom, it might look like we're stacking the decks against this guy.'

'I understand, Wally,' I say. 'No offense taken.'

'Well!' Wally stands, having done his job here for the day. 'We'll all be waiting to hear what transpires.'

He pats my shoulder as he exits. When he leaves, it is just the three of us left – Caleb, myself, and Thomas LaCroix. Like a good prosecutor – like *me* – he jumps right into business. 'They're not going to arraign him until after lunch because of all the publicity,' Tom says. 'Did you see the media when you came in?'

See it? We had to run the gauntlet. If I hadn't known a

service entrance into the court, I never would have gotten Nathaniel inside.

'Anyway, I've already talked to the bailiffs. They're going to clear the other prisoners off the docket before they bring in Szyszynski.' He checks his watch. 'We're scheduled for one o'clock right now, so you've got some time.'

I flatten my hands on the table. 'You will not be putting my son on the stand,' I announce.

'Nina, you know this is just an arraignment. A rubber stamp process. Let's just –'

'I want you to know this, and to know it now. Nathaniel isn't going to be testifying.'

He sighs. 'I've done this for fifteen years. And we're just going to have to see what comes to pass. Right now, you know better than I do what the evidence is. You certainly know better than I do how Nathaniel is faring. But you also know there are some pieces of the puzzle we're waiting on – like the lab reports, and your son's recovery. Six months from now, a year from now . . . Nathaniel might be doing a whole lot better, and taking the stand might not be as much of a hardship.'

'He is five years old. In those fifteen years, Tom, how many cases with a five-year-old witness ended up with a perp in jail for life?'

Not a single one, and he knows it. 'Then we'll wait,' Tom says. 'We have some time, and the defendant is going to want time too, you know that.'

'You can't hold him in jail forever.'

'I'm going to ask for $150,000 bail. And I doubt the Catholic Church will post it for him.' He smiles at me. 'He's not going anywhere, Nina.'

I feel Caleb's hand steal into my lap, and I grab onto it. I think he is supporting me, at first, but then he squeezes my fingers nearly to the point of pain. 'Nina,' he says pleasantly, 'maybe we should just let Mr. LaCroix do his job right now.'

'It's my job too,' I point out. 'I put children on the stand every day, and I watch them fall apart, and then I watch the abusers walk. How can you ask me to forget that, when we're talking about Nathaniel?'

'Exactly – we're talking about Nathaniel. And today he needs a mother more than he needs a mother who is a prosecutor. We need to look at this in steps, and today that step is keeping Szyszynski locked up,' Tom says. 'Let's just focus, and once we clear this hurdle, we can decide what to do next.'

I stare into my lap, where I've nervously pleated my skirt into a thousand wrinkles. 'I know what you're saying.'

'Good, then.'

Lifting my gaze, I smile slightly. 'You're saying the same thing I do, to victims, when I really don't know if I have any chance of securing a conviction.'

To his credit, Tom nods. 'You're right. But I'm not trying to con you. We never know which cases are going to work out, which cases are going to take a plea, which kids will make a turnaround, which kids will heal to the point where a year from now, they're able to contribute in a way they can't that first day.'

I get to my feet. 'But you said it yourself, Tom. Today I'm not supposed to give a damn about those other kids. Today I just care about my own.' I walk to the door before Caleb even has risen from his seat. 'One o'clock,' I say, and it is a warning.

Caleb doesn't catch up to her until they are in the lobby, and then, he has to pull her aside to a small nook, where reporters will not find them. 'What was that all about?'

'I'm protecting Nathaniel.' Nina crosses her arms, daring him to say otherwise.

She seems shaky and unsteady, not at all herself. Maybe it is just the truth of this day. God knows, Caleb isn't faring all that well either. 'We ought to go tell Monica that there's a delay.'

But Nina is busy putting on her coat. 'Can you do it?' she asks. 'I need to run to the office.'

'Now?' Alfred, and the superior court building, is only fifteen minutes away. But still.

'It's something I have to give to Thomas,' she explains.

Caleb shrugs. He watches Nina walk out the front steps. The flashes of several cameras strike her like bullets, freezing her in time as she jogs down the steps. Caleb sees her brush off a reporter with no more effort than she would use to wave away a fly.

He wants to run after her, hold Nina until that wall around her cracks and all the pain spills out. He wants to tell her that she doesn't have to be so strong around him, because they are in this together. He wants to take her downstairs to the bright room with alphabet squares on the floor, sit with their son between them. All she has to do is take off those focused blinders; then she will see that she isn't alone.

Caleb goes so far as to open the glass door, to stick his head outside. By now she is a dot, far across the parking lot. Her name hovers on his lips, but then there is an explosion that blinds him – a newspaper photographer, again. Backing inside, he tries to shake the double vision, but it is a long time before he can see clearly; and so he never witnesses Nina's car leaving the courthouse lot, turning in the opposite direction of her office.

I'm late.

I hurry through the front door of the court, around the line of people waiting to go through the metal detector. 'Hey, Mike,' I say breathlessly, slipping behind the familiar bailiff, who just nods. Our courtroom is to the left; I open the double doors and walk inside.

It is filled with reporters and cameramen, all lined up in the back rows like the bad kids on the rear seats of a bus. This is a big story for York County, Maine. This is a big story for any place.

I walk to the front, where Patrick and Caleb are sitting. They have left a seat on the aisle for me. For a moment I fight my natural inclination – to continue through the gate, and sit at the prosecutor's table with Thomas LaCroix. That is why we 'pass the bar' – we are allowed, by virtue of that test, to work in the front of the courtroom.

I don't know the defense attorney. Probably someone from Portland. Someone the diocese keeps on retainer for things like this. There is a cameraman set up to the right of the defense table, his head bent close to the machine in preparation.

Patrick notices me first. 'Hey,' he says. 'You all right?'

As I expect, Caleb is angry. 'Where have you been? I've tried –'

Whatever he is about to say is interrupted as a bailiff speaks. 'The Honorable Judge Jeremiah Bartlett presiding.'

The judge, of course, I know. He signed the restraining order against Caleb. He instructs us to sit down, and I try, but my body has gone stiff as a board and the seat does not fit me. My eyes take in everything and nothing all at once.

'Are we set for the arraignment on *State v. Szyszynski?*' the judge asks.

Thomas rises smoothly. 'Yes, Your Honor.'

At the defense table, the other attorney stands. 'I'm representing Father Szyszynski, and we're ready, Your Honor.'

I have seen this a thousand times before; one bailiff moves forward toward the bench. He does this to protect the judge. After all, the people brought in as defendants are criminals. Anything could happen.

The door to the holding cell opens, and the priest is led out. His hands are cuffed in front of him. Beside me, I feel Caleb forget to take his next breath. I hold my purse on my lap, a death grip.

The second bailiff leads the priest to the defense table, the inside seat, because he will have to stand up in front of the judge to enter his plea. He is close enough, now, that I could spit at him. I could whisper, and he might hear me.

I tell myself to be patient.

My eyes go to the judge, then to the bailiffs. They are the ones I am worried about. They stand behind the priest, make sure he sits down.

*Move back. Move back move back move back.*

I slide my hand into my purse, past the familiar, to the heat that leaps into my hand. The bailiff takes a step away – this defendant, scum of the earth, still has the right to privacy with his own attorney. There are words moving around the court-room like small insects, distractions I do not really notice.

The minute I stand up, I've jumped off the cliff. The world goes by in a haze of color and light; my weight accelerates, head-over-heels. Then I think, *Falling is the first step in learning how to fly.*

In two steps, I am across the aisle of the courtroom. In a breath, I hold the gun up to the priest's head. I pull the trigger four times.

The bailiff grabs my arm but I won't let go of the weapon. I can't, until I know that I've done it. There is blood spreading, and screams, and then I'm falling again, forward, past the bar, where I am supposed to be. 'Did I get him? Is he dead?'

They slam me onto the ground, and when I open my eyes, I can see him. The priest lies with half his head missing, just a few feet away.

I let go of the gun.

The weight on me takes familiar shape, and then I hear Patrick in my ear. 'Nina, stop. Stop fighting.' His voice brings me back. I see the defense attorney, hiding under the stenog-rapher's table. The press, their cameras flashing like a field of fireflies. The judge, pushing the panic button on his desk and yelling to clear the courtroom. And Caleb, white as snow, wondering who I am.

'Who's got cuffs?' Patrick asks. A bailiff hands him a pair from his belt, and Patrick secures my hands behind me. He lifts me up and bustles me toward the same door through which the priest entered. Patrick's body is unyielding, his chin firm against my ear. 'Nina,' he whispers to me. 'What did you do?'

Once, not long ago, standing in my own home, I had asked Patrick this same question. Now I give his own answer back to him. 'I did what I had to,' I say, and I let myself believe it.

# II

To be once in doubt
Is once to be resolv'd.

– Shakespeare, *Othello*

*Summer camp is a place that hums with crickets and is so green it sometimes hurts my eyes to look.*

*I'm afraid to be here, because it is outside, and because outside there are bees. Bees make my stomach feel like a fist, even seeing one makes me want to run and hide. In my nightmares I picture them sucking my blood like it is honey.*

*My mother tells the camp counselors I'm afraid of bees. They say that in all the years of camp, not a single child has been stung.*

*I think, Someone has to be first.*

*One morning, my counselor – a girl with a macramé necklace that she wears even during swim time – takes us into the woods on a hike. It's time for a circle, she says. She moves one log, to make a bench. She moves a second log, and there are all the yellow jackets.*

*I freeze. The bees cover the counselor's face and arms and belly. She tries to bat them away while she's screaming. I throw myself at her. I slap my hands on her skin. I save her, even while I am being stung and stung.*

*At the end of camp that summer, the counselors give out awards. They are blue ribbons, each one, printed with fat black letters. Mine says Bravest Boy.*

*I still have it.*

# 4

In the moments after, Patrick wonders how he could know that Nina's favorite number is 13, that the scar on her chin came from a sledding crash, that she wished for a pet alligator for three Christmases straight – yet not know that inside her, all this time, was a grenade waiting to explode. 'I did what I had to,' she murmurs, all the way across the slick and bloodied court.

In his arms, she trembles. She feels light as a cloud. Patrick's head whirls. Nina still smells of apples, her shampoo; she still can't walk a straight line – but she is babbling incoherently, not at all in control the way Patrick is accustomed to seeing her. As they cross the threshold into the holding cell, Patrick looks behind him into the courtroom. *Pandemonium.* He's always thought that word sounds like a circus, but here it is now. Brain matter covers the front of the defense attorney's suit. A litter of paper and pocketbooks covers the gallery, as some reporters sob, and others direct their cameramen to film. Caleb stands still as a statue. Bobby, one of the bailiffs, is talking into the radio at his shoulder: 'Yeah, shots were fired, and we need an ambulance.' Roanoke, the other bailiff, hustles a white-faced Judge Bartlett into chambers. 'Clear the court!' the judge yells, and Roanoke answers: 'But we can't, Your Honor. They're all witnesses.'

On the floor, being completely ignored, is the body of Father Szyszynski.

*Killing him was the right thing,* Patrick thinks before he can stop himself. And then immediately afterward: *Oh, God, what has she done?*

'Patrick,' Nina murmurs.

He cannot look at her. 'Don't speak to me.' He will be a witness at – *Christ* – Nina's murder trial. Whatever she tells him, he will have to tell a court.

As an aggressive photographer makes her way toward the holding cell, Patrick moves slightly to block the camera's view of Nina. His job, right now, is to protect her. He just wishes there were someone to protect *him*.

He jostles her in his arms so that he can shut the door. It will be easier to wait out the arrival of the Biddeford Police Department that way. As it swings closed, he sees the paramedics arriving, leaning down over the body.

'Is he dead?' Nina asks. 'I just need you to tell me, Patrick. I killed him, right? How many shots did I get off? I had to do it, you know I had to do it. He's dead, isn't he? The paramedics can't revive him, can they? Tell me they won't. Please, just tell me he's dead. I promise, I'll sit right here and not move if you just go look and see if he's dead.'

'He's dead, Nina,' Patrick says quietly.

She closes her eyes, sways a little. 'Thank God. Oh, God, God, thank God.' She sinks down onto the metal bunk in the small cell.

Patrick turns his back on her. In the courtroom, his colleagues have arrived. Evan Chao, another detective-lieutenant in the department, supervises the securing of the crime scene, yelling over the crescendo of shrieks and sobs. Policemen crouch, dusting for fingerprints, taking photos of the spreading pool of blood and the broken railing where Patrick tackled Nina to get the gun out of her hand. The Maine state police SWAT team arrives, thundering down the center aisle like a tornado. One woman, a reporter sequestered for questioning, glances at what is left of the priest and vomits. It is a grim, chaotic scene; it is the stuff of nightmares, and yet Patrick stares fixedly, far more willing to face this reality than the one crying quietly behind him.

*          *          *

What Nathaniel hates about this particular board game is that all you have to do is spin the spinner the wrong way, and that's it, your little game piece is coasting down that big long slide in the middle. It's true that if you spin the *right* way, you can climb that extra tall ladder . . . but it doesn't always work like that, and before you know it, you've lost.

Monica lets him win, but Nathaniel doesn't like that as much as he thought he would. It makes him feel the way he did when he fell off his bike and had this totally gross cut all across his chin. People looked at him and pretended that there was nothing wrong with him but you could see in their eyes that they really wanted to turn away.

'Are you going to spin, or do I have to wait until you turn six?' Monica teases.

Nathaniel flicks the spinner. *Four.* He moves his little man the right number of spaces and, it figures, winds up on one of those slides. He pauses at the top, knowing that if he only moves three instead, Monica won't say a word.

But before he can decide whether or not to cheat, something catches his attention behind her shoulder. Through the wide glass window of the playroom, he sees one policeman . . . no, two . . . five . . . racing through the hallway. They don't look like Patrick does when he works – all rumply, in a regular shirt and tie. They are wearing shiny boots and silver badges, and their hands are on their guns, just like Nathaniel sees late at night on TV when he comes downstairs to get a drink and his parents don't change the channel fast enough.

'Shoot,' he says softly.

Monica smiles at him. 'That's right, a chute. But you'll have better luck next time, Nathaniel.'

'No . . . shoot.' He curves his fingers into a gun, the sign for the letter *G*. 'You know. Bang.'

He realizes the moment Monica understands him. She looks behind her at the sound of all those running feet, and her eyes go wide. But she turns back to Nathaniel with a smile glued over the question that shivers on her lips. 'It's your spin, right?' Monica says, although they both know his turn has come and gone.

When feeling returns to Caleb's fingers and feet, it comes slowly, an emotional frostbite that leaves his extremities swollen and unfamiliar. He stumbles forward, past the spot where Nina has just shot a man in cold blood, past the people jostling for position so that they can do the jobs they were trained to do. Caleb gives the body of Father Szyszynski a wide berth. His body jerks toward the door where he last saw Nina, being shoved forward into a cell.

Jesus, a *cell*.

A detective who does not recognize him grabs his arm. 'Where do you think you're going?' Silent, Caleb pushes past the man, and then he sees Patrick's face in the small window of the door. Caleb knocks, but Patrick seems to be deciding whether or not to open the door.

At that point, Caleb realizes that all these people, all these detectives, think he might be Nina's accomplice.

His mouth goes dry as sand, so that when Patrick finally does open the door a crack, he can't even request to see his wife. 'Get Nathaniel and go home,' Patrick suggests quietly. 'I'll call you, Caleb.'

Yes, Nathaniel. *Nathaniel.* The very thought of his son, a floor below while all this has been going on, makes Caleb's stomach cramp. He moves with a speed and grace unlikely for someone his size, barreling past people until he reaches the far end of the courtroom, the door at the rear of the aisle. A bailiff stands guard, watching Caleb approach. 'My son, he's downstairs. Please. You have to let me get to him.'

Maybe it is the pain carved into Caleb's face; maybe it is the way his words come out in the color of grief – for whatever reason, the bailiff wavers. 'I swear I'll come right back. But I have to make sure he's all right.'

A nod, one that Caleb isn't meant to see. When the bailiff

looks away, Caleb slips out the door behind him. He takes the stairs two at a time and runs down the hall to the playroom.

For a moment, he stands outside the plate-glass window, watching his son play and letting it bring him back to center. Then Nathaniel sees him and beams, jumping up to open the door and throw himself into Caleb's arms.

Monica's tight face swims into the sea of his vision. 'What happened up there?' she mouths silently.

But Caleb only buries his face against his son's neck, as silent as Nathaniel had been when something happened that he could not explain.

Nina once told Patrick that she used to stand at the side of Nathaniel's crib and watch him sleep. *It's amazing,* she'd said. *Innocence in a blanket.* He understands, now. Watching Nina sleep, you'd never know what had happened just two hours before. You'd never know from that smooth brow what thoughts lay underneath the surface.

Patrick, on the other hand, is absolutely ill. He cannot seem to catch his breath; his stomach knots with each step. And every time he looks at Nina's face, he cannot decide what he'd rather find out: that this morning, she simply went crazy . . . or that she didn't.

As soon as the door opens, I'm wide-awake. I jackknife to a sitting position on the bunk, my hand smoothing the jacket Patrick gave me as a makeshift pillow. It is wool, scratchy; it has left lines pressed into my cheek.

A policeman I don't know sticks his head inside. 'Lieutenant,' he says formally, 'we need you to come give a statement.'

Of course. Patrick's seen it too.

The policeman's eyes are insects on my skin. As Patrick moves toward the door I stand, grab onto the bars of the cell. 'Can you find out if he's dead? Please? I have to know. I have to. I just have to know if he's dead.' My words hit Patrick between the shoulder blades, slow him down. But he doesn't look at me, not as he walks away from the holding cell, past the other policeman, and opens the door.

In the slice of room revealed, I see the activity that Patrick's kept hidden from me for the past few hours. The Murder Winnebago must have arrived – a state police mobile unit that contains everything the cops need to investigate a homicide and the key personnel to do it. Now they cover the courtroom like a mass of maggots, dusting for fingerprints and taking down the names and statements of eyewitnesses. A person shifts, revealing a crimson smear that outlines a splayed, graying hand. As I watch, a photographer leans down, captures the spatter pattern of the blood. My heart trips tight. And I think: *I did this; I did this.*

It is a God's honest fact that Quentin Brown does not fancy driving anywhere, especially long distances, particularly from Augusta to York County. By the time he's in Brunswick he's certain that another moment and his six-foot-five frame will be permanently stunted into the position demanded by this ridiculously tiny Ford Probe. By the time he reaches Portland, he needs to be put into traction. But as an assistant attorney general on the murder team, he has to go where he is summoned. And if someone offs a priest in Biddeford, then Biddeford is where he has to go.

Still, by the time he reaches the district court, he is in a formidable mood, and that's saying something. By normal standards, Quentin Brown is overpowering – add together his shaved head, his unusual height, and his more unusual skin color, given this lily-white state, and most people assume he is either a felon or a vacationing NBA draft pick. But a lawyer? A *black* lawyer? *Not heah,* as the locals say.

In fact, the University of Maine law school heavily recruits students of color, to make up for their rainbow deficiency. Like Quentin, many come; unlike Quentin, they all leave. He's spent twenty years walking into provincial courts and surprising the hell out of the defense attorneys who come expecting someone – or some*thing* – different. And truth be told, Quentin likes it that way.

As always, a path parts for him when he strides into the Biddeford District Court, as people fall back to gape. He walks into the courtroom with the police tape crossing the doors, and continues up the aisle, past the bar. Fully aware that movement has slowed and conversation has stopped, Quentin leans down and examines the dead man. 'For a crazy woman,' he murmurs, appraising, 'she was a damn good shot.' Then Quentin eyeballs the cop who is staring at him as if he's arrived from Mars. 'What's the matter?' he deadpans. 'You never seen someone six-foot-five before?'

A detective walks up to him, swaggering with authority. 'Can Ihelp you?'

'Quentin Brown. From the AG's office.' He extends a hand.

'Evan Chao,' the detective says, working his damnedest not to do a double-take. God, how Quentin loves this moment.

'How many witnesses do we have to the shooting?'

Chao does some arithmetic on a pad. 'We're up to thirty-six, but we've got about fifty people in the back room who haven't given us statements yet. They're all saying the same thing, though. And we have the whole shooting on tape; WCSH was filming the arraignment for the five o'clock news.'

'Where's the gun?'

'Bobby grabbed it, bagged it.'

Quentin nods. 'And the perp?'

'In the holding cell.'

'Good. Let's draft up a complaint for murder.' He glances around, assessing the state of the investigation. 'Where's her husband?'

'With all the other people, waiting to be questioned, I suppose.'

'Do we have any evidence linking him to the crime? Did he participate in any way?'

Chao exchanges a glance with a few police officers, who

murmur among themselves and shrug. 'He hasn't been questioned yet, apparently.'

'Then get him in here,' Quentin says. 'Let's ask him.'

Chao turns to one of the bailiffs. 'Roanoke, find Caleb Frost, will you?'

The older man looks at Quentin and quails. 'He, uh, ain't in there.'

'You know this for a fact,' Quentin says slowly.

'Ayuh. He, well, he asked me if he could go get his kid, but he told me he'd come back.'

'He said *what?*' This is little more than a whisper, but coming from Quentin's great height, it is threatening. 'You let him walk out the door after his wife murdered the man who's charged with molesting his son? What is this, the Keystone Kops?'

'No, sir,' the bailiff replies solemnly. 'It's the Biddeford District Court.'

A muscle jumps in Quentin's jaw. 'Get someone to go find this guy and interview him,' he tells Chao. 'I don't know what he knows; I don't know whether he's involved, but if he needs to be arrested, do it.'

Chao bristles. 'Don't pin this on the police force; it was the bailiff's mistake. Nobody even told me he was in the courtroom.'

*And where else would he be, if his son's abuser was being arraigned?* But Quentin only takes a deep breath. 'Well, we need to deal with the shooter, anyway. Is the judge still here? Maybe we can get him to arraign her.'

'The judge is . . . indisposed.'

'Indisposed,' Quentin repeats.

'Took three Valium after the shots flew, and hasn't woken up yet.'

There is a possibility of getting another judge in, but it is late in the day. And the last thing Quentin wants is to have this woman released because of some stupid bail commissioner. 'Charge her. We'll hold her overnight and arraign her in the morning.'

'Overnight?' Chao asks.

'Yes. Last time I checked, there was still a York County Jail in Alfred.'

The detective looks down at his shoes for a moment. 'Yeah, but . . . well, you know she's a DA?'

Of course he knows, he's known since the moment his office was called to investigate. 'What I know,' Quentin answers, 'is that she's a murderer.'

Evan Chao knows Nina Frost; every detective in Biddeford has worked with her at some time or another. And like every other guy on the force, he doesn't even blame her for what she's done. Hell, half of them wish they'd have the guts to do the same thing, were they in her position.

He doesn't want to be the one to do this, but then again, better him than that asshole Brown. At least he can make sure the next step is as painless as possible for her.

He relieves the officer guarding her and takes up the position himself outside the holding cell. In a more ideal situation, he would take her to a conference room, offer her a cup of coffee, make her comfortable so that she'd be more likely to talk. But the court doesn't have a secure conference room, so this interview will have to be conducted on opposite sides of the bars.

Nina's hair is wild around her face; her eyes are so green they glow. On her arm are deep scratches; it looks as though she's done that to herself. Evan shakes his head. 'Nina, I'm really sorry . . . but I have to charge you with the murder of Glen Szyszynski.'

'I killed him?' she whispers.

'Yes.'

She is transformed by the smile that unwinds across her face. 'Can I see him, please?' she asks politely. 'I promise I won't touch anything, but please, I have to see him.'

'He's gone already, Nina. You can't see him.'

'But I killed him?'

Evan exhales heavily. The last time he'd seen Nina Frost,

she'd been arguing one of his own cases in court – a date rape. She had gotten up in front of the perp and wrung him dry on the witness stand. She had made him look the way she looks, right now. 'Will you give me a statement, Nina?'

'No, I can't. I can't. I did what I had to do, I can't do any more.'

He pulls out a Miranda form. 'I need to read you your rights.'

'I did what I had to do.'

Evan has to raise his voice over hers. 'You have the right to remain silent. Anything you say can be used against you in a court of law. You have the right . . .'

'I can't do any more. I did what I had to do,' Nina babbles.

Finally Evan finishes reading. Through the bars he hands her a pen to sign the paper, but it drops from her fingers. She whispers, 'I can't do any more.'

'Come on, Nina,' Evan says softly. He unlocks the holding cell, leads her through the hallways of the sheriff's office, and outside to a police cruiser. He opens the door for her and helps her inside. 'We can't arraign you till tomorrow, so I've got to take you down to the jail overnight. You're gonna get your own cell, and I'll make sure they take care of you. Okay?'

But Nina Frost has curled up in a fetal position on the back-seat of the cruiser and doesn't seem to hear him at all.

The correctional officer at the booking desk of the jail sucks on a Halls Mentho-Lyptus cough drop while he asks me to narrow my life down to the only things they need to know in a jail: *name, date of birth, height, weight. Eye color, allergies, medications, regular physician.* I answer softly, fascinated by the questions. I usually enter this play in the second act; to see it at its beginning is new for me.

A blast of medicinal mint comes my way, as the sergeant taps his pencil again. 'Distinguishing characteristics?' he asks.

He means birthmarks, moles, tattoos. *I have a scar,* I think silently, *on my heart.*

But before I can answer, another correctional officer unzips my black purse and empties its contents on the desk. Chewing gum, three furry Life Savers, a checkbook, my wallet. The detritus of motherhood: photographs of Nathaniel from last year, a long-forgotten teething ring, a four-pack of crayons pinched from a Chili's restaurant. Two more rounds of ammunition for the handgun.

I grab my arms, suddenly shivering. 'I can't do it. I can't do any more,' I whisper, and try to curl into a ball.

'Well, we're not done yet,' the correctional officer says. He rolls my fingers across an ink pad and makes three sets of prints. He props me up against a wall, hands me a placard. I follow his directions like a zombie; I do not meet his eyes. He doesn't tell me when the flash is going to go off; now I know why in every mug shot a criminal seems to have been caught unaware.

When my vision adjusts after the burst of light, a female guard is standing in front of me. She has one long eyebrow across her forehead and the build of a linebacker. I stumble in her wake into a room not much bigger than a closet, which holds shelves full of neatly folded hazard-orange jail scrubs. The Connecticut prisons had to sell all their brand-new forest-green jumpsuits, I suddenly remember, because the convicts kept escaping into the woods.

The guard hands me a pair of scrubs. 'Get undressed,' she orders.

*I have to do this,* I think, as I hear her snap on the rubber gloves. *I have to do whatever it takes to get out of here.* So I force my mind to go blank, like a screen at the close of a movie. I feel the guard's fingers probe my mouth and my ears, my nostrils, my vagina, my anus. With a jolt, I think of my son.

When it is over, the guard takes my clothes, still damp with the blood of the priest, and bags them. I slowly put on the scrubs, tying them so tight at the waist that I find myself gasping for breath. My eyes dart back and forth as we walk back down the hall. The walls, they're watching me.

In the booking room at the front of the jail again, the female guard leaves me standing in front of a phone. 'Go ahead,' she instructs. 'Make your call.'

I have a constitutional right to a private phone call, but I can feel the weight of their stares. I pick up the receiver and play with it, stroking its long neck. I stare at it as if I have never seen a telephone before.

Whatever they hear, they won't admit to hearing. I have tried to pressure enough correctional officers to come testify, and they never will, because they have to go back and guard these prisoners every day.

For the first time, this works to my advantage.

I meet the gaze of the nearest correctional officer, then slowly shake off the act. Dialing, I wait to be connected to something outside of here. 'Hello?' Caleb says, the most beautiful word in the English language.

'How's Nathaniel?'

*'Nina.* Jesus Christ, what were you doing?'

'How's Nathaniel?' I repeat.

'How the hell do you *think* he is? His mother's been arrested for killing someone!'

I close my eyes. 'Caleb, you need to listen to me. I'll explain everything when I see you. Have you talked to the police?'

'No –'

'Don't. Right now, I'm at the jail. They're holding me here overnight, and I'm going to be arraigned tomorrow.' There are tears coming. 'I need you to call Fisher Carrington.'

'Who?'

'He's a defense attorney. And he's the only person who can get me out of this. I don't care what you have to do, but get him to represent me.'

'What am I supposed to tell Nathaniel?'

I take a deep breath. 'That I'm okay, and that I'll be home tomorrow.'

Caleb is angry; I can hear it in his pause. 'Why should I do this for you, after what you just did to us?'

'If you want there to be an *us*,' I say, 'you'd better do it.'

After Caleb hangs up on me, I hold the phone to my ear, pretending he is still on the other end of the line. Then I replace the receiver, turn around, and look at the correctional officer who is waiting to take me to a cell. 'I had to do it,' I explain. 'He doesn't understand. I can't make him understand. You would have done it, wouldn't you? If it was your kid, wouldn't you have done it?' I make my eyes flicker from left to right, lighting on nothing. I chew my fingernail till the cuticle bleeds.

I make myself crazy, because this is what I want them to see.

It is no surprise when I am led to the solitary cells. In the first place, new prisoners are often put on a suicide watch; in the second place, I put half the women in this jail. The correctional officer slams the door shut behind me, and this becomes my new world: six feet by eight feet, a metal bunk, a stained mattress, a toilet.

The guard moves off, and for the first time this day, I let myself unravel. I have killed a man. I have walked right up to his lying face and shot four bullets into it. The recollection comes in bits and pieces – the click of the trigger past the point of no return; the thunder of the gun; the backward leap of my hand as the gun recoiled, as if it were trying, too late, to stop itself.

His blood was warm where it struck my shirt.

Oh, my God, I have killed a man. I did it for all the right reasons; I did it for Nathaniel; but *I did it.*

My body starts shaking uncontrollably, and this time, it is no act. It is one thing to seem insane for the sake of the witnesses that will be called to testify against me; it is another thing entirely to sift through my own mind and realize what I have been capable of all along. Father Szyszynski will not preside over Mass on Sunday. He will not have his nightly cup of tea or say an evening prayer. I have killed a priest who was not given Last Rites; and I will follow him straight to Hell.

My knees draw up, my chin tucks tight. In the overheated belly of this jail, I am freezing.

'Are you all right, girlfriend?'

The voice floats from across the hall, the second solitary confinement cell. Whoever has been in there watching me has been doing it from the  shadows. I feel heat rise to my face and look up to see a tall black woman, her scrubs knotted above her bellybutton, her toenails painted to orange to match her jail uniform.

'My name's Adrienne, and I'm a real good listener. I don't get to talk to many people.'

Does she think I'm going to fall for that setup? Stoolpigeons are as common in here as professions of innocence, and I should know – I have listened to both. I open my mouth to tell her this, but at second glance, realize I've been mistaken. The long feet, the rippled abdomen, the veins on the backs of the hands – Adrienne isn't a woman at all.

'Your secret,' the transvestite says. 'It's safe with me.'

I stare right at her – his – considerable chest. 'Got a Kleenex?' I ask flatly.

For just a moment, there is a beat of silence. 'That's just a technicality,' Adrienne responds.

I turn away again. 'Yeah, well, I'm still not talking to you.'

Above us, there is the call for lights out. But it never gets dark in jail. It is eternally dusk, a time when creatures crawl from swamps and crickets take over the earth. In the shadows, I can see Adrienne's smooth skin, a lighter shade of night between the bars of her cell. 'What did you do?' Adrienne asks, and there is no mistaking her question.

'What did *you* do?'

'It's the drugs, it's always the drugs, honey. But I'm trying to get off them, I truly am.'

'A drug conviction? Then why did they put you in solitary?'

Adrienne shrugs. 'Well, the boys, I don't belong with them; they just want to beat me up, you know? I'd like to be in with the girls, but they won't let me, because I haven't had the operation yet. I been taking my medicine regular, but they say it don't matter, so long as I've got the wrong kind of plumbing.' She sighs. 'Quite frankly, honey, they don't know what to do with me in here.'

I stare at the cinderblock walls, at the dim safety light on the ceiling, at my own lethal hands. 'They don't know what to do with me either,' I say.

The AG's office puts Quentin up at a Residence Inn that has a small efficiency kitchen, cable TV, and a carpet that smells like cats. 'Thank you,' he says dryly, handing the teenager who doubles as bellman a dollar. 'It's a palace.'

'Whatever,' the kid responds.

It amazes Quentin, the way adolescents are the only group that doesn't blink twice upon seeing him. Then again, he sometimes believes they wouldn't blink twice if a herd of mustangs tore past inches from their Skechered feet.

He doesn't understand them, either as a breed or individually.

Quentin opens the refrigerator, which gives off a dubious odor, and then sinks onto the spongy mattress. Well, it could be the Ritz-Carlton and he'd hate it. Biddeford, in general, makes him edgy.

Sighing, he picks up his car keys and leaves the hotel. Might as well get this over with. He drives without really thinking about where he's going. He knows she's there, of course. The address for the checks has stayed the same all this time.

There is a basketball hoop in the driveway; this surprises him. Somehow, he hasn't thought past last year's debacle to consider that Gideon might have a hobby less embarrassing to a prosecutor. A beat-up Isuzu Trooper with too many rust holes in the running board is parked in the garage. Quentin takes a deep breath, draws himself up to his full height, and knocks on the door.

When Tanya answers, it still hits him like a blow to the chest – her cognac skin; her chocolate eyes, as if this woman is a treat to be savored. But, Quentin reminds himself, even the most exquisite truffles can be bitter on the inside. He takes small comfort in the fact that she steps back when she sees him, too. 'Quentin Brown,' Tanya murmurs, shaking her head. 'To what do I owe this honor?'

'I'm here on a case,' he says. 'Indefinitely.' He's trying to peer behind her, to see what her home looks like inside. Without him in it. 'Thought I'd stop by, since you'd probably be hearing my name around town.'

'Along with other, four letter words,' Tanya mutters.

'Didn't catch that.'

She smiles at him, and he forgets what they were discussing. 'Gideon around?'

'No,' she says, too quickly.

'I don't believe you.'

'And I don't like you, so why don't you take your sorry self back to your little car and –'

'Ma?' The loping voice precedes Gideon, who suddenly appears behind his mother. He is nearly Quentin's height, although he's just turned sixteen. His dark face draws even more closed as he sees who's standing at the doorway. 'Gideon,' Quentin says. 'Hello again.'

'You come to haul my ass back to rehab?' He snorts. 'Don't do me any favors.'

Quentin feels his hands balling into fists. 'I did do you a favor. I pulled enough strings with a judge to keep you out of a juvenile detention facility, even though I took heat for it in my own department.'

'Am I supposed to thank you for that?' Gideon laughs. 'Just like I get down on my knees every night and thank you for being my daddy?'

'Gideon,' Tanya warns, but he shoves past her.

'Later.' He pushes Quentin hard, a threat, as he passes down the steps and gets into the Isuzu. Moments later, the car peels down the street.

'Is he still clean?' Quentin asks.

'Are you asking because you care, or because you don't want that stain on your career again?'

'That's not fair, Tanya –'

'Life never is, Quentin.' For the slightest moment, there is a sadness caught in the corners of her eyes, like the seeds of a dream. 'Go figure.'

She closes the door before he can respond. Moments later Quentin backs carefully out of the driveway. He drives for a full five minutes before he realizes that he has no idea where he is headed.

Lying on his side, Caleb can see the night sky. The moon is so slender it might not even be there the next time he blinks, but those stars, they're flung wide. One bright beacon catches his eye. It's fifty, maybe a hundred light-years away from here. Looking at it, Caleb is staring right into the past. An explosion that happened ages ago, but took this long to affect him.

He rolls onto his back. If only they were all like that.

All that day he's been thinking that Nina is sick; that she needs help, the way someone with a virus or a broken leg needs help. If something in her mind has snapped, Caleb will be the first to understand – he has come close to that himself, when thinking of what has been done to Nathaniel. But when Nina called, she was rational, calm, insistent. She meant to kill Father Szyszynski.

That, in and of itself, doesn't shock Caleb. People are able to hold the greatest scope of emotions inside them – love, joy, determination. It only stands to reason that negative feelings just as staggering can elbow their way in and take over. No, what surprises him is the way she did it. And the fact that she actually thinks this is something she did for Nathaniel.

This is about Nina, through and through.

Caleb closes his eyes to that star, but he still sees it etched on the backs of his eyelids. He tries to remember the moment that Nina told him she was pregnant. 'This wasn't supposed to happen,' she said to him. 'So we can't ever forget that it has.'

There is a rustle of blankets and sheets, and then Caleb

feels heat pressed along the length of his body. He turns, hopeful, praying that this has all been a bad dream and that he can wake up to find Nina safe and sleeping. But on her pillow lies Nathaniel, his eyes shining with tears. 'I want Mommy back,' he whispers.

Caleb thinks of Nina's face when she was carrying Nathaniel, how it was as bright as any star. Maybe that glory faded long ago, maybe it has taken all these light-years to only reach him now. He turns to his son and says, 'I want that too.'

Fisher Carrington stands with his back to the door of the conference room, looking out onto the exercise courtyard. When the correctional officer closes the door behind himself, leaving me there, he turns slowly. He looks just the way he did the last time I saw him, during Rachel's competency hearing: Armani suit, Bruno Magli shoes, thick head of white hair combed away from his sympathetic blue eyes. Those eyes take in my oversize jail scrubs, then immediately return to my face. 'Well,' he says gravely. 'I never imagined I'd talk to you here.'

I walk to one of the chairs in the room and throw myself into it. 'You know what, Fisher? Stranger things have happened.'

We stare at each other, trying to adjust to this role reversal. He is not the enemy anymore; he is my only hope. He is calling the shots; I am just along for the ride. And over this is a veneer of professional understanding: that he will not ask me what I've done, and that I will not have to tell him.

'You need to get me home, Fisher. I want to be back by the time my son sits down for lunch.'

Fisher just nods. He's heard this before. And it doesn't really matter what I want, when all is said and done. 'You know they're going to ask for a Harnish hearing,' he says.

Of course I know this; it is what I would do if I were prosecuting. In Maine, if the state can show probable cause that a capital crime was committed, then the defendant can be held without bail. In jail until the trial.

For months.

'Nina,' Fisher says, the first time he has called me anything other than *counselor.* 'Listen to me.'

But I don't want to listen to him. I want him to listen to me. With great self-control I raise a blank face to his. 'What's next, Fisher?'

He can see right through me, but Fisher Carrington is a gentleman. And so he pretends, just the way I am pretending. He smiles, as if we are old friends. 'Next,' he replies, 'we go to court.'

Patrick stands in the back, behind the throngs of reporters that have come to film the arraignment of the prosecutor who shot a priest in cold blood. This is the stuff of TV movies, of fiction. It is a story to debate at the water cooler with colleagues. In fact, Patrick has been listening to the commentary on more than one channel. Words like *retribution* and *reprisal* slide like snakes from these journalists' mouths. Sometimes, they don't even mention Nina's name.

They talk about the angle of the bullet, the number of paces it took to cross from her seat to the priest's. They give a history of child molestation convictions involving a priest. They do not say that Nina learned the difference between a front-end loader and a grader to satisfy the curiosity of her son. They do not mention that the contents of her pocketbook, catalogued at the jail, included a Matchbox car and a plastic glow-in-the-dark spider ring.

*They don't know her,* Patrick thinks. *And therefore, they don't know why.*

A reporter in front of him with a helmet of blond hair nods vigorously as her cameraman films her impromptu interview of a physiologist. 'The amygdala influences aggression via a pathway of neurons that leads to the hypothalamus,' he says. 'It sends bursts of electrical excitation down the stria terminalis, and that's the trigger of rage. Certainly, there are environmental factors, but without the preexisting pattern . . .'

Patrick tunes them out. A tangible awareness sweeps the gallery, and people begin to take their seats. Cyclopsian cameras blink. Hanging behind, Patrick tucks himself against the wall of the courtroom. He does not want to be recognized, and he isn't quite sure why. Is he ashamed of bearing witness at Nina's shame? Or is he afraid of what she might see in his face?

He should not have come. Patrick tells himself this as the door to the holding cell opens and two bailiffs appear, flanking Nina. She looks tiny and frightened, and he remembers how she shivered against him, her back to his front, as he pushed her from the fray yesterday afternoon.

Nina closes her eyes and then moves forward. On her face is the exact expression she wore at age eleven, a few feet up from the base on a ski lift, the moment before Patrick convinced the operator to let Nina off lest she pass out.

He should not have come, but Patrick also knows he could not have stayed away.

I am to be arraigned in the same courtroom where, yesterday, I murdered a man. The bailiff puts his hand on my shoulder and escorts me through the door. Hands cuffed behind my back, I walk where the priest walked. If I look hard enough, I can see his footsteps glowing.

We march past the prosecutor's table. Five times as many reporters are present today; there are even faces I recognize from *Dateline* and CNN. Did you know that television cameras running in unison sound like the song of cicadas? I turn to the gallery to find Caleb, but behind Fisher Carrington's table there is only a row of empty seats.

I am wearing my prison scrubs and low-heeled pumps. They cannot give you shoes in jail, so you wear whatever you were arrested in. And just yesterday, a lifetime ago, I was a professional woman. But as the heel of my shoe catches on the natty nap of a mat, I stumble and glance down.

We are at the spot where the priest lay dead, yesterday. Where, presumably, the cleaning people who scoured this courtroom could not completely remove the stain of blood from the floor, and covered it with an industrial carpet remnant.

Suddenly I cannot take a single step.

The bailiff grabs my arm more firmly and drags me across the mat to Fisher Carrington's side. There, I remember myself. I sit down in the same seat the priest was sitting in yesterday when I walked up and shot him. It's warm beneath my thighs – lights beating down on the wood from the courtroom ceiling, or maybe just an old soul that hasn't had the time to move on. The moment the bailiff steps away, I feel a rush of air at the nape of my neck, and I whip around, certain there will be someone waiting with a bullet for me.

But there is no bullet, no sudden death. There are only the eyes of everyone in that courtroom, burning like acid. For their viewing pleasure, I start to bite my nails, twitch in my seat. Nervousness can pass for crazy.

'Where is Caleb?' I whisper to Fisher.

'I have no idea, but he came to my office this morning with the retainer. Keep your head straight.' Before I can answer, the judge raps his gavel.

I do not know this judge. Presumably, they've brought him in from Lewiston. I do not know the AG either, sitting in my usual spot at the prosecution desk. He is enormous, bald, fearsome. He glances at me only once, and then his eyes move on – he has already dismissed me for crossing over to the dark side.

What I want to do at that moment is walk over to this prosecutor and tug on his sleeve. *Don't judge me,* I'd say, *until you've seen the view from here. You are only as invincible as your smallest weakness, and those are tiny indeed – the length of a sleeping baby's eyelash, the span of a child's hand. Life turns on a dime, and – it turns out – so does one's conscience.*

'Is the state ready to proceed?' the judge asks.

The assistant attorney general nods. 'Yes, Your Honor.'

'Is the defense attorney ready to proceed?'

'Yes, Your Honor,' Fisher says.

'Will the defendant please come forward?'

I don't stand, at first. It is not a conscious rebuff; I'm just

not used to being the one who rises at this point in the arraignment. The bailiff hauls me out of my seat, wrenching my arm
in the process.

Fisher Carrington remains in his chair, and my whole body
grows cold. This is his chance to insult me. When a defendant
stands and the attorney stays seated, it is a clear sign to insiders
that he doesn't give a damn about the client. As I lift my chin
and turn away, resolved, Fisher slowly unfolds from his chair.
He is a solid presence along my right side, a fortifying wall.
He turns to me and raises an eyebrow, questioning my faith.

'Please state your name?'

I take a deep breath. 'Nina Maurier Frost.'

'Will the clerk please read the charge?' the judge asks.

'The state of Maine hereby charges that on or about the
thirtieth day of October, 2001, the defendant, Nina Maurier
Frost, did slay and murder Glen Szyszynski in Biddeford, in
the County of York, Maine. How do you plead?'

Fisher smooths a hand down his tie. 'We're going to enter
a plea of not guilty, Your Honor. And I'm putting the court
and state on notice that we may be entering a plea of not guilty
by reason of insanity at a later date.'

None of this surprises the judge. It does not surprise me
either, although Fisher and I have not discussed an insanity
defense. 'Mr. Brown,' the judge says, 'when would you like to
schedule a Harnish hearing?'

This is expected, too. In the past I have seen *State v. Harnish*
as a godsend, keeping felons temporarily off the street while I'm
working to permanently lock them up. After all, do you really
want someone who's committed a capital crime walking free?

Then again, in the past, I have not been the criminal in
question.

Quentin Brown looks at me, then turns to the judge. His
eyes, obsidian, do not give anything away. 'Your Honor, at this
time, due to the severity of the crime and the open nature in
which it was committed in this very courtroom, the state is
asking for bail in the amount of $500,000 with surety.'

The judge blinks at him. Stunned, Fisher turns to Brown. I want to stare at him, too, but I can't, because then he will know that I'm sane enough to understand this unexpected gift. 'Am I understanding, Mr. Brown, that the state is waiving its right for a Harnish hearing?' the judge clarifies. 'That you wish to *set* bail in this case, as opposed to *denying* it?'

Brown nods tightly. 'May we approach, please?'

He takes a step forward, and so does Fisher. Out of long habit, I take a step forward too, but the bailiffs standing behind me grab my arms.

The judge puts his hand over the microphone so that the cameras cannot hear the conversation, but I can, even from a few feet away. 'Mr. Brown, I understood that your evidence in this case was rather good.'

'Judge, to tell you the truth, I don't know whether she has a successful insanity plea or not . . . but I can't in good faith ask this court to hold her without bail. She's been a prosecutor for ten years. I don't think she's going to flee, and I don't think she's a risk to society. With all due respect, Your Honor, I've run that past my boss and her boss, and I'm asking the court to please do this without making it an issue for the press to devour.'

Fisher immediately turns with a gracious smile. 'Your Honor, I'd like to let Mr. Brown know that my client and I appreciate his sensitivity. This is a difficult case for everyone involved.'

Me, I feel like dancing. To have the Harnish hearing waived is a tiny miracle. 'The state is asking for bail in the amount of $500,000. What are the defendant's ties to this state, Mr. Carrington?' the judge asks.

'Your Honor, she's a lifelong resident of Maine. She has a small child here. The defendant would be happy to turn in her passport and agree to not leave the state.'

The judge nods. 'Given the fact that she's worked as a prosecutor for so long, as a condition of the defendant's bail I am also going to bar her from speaking with any employees currently working at the York County District Attorney's office until the completion of this case, to ensure that she doesn't have any access to information.'

'That's fine, Your Honor,' Fisher says on my behalf.

Quentin Brown jumps in. 'In addition to bail, Judge, we're asking for a special condition of a psychiatric evaluation.'

'We have no problem with that,' Fisher answers. 'We'd like one of our own, with a private psychiatrist.'

'Does it matter to the state whether a private or a state psychiatrist is used, Mr. Brown?' the judge asks.

'We want a state psychiatrist.'

'Fine. I'll make that a condition of bail, as well.' The judge writes something down in his file. 'But I don't believe $500,000 is necessary to keep this woman in the state. I'm setting bail at $100,000 with surety.'

What happens next is a whirlwind: hands on my arms, pushing me back in the direction of the holding cell; Fisher's face telling me he'll call Caleb about the bail; reporters stampeding up the aisles and into the hall to phone their affiliates. I am left in the company of a deputy sheriff so thin his belt is notched like a pegboard. He locks me into the cell and then buries his face in *Sports Illustrated*.

I'm going to get out. I'm going to be back home, having lunch with Nathaniel, just like I told Fisher Carrington yesterday.

Hugging my knees to my chest, I start to cry. And let myself believe I just might get away with this.

The day it first happened, they had been learning about the Ark. It was this huge boat, Mrs. Fiore told Nathaniel and the others. Big enough to fit all of them, their parents, and their pets. She gave everyone a crayon and a piece of paper to draw their favorite animal. 'Let's see what we come up with,' she had said, 'and we'll show them all to Father Glen before his story.'

Nathaniel sat next to Amelia Underwood that day, a girl who always smelled of spaghetti sauce and the stuff that gets caught in bathtub drains. 'Did elephants go on the boat?' she asked, and Mrs. Fiore nodded. 'Everything.'

'Raccoons?'

'Yes.'

'Narwhals?' That from Oren Whitford, who was already reading chapter books when Nathaniel wasn't even sure which way the loop went on a *b* and a *d*.

'Uh-huh.'

'Cockroaches?'

'Unfortunately,' Mrs. Fiore said.

Phil Filbert raised his hand. 'How about the holy goats?'

Mrs. Fiore frowned. 'That's the Holy Ghost, Philip, which is something totally different.' But then she reconsidered. 'I suppose it was there too, though.'

Nathaniel raised his hand. The teacher smiled at him. 'What animal are you thinking of?'

But he wasn't thinking of an animal at all. 'I need to go pee,' he said, and all the other kids laughed. Heat spread across his face, and he grabbed the block of wood that Mrs. Fiore gave him for a bathroom pass and darted out the door. The bathroom was at the end of the hall, and Nathaniel lingered in there, flushing the toilet a bunch of times just to hear the sound of it; washing his hands with so much soap bubbles rose in the sink like a mountain.

He was in no rush to get back to Sunday school. In the first place, everyone would still be laughing at him, and in the second place, Amelia Underwood stank worse than the little cakes inside the bathroom urinals. So he wandered down the hall a little farther, to Father Glen's office. The door was usually locked, but right now, there was a crack just big enough for someone like Nathaniel to slip through. Without hesitation, he crept inside.

The room smelled of lemons, just like the main part of the church. Nathaniel's mother said that was because a lot of ladies volunteered to scrub the pews until they were shining, so he figured they probably came into the office and scrubbed too.

There were no pews, though – only row after row of book-shelves. There were so many letters jammed onto the spines of the books that it made Nathaniel dizzy to try to sort them all out. He turned his attention instead to a picture hanging on the wall, of a man riding a white stallion, and spearing a dragon through its heart.

Maybe dragons hadn't fit onto the Ark, which was why no one ever saw them anymore.

'St. George was awfully brave,' a voice said behind him, and Nathaniel realized he was not alone. 'And you?' the priest asked with a slow smile. 'Are you brave too?'

If Nina had been his wife, Patrick would have sat in the front row of the gallery. He would have made eye contact with her the second she walked through the door of the courtroom, to let her know that no matter what, he was there for her. He wouldn't have needed someone to come to his house and spoon-feed him the outcome of the arraignment.

By the time Caleb answers the doorbell, Patrick is furious at him all over again.

'She's out on bail,' Patrick says without preamble. 'You'll have to get a check for ten thousand dollars to the courthouse.' He stares Caleb down, his hands jammed into the pockets of his jacket. 'I assume you can do that. Or were you planning to leave your wife high and dry twice in one day?'

'You mean the way she left *me?*' Caleb retorts. 'I couldn't go. I had no one to watch Nathaniel.'

'That's bullshit. You could have asked me. In fact, I'll watch him right now. You go ahead, get Nina. She's waiting.' He crosses his arms, calling Caleb's bluff.

'I'm not going,' Caleb says, and in less than a breath Patrick pins him against the doorframe.

'What the fuck is the matter with you?' he grits out. 'She needs you now.'

Caleb, bigger and stronger, pushes back. He balls a fist, sends Patrick flying into the hedge on the path. 'Don't you tell me what *my* wife needs.' In the background is the sound of a tiny voice, calling for his father. Caleb turns, walks inside, closes the door behind him.

Sprawled in the bushes, Patrick tries to catch his breath. He gets to his feet slowly, extricating leaves from his clothing. What is he supposed to do now? He cannot leave Nina in jail, and he doesn't have the cash to bail her out himself.

Suddenly the door opens again. Caleb stands there, a check in hand. Patrick takes it and Caleb nods in gratitude, neither one alluding to the fact that only minutes ago, they were willing to kill. This is the currency of apology; a deal transacted in the name of the woman who has unbalanced both of their lives.

I'm ready to give Caleb a piece of my mind for missing the arraignment, but it's going to have to wait until after I've held Nathaniel so close that he starts to melt into me. Fidgety, I wait for the deputy to unlock the holding cell and escort me into the anteroom of the sheriff's department. There is a familiar face there, but it's the wrong one.

'I posted bail,' Patrick says. 'Caleb gave me a check.'

'He . . .' I start to speak, and then remember who is standing in front of me. It may be Patrick, but still. I turn to him, wide-eyed, as he leads me out the service entrance of the court-house, to avoid the press. 'Is he really dead? Do you promise me he's really dead?'

Patrick grabs my arm and turns me toward him. 'Stop.' Pain pulls his features tight. 'Please, Nina. Just stop.'

He knows; of course he knows. This is Patrick. In a way it is a relief to no longer have to pretend with him; to have the opportunity to talk to someone who will understand. He leads me through the bowels of the building to a service entrance, and ducks me into his waiting Taurus. The parking lot is filled with news vans, satellite dishes mounted on top like strange birds. Patrick tosses something heavy in my lap, a thick edition of the *Boston Globe*.

ABOVE THE LAW, the headline reads. And a subtitle: *Priest*

*Murdered in Maine; A District Attorney's Biblical Justice.* There
is a full-color photo of me being tackled by Patrick and the
bailiffs. In the right-hand corner is Father Szyszynski, lying in
a pool of his own blood. I trace Patrick's grainy profile. 'You're
famous,' I say softly.

Patrick doesn't answer. He stares out at the road, focused
on what lies ahead.

I used to be able to talk to him about anything. That cannot
have changed, just because of what I've done. But as I look
out the window I see it is a different world – two-legged cats
prance down the street, Gypsies twirl up driveways, zombies
knock on doors. Somehow I've forgotten about Halloween;
today nobody is the person he was just a day ago. 'Patrick,' I
begin.

He cuts me off with a slash of his hand. 'Nina, it's already
bad enough. Every time I think about what you did, I remember
the night before, at Tequila Mockingbird. What I said to you.'

*People like that, they ought to be shot.* I hadn't remembered his
words until now. Or had I? I reach across the seat to touch his
shoulder, to reassure him that this isn't his fault, but he recoils
from me. 'Whatever you're thinking, you're wrong. I –'

Suddenly Patrick wrenches the car to the shoulder of the
road. 'Please, don't tell me anything. I'm going to have to testify
during your trial.'

But I have always confided in Patrick. To crawl back behind
my shell of insanity seems even crazier; a costume two sizes
too small. I turn with a question in my eyes, and as usual, he
responds before I can even put it into words. 'Talk to Caleb
instead,' he says, and he pulls back into the midday trickle of
traffic.

Sometimes when you pick up your child you can feel the map
of your own bones beneath your hands, or smell the scent of
your skin in the nape of his neck. This is the most extraordinary thing about motherhood – finding a piece of yourself separate and apart that all the same you could not live without. It is

the feeling you get when you place the last scrap of the thousand-piece jigsaw puzzle; it is the last footfall in a photo-finish race; exhilaration and homecoming and stunned wonder, caught between those stubby fingers and the spaces where baby teeth have given way. Nathaniel barrels into my arms with the force of a hurricane, and just as easily sweeps me off my feet. 'Mommy!'

*Oh,* I think, *this is why.*

Over my son's head, I notice Caleb. He stands at a distance, his face impassive. I say, 'Thank you for the check.'

'You're famous,' Nathaniel tells me. 'Your picture was in the paper.'

'Buddy,' Caleb asks, 'you want to pick out a video and watch it in my room?'

Nathaniel shakes his head. 'Can Mommy come?'

'In a little while. I have to talk to Daddy first.'

So we go through the motions of parenting; Caleb settling Nathaniel on the great ocean of our bedspread, while I push the buttons that set a Disney tape into motion. It seems natural that while he waits here, entranced by fantasy, Caleb and I go into his little boy's room to make sense of what's real. We sit on the narrow bed, surrounded by a bevy of appliquéd Amazon tree frogs, a rainbow of poisonous color. Overhead, a caterpillar mobile drifts without a care in the world. 'What the hell were you doing, Nina?' Caleb says, the opening thrust. 'What were you *thinking?*'

'Have the police talked to you? Are you in trouble?'

'Why would I be?'

'Because the police don't know you weren't planning this with me.'

Caleb folds in on himself. 'Is that what you did? Plan it?'

'I planned to make it look unplanned,' I explain. 'Caleb, he hurt Nathaniel. He *hurt* him. And he was going to get away with it.'

'You don't know that –'

'I do. I see it every day. But this time, it was *my* baby. *Our* baby. How many years do you think Nathaniel will have nightmares about this? How many years will he be in therapy? Our son is never going to be the way he was. Szyszynski took away a piece of him that we'll never get back. So why shouldn't I have done the same to him?' *Do unto others,* I think, *as you would have them do unto you.*

'But Nina. You . . .' He cannot even say it.

'When you found out, when Nathaniel said his name, what was the first thought that ran through your mind?'

Caleb looks into his lap. 'I wanted to kill him.'

'*Yes.*'

He shakes his head. 'Szyszynski was headed to a trial. He would have been punished for what he did.'

'Not enough. There is no sentence a judge could pass down that would make up for this and you know it. I did what any parent would want to do. I just have to look crazy to get away with it.'

'What makes you think you *can?*'

'Because I know what it takes to be declared legally insane. I watch these defendants come in and I can tell you right away who's going to get convicted and who's going to walk. I know what you have to say, what you have to do.' I look Caleb right in the eye. 'I am an attorney. But I shot a man in front of a judge, in front of a whole court. Why would I do that, if I weren't crazy?'

Caleb is quiet for a moment, turning the truth over in his hands. 'Why are you telling me this?' he asks softly.

'Because you're my husband. You can't testify against me during my trial. You're the only one I *can* tell.'

'Then why didn't you tell me what you were going to do?'

'Because,' I reply, 'you would have stopped me.'

When Caleb gets up and walks to the window, I follow him. I place my hand gently on his back, in the hollow that seems so vulnerable, even in a man full-grown. 'Nathaniel deserves this,' I whisper.

Caleb shakes his head. 'No one deserves this.'

★          ★          ★

As it turns out, you can function while your heart is being torn to shreds. Blood pumps, breath flows, neurons fire. What goes missing is the affect; a curious flatness to voice and actions that, if noted, speak of a hole so deep inside there's no visible end to it. Caleb stares at this woman who just yesterday was his wife and sees a stranger in her place. He listens to her explanations and wonders when she took up this foreign language, this tongue that makes no sense.

Of course, it is what any parent would want to do to the devil who preys upon a child. But 99.9 percent of those parents don't act on it. Maybe Nina thinks she was avenging Nathaniel, but it was at the reckless expense of her own life. If Szyszynski had gone to jail, they would be patchwork and piecemeal, but they would still be a family. If Nina goes to jail, Caleb loses a wife. Nathaniel loses his mother.

Caleb feels fire pooling like acid in the muscles of his shoulders. He is furious and stunned and maybe a little bit awed. He has traveled every inch of this woman, he understands what makes her cry and what brings her to rapture; he recognizes every cut and curve of her body; but he doesn't know her at all.

Nina stands expectantly beside him, waiting for him to tell her she did the right thing. Funny, that she would flout the law, but still need his approval. For this reason, and all the others, the words she wants to hear from him will not come.

When Nathaniel walks into the room with the dining room tablecloth wrapped around his shoulders, Caleb latches onto him. In this storm of strangeness, Nathaniel is the one thing he can recognize. 'Hey!' Caleb cries with too much enthusiasm, and he tosses the boy into the air. 'That's some cape!'

Nina turns too, a smile placed on her face where the earnestness was a moment before. She reaches for Nathaniel, too, and out of pure spite, Caleb hefts the child high on his shoulders where she cannot reach.

'It's getting dark,' Nathaniel says. 'Can we go?'

'Go where?'

In answer, Nathaniel points out the window. On the street below is a battalion of tiny goblins, miniature monsters, fairy princesses. Caleb notices, for the first time, that the leaves have all fallen; that grinning pumpkins roost like lazy hens on the stone walls of his neighbor's home. How could he have missed the signs of Halloween?

He looks at Nina, but she has been just as preoccupied. As if on cue, the doorbell rings. Nathaniel wriggles on Caleb's shoulders. 'Get it! Get it!'

'We'll have to get it later.' Nina tosses him a helpless look; there is no candy in this house. There is nothing left that's sweet.

Worse, yet, there is no costume. Caleb and Nina realize this at the same moment, and it sews them close. They both recall Nathaniel's previous Halloweens in descending order: knight in shining armor, astronaut, pumpkin, crocodile, and, as an infant, caterpillar. 'What would you like to be?' Nina asks.

Nathaniel tosses his magical tablecloth over his shoulder. 'A superhero,' he says. 'A new one.'

Caleb is fairly sure they could muster up Superman on short notice. 'What's wrong with the old ones?'

Everything, it turns out. Nathaniel doesn't like Superman because he can be felled by Kryptonite. Green Lantern's ring doesn't work on anything yellow. The Incredible Hulk is too stupid. Even Captain Marvel runs the risk of being tricked into saying the word *Shazam!* and turning himself back into young Billy Batson.

'How about Ironman?' Caleb suggests.

Nathaniel shakes his head. 'He could rust.'

'Aquaman?'

'Needs water.'

'Nathaniel,' Nina says gently, 'nobody's perfect.'

'But they're *supposed* to be,' Nathaniel explains, and Caleb understands. Tonight, Nathaniel needs to be invincible. He needs to know that what happened to him could never, ever happen again.

'What we need,' Nina muses, 'is a superhero with no Achilles' heel.'

'A what?' Nathaniel says.

She takes his hand. 'Let's see.' From his closet, she extracts a pirate's bandanna, and wraps this rakishly around Nathaniel's head. She crisscrosses a spool of yellow crime-scene tape Patrick once brought around Nathaniel's chest. She gives him swimming goggles, tinted blue, for X-ray vision, and pulls a pair of red shorts over his sweatpants because this is Maine, after all, and she is not about to let him go out half-dressed in the cold. Then she surreptitiously motions to Caleb, so that he pulls off his red thermal shirt and hands it to her. This she ties around Nathaniel's neck, a second cape. 'Oh, my gosh, do you see who he looks like?'

Caleb has no idea, but he plays along. 'I can't believe it.'

'Who? Who!' Nathaniel is fairly dancing with excitement.

'Well, IncrediBoy, of course,' Nina answers. 'Didn't you ever see his comic book?'

'No . . .'

'Oh, he's the most super superhero. He's got these two capes, see, which allow him to fly farther and faster.'

'Cool!'

'And he can pull people's thoughts right out of their heads, before they even speak them. In fact, you look so much like him, I bet you've got that superpower already. Go ahead.' Nina squinches her eyes shut. 'Guess what I'm thinking.'

Nathaniel frowns, concentrating. 'Um . . . that I'm as good at this as IncrediBoy?'

She slaps her forehead. 'Oh my *gosh!* Nathaniel, how'd you *do* that!'

'I think I got his X-ray vision, too,' Nathaniel crows. 'I can see through houses and know what candy people are giving out!' He dashes forward, heading for the stairs. 'Hurry up, okay?'

With the buffer of their son gone, Caleb and Nina smile uncomfortably at each other again. 'What are you going to do when he can't see through doors?' Caleb asks.

'Tell him it's a glitch in his optical sensor that needs to be checked out.'

Nina walks out of the room, but Caleb stays upstairs a moment longer. From the window, he watches his ragtag son leap off the porch in a single bound – grace born of confidence. Even from up here, Caleb can see Nathaniel's smile, can hear the sharp start of his laugh. And he wonders if maybe Nina is right; if a superhero is nothing but an ordinary person who believes that she cannot fail.

*She is holding the gun that's a blow-dryer up to her head, when I ask. 'What's the next thing after love?'*

*'What?'*

*The stuff I need to say is all tangled. 'You love Mason, right?'*

*The dog hears his name and smiles. 'Well, sure,' she says.*

*'And you love Daddy more than that?'*

*She looks down at me. 'Yes.'*

*'And you love me even higher?'*

*Her eyebrows fly. 'True.'*

*'So what comes after that?'*

*She lifts me and puts me on the edge of the sink. The countertop is warm where the blow-dryer has been sitting; it just might be alive. For a minute, she thinks hard. 'The next thing after love,' she tells me, 'is being a mom.'*

# 5

At one point in my life, I had wanted to save the world. I'd listened, dewy-eyed, to law school professors and truly believed that as a prosecutor, I had a chance to rid the planet of evil. This was before I understood that when you have five hundred open cases, you make the conscious decision to plead as many as you can. It was before I realized that righteousness has less to do with a verdict than persuasion. Before I realized that I had not chosen a crusade, but only a job.

Still, it never entered my mind to be a defense attorney. I couldn't stomach the thought of standing up and lying on behalf of a morally depraved criminal, and as far as I was concerned most of them were guilty until proven innocent. But sitting in Fisher Carrington's sumptuous paneled office, being handed Jamaican coffee, $27.99 per pound, by his trim and efficient secretary, I start to understand the attraction.

Fisher comes out to meet me. His Newman-blue eyes twinkle, as if he couldn't be more delighted to find me sitting in his antechamber. And why shouldn't he be? He could charge me an arm and a leg and knows I will pay it. He has the chance to work on a high-profile murder that will net him a ton of new business. And finally, it's a departure from your run-of-the-mill case, the kind Fisher can do in his sleep.

'Nina,' he says. 'Good to see you.' As if, less than twenty-four hours ago, we hadn't met each other in the conference room of a jail. 'Come back to my office.'

It is heavily paneled, a man's room that conjures the smell of cigar smoke and snifters of brandy. He has the same books of statutes lining his shelves that I do, and somehow that is comforting. 'How's Nathaniel?'

'Fine.' I take a seat in an enormous leather wing chair and let my eyes wander.

'He must be happy to have his mother home.'

*More than his father is,* I think. My attention fixes on a small Picasso sketch on the wall. Not a lithograph – the real thing.

'What are you thinking?' Fisher asks, sitting down across from me.

'That the state doesn't pay me enough.' I turn to him. 'Thank you. For getting me out yesterday.'

'Much as I'd like to take the credit, that was a gift horse prancing in, and you know it. I didn't expect leniency from Brown.'

'I wouldn't expect it again.' I can feel his eyes on me, measuring. As compared to my behavior at yesterday's brief meeting, I'm under much greater control.

'Let's get down to business,' Fisher announces. 'Did you give the police a statement?'

'They asked. I repeated that I'd done all I could do. That I couldn't do any more.'

'You said this how many times?'

'Over and over.'

Fisher sets down his Waterman and folds his hands. His expression is a curious mix of morbid fascination, respect, and resignation. 'You know what you're doing,' he says, a statement.

I look at him over the rim of my coffee mug. 'You don't want to ask me that.'

Leaning back in his chair, Fisher grins. He has dimples, two in each cheek. 'Were you a drama major before you got to law school?'

'Sure,' I say. 'Weren't you?'

There are so many questions he wants to ask me; I can see them fighting inside of him like small soldiers desperate to join this fray. I can't blame him. By now, he knows I'm sane; he knows the game I have chosen to play. This is equivalent to having a Martian land in one's backyard. You can't possibly walk away without poking it once, to see what it's made of inside.

'How come you had your husband call me?'

'Because juries love you. People believe you.' I hesitate, then give him the truth. 'And because I hated going up against you.'

Fisher accepts this as his due. 'We need to prepare an insanity defense. Or go with extreme anger.'

There are no different degrees of murder in Maine, and the mandatory sentence is twenty-five years to life. Which means if I am to be acquitted, I have to be not guilty – (difficult to prove, given that the act is on film); not guilty by reason of insanity; or under the influence of extreme anger brought on by adequate provocation. That final defense reduces the crime to manslaughter, a lesser charge. It's somewhat amazing that in this state, it is legal to kill someone if they piss you off enough and if the jury agrees you had good reason to be pissed off, but there you have it.

'My advice is to argue both,' Fisher suggests. 'If –'

'No. If you argue both, it looks sleazy to the jury. Trust me. It seems like even *you* can't make up your mind why I'm not guilty.' I think about this for a minute. 'Besides, having twelve jurors agree on what justifies provocation is more of a long shot than having them recognize insanity when a prosecutor shoots a man right in front of a judge. And winning on extreme anger isn't an out-and-out win – it only lessens the conviction. If you get me off on an insanity charge, it's a complete acquittal.'

My defense is starting to form in my mind. 'Okay.' I lean forward, ready to let him in on my plan. 'We're going to get a call from Brown for the state psychiatric investigation. We can go to that shrink first, and based on that report, we can find someone to use as our own psychiatric expert.'

'Nina,' Fisher says patiently. 'You are the client. I am the attorney. Understand that now, or this isn't going to work.'

'Come on, Fisher. I know exactly what to do.'

'No, you don't. You're a prosecutor, and you don't know the first thing about running a defense.'

180 *Jodi Picoult*

'It's all about putting on a good act, right? And haven't I already done that?' Fisher waits until I settle back in my chair with my arms crossed over my chest, defeated. 'All right, fine. Then what are we going to do?'

'Go to the state psychiatrist,' Fisher says dryly. 'And then find someone to use as our own psychiatric expert.' When I lift my brows, he ignores me. 'I'm going to ask for all the information Detective Ducharme put together on the investigation involving your son, because that was what led you to believe you needed to kill this man.'

*Kill this man.* The phrase sends a shiver down my spine. We toss these words about so easily, as if we are discussing the weather, or the Red Sox scores.

'Is there anything else you can think of that I need to ask for?'

'The underwear,' I tell him. 'My son's underwear had semen on it. It was sent out for DNA testing but hasn't come back yet.'

'Well, that doesn't really matter anymore –'

'I want to see it,' I announce, brooking no argument. 'I need to see that report.'

Fisher nods, makes a note. 'Fine, then. I'll request it. Anything else?' I shake my head. 'All right. When I get the discovery in, I'll call you. In the meantime, don't leave the state, don't talk to anyone in your office, don't screw up, because you're not going to get a second chance.' He stands, dismissing me.

I walk to the door, trailing my fingers over the polished wainscoting. With my hand on the knob, I pause, then look over my shoulder. He is making notes inside my file, just the way I do when I begin a case. 'Fisher?' He glances up. 'Do you have any children?'

'Two. One daughter's a sophomore at Dartmouth, the other is in high school.'

It is suddenly hard to swallow. 'Well,' I say softly. 'That's good to know.'

&#9733;     &#9733;     &#9733;

*Lord have mercy. Christ have mercy.*

None of the reporters or parishioners who have come to Father Szyszynski's funeral Mass at St. Anne's recognize the woman draped in black and sitting in the second-to-last row of the church, not responding to the Kyrie. I have been careful to hide my face with a veil; to keep my silence. I have not told Caleb where I am headed; he thinks I am coming home after my appointment with Fisher. But instead I sit in a state of mortal sin, listening to the archbishop extol the virtues of the man I killed.

He may have been accused, but he was never convicted. Ironically, I have turned him into a victim. The pews are crushed with his flock, coming to pay their last respects. Everything is silver and white – the vestments of the clergy that have come to send Szyszynski off to God, the lilies lining the aisle, the altar boys who led the procession with their tapers, the pall over the casket – and the church looks, I imagine, like Heaven does.

The archbishop prays over the gleaming coffin, two priests beside him waving the censer and the Holy Water. They seem familiar; I realize they are the ones that recently visited the parish. I wonder if one of them will take over, now that there is no priest.

*I confess to Almighty God, and to you here present, that I have sinned through my own fault.*

The sweet smoke of candles and flowers makes my head swim. The last funeral Mass I attended was my father's, one with far less pageantry than this, although the service bled by in the same stream of disbelief. I can remember the priest who had put his hands over mine and offered me the greatest condolence he could: 'He's with God, now.'

As the Gospel is read, I look around the congregation. Some of the older women are sobbing; most are staring at the archbishop with the solemnity he commands. If Szyszynski's body belongs to Christ, then who controlled his mind? Who placed in that brain the seed to hurt a child? What made him pick mine?

Words jump out at me: *commend his soul; with his Maker; Hosanna in the highest.*

The organ's notes throb, and then the archbishop stands to deliver the eulogy. 'Father Glen Szyszynski,' he begins, 'was well loved by his congregation.'

I cannot say why I came here; why I knew that I would swim an ocean, break through fetters, run cross-country if need be to witness Szyszynski's burial. Maybe it is closure for me; maybe it is the proof I still need.

*This is My Body.*

I picture his face in profile, the minute before I pulled the trigger.

*This is the cup of My Blood.*

His skull, shattered.

Into the silence I gasp, and the people sitting on either side of me turn, curious.

When we stand like automatons and file into the aisle to take Communion, I find my feet moving before I can remember to stop them. I open my mouth for the priest holding the Host. 'Body of Christ,' he says, and he looks me in the eye.

'Amen,' I answer.

When I turn my gaze falls on the front left pew, where a woman in black is bent over at the waist, sobbing so hard she cannot catch her breath. Her iron-gray curls wilt beneath her black cloche hat; her hands are knotted so tightly around the edge of the pew I think she may splinter the wood. The priest who has given me Communion whispers to another clergyman, who takes over as he goes to comfort her. And that is when it hits me:

Father Szyszynski was someone's son, too.

My chest fills with lead and my legs melt beneath me. I can tell myself that I have gotten retribution for Nathaniel; I can say that I was morally right – but I cannot take away the truth that another mother has lost her child because of me.

Is it right to close one cycle of pain if it only opens up another one?

The church starts to spin, and the flowers are reaching for my ankles. A face as wide as the moon looms in front of me, speaking words that I cannot hear. *If I faint, they will know who I am. They will crucify me.* I summon all the strength I have left to shove aside the people in my way, to lurch down the aisle, to push open the double doors of St. Anne's and break free.

Mason, the golden retriever, has been called Nathaniel's dog for as long as Nathaniel can remember, although he was part of the family for ten months before Nathaniel was even born. And the strange thing is, if it had been the other way around – if *Nathaniel* had gotten here first – he would have told his parents that he really wanted a cat. He likes the way you can drape a kitten over your arm, the same way you'd carry a coat if you got too hot. He likes the sound they make against his ear, how it makes his skin hum, too. He likes the way they don't take baths; he likes the fact that they can fall from a great height, but land on their feet.

He asked for a kitten one Christmas, and although Santa had brought him everything else, the cat didn't happen. It was Mason, he knew. The dog had a habit of bringing in gifts – the skull of a mouse he'd chewed clean, the body of a thrashed snake found at the end of the drive, a toad caught in the bowl of his mouth. *God knows,* Nathaniel's mother said, *what he'd do to a kitten.*

So that day when he wandered in the basement of the church, the day he'd been looking at the dragon painting in Father Glen's office, the first thing Nathaniel noticed was the cat. She was black, with three white paws, as if she'd stepped into paint and realized, partway through, that it wasn't such a good idea. Her tail twitched like a snake charmer's cobra. Her face was no bigger than Nathaniel's palm.

'Ah,' the priest said. 'You like Esme.' He reached down and scratched between the cat's ears. 'That's my girl.' Scooping the cat into his arms, he sat down on the couch beneath the painting of the dragon. Nathaniel thought he was very brave. Had it been him, he'd be worried about the monster coming to life, eating him whole. 'Would you like to pet her?'

Nathaniel nodded, his throat so full of his good fortune that he couldn't even speak. He came closer to the couch, to the small ball of fur in the priest's lap. He placed his hand on the kitten's back, feeling the heat and the bones and the heart of her. 'Hi,' he whispered. 'Hi, Esme.'

Her tail tickled Nathaniel under the chin, and he laughed. The priest laughed too, and put his hand on the back of Nathaniel's neck. It was the same spot where Nathaniel was petting the cat, and for a moment he saw something like the endless mirror in a carnival's fun house – him touching the cat, and the priest touching him, and maybe even the big invisible hand of God touching the priest. Nathaniel lifted his palm, took a step back.

'She likes you,' the priest said.

'For real?'

'Oh, yes. She doesn't act this way around most of the children.'

That made Nathaniel feel tall all over. He scratched the cat's ears again, and he would have sworn she smiled.

'That's it,' the priest encouraged. 'Don't stop.'


Quentin Brown sits at Nina's desk in the district attorney's office, wondering what's missing. For lack of space, he has been given her office as a base of operations, and the irony has not been lost on him that he will be planning the conviction of this woman from the very seat in which she once sat. What he has learned, from observation, is that Nina Frost is a neat-freak – her paper clips, for the love of God, are sorted by size in small dishes. Her files are alphabetized. There is not a clue to be found – no crumpled Post-it with the name of a gun dealer; not even a doodle of Father Szyszynski's face on the blotter. *This could be anyone's workspace,* Quentin thinks, *and therein lies the problem.*

What kind of woman doesn't keep a picture of her kid or her husband on her desk?

He mulls over what this might or might not mean for a moment, then takes out his wallet. From the folds he pulls a worn baby photo of Gideon. They'd had it taken at Sears. To get that smile on the boy's face, Quentin had pretended to hit Tanya on the head with a Nerf football, and he'd inadvertently knocked out her contact lens. He sets the photograph square, now, in the corner of Nina Frost's blotter, as the door opens.

Two Biddeford detectives enter – Evan Chao and Patrick Ducharme, if Quentin recalls correctly. 'Come in,' he says, gesturing to the seats across from him. 'Take a seat.'

They form a solid block, their shoulders nearly touching. Quentin lifts a remote control and turns on a television/VCR on the shelf behind them. He has already watched the tape a thousand times himself, and imagines that the two detectives have seen it as well. Hell, most of New England has seen it by now; it was run on all the CBS news affiliates. Chao and Ducharme turn, mesmerized by the sight of Nina Frost on the small screen, walking with a preternatural grace toward the railing of the gallery and lifting a handgun. In this version, the unedited one, you can see the right side of Glen Szyszynski's head exploding.

'Jesus,' Chao murmurs.

Quentin lets the tape run. This time, he isn't watching it – he's watching the reactions of the detectives. He doesn't know Chao or Ducharme from a hole in the wall, but he can tell you this – they've worked with Nina Frost for seven years; they've worked with Quentin for twenty-four hours. As the camera tilts wildly, coming to rest on the scuffle between Nina and the bailiffs, Chao looks into his lap. Ducharme stares resolutely at the screen, but there is no emotion on his face.

With one click, Quentin shuts off the TV. 'I've read the witness statements, all 124 of them. And, naturally, it doesn't hurt to have the entire fiasco in living color.' He leans forward, his elbows on Nina's desk. 'The evidence is solid here. The only question is whether she is or isn't guilty by reason of insanity. She'll either run with that, or extreme anger.' Turning to Chao, he asks, 'Did you go to the autopsy?'

'Yeah, I did.'

'And?'

'They already released the body to the funeral home, but they won't give me a report until the victim's medical records arrive.'

Quentin rolls his eyes. 'Like there's a question here about the cause of death?'

'It's not that,' Ducharme interrupts. 'They like to have all the medical records attached. It's the office protocol.'

'Well, tell them to hurry up,' Quentin says. 'I don't care if Szyszynski had full-blown AIDS . . . that isn't what he died of.' He opens a file on his desk and waves a paper at Patrick Ducharme. 'What the hell was this?'

He lets the detective read his own report about the interrogation of Caleb Frost, under suspicion for molesting his own son. 'The boy was mute,' Patrick explains. 'He was taught basic sign language, and when we pressed him to ID the perp, he kept making the sign for *father*.' Patrick hands back the paper. 'We went to Caleb Frost first.'

'What did she do?' Quentin asks. There is no need to spell out to whom he's referring.

Patrick rubs a hand over his face, muttering into his hand.

'I didn't quite catch that, Detective,' Quentin says.

'She got a restraining order against her husband.'

'*Here?*'

'In Biddeford.'

'I want a copy of that.'

Patrick shrugs. 'It was vacated.'

'I don't care. Nina Frost shot the man she was convinced molested her son. But just four days earlier, she was convinced it was a different man. Her lawyer's going to tell a jury that she killed the priest because he was the one who hurt her child . . . but how sure *was* she?'

'There was semen,' Patrick says. 'On her son's underwear.'

'Yes.' Quentin rifles through some more pages. 'Where's the DNA on that?'

'At the lab. It should be back this week.'

Quentin's head comes up slowly. 'She didn't even see the DNA results on the underwear before she shot the guy?'

A muscle jumps along Patrick's jaw. 'Nathaniel *told* me. Her son. He made a verbal ID.'

'My five-year-old nephew tells me the tooth fairy's the one who brought him a buck, but that doesn't mean I *believe* him, Lieutenant.'

Before he has even finished his sentence, Patrick is out of his chair, leaning across the desk toward Quentin. 'You don't know Nathaniel Frost,' he bites out. 'And you have no right to question my professional judgment.'

Quentin stands, towering over the detective. 'I have every right. Because reading your file on the investigation, it sure looks to me like you fucked up simply because you were giving a DA who jumped to conclusions special treatment. And I'll be damned if I'm going to let you do that again while we prosecute her.'

'She didn't jump to conclusions,' Patrick argues. 'She knew exactly what she was doing. Christ, if it were my kid, I would have done the same thing.'

'Both of you listen to me. Nina Frost is a murder suspect. She made the choice to commit a criminal act. She killed a man in cold blood in front of a courtroom of people. Your job is to uphold laws, and no one – *no one* – gets to bend those to their own advantage, not even a district attorney.' Quentin turns to the first policeman. 'Is that clear, Detective Chao?'

Chao nods tightly.

'Detective Ducharme?'

Patrick meets his eye, sinks into his chair. It is not until long after the detectives have left the office that Quentin realizes Ducharme never actually answered.

*     *     *

Getting ready for winter, in Caleb's opinion, is only wishful thinking. The best preparation in the world isn't going to keep a storm from catching you unaware. The thing about nor'easters is that you don't always see them coming. They head out to sea, then turn around and batter Maine hard. There have been times in recent years that Caleb has opened the front door to find a chest-high drift of snow; has dug his way free with a shovel kept in the front closet to find a world that looks nothing like it did the night before.

Today, he is readying the house. That means hiding Nathaniel's bike in the garage, and unearthing the Flexible Flyer and the cross-country skis instead. Caleb has covered the shrubs in the front of the house with triangular wooden horses, little hats to keep their fragile branches from the ice and snow that slide off the roof.

All that is left, now, is storing enough chopped wood to last through the winter. He's brought in three loads now, stacking them in crosshatches in the basement. Slivers of oak jab his thick gloves as he moves in rhythm, taking a pair of split logs from the pile dumped down the bulkhead and laying them neatly in place. Caleb feels a wistfulness press in on him, as if each growing inch of the woodpile is taking away something summerish – a bright flock of goldfinches, a raging stream, the steam of loam overturned by a tiller. All winter long, when he burns these stacks, Caleb imagines it like a puzzle. With each log he tosses on a fire, he is able to remember the song of a cricket, or the arc of stars in the July sky. And so on, until the basement is empty again, and springtime has flung itself, jubilant, over his property.

'Do you think we'll make it through the winter?'

At Nina's voice, Caleb startles. She has come down the basement stairs and stands at the bottom with her arms crossed, surveying the stacks of wood. 'Doesn't seem like much,' she adds.

'I've got plenty.' Caleb places two more logs. 'I just haven't brought it all in yet.'

He is aware of Nina's eyes on him as he turns and bends, lifts a large burl into his arms, and deposits it at the top of a tall stack. 'So.'

'Yes,' she answers.

'How was the lawyer's?'

She shrugs. 'He's a defense attorney.'

Caleb assumes this is meant as an insult. As always in legal matters, he doesn't know what to say in response. The basement is only half full, but Caleb is suddenly aware of how big he is, and how close he is to Nina, and how the room does not seem able to hold both of them. 'Are you going back out again? Because I need to go to the hardware store to get that tarp.'

He doesn't need a tarp; he has four of them stored in the garage. He does not even know why those words have flown from his mouth, like birds desperate to escape through a chimney flue. And yet, he keeps speaking: 'Can you watch Nathaniel?'

Nina goes still in front of his eyes. 'Of course I can watch Nathaniel. Or do you think I'm too unstable to take care of him?'

'I didn't mean it like that.'

'You did, Caleb. You may not want to admit it, but you did.' There are tears in her eyes. But because he cannot think of the words that might take them away, Caleb simply nods and walks past her, their shoulders brushing as he makes his way up the stairs.

He doesn't drive to the hardware store, naturally. Instead he finds himself meandering across the county on back roads, pulling into Tequila Mockingbird, the little bar that Nina talks about from time to time. He knows she meets Patrick there for lunch every week; he even knows that the ponytailed bartender is named Stuyvesant. But Caleb has never set foot in the place, and when he walks through the door into the nearly empty afternoon room, he feels like a secret is swelling beneath his ribs – he knows so much more about this place than it knows about him.

'Afternoon,' Stuyvesant says, as Caleb hovers at the bar. Which seat does Nina take? He stares at each of them, lined up like teeth, trying to divine the one. 'What can I get you?'

Caleb drinks beer. He's never been much for hard liquor. But he asks for a shot of Talisker, a bottle he can read across the bar whose name sounds just as soothing on the tongue as, he imagines, the whiskey it describes. Stuyvesant sets it down in front of him with a bowl of peanuts. There is a businessman sitting three stools away, and a woman trying not to cry as she writes a letter at a booth. Caleb lifts the glass to the bartender. '*Sláinte*,' he says, a toast he once heard in a movie.

'You Irish?' Stuyvesant asks, running a cloth around the polished hood of the bar.

'My father was.' In fact, Caleb's parents had both been born in America, and his ancestry was Swedish and British.

'No kidding.'This from the businessman, glancing over. 'My sister lives in County Cork. Gorgeous place.' He laughs. 'Why on earth did you come over here?'

Caleb takes a sip of his whiskey. 'Didn't have much choice,' he lies. 'I was two years old.'

'You live in Sanford?'

'No. Here on business. Sales.'

'Aren't we all?'The man lifts his beer. 'God bless the corporate expense account, right?' He signals to Stuyvesant. 'Another round for us,' he says, and then to Caleb: 'My treat. Or rather, my company's.'

They talk about the upcoming Bruins season, and the way it feels like snow already.They debate the merits of the Midwest, where the businessman lives, versus New England. Caleb doesn't know why he is not telling the businessman the truth – but prevarication comes so easily, and the knowledge that this man will buy anything he says right now is oddly liberating. So Caleb pretends he's from Rochester, New Hampshire, a place he has never actually been. He fabricates a company name, a product line of construction equipment, and a history of distinguished achievement. He lets the lies tumble from his lips, gathers them like marker chips at a casino, almost giddy to see how many he can stack before they come crashing down.

The man glances at his watch and swears. 'Gotta call home. If I'm late, my wife assumes I've wrapped my rental car around a tree. You know?'

'Never been married,' Caleb shrugs, and drinks the Talisker through the sieve of his teeth, like baleen.

'Smart move.' The businessman hops off the stool, headed toward the rear of the bar, a pay phone from which Nina has called Caleb once or twice when her own cell phone's battery died. As he passes, he holds out his hand. 'Name's Mike Johanssen, by the way.'

Caleb shakes. 'Glen,' he answers. 'Glen Szyszynski.'

He remembers too late that he is supposed to be Irish, not Polish. That Stuyvesant, who lives here, will surely pick up on the name. But neither of these things matters. By the time the businessman returns and Stuyvesant thinks twice, Caleb has left the bar, more comfortable wearing another man's unlikely identity than he feels these days in his own.

The state psychiatrist is so young that I have a profound urge to reach across the desk separating us and smooth his cowlick. But if I did that, Dr. Storrow would probably die of fright, certain I mean to strangle him with the strap of my purse. It is why he chose to meet me at the court in Alfred, and I can't say I blame him. All of this man's clients are either insane or homicidal, and the safest place to conduct his interview – in lieu of jail – is a public venue with plenty of bailiffs milling around.

I have dressed with great deliberation, not in my usual conservative suit, but in khaki pants and a cotton turtleneck and loafers. When Dr. Storrow looks at me, I don't want him to be thinking *lawyer.* I want him to remember his own mother, standing on the sidelines of his soccer game, cheering him to victory.

The first time he speaks, I expect his voice to crack. 'You were a prosecutor in York County, weren't you, Ms. Frost?'

I have to think before I answer. How crazy is crazy? Should

I seem to have trouble understanding him, should I start gnawing the collar of my shirt? It will be easy to deceive a shrink as inexperienced as Storrow . . . but that is no longer the issue. Now, I need to make sure that the insanity is temporary. That I get, as we call it, acquitted without being committed. So I smile at him. 'Call me Nina,' I offer. 'And yes.'

'Okay,' Dr. Storrow says. 'I have this questionnaire, um, to fill out, and give to the court.' He takes out a piece of paper I have seen a thousand times, fill-in-the-blanks, and begins to read. 'Did you take any medication before you came here today?'

'No.'

'Have you ever been charged with a crime before?'

'No.'

'Have you ever been to court before?'

'Every day,' I say. 'For the past ten years.'

'Oh . . .' Dr. Storrow blinks at me, as if he's just remembered who he is talking to. 'Oh, that's right. Well, I still need to ask you these questions, if that's okay.' He clears his throat. 'Do you understand what the role of the judge is in a trial?'

I raise one eyebrow.

'I'm going to take that as a yes,' Dr. Storrow scribbles on his form. 'Do you know what the role of the prosecutor is?'

'Oh, I think I have a pretty good idea.'

*Do you know what the defense attorney does? Do you understand that the state is trying to prove you guilty beyond a reasonable doubt?* The questions come, silly as cream pies thrown at the face of a clown. Fisher and I will use this ridiculous rubber stamp interview to our advantage. On paper, without the inflection of my voice, my answers will not look absurd – they will only seem a little evasive, a little strange. And Dr. Storrow is too inexperienced to communicate on the stand that all along I knew exactly what he was talking about.

'What should you do if something happens in court that you don't understand?'

I shrug. 'I'd have my attorney ask what legal precedent they were following, so that I could look it up.'

'Do you understand that anything you say to your lawyer, he can't repeat?'

'Really?'

Dr. Storrow puts down the form. With a perfectly straight face, he says, 'I think we can move on.' He looks at my purse, from which I once pulled a gun. 'Have you ever been diagnosed with a psychiatric illness?'

'No.'

'Have you ever been on any medication for psychiatric problems?'

'No.'

'Do you have a history of emotional breakdown triggered by stress?'

'No.'

'Have you ever owned a gun before?'

I shake my head.

'Have you ever been to counseling of any kind?'

That question gives me pause. 'Yes,' I admit, thinking back to the confessional at St. Anne's. 'It was the worst mistake of my life.'

'Why?'

'When I found out my son had been sexually abused, I went to confession at my church. I talked to my priest about it. And then I found out that he was the bastard who did it.'

My language makes a blush rise above the collar of his button-down shirt. 'Ms. Frost – Nina – I need to ask you some questions about the day that . . . that everything happened.'

I start to pull at the sleeves of my turtleneck. Not a lot, just so that fabric covers my hands. I look into my lap. 'I had to do it,' I whisper.

I am getting so good at this.

'How were you feeling that day?' Dr. Storrow asks. Doubt ices his voice; just moments ago, I was perfectly lucid.

'I had to do it . . . you understand. I've seen this happen too many times. I couldn't lose him to this.' I close my eyes, thinking of every successful insanity defense I've ever heard proposed to a court. 'I didn't have a choice. I couldn't have stopped myself . . . it was like I was watching someone else do it, someone else reacting.'

'But you knew what you were doing,' Dr. Storrow replies, and I have to catch myself before my head snaps up. 'You've prosecuted people who've done horrible things.'

'I didn't do a horrible thing. I saved my son. Isn't that what mothers are supposed to do?'

'What do *you* think mothers are supposed to do?' he asks.

*Stay awake all night when an infant has a cold, as if she might be able to breathe for him. Learn how to speak Pig Latin, and make a pact to talk that way for an entire day. Bake at least one cake with every ingredient in the pantry, just to see how it will taste.*

*Fall in love with your son a little more every day.*

'Nina?' Dr. Storrow says. 'Are you all right?'

I look up and nod through my tears. 'I'm sorry.'

'Are you?' He leans forward. 'Are you truly sorry?'

We are not talking about the same thing anymore. I imagine Father Szyszynski, on his way to Hell. I think of all the ways to interpret those words, and then I meet Dr. Storrow's gaze. 'Was he?'

Nina has always tasted better than any other woman, Caleb thinks, as his lips slip down the slope of one shoulder. Like honey and sun and caramel – from the roof of her mouth to the hollow behind her knee. There are times Caleb believes he could feast on his wife and never feel that he is getting enough.

Her hands come up to clutch his shoulder, and in the half dark her head falls back, making the line of her throat a land-scape. Caleb buries his face there, and tries to navigate by touch. Here, in this bed, she is the woman he fell in love with a lifetime ago. He knows when she is going to touch him, and where. He can predict each of her moves.

Her legs fall open to either side of him, and Caleb presses himself against her. He arches his back. He imagines the moment he will be inside her, how the pressure will build and build and explode like a bullet.

At that moment Nina's hand slips between their bodies to cup him, and just like that, Caleb goes soft. He tries grinding against her. Nina's fingers play over him like a flutist's, but nothing happens.

Caleb feels her hand come up to his shoulder again, feels the cold air of its absence on his balls. 'Well,' Nina says, as he rolls to his back beside her. 'That's never happened before.'

He stares at the ceiling, at anything but this stranger beside him. *It's not the only thing,* he thinks.

On Friday afternoon, Nathaniel and I go grocery shopping. The P&C is a gastronomic fest for my son: I move from the deli counter, where Nathaniel gets a free slice of cheese; to the cookie aisle, where we pick up the box of Animal Crackers; to the breads, where Nathaniel works his way through a plain bagel. 'What do you think, Nathaniel?' I ask, handing him a few grapes from the bunch I've just put in the cart. 'Should I pay $4.99 for a honeydew?'

I pick up the melon and sniff at the bottom. In truth, I have never been a good judge of fruit. I know it's all about softness and scent, but in my opinion some with the sweetest insides have been hard as a rock on the surface.

Suddenly, the bagel Nathaniel's been eating falls into my hand. 'Peter!' he yells, waving from his harness in the shopping cart. 'Peter! Hey, Peter!'

I look up to find Peter Eberhardt walking down the produce aisle, holding a bag of chips and a bottle of Chardonnay. Peter, whom I have not seen since the day I had my restraining order against Caleb vacated. There is so much I want to say to him – to ask him, now that I am not in the office to find out myself – but the judge has specifically prohibited me from speaking to my own colleagues as a condition of bail.

Nathaniel, of course, doesn't know that. He just understands that Peter – a man who keeps Charms lollipops on his desk, who can do the best impression of a duck sneezing, whom he hasn't seen in weeks – is suddenly standing six feet away. 'Peter,' Nathaniel calls again, and holds out his arms.

Peter thinks twice. I can see it in his face. But then again, he adores Nathaniel. All the reason in the world cannot stand up to my son's smile. Peter lays his bag of chips and bottle of wine on top of a display of Red Delicious apples and gives Nathaniel a bear hug. 'Listen to you!' he crows. 'That voice is back to a hundred percent working order, isn't it?'

Nathaniel giggles when Peter opens up his mouth to check inside. 'Does the volume work too?' he asks, pretending to twist a knob on Nathaniel's belly, so that he laughs louder and louder.

Then Peter turns to me. 'He sounds great, Nina.' Four words, but I know what he is really saying: *You did the right thing.*

'Thanks.'

We look at each other, measuring what can and cannot be said. And because we are so busy making a commodity of our friendship, I never notice another grocery cart approaching. It pings against the rear of mine gently, just loud enough to make me look up, so that I can see Quentin Brown smiling beside a sea of navel oranges. 'Well, well,' he says. 'Aren't things ripe here?' He pulls a cell phone out of his breast pocket and dials. 'Get a squad car down here now. I'm making an arrest.'

'You don't understand,' I insist, as he puts away his phone.

'What's so difficult to grasp? You're in blatant violation of your bail agreement, Ms. Frost. Is this or is this not a colleague from the district attorney's office?'

'For Christ's sake, Quentin,' Peter interjects. 'I was talking to the kid. He called me over.'

Quentin grabs my arm. 'I took a chance on you, and you made me look like a fool.'

'Mommy?' Nathaniel's voice rises to me like steam.

'It's okay, sweetie.' I turn to the assistant attorney general and speak through my teeth. 'I will come with you,' I say in an undertone. 'But please have the decency to do this without traumatizing my child any more.'

'I didn't speak to her,' Peter yells. 'You can't do this.'

When Quentin turns, his eyes go as dark as plums. 'I believe, Mr. Eberhardt, that the exact words you *didn't* speak were:

"He sounds great, Nina." *Nina*. As in the name of the woman you weren't talking to. And frankly, even if you were stupid enough to approach Ms. Frost, it was her responsibility to take her cart and walk away from you.'

'Peter, it's all right.' I talk fast, because I can hear the sirens outside the store already. 'Get Nathaniel home to Caleb, will you?'

Then two policemen come running into the aisle, their hands on the butts of their guns. Nathaniel's eyes go wide at the show, until he realizes what they are doing. 'Mommy!' he screams, as Quentin orders me to be handcuffed.

I face Nathaniel, smiling so hard my face may break. 'It's fine. See? I'm fine.' My hair falls out of its clip as my hands are pulled behind me. 'Peter? Take him *now.*'

'Come on, bud,' Peter soothes, pulling Nathaniel out of the cart. His shoes get caught on the metal rungs, and Nathaniel starts fighting in earnest. His arms reach out to me and he starts crying so violently he begins to hiccup. *'Mommeeeee!'*

I am marched past the gaping shoppers, past the slack-jawed stockboys, past the cashiers who pause in midair with their electronic scanners. The whole way, I can hear my son. His shrieks follow me through the parking lot, to the squad car. The lights are spinning on its roof. Once, long before all this, Nathaniel pointed to a cruiser in pursuit, and called it a zooming holiday.

'I'm sorry, Nina,' one of the policemen says as he ducks me inside. Through the window I can see Quentin Brown, arms crossed. *Orange juice*, I think. *Roast beef and sliced American cheese. Asparagus, Ritz crackers, milk. Vanilla yogurt.* This is my litany the whole way back to jail: the contents of my abandoned shopping cart, slowly going bad, until some kind soul has the inclination to put them back where they belong.

Caleb opens the door to find his son sobbing in Peter Eberhardt's arms. 'What happened to Nina?' he immediately asks, and reaches for Nathaniel.

'The guy's an asshole,' Peter says desperately. 'He's doing this to leave his mark on the town. He's –'

'Peter, *where's my wife?*'

The other man winces. 'Back in jail. She violated her bail agreement, and the assistant attorney general had her arrested.'

For a moment, Nathaniel feels like a lead weight. Caleb staggers under the responsibility of bearing him, then finds his footing. Nathaniel is still crying, more quietly now, a river that runs down the back of his shirt. Caleb makes small circles on the child's spine. 'Back up. Tell me what happened.'

Caleb picks out select words: *grocery, produce, Quentin Brown.* But he can barely hear Peter over the roar in his own head, one single phrase: *Nina, what have you done now?* 'Nathaniel called me over,' Peter explains. 'I was so psyched to hear him talking again, I couldn't just ignore him.'

Caleb shakes his head. 'You . . . you were the one who approached her?'

Peter is a foot shorter than Caleb and feels every inch of it at that moment. He takes a step backward. 'I never would have gotten her in trouble, Caleb, you know that.'

Caleb pictures his son screaming, his wife being sandwiched between policemen, a barrage of fruit spilled on the floor in this fray. He knows it is not Peter's fault, not entirely. It takes two to have a conversation; Nina should have simply walked away.

But as Nina would tell him, she probably wasn't thinking at the time.

Peter places a hand on Nathaniel's calf and rubs gently. It only sets the child off again; screams ricochet around the porch and peal off the thick bare branches of trees. 'Jesus, Caleb, I'm sorry. It's ridiculous. We didn't do anything.'

Caleb turns so that Peter can see Nathaniel's back, heaving with the force of his fear. He touches the damp cap of his son's hair. 'You didn't do anything?' Caleb challenges, and leaves Peter standing outside.

★　　　★　　　★

I move stiffly as I'm led to the solitary cells again, but I cannot tell what's made me numb – my arrest, or the simple cold. The furnace at the jail has broken, and the correctional officers are all wearing heavy coats. Inmates usually clad in shorts or under-wear have put on sweaters; having none, I sit shivering in my cell after the door is locked behind me.

'Honey.'

I close my eyes, turn in to the wall. Tonight, I don't feel like dealing with Adrienne. Tonight I have to find a way to under-stand that Quentin Brown has screwed me. Getting released on bail the first time was a miracle; good fortune rarely strikes twice in the same spot.

I wonder if Nathaniel is all right. I wonder if Fisher has spoken to Caleb. This time, being booked, I chose my attorney as my one phone call. It was the coward's way out.

Caleb will say this is my fault. That is, if he's still speaking to me.

'Honey, your teeth are chattering so hard you're gonna give yourself a root canal. Here.' Something swishes near the bars; I turn to see Adrienne tossing me a sweater. 'It's angora. Don't be stretching it out.'

With jerky movements, I tug on the sweater, which I couldn't stretch in my wildest imaginings, Adrienne being six inches and two cup sizes larger than me. I am still shaking, but at least now I know it has nothing to do with the cold.

As the guards call lights out, I try to think of heat. I remember how Mason, when he was a puppy, would lie on my feet with his soft belly hot against my bare toes. And the beach in St. Thomas, where Caleb buried me up to my neck in the hot sand on our honeymoon. Pajamas, pulled off Nathaniel's body in the early morning, still warm and smelling of sleep.

Across the corridor Adrienne chews Wintergreen Life Savers. They give off green sparks in the near dark, as if she has learned how to make her own lightning.

Even in the muffled silence of jail, I can hear Nathaniel screaming for me as I am being handcuffed. Nathaniel, who had been doing so well – edging toward normal – what will this do to him? Will he wait for me at a window, even when I don't come home? Will he sleep next to Caleb, to chase away nightmares?

I rerun my actions at the grocery store like the loop of a security camera's video – what I did, what I should have done. I might have appointed myself to be Nathaniel's protector, but today I did not do a crackerjack job of it. I assumed that talking to Peter was harmless . . . and instead that one action might have set Nathaniel back by leaps and bounds.

A few feet away, in Adrienne's cell, sparks dance like fire-flies. Things aren't always what they seem.

For example, I have always believed I know what is best for Nathaniel.

But what if it turns out I've been wrong?

'I put in some hot chocolate to go with your whipped cream,' Caleb says, a lame joke, as he sets the mug down on Nathaniel's nightstand. Nathaniel doesn't even turn to him. He faces the wall, wrapped like a cocoon, his eyes so red from crying that he does not look like himself.

Caleb pulls off his shoes and gets right onto Nathaniel's bed, then wraps his arms tight around the boy. 'Nathaniel, it's okay.'

He feels that tiny head shake once. Coming up on an elbow, Caleb gently turns his son onto his back. He grins, trying so hard to pretend that this is entirely ordinary, that Nathaniel's whole world has not become a snow globe, waved intermittently every time things begin to settle. 'What do you say? You want some of this cocoa?'

Nathaniel sits up slowly. He brings his hands out from underneath the covers and curls them into his body. Then he raises his palm, fingers outstretched, and sets his thumb on his chin. *Want Mommy.*

Caleb's whole body goes still. Nathaniel hasn't been very forthcoming since Peter brought him home, except for the crying. He stopped sobbing sometime between when Caleb bathed him and got him into his pajamas. But surely he can talk, if he wants to. 'Nathaniel, can you tell me what you want?'

That hand sign, again. And a third time.

'Can you say it, buddy? I know you want Mommy. Say it for me.'

Nathaniel's eyes shine, and the tears spill over. Caleb grabs the boy's hand. 'Say it,' he begs. 'Please, Nathaniel.'

But Nathaniel doesn't utter a word.

'Okay,' Caleb murmurs, releasing Nathaniel's hand into his lap. 'It's okay.' He smiles as best he can, and gets off the bed. 'I'm going to be right back. In the meantime, you can start on that hot chocolate, all right?'

In his own bedroom, Caleb picks up the phone. Dials a number from a card in his wallet. Pages Dr. Robichaud, the child psychiatrist. Then he hangs up, balls his hand into a fist, and punches a hole in the wall.

Nathaniel knows this is all his fault. Peter said it wasn't, but he was lying, the way grown-ups do in the middle of the night to make you stop thinking about something awful living under the bed. They'd taken the bagel out of the store without letting the machine ring up its numbers; they'd driven to his house without his car seat; even just now, his dad had brought cocoa to the bedroom when no food was ever allowed upstairs. His mother was gone, all the rules were getting broken, and it was because of Nathaniel.

He had seen Peter and said hi, which turned out to be a bad thing. A very, very bad thing.

This is what Nathaniel knows: He talked, and the bad man grabbed his mother's arm. He talked, and the police came. He talked, and his mother got taken away.

So he will never talk again.

By Saturday morning, they have fixed the heat. They've fixed it so well that it is nearly eighty degrees inside the jail. When

I am brought to the conference room to meet Fisher, I'm wearing a camisole and scrub pants, and sweating. Fisher, of course, looks perfectly cool, even in his suit and tie. 'The earliest I can even get to a judge for a revocation hearing is Monday,' he says.

'I need to see my son.'

Fisher's face remains impassive. He is just as angry as I would be, in his shoes – I have just complicated my case irreparably. 'Visiting hours are from ten to twelve today.'

'Call Caleb. Please, Fisher. Please, do whatever you have to do to make him bring Nathaniel down here.' I sink into the chair across from him. 'He is five years old, and he saw me being taken away by the police. Now he has to see that I'm all right, even in here.'

Fisher promises nothing. 'I don't have to tell you that your bail is going to be revoked. Think about what you want me to say to the judge, Nina, because you don't have any chances left.'

I wait until he meets my eye. 'Will you call home for me?'

'Will you admit that I'm in charge?'

For a long moment, neither of us blinks, but I break first. I stare at my lap until I hear Fisher close the door behind him.

Adrienne knows I'm anxious as visiting hours come to an end – nearly noon, and still I have not been called to see anyone. She lies on her stomach, painting her nails fluorescent orange. In honor of hunting season, she said. As the correctional officer walks past for his quarter-hour check, I stand up. 'Are you sure no one's come yet?'

He shakes his head, moves on. Adrienne blows on her fingers to dry the polish. 'I got extra,' she says, holding up the bottle. 'You want me to roll it across?'

'I don't have any nails. I bite mine.'

'Now, that is a travesty. Some of us just don't have the sense to make the most of what God gives us.'

I laugh. 'You're one to talk.'

'In my case, honey, when it came to passing out the right stuff, God was having a senior moment.' She sits down on her lower bunk and takes off her tennis shoes. Last night, she did her toenails, tiny American flags. 'Well, fuck me,' Adrienne says. 'I smudged.'

The clock has not moved. Not even a second, I'd swear it.

'Tell me about your son,' Adrienne says when she sees me looking down the hallway again. 'I always wanted to have me one of them.'

'I would have figured you'd want a girl.'

'Honey, us ladies, we're high maintenance. A boy, you know exactly what you're getting.'

I try to think of the best way to describe Nathaniel. It is like trying to hold the ocean in a paper cup. How do I explain a boy who eats his food color by color; who wakes me in the middle of the night with a burning need to know why we breathe oxygen instead of water; who took apart a microcassette recorder to find his voice, trapped inside? I know my son so well, I surprise myself – there are too many words to choose from.

'Sometimes when I hold his hand,' I answer slowly, finally, 'it's like it doesn't fit anymore. I mean, he's only five, you know? But I can feel what's coming. Sometimes his palm's just a little too wide, or his fingers are too strong.' Glancing at Adrienne, I shrug. 'Each time I do it, I think this may be the last time I hold his hand. That next time, he may be holding mine.'

She smiles softly at me. 'Honey, he ain't coming today.'

It is 12:46 P.M., and I have to turn away, because Adrienne is right.

The CO wakes me up in the late afternoon. 'Come on,' he mutters, and slides open the door of my cell. I scramble upright, rubbing the sleep from my eyes. He leads me down a hallway to a part of the jail I have not yet visited. A row of small rooms, mini-prisons, are on my left. The guard opens one and guides me inside.

It is no bigger than a broom closet. Inside, a stool faces a Plexiglas window. A telephone receiver is mounted to the wall at its side. And on the other side of the glass, in a twin of a room, sits Caleb.

'Oh!' The word comes on a cry, and I lurch for the telephone, picking it up and holding it to my ear. 'Caleb,' I say, knowing he can see my face, read my words. 'Please, please, pick up the phone.' I pantomime over and over. But his face is chiseled and hard; his arms crossed tight on his chest. He will not give me this one thing.

Defeated, I sink onto the stool and rest my forehead against the Plexiglas. Caleb bends down to pick something up, and I realize that Nathaniel has been there all along, beneath the counter where I could not see him. He kneels on the stool, eyes wide and wary. He hesitantly touches the glass, as if he needs to know that I am not a trick of the light.

At the beach once, we found a hermit crab. I turned it over so that Nathaniel could see its jointed legs scrambling. *Put him on your palm,* I said, *and he'll crawl.* Nathaniel had held out his hand, but every time I went to set the crab on it, he jerked away. He wanted to touch it, and he was terrified to touch it, in equal proportions.

So I wave. I smile. I fill my little cubicle with the sound of his name.

As I did with Caleb, I pick up the telephone receiver. 'You too,' I mouth, and I do it again, so Nathaniel can see how. But he shakes his head, and instead raises his hand to his chin. *Mommy,* he signs.

The receiver falls out of my hand, a snake that strikes the wall beside it. I do not even need to look at Caleb for verification; just like that, I know.

So with tears running down my face, I hold up my right hand, the *I-L-Y* combination that means *I love you.* I catch my breath as Nathaniel raises one small fist, unfurls the fingers like signal flags to match mine. Then, a peace sign, the number two handshape. *I love you, too.*

By now, Nathaniel is crying. Caleb says something to him that I cannot hear, and he shakes his head. Behind them, the guard opens the door.

Oh, God, I am losing him.

I rap on the glass to get his attention. Push my face up against it, then point to Nathaniel and nod. He does what I've asked, turning his cheek so that it touches the transparent wall.

I lean close, kiss the barrier between us, and pretend it isn't there. Even after Caleb's carried him from the visiting room, I sit with my temple pressed to the glass, convincing myself I can still feel Nathaniel on the other side.

It didn't happen just that once. Two Sundays afterward, when Nathaniel's family went to Mass, the priest came into the little room where Miss Fiore was reading everyone a story about a guy with a slingshot who took down a giant. 'I need a volunteer,' he said, and even though all the hands went up, he looked right at Nathaniel.

'You know,' he said in the office, 'Esme missed you.'

'She did?'

'Oh, absolutely. She's been saying your name for days now.'

Nathaniel laughed. 'She has not.'

'Listen.' He cupped his ear, leaned in to the cat on the couch. 'There you go.'

Nathaniel listened, but only heard a faint mew.

'Maybe you have to get closer,' the priest said. 'Climb up here.'

For just a moment, Nathaniel hesitated, remembered. His mother had told him about going off alone with strangers. But this wasn't really a stranger, was it? He sat down in the priest's lap, and pressed his ear right against the belly of the cat. 'That's a good boy.'

The man shifted his legs, the way Nathaniel's father sometimes did when he was sitting on his knee and his foot fell asleep. 'I could move,' Nathaniel suggested.

'No, no.' The priest's hand slipped down Nathaniel's back, over his bottom, to rest in his own lap. 'This is fine.'

But then Nathaniel felt his shirt being untucked. Felt the long fingers of the priest, hot and damp, against his spine. Nathaniel did not know how to tell him no. His head was filled with a memory: a fly caught in the car one day when they were driving, which kept slamming itself into the windows in a desperate effort to get out. 'Father?' Nathaniel whispered.

'I'm just blessing you,' he replied. 'A special helper deserves that. I want God to know that every time He sees you.' His fingers stilled. 'You *do* want that, don't you?'

A blessing was a good thing, and for God to keep an extra eye on him – well, it was what his mother and father would want, Nathaniel was sure of it. He turned his attention back to the lazy cat, and that was when he heard it – just a puff of breath – Esme, or maybe not Esme, sighing his name.

The second time I am called out by a correctional officer is Sunday afternoon. He takes me upstairs to the conference rooms, where inmates meet privately with their attorneys. Maybe Fisher has come to see how I am holding up. Maybe he wants to discuss tomorrow's hearing.

But to my surprise, when the door is unlocked, Patrick is waiting inside. Spread out on the conference table are six containers of take-out Chinese food. 'I got everything you like,' he says. 'General Tso's chicken, vegetable lo mein, beef with broccoli, Lake Tung Ting shrimp, and steamed dumplings. Oh, and that crap that tastes like rubber.'

'Bean curd.' I lift my chin a notch, challenging him. 'I thought you didn't want to talk to me.'

'I don't. I want to eat with you.'

'Are you sure? Think of all the things I could say while your mouth is full, before you have a chance to –'

'Nina.' Patrick's blue eyes seem faded, weary. 'Shut up.'

But even as he scolds me, he holds out his hand. It rests on the table, extended, an offering more tantalizing than anything else before me.

I sit across from him and grab on. Immediately, Patrick

squeezes, and that's my undoing. I lay my cheek on the cold, scarred table, and Patrick strokes my hair. 'I rigged your fortune cookie,' he confesses. 'It says you'll be acquitted.'

'What does yours say?'

'That you'll be acquitted.' Patrick smiles. 'I didn't know which one you'd pick.'

My eyes drift shut as I let down my guard. 'It's okay,' Patrick tells me, and I believe him. I place his palm against my burning face, as if shame is something he might carry in the cup of his hand, fling someplace far away.

When you call someone on the prison pay phone, they know it. Every thirty seconds a voice gets on the line, informing the person on the other end that this transmission is taking place from the Alfred County Jail. I use the fifty cents Patrick gave me that afternoon, and make the call on my way to the shower. 'Listen,' I say, the minute I reach Fisher at his home number. 'You wanted me to tell you what to say on Monday morning.'

'Nina?' In the background I hear the laughter of a woman. The sound of glasses, or china, in a sink.

'I need to talk to you.'

'You've caught us in the middle of dinner.'

'Well, for God's sake, Fisher.' I turn my back as a line of men straggles in from the outside courtyard. 'Why don't I just call back then when it's more convenient for you, because I'm sure I'll have another opportunity, in, oh, three or four days.'

I hear the distant noise growing more faint; the click of a door. 'All right. What is it?'

'Nathaniel isn't speaking. You need to get me out of here, because he's falling apart.'

'He isn't speaking? Again?'

'Caleb brought him yesterday. And . . . he's signing.'

Fisher considers this. 'If we get Caleb down here to testify, and Nathaniel's psychiatrist —'

'You'll have to subpoena him.'

'The psychiatrist?'

'Caleb.'

If this surprises him, he doesn't admit it. 'Nina, the fact is, you messed up. I'm going to try to get you out. I still think it's unlikely. But if you want me to give it a shot, you're going to have to sit tight for a week.'

'A *week?*' My voice rises. 'Fisher, this is my son we're talking about. Do you know how much worse Nathaniel might get in a week?'

'I'm counting on it.'

A voice cuts in. *This call is being made from the Alfred County Jail. If you wish to continue, please deposit another twenty-five cents.*

By the time I tell Fisher to go screw himself, the line has already been disconnected.

Adrienne and I are given a half hour together outside in the exercise courtyard. We walk the perimeter, and then when we get cold, we stand with our backs to the wind beneath the high brick wall. When the CO goes inside, Adrienne smokes cigarettes that she makes by burning down orange peels she collects from the cafeteria trash, and rolling the ash in onion-skin pages torn from *Jane Eyre*, a book her Aunt Lu sent for her birthday. She has already ripped through page 298. I told her to ask for *Vanity Fair* next year.

I sit cross-legged on the dead grass. Adrienne kneels behind me, smoking, her hands in my hair. When she gets out, she wants to be a cosmetologist. Her nail makes a part from my temple to the nape of my neck. 'No pigtails,' I instruct.

'Don't insult me.' She makes another part, parallel to the first, and begins to braid in tight rows. 'You've got fine hair.'

'Thank you.'

'It wasn't a compliment, honey. Look at this . . . slips right out of my fingers.'

She pulls and tugs, and several times I have to wince. If only it were that easy to tighten up the tangles inside my head, too. Her glowing cigarette, smoked down to within an inch, sails over my shoulder and lands on the basketball court. 'There,' Adrienne says. 'Ain't you the bomb.'

Of course, I can't see. I touch my hands to the knobs and ridges the braids have made on my scalp, and then, just because I am feeling mean-spirited, begin to unravel all Adrienne's hard work. She shrugs, then sits down next to me. 'Did you always want to be a lawyer?'

'No.' Who does, after all? What kid considers being an attorney a glamorous vocation? 'I wanted to be the man at the circus who tames the lions.'

'Oh, don't I know it. Those sequined costumes were something.'

For me, it hadn't been about the outfits. I'd loved the way Gunther Gebel-Williams could walk into a cage full of beasts and make them think they were house cats. In this, I realize, my actual profession has not fallen that far off the mark. 'How about you?'

'My daddy wanted me to be the center for the Chicago Bulls. Me, I was angling for Vegas showgirl.'

'Ah.' I draw up my knees, wrap my arms around them. 'What does your daddy think now?'

'He ain't doing much thinking, I imagine, six feet under.'

'I'm sorry.'

Adrienne glances up. 'Don't be.'

But she has retreated somewhere else, and to my surprise, I find I want her back. The game that Peter Eberhardt and I used to play swims into my mind, and I turn to Adrienne. 'Best soap opera,' I challenge.

'What?'

'Just play along with me. Give your opinion.'

'*The Young and the Restless*,' Adrienne replies. 'Which, by the way, those fool boys in Minimum don't even have the good sense to listen to on their TV at one P.M.'

'Worst crayon color?'

'Burnt sienna. What is *up* with that, anyway? They might as well call it Vomit.' Adrienne grins, a flash of white in her face. 'Best jeans?'

'Levi's 501s. Ugliest CO?'

'Oh, the one who comes on after midnight that needs to bleach her moustache. You ever see the size of her ass? *Hello, honey,* let me introduce you to Miss Jenny Craig.'

Then we are both laughing, lying back on the cold ground and feeling winter seep into us by osmosis. When we finally catch our breath, there is a hollow in my chest, a sinking feeling that here, of all places, I should not be capable of joy. 'Best place to be?' Adrienne asks after a moment.

*On the other side of this wall. In my bed, at home. Anywhere with Nathaniel.*

'Before,' I answer, because I know she'll understand.

In one of Biddeford's coffee shops, Quentin sits on a stool too small for a gnome. One sip from his mug, and hot chocolate burns the roof of his mouth. 'Holy shit,' he mutters, holding a napkin to his mouth, just as Tanya walks in the door in her nurse's outfit – scrubs, printed with tiny teddy bears.

'Just shut up, Quentin,' she says, sliding onto the stool beside him. 'I'm not in the mood to hear you make fun of my uniform.'

'I wasn't.' He gestures to the mug, then just gives up the battle. 'What can I get you?'

He orders Tanya a decaf mochaccino. 'You like it, then?' he asks.

'Coffee?'

'Nursing.'

He had met Tanya at the University of Maine when she was a student, too. *What's this,* he'd asked at the end of their first date, trailing his fingers over her collarbone. *A clavicle,* she said. *And this?* His hand had run down the xylophone of her spine. *The coccyx.* He'd spread his fingers over the curve of her hip. *This is the part of you I like best,* he said. Her head had fallen back, her eyes drifting shut as he bared the skin and kissed her there. *Ilium,* she'd whispered.

Nine months later, there had been Gideon. They were married, a mistake, six days before he was born. They stayed married for less than a year. Since then Quentin had supported his son financially, if not emotionally.

'I must hate it, if I've stuck with it that long,' Tanya says, and it takes Quentin a moment to realize that she is only answering his question. Something must have crossed his face, because she touches her hand to his. 'I'm sorry, that was rude. And here you were just being polite.'

Her coffee arrives. She blows on it before taking a sip. 'Saw your name in the paper,' Tanya says. 'They got you down here for that priest's murder.'

Quentin shrugs. 'Pretty simple case, actually.'

'Well, sure, if you look at the news.' But Tanya shakes her head, all the same.

'What's that supposed to mean?'

'That the world isn't black and white, but you never did learn that.'

He raises his brows. 'I didn't learn it? Who threw whom out?'

'Who found whom screwing that girl who looked like a mouse?'

'There were mitigating circumstances,' Quentin says. 'I was drunk.' He hesitates, then adds, 'And she looked more like a rabbit, really.'

Tanya rolls her eyes. 'Quentin, it's been sixteen and a half years and you're still being a lawyer about it.'

'Well, what do you expect?'

'For you to be a man,' Tanya replies simply. 'For you to admit that even the Great and Powerful Brown is capable of making a mistake once or twice a century.' She pushes away her mug, although she isn't even half-finished. 'I've always wondered if you're so good at what you do because it takes the heat off you. You know, if making everyone else walk the straight and narrow makes you righteous by association.' She fishes in her purse and slaps five dollars on the counter. 'Think about that when you're prosecuting that poor woman.'

'What the hell is that supposed to mean?'

'Can you even imagine what she was feeling, Quentin?' Tanya asks, her head tipped to the side. 'Or is that kind of connection to a child beyond you?'

He stands when she does. 'Gideon wants nothing to do with me.'

Tanya buttons her coat, already halfway to the door. 'I always said he got your intelligence,' she says, and then, once again, she slips right through his grasp.

By Thursday, Caleb has established a routine. He gets Nathaniel up, feeds him breakfast, and takes him for a walk with the dog. They drive to whatever site Caleb might be working at that morning, and while he builds walls Nathaniel sits in the bed of the truck and plays with a shoebox full of Legos. They eat lunch together, peanut butter and banana sandwiches or Thermoses of chicken soup, and soda that he's packed in the cooler. And then they go to Dr. Robichaud's office, where the psychiatrist tries, unsuccessfully, to get Nathaniel to speak again.

It is a ballet, really – a story they are crafting without words, but comprehensible to anyone who sees Caleb and his silent son moving slowly through their days. To his surprise, this is even beginning to feel like normal. He likes the quiet, because when there are no words to be had, you can't tangle yourself up in the wrong ones. And if Nathaniel isn't talking, at least he isn't crying anymore.

Caleb keeps blinders on, moving from one task to the next, getting Nathaniel fed and clothed and tucked in, and there-fore only has a few moments each day to let his mind wander. Usually, this is when he is lying in bed, with the space beside him where Nina used to be. And even when he tries to keep himself from thinking it, the truth fills his mouth, bitter as a lemon: Life is easier, without her here.

On Thursday, Fisher brings me the discovery to read. This consists of 124 eyewitness accounts that describe my murder of Father Szyszynski, Patrick's report on the molestation, my own incoherent statement to Evan Chao, and the autopsy report.

I read Patrick's file first, feeling like a beauty queen poring over her scrapbook. Here is the explanation for everything else that sits in a stack at my side. Next, I read the statements of all the people who were in the courtroom the day of the murder. Of course, I save the best for last – the autopsy report, which I hold as reverently as if it were the Dead Sea Scrolls.

First I look at the pictures. I stare at them so hard that when I close my eyes I can still see the ragged edge where the priest's face was simply gone now. I can envision the creamy color of his brain. His heart weighed 350 grams, or so says Dr. Vern Potter, coroner.

'Dissection of the coronary arteries,' I read aloud, 'reveals narrowing of the lumen by atherosclerotic plaque. The most significant narrowing is in the left anterior descending coronary, where the lumen is narrowed by about 80 percent of the cross-sectional area.'

*Lumen.* I repeat this word, and the others that are all that are left of this monster: *no evidence of thrombus; the gallbladder serosa is smooth and glistening; the bladder is slightly trabeculated.*

The stomach contains partly digested bacon and a cinnamon roll.

Powder burns from the gun form a corona around the small hole in the rear of his head, where the bullet entered. There is a zone of necrosis around the bullet tract. Only 816 grams of his brain were left intact. There were contusions of the cerebellar tonsils bilaterally. Cause of death: Gunshot wound to head. Manner of death: Homicide.

This language is foreign, and I am suddenly, miraculously fluent. I touch my fingers to the autopsy report. Then I remember the twisted face of his mother, at the funeral.

Attached to this file is another one, with the name of a local physician's office stamped on its side. This must be Father Szyszynski's medical history. It is a thick file, far more than fifty years of routine checkups, but I don't bother to crack it open. Why should I? I have done what all those ordinary flus and hacking coughs and aches and cramps could not.

I killed him.

'This is for you,' the paralegal says, handing Quentin a fax. He looks up, takes the pages, and then stares down at them, confused. The lab report has Szyszynski's name on it; but has nothing to do with his case. Then he realizes: It is from the previous case, the closed case – the one involving the defendant's son. He glances at it, shrugging at the results, which are no great surprise. 'It's not mine,' Quentin says.

The paralegal blinks at him. 'So what am I supposed to do with it?'

He starts to hand it back to the woman, then puts it on the edge of his desk instead. 'I'll take care of it,' he answers, and buries himself in his work again until she leaves his office.

There are a thousand places Caleb would rather be – in a prisoner-of-war's hovel, for example; or standing in an open field during a tornado. But he had to be present today, the subpoena said so. He stands in the courtroom cafeteria in his one jacket and threadbare tie, holding a cup of coffee so hot it is burning his palm, and tries to pretend that his hands aren't shaking with nerves.

Fisher Carrington is not such a bad guy, he thinks. At least, he's not nearly the demon that Nina has made him out to be. 'Relax, Caleb,' the attorney says. 'This will be over before you know it.' They make their way to the exit. Court will convene in five minutes; even now, they might be bringing Nina in.

'All you have to do is answer the questions we've already gone over, and then Mr. Brown will ask a few of his own. No one's expecting you to do anything but tell the truth. Okay?'

Caleb nods, tries to take a sip of the fire that is his coffee. He doesn't even like coffee. He wonders what Nathaniel is doing with Monica, downstairs in the playroom. He tries to distract himself by picturing an intricate brick pattern he created for a former insurance CEO's patio. But reality crouches like a tiger in the corner of his mind: In minutes, he is going to be a witness. In minutes, dozens of reporters and curious citizens and a judge will be hanging on the words of a man who much prefers silence. 'Fisher,' he begins, then takes a deep breath. 'They can't ask me anything, you know, that she told me . . . can they?'

'Anything Nina told you?'

'About . . . about what she did.'

Fisher stares at Caleb. 'She talked to you about it?'

'Yeah. Before she –'

'Caleb,' the lawyer interrupts smoothly, 'don't tell me, and I'll make sure you don't have to tell anyone else.'

He disappears through a doorway before Caleb can even measure the strength of his relief.

As Peter takes the stand for Quentin Brown at my bail revocation hearing, he shoots me a look of apology. He can't lie, but he doesn't want to be the one responsible for landing me in jail. To make this easier on him, I try not to catch his eye. I concentrate instead on Patrick, sitting somewhere behind me, so close I can smell the soap he uses. And on Brown, who seems too big to be pacing this tiny courtroom.

Fisher puts his hand on my leg, which has been jiggling nervously without my even noticing. 'Stop,' he mouths.

'Did you see Nina Frost that afternoon?' Quentin asks.

'No,' Peter says. 'I didn't see her.'

Quentin raises his brows in absolute disbelief. 'Did you walk up to her?'

'Well, I was coming down the produce aisle, and her cart happened to be placed along the path I was taking. Her son was sitting in it. He's the one I approached.'

'Did Ms. Frost walk up to the cart as well?'

'Yes, but she was moving closer to her son. Not to me.'

'Just answer the questions as I ask them.'

'Look, she was standing next to me, but she didn't speak to me,' Peter says.

'Did you speak to her, Mr. Eberhardt?'

'No.' Peter turns to the judge. 'I was talking to Nathaniel.'

Quentin touches a stack of papers on the prosecutor's table. 'You have access to the information in these files?'

'As you know, Mr. Brown, I'm not working on her case. *You* are.'

'But I'm working in her former office, the one right next to yours, aren't I?'

'Yes.'

'And,' Quentin says, 'there aren't any locks on those doors, are there?'

'No.'

'So I guess you think she approached you so that she could squeeze the Charmin?'

Peter narrows his eyes. 'She wasn't trying to get into trouble, and neither was I.'

'And now you're trying to help her out of all that trouble, aren't you?'

Before he can answer, Quentin turns over the witness to the defense. Fisher gets up, buttoning his jacket. I feel a line of sweat break out on my spine. 'Who spoke first, Mr. Eberhardt?' he asks.

'Nathaniel.'

'What did he say?'

Peter looks at the railing. He knows by now, too, that Nathaniel has gone mute again. 'My name.'

'If you didn't want Nina to get into trouble, why didn't you just turn around and walk away?'

'Because Nathaniel wanted me. And after . . . after the abuse, he stopped talking for a while. This was the first time I'd heard him speak since all that happened. I couldn't just do an about-face and walk away.'

'Was it at that exact moment that Mr. Brown rounded the corner and saw you?'

'Yes.'

Fisher clasps his hands behind his back. 'Did you ever speak to Nina about her case?'

'No.'

'Did you give her any inside information about her case?'

'No.'

'Did she ask you for any?'

'No.'

'Are you working on Nina's case at all?'

Peter shakes his head. 'I will always be her friend. But I understand my job, and my duties as an officer of this court. And the last thing I'd want to do is involve myself in this case.'

'Thank you, Mr. Eberhardt.'

Fisher settles into place beside me at the defense table, as Quentin Brown glances up at the judge. 'Your Honor, the state rests.'

*That makes one of us,* I think.

Caleb's gaze is drawn to her, and he is shocked. His wife, the one who always looks crisp and fresh and coordinated, sits in bright orange scrubs. Her hair is a cloud about her head; her eyes are shadowed with circles. There is a cut on the back of her hand and one of her shoelaces has come untied. Caleb has the unlikely urge to kneel before her, to double-knot it, to bury his head in her lap.

You can hate someone, he realizes, and be crazy about her at the same time.

Fisher catches his eye, pulling Caleb back to this responsibility. If he screws up, Nina may not be allowed to come home. Then again, Fisher has told him that even if he is flawless on the stand, she may still be locked up in jail pending trial. He clears his throat and imagines himself in an ocean of language, trying to keep his head above water.

'When did Nathaniel start speaking again, after you found out about the abuse?'

'About three weeks ago. The night Detective Ducharme came to talk to him.'

'Had his verbal ability increased since that night?'

'Yes,' Caleb answers. 'He was pretty much back to normal.'

'How much time was his mother spending with him?'

'More than usual.'

'How did Nathaniel seem to you?'

Caleb thinks for a moment. 'Happier,' he says.

Fisher moves, so that he is standing behind Nina. 'What changed after the incident at the grocery store?'

'He was hysterical. He was crying so hard he couldn't breathe, and he wouldn't talk at all.' Caleb looks into Nina's eyes, hands her this phrase like a gift. 'He kept making the sign for *Mommy.*'

She makes a small sound, like a kitten. It renders him speechless; he has to ask Fisher to repeat his next question. 'Has he spoken at all in the past week?'

'No,' Caleb replies.

'Have you taken Nathaniel to see his mother?'

'Once. It was very . . . hard on him.'

'How do you mean?'

'He didn't want to leave her,' Caleb admits. 'I had to physically drag him away when the time was up.'

'How is your son sleeping at night?'

'He won't, unless I take him into bed with me.'

Fisher nods gravely. 'Do you think, Mr. Frost, that he needs his mother back?'

Quentin Brown stands immediately. 'Objection!'

'This is a bail hearing, I'll allow it,' the judge replies. 'Mr. Frost?'

Caleb sees answers swimming in front of him. There are so many, which is the one he should choose? He opens his mouth, then closes it to start over.

At that moment he notices Nina. Her eyes are bright on his, feverish, and he tries to remember why this seems so familiar. Then it comes to him: this is the way she looked weeks ago when she was trying to convince a mute Nathaniel that all he had to do was speak from the heart; that any word was better than none. 'We both need her back,' Caleb says, the right thing after all.

Halfway through Dr. Robichaud's testimony, I realize that this is the trial we would have had to convict the priest, had I not killed him. The information being presented focuses on the molestation of Nathaniel, and the consequences. The psychiatrist walks the court through her introduction to Nathaniel, his sexual abuse evaluation, his therapy sessions, his use of sign language. 'Did Nathaniel ever reach a point where he could talk again?' Fisher asks.

'Yes, after he verbally disclosed the name of his abuser to Detective Ducharme.'

'Since then, as far as you know, has he been talking normally?'

The psychiatrist nods. 'More and more so.'

'Did you see him this past week, Doctor?'

'Yes. His father called me, very upset, on Friday night. Nathaniel had stopped speaking again. When I saw him on Monday morning, he'd regressed considerably. He's withdrawn and uncommunicative. I couldn't even get him to sign.'

'In your expert opinion, is the separation from his mother causing Nathaniel psychological damage?'

'No question,' Dr. Robichaud says. 'In fact, the longer it goes on, the more permanent the damage might be.'

As she gets down from the stand, Brown gets up to do his closing. He starts by pointing at me. 'This woman has a blatant disregard for rules, and clearly, this isn't the first time. What she should have done the moment she saw Peter Eberhardt was turn around and walk the other way. But the fact is, she didn't.' He turns to the judge. 'Your Honor, you were the one who imposed the condition that Nina Frost not have contact with members of the district attorney's office, because you were concerned about treating her differently than other defendants. But if you let her go without sanction, you'll be doing just that.'

Even on edge, as I am, I realize that Quentin's made a tactical mistake. You can make suggestions to a jury . . . but you never, *ever* tell the judge what to do.

Fisher rises. 'Your Honor, what Mr. Brown saw in the produce department was nothing more than sour grapes. The reality of the matter is that no information was exchanged. In fact, there's no evidence that information was even sought.'

He puts his hands on my shoulders. I have seen him do this with other clients; in my office, we used to call it his Grandfather Stance. 'This was an unfortunate misunderstanding,' Fisher continues, 'but that's all it is. Nothing more, nothing less. And if, as a result, you keep Nina Frost from her child, you may wind up sacrificing that child. Certainly after what everyone's been through, that's the last thing this court would like to see happen.'

The judge lifts his head and looks at me. 'I'm not going to keep her away from her son,' he rules. 'However, I'm also not going to give her the opportunity to violate the rules of this court again. I release Ms. Frost on the condition that she be on home confinement. She'll wear an electronic bracelet, and will be subject to all the rules of probation and parole with regards to electronic monitoring. Ms. Frost.' He waits for me to nod. 'You are not to leave the house, except to meet with your attorney or to come to court. For those times, and only those times, the bracelet will be reprogrammed accordingly. And God help me, if I have to patrol your street myself to make sure you're adhering to these provisions, I will.'

My new wrist cuff works through telephone lines. If I move 150 feet away from my house, the bracelet makes an alarm go off. A probation officer may visit me at any time, demand a sample of my blood or urine to make sure I have not had any drugs or alcohol. I opt to wear my scrubs home, and ask the deputy sheriff to instruct that my old clothes be given, a gift, to Adrienne. They'll be short and tight – in other words, a perfect fit for her.

'You have nine lives,' Fisher murmurs as we walk out of the parole office, where my cuff has been computer-programmed.

'Seven left,' I sigh.

'Let's hope we don't have to use them all.'

'Fisher.' I stop walking as we reach the staircase. 'I just wanted to tell you . . . I couldn't have done that any better.'

He laughs. 'Nina, I think you'd actually choke if you had to say the word *thanks*.'

We walk side by side upstairs, toward the lobby. Fisher, a gentleman to the last, pushes open the heavy fire door of the stairwell and holds it while I step through.

The immediate burst of light as the cameras explode renders me blind, and it takes a moment for the world to come back to me. When it does, I realize that in addition to the reporters, Patrick and Caleb and Monica are waiting. And then, emerging from a spot behind his father's big body, I see my son.

She is wearing funny orange pajamas and her hair looks like a swallow's nest Nathaniel once found behind the soda bottles in the garage, but her face is his mother's and her voice, when it says his name, is his mother's too. Her smile is a hook in him; he can feel the catch in his throat as he swallows it and lets himself be reeled across the space between them. *Mommy.* Nathaniel's arms rise up from his sides. He stumbles over a wire, and someone's foot, and then he is running.

She falls to her knees and that only makes the tug stronger. Nathaniel's so close that he can see she is crying, and this isn't even very clear because he is crying too. He feels the hook coming free, drawing out the silence that has swelled in his belly for a week now, and the moment before he reaches her embrace it bursts from his lips in a rusty, trebled joy. 'Mommy, Mommy, Mommy!' Nathaniel shouts, so loud that it drowns out everything but the drum of his mother's heart beneath his ear.

He's gotten bigger in a week. I heft Nathaniel into my arms, smiling like a fool, as the cameras capture every move. Fisher has corralled the reporters, is even now preaching to them. I bury my face in Nathaniel's sweet neck, matching my memory with what is real.

Suddenly Caleb stands beside us. His face is as inscrutable as it was the last time we were alone, on opposite sides of a glass visitation booth at jail. Although his testimony helped free me, I know my husband. He did what was expected, but it was not necessarily something he wanted to do. 'Caleb,' I begin, flustered. 'I . . . I don't know what to say.'

To my surprise, he offers an olive branch: a crooked smile. 'Well, that's a first. No wonder so many reporters are around.' Caleb's grin slides more firmly into place; and at the same time, he anchors his arm around my shoulders, guides me one step closer to home.

*These are the jokes I know.*
*What's in the middle of a jellyfish?*
*A jellybutton.*

*Why didn't the skeleton cross the road?*
*It didn't have the guts.*

*Why did the cookie go to the hospital?*
*It felt crumby.*

*What do lizards put on their kitchen floors?*
*Reptiles.*

*What do you call a blind dinosaur?*
*An I-don't-think-he-saurus.*

*There is one more:*
*Knock knock.*
*Who's there?*
*Sadie.*
*Sadie who?*
*Sadie magic word, Nathaniel, and then you'll be allowed to go.*
*When he told it to me, I didn't laugh.*

# 6

And just like that, I have fallen back into my former life. The three of us sit around the breakfast table, like any other family. With his finger, Nathaniel traces the letters in the headline of the morning paper. '*M*,' he says quietly. '*O, M . . .*' Over my coffee cup, I look at the photograph. There I am, holding Nathaniel, Caleb at my side. Fisher, somehow, has managed to get his face in the picture too. In the distance, a few steps behind, is Patrick; I recognize him only by his shoes. Across the top, in screaming black letters: MOMMY.

Caleb takes Nathaniel's empty cereal bowl away as he runs off into the playroom, where he has set up two armies of plastic dinosaurs for a Jurassic war. I glance at the paper. 'I'm the poster child for bad parenting,' I say.

'Beats being the local Maine murderess.' He nods to the table. 'What's in the envelope?'

The manila mailer is the interoffice kind, tied shut with red floss. I found it stuffed between the Local and Sports sections of the paper. I flip it over, but there is no return address, no marking of any kind.

Inside is a report from the state lab, the kind of chart I have seen before. A table with results in eight columns, each a different location on human DNA. And two rows of numbers that are identical at every single spot.

*Conclusions: The DNA profile detected on the underpants is consistent with the DNA profile of Szyszynski. As a result, he cannot be eliminated as a possible contributor of the genetic material detected in this stain. The chances of randomly selecting an unrelated individual who matches the genetic material found in the*

*underwear are greater than one in six billion, which is approxi-*
*mately the world population.*

Or in English: Father Szyszynski's semen was found on my
son's underwear.

Caleb peers over my shoulder. 'What's that?'

'Absolution,' I sigh.

Caleb takes the paper from my hands, and I point to the
first row of numbers. 'This shows the DNA from Szyszynski's
blood sample. And the line below it shows the DNA from the
stain on the underpants.'

'The numbers are the same.'

'Right. DNA is the same all over your body. That's why, if the
cops arrest a rapist, they draw blood – can you imagine how ridiculous it would be to ask the guy to give a semen sample? The idea
is, if you can match the suspect's blood DNA to evidence, you're
almost guaranteed a conviction.' I look up at him. 'It means that
he did it, Caleb. He was the one. And . . .' My voice trails off.

'And what?'

'And I did the right thing,' I finish.

Caleb puts the paper facedown on the table and gets up.

'What?' I challenge.

He shakes his head slowly. 'Nina, you didn't do the right
thing. You said it yourself. If you match the DNA in the suspect's
blood to the evidence, you're guaranteed a conviction. So if
you'd waited, he would have gotten his punishment.'

'And Nathaniel would still have had to sit in that courtroom, reliving every minute of what happened to him, because
that lab report would mean nothing without his testimony.' To
my embarrassment, tears rise in my eyes. 'I thought Nathaniel
had been through enough without that.'

'I know what you thought,' Caleb says softly. 'That's the
problem. What about the things Nathaniel's had to deal with
*because* of what you did? I'm not saying you did the wrong
thing. I'm not even saying it wasn't something I'd thought of
doing, myself. But even if it was the just thing to do . . . or the
fitting thing . . . Nina, it still wasn't the *right* thing.'

He puts on his boots and opens the kitchen door, leaving me alone with the lab results. I rest my head on my hand and take a deep breath. Caleb's wrong, he *has* to be wrong, because if he isn't, then –

My thoughts veer away from this as the manila envelope draws my eye. Who left this for me, cloak-and-dagger? Someone on the prosecution's side would have fielded it from the lab. Maybe Peter dropped it off, or a sympathetic paralegal who thought it might go to motive for an insanity defense. At any rate, it is a document I'm not supposed to have.

Something, therefore, I can't share with Fisher.

I pick up the phone and call him. 'Nina,' he says. 'Did you see the morning paper?'

'Hard to miss. Hey, Fisher, did you ever see the DNA results on the priest?'

'You mean the underwear sample? No.' He pauses. 'It's a closed case, now, of course. It's possible somebody told the lab not to bother.'

Not likely. The staff in the DA's office would have been far too busy to see to a detail like that. 'You know, I'd really like to see the report. If it did come back.'

'It doesn't really have any bearing on your case –'

'Fisher,' I say firmly, 'I'm asking you politely. Have your paralegal call Quentin Brown to fax the report over. I need to see it.'

He sighs. 'All right. I'll get back to you.'

I place the receiver back in its cradle, and sit down at the table. Outside, Caleb splits wood, relieving his frustration with each heavy blow of the ax. Last night, feeling his way under the covers with one warm hand, he'd brushed the plastic lip of my electronic monitoring bracelet. That was all, and then he'd rolled onto one side away from me.

Picking up my coffee, I read the twin lines on the lab report again. Caleb is mistaken, that's all there is to it. All these letters and numbers, they are proof, in black and white, that I am a hero.

\*       \*       \*

Quentin gives the lab report another cursory glance and then puts it on a corner of his desk. No surprises there; everyone knows why she killed the priest. The point is, none of this matters anymore. The trial at hand isn't about sexual abuse, but murder.

The secretary, a harried, faded blonde named Rhonda or Wanda or something like that, sticks her head in the door. 'Does no one knock in this building?' Quentin mutters, scowling.

'You take the lab report on Szyszynski?' she asks.

'It's right here. Why?'

'Defense attorney just called; he wants a copy faxed over to his office yesterday.'

Quentin hands the papers to the secretary. 'What's the rush?'

'Who knows.'

It makes no sense to Quentin; Fisher Carrington must realize that the information will not make or break his case. But then again, it doesn't matter at all for the prosecution – Nina Frost is facing a conviction, he's certain, and no lab report about a dead man is going to change that. By the time the secretary has closed the door behind herself, Quentin has put Carrington's request out of his mind.

Marcella Wentworth hates snow. She had enough of it, growing up in Maine, and then working there for nearly a decade. She hates waking up and knowing you have to shovel your way to your car; she hates the sensation of skis beneath her feet; she hates the uncontrollable feel of wheels spinning out on black ice. The happiest day of Marcella's life, in fact, was the day she quit her job at the Maine State Lab, moved to Virginia, and threw her Sorrel boots into a public trash bin at a highway McDonald's.

She has worked for three years now at CellCore, a private lab. Marcella has a year-round tan and only one medium-weight winter coat. But at her workstation she keeps a post-card Nina Frost, a district attorney, sent her last Christmas –

a cartoon depicting the unmistakable mitten shape of her birth state, sporting googly eyes and a jester's hat. *Once a Mainiac, always a Mainiac,* it reads.

Marcella is looking at the postcard, and thinking that there may already be a dusting on the ground up there by now, when Nina Frost calls.

'You're not going to believe this,' Marcella says, 'but I was just thinking about you.'

'I need your help,' Nina answers. All business – but then, that has always been Nina. Once or twice since Marcella left the state lab, Nina called to consult on a case, just for the purpose of verification. 'I've got a DNA test I need checked.'

Marcella glances at the overwhelming stack of files piling her in-box. 'No problem. What's the story?'

'Child molestation. There's a known blood sample and then semen on a pair of underwear. I'm not an expert, but the results looks pretty cut and dried.'

'Ah. I'm guessing they don't jive, and you think the state lab screwed up?'

'Actually, they do jive. I just need to be absolutely certain.'

'Guess you really don't want this one to walk,' Marcella muses.

There is a hesitation. 'He's dead,' Nina says. 'I shot him.'

Caleb has always liked chopping wood. He likes the Herculean moment of hefting the ax, of swinging it down like a man measuring his strength at a carnival game. He likes the sound of a log being broken apart, a searing crack, and then the hollow *plink* of two halves falling to opposite sides. He likes the rhythm, which erases thought and memory.

Maybe by the time he has run out of wood to split, he will feel ready to go back inside and face his wife.

Nina's single-mindedness has always been attractive – especially to a man who, in so many matters, is naturally hesitant. But now the flaw has been magnified to the point of being grotesque. She simply cannot let go.

Once, Caleb had been hired to build a brick wall in a town park. As he'd worked, he'd gotten used to the homeless man who lived beneath the birthday pavilion. His name was Coalspot, or so Caleb had been told. He was schizophrenic but harmless. Sometimes, Coalspot would sit on the park bench next to Caleb as he worked. He spent hours unlacing his shoe, taking it off, scraping at his heel, and then putting his shoe back on. 'Can you see it?' the man asked Caleb. 'Can you see the hole where the poison's leaking?'

One day a social worker arrived to take Coalspot to a shelter, but he wouldn't go. He insisted he would infect everyone else; the poison was contagious. After three hours, the woman had reached the end of her rope. 'We try to help them,' she sighed to Caleb, 'and this is what we get.'

So Caleb sat down beside Coalspot. He took off his own work boot and sock, pointed to his heel. 'You see?' he said. 'Everyone already has one.'

After that, the homeless man went off, easy as a kitten. It didn't matter there was no poisonous hole – just at that moment, Coalspot truly believed there was one. And that for a second, Caleb had told the man he was right.

Nina is like that, now. She has redefined her actions so that they make sense to her, if not to anyone else. To say that she killed a man in order to protect Nathaniel? Well, whatever trauma he might suffer as a witness couldn't be nearly as bad as watching his mother get handcuffed and carted off to jail.

Caleb knows that Nina is looking for vindication, but he can't do what he did with Coalspot – look her in eye and tell her that yes, he understands. He can't look her in the eye, period.

He wonders if the reason he's putting up a wall between them is so that, when she is sentenced, it is easier to let her go.

Caleb takes another log and sets it on end on the chopping block. As the ax comes down, the wood cleaves into two neat pieces, and sitting in the center is the truth. What Nina has done doesn't make Caleb feel morally superior, by default. It makes him a coward, because he wasn't the one brave enough to cross the line from thought to deed.

There are parts of it Nathaniel can't remember – like what he said when Nathaniel first shook his head no; or which one of them unbuttoned his jeans. What he can still think of, sometimes even when he is trying his hardest not to, is how the air felt cold when his pants came off, and how hot his hand was after that. How it hurt, it hurt so bad, even though he had said it wouldn't. How Nathaniel had held Esme so tight she cried; how in the mirror of her gold eyes he saw a little boy who no longer was him.

It will make Nina happy.

Those are Marcella's first thoughts when she reads the DNA results, and sees that the semen stain and the priest's blood are indistinguishable from each other. No scientist will ever say it quite this way in testimony, but the numbers – and the stats – speak for themselves: This is the perp, no question.

She picks up the phone to tell Nina so, tucking it under her chin so that she can rubber-band the medical files that came attached to the lab report. Marcella hasn't bothered to scan these; it is pretty clear from what Nina said that the priest died as a result of the gunshot wound. But still, Nina has asked Marcella for a thorough review. She sighs, then puts back the receiver and opens the thick folder.

Two hours later, she finishes reading. And realizes that in spite of her best intentions to stay away, she'll be heading back to Maine.

Here is what I have learned in a week: A prison, no matter what shape and size, is still a prison. I find myself staring out windows along with the dog, itching to be on the other side of the glass. I would give a fortune to do the most mundane of errands: run to the bank, take the car to Jiffy Lube, rake leaves.

Nathaniel has gone back to school. This is Dr. Robichaud's suggestion, a step toward normalcy. Still, I can't help but wonder if Caleb had some small part in this; if he really doesn't like the thought of leaving me alone with my son.

One morning, before I could think twice, I walked halfway down the driveway to pick up the newspaper before I remembered the electronic bracelet. Caleb found me on the porch, sobbing, waiting for the sirens I was certain would come. But through some miracle, the alarm did not go off. I spent six seconds in the fresh air, and no one was the wiser.

To occupy myself, sometimes I cook. I have made *penne alla rigata*, coq au vin, potstickers. I choose dishes from foreign places, anywhere but here. Today, though, I am cleaning the house. I have already emptied the coat closet and the kitchen pantry, restocked their items in order of frequency of use. Up in the bedroom, I've tossed out shoes I forgot I ever bought, and have aligned my suits in a rainbow, from palest pink to deepest plum to chocolate.

I am just weeding through Caleb's dresser when he comes in, stripping off a filthy shirt. 'Do you know,' I say, 'that in the hall closet is a brand-new pair of cleats fives sizes bigger than Nathaniel's foot?'

'Got them at a garage sale. Nathaniel'll grow into them.'

After all this, doesn't he understand that the future doesn't necessarily follow in a straight, unbroken line?

'What are you doing?'

'Your drawers.'

'I like my drawers.' Caleb takes a torn shirt I've put aside and stuffs it back in all wrinkled. 'Why don't you take a nap? Read, or something?'

'That would be a waste of time.' I find three socks, all without mates.

'Why is just taking time a waste of it?' Caleb asks, shrugging into another shirt. He grabs the socks I've segregated and puts them into his underwear drawer again.

'Caleb. You're ruining it.'

'How? It was fine to start with!' He jams his shirt into the waist of his jeans, tightens his belt again. 'I like my socks the way they are,' Caleb says firmly. For a moment he looks as if he is going to add to that, but then shakes his head and runs down the stairs. Shortly afterward, I see him through the window, walking in the bright, cold sun.

I open the drawer and remove the orphan socks. Then the torn shirt. It will take him weeks to notice the changes, and one day he will thank me.

'Oh, my God,' I cry, glancing out the window at the unfamiliar car that pulls up to the curb. A woman gets out – pixie-small, with a dark cap of hair and her arms wrapped tight against the cold.

'What?' Caleb runs into the room at my exclamation. 'What's the matter?'

'Nothing. Absolutely nothing!' I throw open the door and smile widely at Marcella. 'I can't believe you're here!'

'Surprise,' she says, and hugs me. 'How are you doing?' She tries not to look, but I see it – the way her eyes dart down to try and find my electronic bracelet.

'I'm . . . well, I'm great right now. I certainly never expected you to bring me my report in person.'

Marcella shrugs. 'I figured you might enjoy the company. And I hadn't been back home for a while. I missed it.'

'Liar,' I laugh, pulling her into the house, where Caleb and Nathaniel are watching with curiosity. 'This is Marcella Wentworth. She used to work at the state lab, before she bailed on us to join the private sector.'

I'm positively beaming. It's not that Marcella and I are so very close; it's just that these days, I don't get to see that many people. Patrick comes, from time to time. And there's my family, of course. But most of my friends are colleagues, and after the revocation hearing, they're keeping their distance.

'You up here on business or pleasure?' Caleb asks.

Marcella glances at me, unsure of what she should say.

'I asked Marcella to take a look at the DNA test.'

Caleb's smile fades just the slightest bit, so that only if you know him as well as I do would you even catch the dimming. 'You know what? Why don't I take Nathaniel out, so that you two can catch up?'

After they leave, I lead Marcella into the kitchen. We talk about the temperature in Virginia at this time of year, and when we had our first frost. I make us iced tea. Then, when I can stand it no longer, I sit down across from her. 'It's good news, isn't it? The DNA, it's a match?'

'Nina, did you notice anything when you read the medical file?'

'I didn't bother, actually.'

Marcella draws a circle on the table with her finger. 'Father Szyszynski had chronic myeloid leukemia.'

'Good,' I say flatly. 'I hope he was suffering. I hope he puked his insides out every time he got chemotherapy.'

'He wasn't getting chemo. He had a bone marrow transplant about seven years ago. His leukemia was in remission. For all intents and purposes, he was cured.'

I stiffen a little. 'Is this your way of telling me I ought to feel guilty for killing a man who was a cancer survivor?'

'No. It's . . . well, there's something about the treatment of leukemia that factors into DNA analysis. Basically, to cure it, you need to get new blood. And the way that's done is via bone marrow transplant, since bone marrow is what makes blood. After a few months, your old bone marrow has been replaced completely by the donor's bone marrow. Your old blood is gone, and the leukemia with it.' Marcella looks up at me. 'You follow?'

'So far.'

'Your body can use this new blood, because it's healthy. But it's not your blood, and at the DNA level, it doesn't look like your blood used to. Your skin cells, your saliva, your semen – the DNA in those will be what you were born with, but the DNA in your new blood comes from your donor.' Marcella puts her hand on top of mine. 'Nina, the lab results were accurate. The DNA in Father Szyszynski's blood sample matched the semen in your son's underwear. But the DNA in Father Szyszynski's blood isn't really his.'

'No,' I say. 'No, this isn't the way it works. I was just explaining it the other day to Caleb. You can get DNA from any cell in your body. That's why you can use a blood sample to match a semen sample.'

'Ninety-nine point nine percent of the time, yes. But this is a very, very specific exception.' She shakes her head. 'I'm sorry, Nina.'

My head swings up. 'You mean . . . he's still alive?'

She doesn't have to answer.

I have killed the wrong man.

After Marcella leaves, I pace like a lion in a cage of my own making. My hands are shaking; I can't seem to get warm. What have I done? I killed a man who was innocent. A *priest*. A person who came to comfort me when my world cracked apart; who loved children, Nathaniel included. I killed a man who fought cancer and won, who deserved a long life. I committed murder and I can no longer even justify my actions to myself.

I have always believed there is a special place in Hell for the worst ones – the serial killers, the rapists who target kids, the sociopaths who would just as soon lie as cut your throat for the ten dollars in your wallet. And even when I have not secured convictions for them, I tell myself that eventually, they will get what's coming to them.

So will I.

And the reason I know this is because even though I cannot find the strength to stand up; even though I want to scratch at myself until this part of me has been cut away in ribbons, there is another part of me that is thinking: *He is still out there.*

I pick up the phone to call Fisher. But then I hang it up. He needs to hear this; he could very well find out by himself. But I don't know how it will play in my trial, yet. It could make the prosecution more sympathetic, since their victim is a true victim. Then again, an insanity defense is an insanity defense. It doesn't matter if I killed Father Szyszynski or the judge or every spectator in that courtroom – if I were insane at the time, I still wouldn't be guilty.

In fact, this might make me look crazier.

I sit down at the kitchen table and bury my face in my hands. The doorbell rings and suddenly Patrick is in the kitchen, too big for it, frantic from the message I've left on his beeper. 'What?' he demands, absorbing in a single glance my position, and the quiet of the household. 'Did something happen to Nathaniel?'

It is such a loaded question, that I can't help it – I start to laugh. I laugh until my stomach cramps, until I cannot catch my breath, until tears stream from my eyes and I realize I am sobbing. Patrick's hands are on my shoulders, my forearms, my waist, as if the thing that has broken inside me might be as simple as a bone. I wipe my nose on the back of my sleeve and force myself to meet his gaze. 'Patrick,' I whisper, 'I screwed up. Father Szyszynski . . . he didn't . . . he wasn't –'

He calms me down and makes me tell him everything. When I finish, he stares at me for a full thirty seconds before he speaks. 'You're kidding,' Patrick says. 'You shot the wrong guy?'

He doesn't wait for an answer, just gets up and starts to pace. 'Nina, wait a second. Things get screwed up in labs; it's happened before.'

I grab onto this lifeline. 'Maybe that's it. Some medical mistake.'

'But we had an ID before we ever had the semen evidence.' Patrick shakes his head. 'Why would Nathaniel have said his name?'

Time can stop, I know that now. It is possible to feel one's heart cease beating, to sense the blood hover in one's veins. And to have the awful, overwhelming sense that one is trapped in this moment, and there is just no way out of it. 'Tell me again.' My words spill like stones. 'Tell me what he told you.'

Patrick turns to me. 'Father Glen,' he replies. 'Right?'

★          ★          ★

Nathaniel remembers feeling dirty, so dirty that he thought he could take a thousand showers and still need to clean himself again. And the thing of it was, the dirty part of him was under his skin; he would have to rub himself raw before it was gone.

It burned down *there*, and even Esme wouldn't come near him. She purred and then hopped onto the big wooden desk, staring. *This is your fault*, she was saying. Nathaniel tried to get his pants, but his hands were like clubs, unable to pick up anything. His underwear, when he finally managed to grab it, was all wet, which made no sense because Nathaniel hadn't had an accident, he just knew it. But the priest had been looking at his underpants, holding them. He'd liked the baseball mitts.

Nathaniel didn't want to wear them again, ever.

'We can fix that,' the priest said, in a voice soft as a pillow, and he disappeared for a moment. Nathaniel counted to thirty-five, and then did it again, because that was as high as he could go. He wanted to leave. He wanted to hide under the desk or in the file cabinet. But he needed underpants. He couldn't get dressed without them, they came first. That was what his mom said when he forgot sometimes, and she made him go upstairs to put them on.

The priest came back with a baby pair, not like his dad's, which looked like shorts. He'd gotten these, Nathaniel was sure, from the big box that held all the greasy coats and smelly sneakers people had left behind in the church. *How could you leave without your sneakers, and never notice?* Nathaniel always had wanted to know. For that matter, how could you forget your underpants?

These were clean and had Spiderman on them. They were too tight, but Nathaniel didn't care. 'Let me take the other pair,' the priest said. 'I'll wash them and give them back.'

Nathaniel shook his head. He pulled on his sweatpants and tucked the boxers into the kangaroo part of his sweatshirt, turning the icky side so that he didn't have to touch it. He felt the priest pet his hair and he went perfectly still, like granite, with the same thick, straight feelings inside.

'Do you need me to walk you back?'

Nathaniel didn't answer. He waited until the priest had picked up Esme and left; then he walked down the hall to the boiler room. It was creepy inside – no light switch, and cobwebs, and once even the skeleton of a mouse that had died. No one ever went in there, which is why Nathaniel did, and stuffed the bad underwear way behind the big machine that hummed and belched heat.

When Nathaniel went back to his class, Father Glen was still reading the Bible story. Nathaniel sat down, tried to listen. He paid careful attention, even when he felt someone's eyes on him. When he looked up, the other priest was standing in the hallway, holding Esme and smiling. With his free hand he raised a finger to his lips. *Shh. Don't tell.*

That was the moment Nathaniel lost all his words.

The day my son stopped speaking, we had gone to church. Afterward, there was a fellowship coffee – what Caleb liked to call Bible Bribery, a promise of doughnuts in return for your presence at Mass. Nathaniel moved around me as if I were a maypole, turning this way and that as he waited for Father Szyszynski to call the children together to read.

This coffee was a celebration, of sorts – two priests who had come to study at St. Anne's for some sort of Catholic edification were going back to their own congregations. A banner blew from the base of the scarred table, wishing them well. Since we were not regular churchgoers, I had not really noticed the priests doing whatever it was they were supposed to be doing. Once or twice I'd seen one from behind and made the assumption it was Father Szyszynski, only to have the man turn around and prove me wrong.

My son was angry because they had run out of powdered sugar doughnuts. 'Nathaniel,' I said, 'stop pulling on me.'

I'd tugged him off my waist, smiling apologetically at the couple that Caleb was speaking to; acquaintances we had not seen in months. They had no children, although they were our ages, and I imagine that Caleb liked talking to them for the same reason I did – there was that amazing *What if* permeating the conversation, as if Todd and Margaret were a funhouse mirror in which Caleb and I could see who else we might have become, had I never conceived. Todd was talking about their upcoming trip to Greece; how they were chartering a boat to take them from island to island.

Nathaniel, for reasons I could not fathom, sank his teeth into my hand.

I jumped, more shocked than hurt, and grabbed Nathaniel by the wrist. I was caught in that awful limbo of public discipline – a moment when a child has done something truly punishable but escapes without penalty because it isn't politically correct to give him the quick smack on his behind that he deserves. 'Don't you ever do that again,' I said through my teeth, trying for a smile. 'Do you hear me?'

Then I noticed all the other kids hurrying down the stairs after Father Szyszynski, a Pied Piper. 'Go,' I urged. 'You don't want to miss the story.'

Nathaniel buried his face underneath my sweater, his head swelling my belly again, a mock pregnancy. 'Come on. All your friends are going.'

I had to peel his arms from around me, push him in the right direction. Twice he looked back, and twice I had to nod, encouraging him to get a move on. 'I'm sorry,' I said to Margaret, smiling. 'You were talking about Corsica?'

Until now, I did not remember that one of the other priests, the taller one who carried a cat as if it were part of his clerical attire, hurried down the steps after the children. That he caught up to Nathaniel and put his hand on his shoulder with the comfort of someone who had done it before.

*Nathaniel said his name.*

A memory bursts and stings my eyes: *What's the opposite of left?*

*White.*

*What's the opposite of white?*

*Bwack.*

I remember the priest at Father Szyszynski's funeral who had stared through my veil as he handed me the Host, as if my features were familiar. And I remember the sentences printed carefully on a banner beneath the coffee table on that last day, before Nathaniel stopped speaking. PEACE BE WITH YOU, FATHER O'TOOLE. PEACE BE WITH YOU, FATHER GWYNNE.

Tell me what he told you, I'd asked Patrick.

*Father Glen.*

Maybe that is what Patrick heard. But that isn't how Nathaniel would have said it.

'He wasn't saying Father *Glen*,' Nina murmurs to Patrick. 'He was saying Father *Gwynne*.'

'Yeah, but you know how Nathaniel talks. His *L*'s always come out wrong.'

'Not this time,' Nina sighs. 'This time he was saying it right. Gwen. Gwynne. They're so close.'

'Who the hell is Gwynne?'

Nina rises, her hands splayed through her hair. 'He's the one, Patrick. He's the one who hurt Nathaniel and he's still, he could still be doing this to a hundred other boys, and –' She wilts, stumbling against the wall. Patrick steadies her with one hand, and he is startled to feel her shaking so hard. His first instinct is to reach for her. His second, smarter response is to let her take a step away.

She slides down the side of the refrigerator until she is sitting on the floor. 'He's the bone marrow donor. He *has* to be.'

'Does Fisher know about this yet?' She shakes her head. 'Caleb?'

In that moment, he thinks of a story he read long ago in school, about the start of the Trojan War. Paris was given a choice to be the richest man in the world, the smartest man in the world, or the chance to love another man's wife. Patrick, fool that he is, would make the same mistake. For with her hair in knots, her eyes red and swollen, her sorrow cracked open in her lap, Nina is every bit as beautiful to him now as Helen was back then.

She lifts her face to his. 'Patrick . . . what am I going to do?'

It shocks him into a response. 'You,' Patrick says clearly, 'are not going to *do* anything. You are going to sit in this house because you're on trial for a man's murder.' When she opens her mouth to argue, Patrick holds up his hand. 'You've already been locked up once, and look what happened to Nathaniel. What do you think's going to happen to him if you walk out that door for more vigilante justice, Nina? The only way you can keep him safe is to stay with him. Let me . . .' He hesitates, knowing that on the edge of this cliff, the only way out is to retreat, or to jump. 'Let me take care of it.'

She knows exactly what he has just vowed. It means going against his department, going against his own code of ethics. It means turning his back on the system, like Nina has. And it means facing the consequences. Like Nina. He sees the wonder in her face, and the spark that lets him know how tempted she is to take him up on his offer. 'And risk losing your job? Going to jail?' she says. 'I can't let you do something that stupid.'

*What makes you think I haven't already?* Patrick doesn't say the words aloud, but he doesn't have to. He crouches down and puts his hand on Nina's knee. Her hand comes up to cover his. And he sees it in her eyes: She *knows* how he feels about her, she has always known. But this is the first time she has come close to admitting it.

'Patrick,' she says quietly, 'I think I've already ruined the lives of enough people I love.'

When the door bursts open and Nathaniel tumbles into the kitchen on a whirl of cold air, Patrick comes to his feet. The boy smells of popcorn and is carrying a stuffed frog inside his winter coat. 'Guess what,' he says. 'Daddy took me to the arcade.'

'You're a lucky guy,' Patrick answers, and even to his own ears, his voice sounds weak. Caleb comes in, then, and closes the door behind him. He looks from Patrick to Nina, and smiles uncomfortably. 'I thought you were visiting with Marcella.'

'She had to go. She was meeting someone else. As she was leaving, Patrick stopped by.'

'Oh.' Caleb rubs the back of his neck. 'So . . . what did she say?'

'Say?'

'About the DNA.'

Before Patrick's very eyes, Nina changes. She flashes a polished smile at her husband. 'It's a match,' she lies. 'A perfect match.'

From the moment I step outside, the world is magic. Air cold enough to make my nostrils stick together; a sun that trembles like a cold yolk; a sky so wide and blue that I cannot keep it all in my eyes. Inside smells different from outside, but you don't notice until one of them is taken away from you.

I am on my way to Fisher's office, so my electronic bracelet has been deactivated. Being outside is so glorious that it almost supersedes the secret I am hiding. As I slow for a stoplight I see the Salvation Army man swinging his bell, his bucket swaying gently. This is the season of charity; surely there will be some left for me.

Patrick's offer swims through my mind like smoke, making it difficult to see clearly. He is the most moral, upstanding man I know – he would not have offered lightly to become my one-man posse. Of course, I cannot let him do this. But I also can't stop hoping that maybe he will ignore me and do it anyway. And immediately, I hate myself for even thinking such a thing.

I tell myself, too, that I don't want Patrick to go after Gwynne for another reason, although it is one I will admit only in the darkest corners of the night: Because I want to be the one. Because this was *my* son, *my* grievance, *my* justice to mete out.

When did I become this person – a woman who has the capacity to commit murder, to want to murder again, to get what she wants without caring who she destroys in the process?

Was this always a part of me, buried, waiting? Maybe there is a seed of malfeasance even in the most honest of people – like Patrick – that requires a certain combination of circumstances to bloom. In most of us, then, it lies dormant forever. But for others, it blossoms. And once it does, it takes over like loosestrife, choking out rational thought, killing compassion.

So much for Christmas spirit.

Fisher's office is decorated for the holidays too. Swaths of garland drape the fireplace; there is mistletoe hanging square over the secretary's desk. Beside the coffee urn sits a jug of hot mulled cider. While I wait for my attorney to retrieve me, I run my hand over the leather cushion of the couch, simply for the novelty of touching something other than the old sage chenille sofa in my living room at home.

What Patrick said about labs making mistakes has stayed with me. I will not tell Fisher about the bone marrow tranpslant, not until I know for sure that Marcella's explanation is right. There is no reason to believe that Quentin Brown will dig up this obscure glitch about DNA; so there is no reason to trouble Fisher yet with information he might never need to know.

'Nina.' Fisher strides toward me, frowning. 'You're losing weight.'

'It's called prisoner-of-war chic.' I fall into step beside him, measuring the dimensions of this hall and that alcove, simply because they are unfamiliar to me. In his office, I stare out the window, where the fingers of bare branches rap a tattoo against the glass.

Fisher catches the direction of my gaze. 'Would you like to go outside?' he asks quietly.

It is freezing, nearly zero. But I am not in the habit of handing back gifts. 'I would love that.'

So we walk in the parking lot behind the law offices, the wind kicking up small tornadoes of brown leaves. Fisher holds a stack of papers in his gloved hands. 'We've gotten the state's psychiatric evaluation back. You didn't quite answer his questions directly, did you?'

'Oh, come on. *Do you know the role of a judge in the court-room?* For God's sake.'

A small grin plays over Fisher's mouth. 'All the same, he found you competent and sane at the time of the offense.'

I stop walking. What about now? Is it crazy to want to finish the job once you've found out you didn't succeed the first time? Or is that the sanest thing in the world?

'Don't worry. I think we can chew this guy up and rip his report to shreds – but I also would like a forensic shrink to say you were insane then, and aren't now. The last thing I want is a jury thinking you're still a threat.'

But I am. I imagine shooting Father Gwynne, getting it right this time. Then I turn to Fisher, my face perfectly blank. 'Who do you want to use?'

'How about Sidwell Mackay?'

'We joke about him in the office,' I say. 'Any prosecutor can get through him in five minutes flat.'

'Peter Casanoff?'

I shake my head. 'Pompous windbag.'

Together we turn our backs to the wind, trying to make a very logical decision about whom we can find to call me insane. Maybe this will not be so difficult after all. What rational woman still sees the wrong man's blood on her hands every time she looks down, but spends an hour in the shower imagining how she might kill the *right* man?

'All right,' Fisher suggests. 'How about O'Brien, from Portland?'

'I've called him a couple of times. He seems all right, maybe a little squirmy.'

Fisher nods in agreement. 'He's going to come off like an academic, and I think that's what you need, Nina.'

I offer him my most complacent smile. 'Well, Fisher. You're the boss!'

He gives me a guarded look, then hands over the psychiatric report. 'This is the one the state sent. You need to remember what you told him before you go see O'Brien.'

So defense attorneys *do* ask their clients to memorize what they said to the state psychiatrist.

'We've got Judge Neal coming down, by the way.'

I cringe. 'Oh, you've got to be kidding.'

'Why?'

'He's supposed to be incredibly gullible.'

'How lucky for you, then, that you're a defendant,' Fisher says dryly. 'Speaking of which . . . I don't believe we're going to put you on the stand.'

'I wouldn't expect you to, after two psychiatrists testify.' But I am thinking, *I cannot take the stand now, not knowing what I know.*

Fisher stops walking and faces me. 'Before you start telling me how you think your defense ought to be handled, Nina, I want to remind you you're looking at insanity from a prosecutor's perspective, and I –'

'You know, Fisher,' I interrupt, glancing at my watch, 'I can't really talk about this today.'

'Is the coach turning into a pumpkin?'

'I'm sorry. I just can't.' My eyes slide away from his.

'You can't put it off forever. Your trial will start in January, and I'll be gone over the holidays with my family.'

'Let me get examined first,' I bargain. 'Then we can sit down.'

Fisher nods. I think of O'Brien, of whether I can convince him of my insanity. I wonder if, by then, it will be an act.

For the first time in a decade, Quentin takes a long lunch. No one will notice at the DA's office; they barely tolerate his presence, and in his absence, probably dance on the top of his desk. He checks the directions he's downloaded from the computer and swings his car into the parking lot of the high school. Teens sausaged into North Face jackets give him cursory glances as he passes. Quentin walks right through the middle of a hackeysack game without breaking stride, and continues around the back of the school.

There is a shoddy football stadium, an equally shoddy track, and a basketball court. Gideon is doing an admirable job of guarding some pansy-ass center six inches shorter than him. Quentin puts his hands into the pockets of his overcoat and watches his son steal the ball and shoot an effortless three-pointer.

The last time his son had picked up the phone to get in touch, he'd been calling from jail, busted for possession. And although it cost Quentin plenty of snide comments about nepotism, he'd gotten Gideon's sentence transmuted to a rehab facility. That hadn't been good enough for Gideon, though, who'd wanted to be released scot-free. 'You're no use as a father,' he'd told Quentin. 'I should have known you'd be no use as a lawyer, either.'

Now, a year later, Gideon high-fives another player and then turns around to see Quentin watching. 'Shit, man,' he mutters. 'Time.' The other kids fall to the sidelines, sucking on water bottles and shrugging off layers of clothes. Gideon approaches, arms crossed. 'You come here to make me piss in some cup?'

Shrugging, Quentin says, 'No, I came to see you. To talk.'

'I got nothing to say to you.'

'That's surprising,' Quentin responds, 'since I have sixteen years' worth.'

'Then what's another day?' Gideon turns back toward the game. 'I'm busy.'

'I'm sorry.'

The words make the boy pause. 'Yeah, right,' he murmurs. He storms back to the basketball court, grabbing the ball and spinning it in the air – to impress Quentin, maybe? 'Let's go, let's go!' he calls, and the others rally around him. Quentin walks off. 'Who was that, man?' he hears one of the boys ask Gideon. And Gideon's response, when he thinks Quentin is too far away to hear: 'Some guy who needed directions.'

From the window of the doctor's office at Dana-Farber, Patrick can see the ragtag edge of Boston. Olivia Bessette, the oncologist listed on Father Szyszynski's medical reports, has turned out to be considerably younger than Patrick expected – not much older than Patrick himself. She sits with her hands folded, her curly hair pulled into a sensible bun, one rubber-soled white clog tapping lightly on the floor. 'Leukemia only affects the blood cells,' she explains, 'and chronic myeloid leukemia tends to have an onset in patients in their forties and fifties – although I've had some cases with patients in their twenties.'

Patrick wonders how you sit on the edge of a hospital bed and tell someone they are not going to live. It is not that different, he imagines, from knocking on a door in the middle of the night and informing a parent that his son has been killed in a drunk driving accident. 'What happens to the blood cells?' he asks.

'Blood cells are all programmed to die, just like we are. They start out at a baby stage, then grow up to be a little more functional, and by the time they get spit out of the bone marrow they are adult cells. By then, white cells should be able to fight infection on your behalf, red blood cells should be able to carry oxygen, and platelets should be able to clot your blood. But if you have leukemia, your cells never mature . . . and they never die. So you wind up with a proliferation of white cells that don't work, and that overrun all your other cells.'

Patrick is not really going against Nina's wishes, being here. All he's doing is clarifying what they know – not taking it a step farther. He secured this appointment on a ruse, pretending that he is working on behalf of the assistant attorney general. Mr. Brown, Patrick explained, has the burden of proof. Which means they need to be a hundred percent sure that Father Szyszynski didn't drop dead of leukemia the moment that his assailant pulled out a gun. Could Dr. Bessette, his former oncologist, offer any opinions?

'What does a bone marrow transplant do?' Patrick asks.

'Wonders, if it works. There are six proteins on all of our cells, human leukocyte antigens, or HLA. They help our bodies recognize you as you, and me as me. When you're looking for a bone marrow donor, you're hoping for all six of these proteins to match yours. In most cases, this means siblings, half-siblings, maybe a cousin – relatives seem to have the lowest instance of rejection.'

'Rejection?' Patrick asks.

'Yes. In essence, you're trying to convince your body that the donor cells are actually yours, because you have the same six proteins on them. If you can't do that, your immune system will reject the bone marrow transplant, which leads to Graft Versus Host disease.'

'Like a heart transplant.'

'Exactly. Except this isn't an organ. Bone marrow is harvested from the pelvis, because it's the big bones in your body that make blood. Basically, we put the donor to sleep and then stick needles into his hips about 150 times on each side, suctioning out the early cells.'

He winces, and the doctor smiles a little. 'It *is* painful. Being a bone marrow donor is a very selfless thing.'

*Yeah, this guy was a fucking altruist,* Patrick thinks.

'Meanwhile, the patient with leukemia has been taking immunosuppressants. The week before the transplant, he's given enough chemotherapy to kill all the blood cells in his body. It's timed this way, so that his bone marrow is empty.'

'You can live like that?'

'You're at huge risk for infection. The patient still has his own living blood cells . . . he's just not making any new ones. Then he gets the donor marrow, through a simple IV. It takes about two hours, and we don't know how, but the cells manage to find their way to the bone marrow in his own body and start growing. After about a month, his bone marrow has been entirely replaced by his donor's.'

'And his blood cells would have the donor's six proteins, that HLA stuff?' Patrick asks.

'That's right.'

'How about the donor's DNA?'

Dr. Bessette nods. 'Yes. In all respects, his blood is really someone else's. He's just fooling his body into believing it's truly his.'

Patrick leans forward. 'But if it takes – if the cancer goes into remission – does the patient's body start making his own blood again?'

'No. If it did, we'd consider it a rejection of the graft, and the leukemia would return. We *want* the patient to keep producing his donor's blood forever.' She taps the file on her desk. 'In Glen Szyszynski's case, five years after the transplant, he was given a clean bill of health. His new bone marrow was working quite well, and the chance of a recurrence of leukemia was less than ten percent.' Dr. Bessette nods. 'I think the prosecution can safely say that however the priest died, it wasn't of leukemia.'

Patrick smiles at her. 'Guess it felt good to have a success story.'

'It always does. Father Szyszynski was lucky to have found a perfect match.'

'A perfect match?'

'That's what we call it when a donor's HLA corresponds to all six of the patient's HLA.'

Patrick takes a quick breath. 'Especially when they're not related.'

'Oh,' Dr. Bessette says. 'But that wasn't the case here. Father Szyszynski and his donor were half-brothers.'

Francesca Martine came to the Maine State Lab by way of New Hampshire, where she'd been working as a DNA scientist until something better came along. That something turned out *not* to be the ballistics expert who broke her heart. She moved north, nursing her wounds, and discovered what she'd always known – safety came in gels and Petri dishes, and numbers never hurt you.

That said, numbers also couldn't explain the visceral reaction she has the minute she first meets Quentin Brown. On the phone, she imagined him like all the other state drones – harried and underpaid, with skin a sickly shade of gray. But from the moment he walks into her lab, she cannot take her eyes off him. He is striking, certainly, with his excessive height and his mahogany complexion, but Frankie knows that isn't the attraction. She feels a pull between them, magnetism honed by the common experience of being different. She is not black, but she's often been the only woman in the room with an IQ of 220.

Unfortunately, if she wants Quentin Brown to study her closely, she'll have to assume the shape of a forensic lab report. 'What was it that made you look at this twice?' Frankie asks.

He narrows his eyes. 'How come you're asking?'

'Curiosity. It's pretty esoteric stuff for the prosecution.'

Quentin hesitates, as if wondering whether to confide in her. *Oh, come on*, Frankie thinks. *Loosen up.* 'The defense asked to take a look at it, specifically. Immediately. And it didn't seem to merit that kind of request. I don't see how the DNA results here make a difference for us *or* for them.'

Frankie crosses her arms. 'The reason they were interested isn't because of the lab report I issued. It's because of what's in the medical files.'

'I'm not following you.'

'You know the way the DNA report says that the chances of randomly selecting an unrelated individual who matches this genetic material are one in six billion?'

Quentin nods.

'Well,' Frankie explains, 'you just found the one.'

It costs approximately two thousand dollars of taxpayer money to exhume a body. 'No,' Ted Poulin says flatly. As the attorney general of Maine, and Quentin's boss, that ought to be that. But Quentin isn't going to give up without a fight, not this time.

He grips the receiver of the phone. 'The DNA scientist at the state lab says we can do the test on tooth pulp.'

'Quentin, it doesn't matter for the prosecution. She killed him. Period.'

'She killed a guy who molested her son. I have to change him from a sexual predator into a victim, Ted, and this is the way to do it.'

There is a long silence on the other end. Quentin runs his fingertips along the grain of wood on Nina Frost's desk. He does this over and over, as if he is rubbing an amulet.

'There's no family to fight it?'

'The mother gave consent already.'

Ted sighs. 'The publicity is going to be outrageous.'

Leaning back in his chair, Quentin grins. 'Let me take care of it,' he offers.

Fisher storms into the district attorney's office, uncharacteristically flustered. He has been there before, of course, but who knows where the hell they've ensconced Quentin Brown while he's prosecuting Nina's case. He has just opened up his mouth to ask the secretary when Brown himself walks out of the small kitchen area, carrying a cup of coffee. 'Mr. Carrington,' he says pleasantly. 'Looking for me?'

Fisher withdraws the paperwork he's received that morning from his breast pocket. The Motion to Exhume. 'What is this?'

Quentin shrugs. 'You must know. You're the one who asked for the DNA records to be rushed over, after all.'

Fisher has no idea why, in fact. The DNA records were rushed over at Nina's behest, but he'll be damned if he lets Brown know this. 'What are you trying to do, counselor?'

'A simple test that proves the priest your client killed wasn't the same guy who abused her kid.'

Fisher steels his gaze. 'I'll see you in court tomorrow morning,' he says, and by the time he gets into his car to drive to Nina's home, he has begun to understand how an ordinary human might become frustrated enough to kill.

'Fisher!' I say, and I'm actually delighted to see the man. This amazes me – either I have truly bedded down with the Enemy, or I've been under house arrest too long. I throw open the door to let him in, and realize that he is furious. 'You knew,' he says, his voice calm and that much more frightening for all its control. He hands me a motion filed by the assistant attorney general.

My insides begin to quiver; I feel absolutely sick. With tremendous effort I swallow and meet Fisher's eye – better to come clean eventually, than to not come clean at all. 'I didn't know if I should tell you. I didn't know if the information was going to be important to my case.'

'That's *my* job!' Fisher explodes. 'You are paying me for a reason, Nina, and it's because you know on some level, although apparently not a conscious one, that I am qualified to get you acquitted. In fact, I'm more qualified to do that than any other attorney in Maine . . . *including* you.'

I look away. At heart, I am a prosecutor, and prosecutors don't tell defense attorneys everything. They dance around each other, but the prosecutor is always the one who leads, leaving the other lawyer to find his footing.

Always.

'I don't trust you,' I say finally.

Fisher fields this like a blow. 'Well, then. We're even.'

We stare at each other, two great dogs with their teeth bared. Fisher turns away, angry, and in that moment I see my face in the reflection of the window. The truth is, I'm not a prosecutor anymore. I'm not capable of defending myself. I'm not sure I even want to.

'Fisher,' I call out when he is halfway out the door. 'How badly will this hurt me?'

'I don't know, Nina. It doesn't make you look any less crazy, but it's also going to strip you of public sympathy. You're not a hero anymore, killing a pedophile. You're a hothead who knocked off an innocent man – a *priest*, no less.' He shakes his head. 'You're the prime example of why we have laws in the first place.'

In his eyes, I see what's coming – the fact that I am no longer a mother doing what she had to for her child, but simply a reckless woman who thought she knew better than anyone else. I wonder if camera flashes feel different on your skin when they capture you as a criminal, instead of a victim. I wonder if parents who once fathomed my actions – even if they disagreed with them – will look at me now and cross the street, just in case faulty judgment is contagious.

Fisher exhales heavily. 'I can't keep them from exhuming the body.'

'I know.'

'And if you keep hiding information from me, it *will* hurt you, because I won't know how to work with it.'

I duck my head. 'I understand.'

He raises his hand in farewell. I stand on the porch and watch him go, hugging myself against the wind. When his car heads down the street, its exhaust freezes, a sigh caught in the cold. With a deep breath I turn to find Caleb standing not three feet behind me. 'Nina,' he says, 'what was that?'

Pushing past him, I shake my head, but he grabs my arm and will not let me go. 'You lied to me. *Lied* to me!'

'Caleb, you don't understand –'

He grasps my shoulders and shakes me once, hard. 'What is it I don't understand? That you killed an innocent man? Jesus, Nina, when is it going to hit you?'

Once, Nathaniel asked me how the snow disappears. It is like that in Maine – instead of melting over time, it takes one warm day for drifts that are thigh-high in the morning to evaporate by the time the sun goes down. Together we went to the library to learn the answer – *sublimation*, the process by which something solid vanishes into thin air.

With Caleb's hands holding me up, I fall apart. I let out everything I have been afraid to set free for the past week. Father Szyszynski's voice fills my head; his face swims in front of me. 'I know,' I sob. 'Oh, Caleb, I know. I thought I could do this. I thought I could take care of it. But I made a mistake.' I fold myself into the wall of his chest, waiting for his arms to come around me.

They don't.

Caleb takes a step back, shoves his hands in his pockets. His eyes are red-rimmed, haunted. 'What's the mistake, Nina? That you killed a man?' he asks hoarsely. 'Or that you didn't?'

'It's a shame, is what it is,' the church secretary says. Myra Lester shakes her head, then hands Patrick the cup of tea she's made him. 'Christmas Mass just around the corner, and us without a chaplain.'

Patrick knows that the best road to information is not always the one that's paved and straightforward, but the one that cuts around back and is most often forgotten as an access route. He also knows, from his long-lapsed days of growing up Catholic, that the collective memory – and gossip mill – most often is the church secretary. So he offers his most concerned expression, the one that always got him a pinch on the cheek from his elderly aunts. 'The congregation must be devastated.'

'Between the rumors flying around about Father Szyszynski, and the way he was killed – well, it's most un-Christian, that's all I have to say about it.' She sniffs, then settles her considerable bottom on a wing chair in the rectory office.

He would like to have assumed a different persona, now – a newcomer to Biddeford, for example, checking out the parish – but he has already been seen in his capacity as a detective, during the sexual abuse investigation. 'Myra,' Patrick says, then looks up at her and smiles. 'I'm sorry. I meant Mrs. Lester, of course.'

Her cheeks flame, and she titters. 'Oh, no, you feel free to call me whatever you like, Detective.'

'Well, Myra, I've been trying to get in touch with the priests that were visiting St. Anne's shortly before Father Szyszynski's death.'

'Oh, yes, they were lovely. Just lovely! That Father O'Toole, he had the most scrumptious Southern accent. Like peach schnapps, that's what I thought of every time he spoke . . . Or was that Father Gwynne?'

'The prosecution's hounding me. I don't suppose you'd have any idea where I could find them?'

'They've gone back to their own congregations, of course.'

'Is there a record of that? A forwarding address, maybe?'

Myra frowns, and a small pattern of lines in the shape of a spider appears on her forehead. 'I'm sure there must be. Nothing in this church goes on without me knowing the details.' She walks toward all the ledgers and logs stacked behind her desk. Flipping through the pages of a leather-bound book, she finds an entry and smacks it with the flat of her hand. 'It's right here. Fathers Brendan O'Toole, from St. Dennis's, in Harwich, Massachusetts, and Arthur Gwynne, due to depart this afternoon as per the See of Portland.' Myra scratches her hair with the eraser of a pencil. 'I suppose the other priest could have come from Harwich, too, but that wouldn't explain the peach schnapps.'

'Maybe he moved as a child,' Patrick suggests. 'What's the Sea of Portland?'

'See, *S-E-E*. It's the governing diocese hereabouts in Maine, of course.' She lifts her face to Patrick's. 'They're the ones who sent the priests to us in the first place.'

Midnight, in a graveyard, with an unearthed casket – Patrick can think of a thousand places he'd rather be. But he stands beside the two sweating men who have hauled the coffin from the ground and set it beside Father Szyszynski's resting place, like an altar in the moonlight. He has promised to be Nina's eyes, Nina's legs. And if necessary, Nina's hands.

They are all wearing Hazmat suits – Patrick and Evan Chao, Fisher Carrington and Quentin Brown, Frankie Martine, and the medical examiner, Vern Potter. In the black circle beyond their flashlights, an owl screams.

Vern jumps a foot. 'Holy sweet Jesus. Any minute now I keep expecting the zombies to get up from behind the tombstones. Couldn't we have done this in broad daylight?'

'I'll take zombies over the press any day,' Evan Chao mutters. 'Get it over with, Vern.'

'Hokey-dokey.' The medical examiner takes a crowbar and pries open Father Szyszynski's casket. The foul air that puffs from its insides has Patrick gagging. Fisher Carrington turns away and holds a handkerchief to his face mask. Quentin walks off briskly to vomit behind a tree.

The priest does not look all that different. Half of his face is still missing. His arms lie at his sides. His skin, gray and wrinkled, has not yet decomposed. 'Open wide,' Vern murmurs, and he ratchets down the jaw, reaches inside, and pulls out a molar with a pair of tooth pliers.

'Get me a couple wisdom teeth, too,' Frankie says. 'And hair.'

Evan nods to Patrick, calling him aside. 'You believe this?' he asks.

'Nope.'

'Maybe the bastard's just getting what he deserves.'

Patrick is stunned for a moment, until he remembers: There is no reason to believe Evan would know what Patrick knows – that Father Szyszynski was innocent. 'Maybe,' he manages.

A few minutes later, Vern hands a jar and an envelope to Frankie. Quentin hurries away with her, Fisher close behind. The ME closes the casket and turns to the grave diggers. 'You can put him back now,' he instructs, then turns to Patrick. 'On your way out?'

'In a sec.' Patrick watches Vern go, then turns to the grave, where the two big men have dropped the coffin again and are starting to shovel dirt over it again. He waits until they are finished, because he thinks someone should.

By the time Patrick gets to the Biddeford District Court, he wonders whether Father Arthur Gwynne ever existed at all. He's driven from the graveyard, where the body was being exhumed, to the Catholic See in Portland . . . where he was told by the chancellor that their records only showed Father O'Toole coming to visit Biddeford. If Father Gwynne was at the church too, it might have been a personal connection to the Biddeford chaplain that brought him there. Which, of course, is exactly what Patrick needs to confirm.

The probate clerk hands him a copy of the priest's Last Will and Testament, which became a public record a month ago, when it was filed with the court. The document is simple to a fault. Father Szyszynski left fifty percent of his estate to his mother. And the rest to the executor of his will: Arthur Gwynne, of Belle Chasse, Louisiana.

Enamel is the strongest material naturally found in the human body, which makes it a bitch to crack open. To this end, Frankie soaks the extracted molar in liquid nitrogen for about five minutes, because frozen, it is more likely to shatter. 'Hey, Quentin,' she says, grinning at the attorney, waiting impatiently. 'Can you break a dollar?'

He fishes in his pockets, but shakes his head. 'Sorry.'

'No problem.' She takes a buck from her wallet and floats it in the liquid nitrogen, then pulls it out, smashes it on the counter, and laughs. 'I can.'

He sighs. 'Is this why it takes so long to get results from the state lab?'

'Hey, I'm letting you cut in line, aren't I?' Frankie removes the tooth from its bath and sets it in a sterile mortar and pestle. She grinds at it, pounding harder and harder, but the tooth will not crack.

'Mortar and pestle?' Quentin asks.

'We used to use the ME's skull saw, but we had to get a new blade every time. Plus, the cutting edge gets too hot, and denatures the DNA.' She glances at him over her protective goggles. 'You don't want me to screw up, do you?' Another whack, but the tooth remains intact. 'Oh, for God's sake.' Frankie plucks a second tooth out of the liquid nitrogen. 'Come with me. I want to get this over with.'

She double-bags the tooth in Ziplocs and leads Quentin to the stairwell, all the way to the basement garage of the laboratory. 'Stand back,' she says, and then squats, setting the bag on the floor. Taking a hammer out of the pocket of her lab coat, Frankie begins to pound, her own jaw aching in sympathy. The tooth shatters on the fourth try, its pieces splintering into the plastic bag.

'Now what?' Quentin asks.

The pulp is brownish, slight . . . but most definitely there. 'Now,' she says, 'you wait.'

Quentin, who is unused to staying up in graveyards all night and then driving to the lab in Augusta, falls asleep on a bank of chairs in the lobby. When he feels a cool hand on the back of his neck, he startles awake, sitting up so quickly he is momentarily dizzy. Frankie stands before him, holding out a report. 'And?' he asks.

'The tooth pulp was chimeric.'

'English?'

Frankie sits down beside him. 'The reason we test tooth pulp is because it has blood cells in it . . . but also tissue cells. For you and me and most people, the DNA in both of those cells will be the same. But if someone gets a bone marrow transplant, they're going to show a mixture of two DNA profiles in their tooth pulp. The first profile will be the DNA they were born with, and that'll be in the tissue cells. The second profile will be the DNA that came from their marrow donor, and will be in the blood cells. In this sample, the suspect's tooth pulp yielded a mixture.'

Quentin frowns at the numbers on the page. 'So –'

'So here's your proof,' Frankie says. 'Somebody else perved that kid.'

After Fisher calls me with the news, I go right into the bathroom and throw up. Again, and again, until there is nothing left in my stomach but the guilt. The truth is, a man was killed by my own hand, a man who deserved no punishment. What does this make me?

I want to shower until I don't feel dirty; I want to strip off my own skin. But the horror is at the heart of me. Cut a gut feeling, watch yourself bleed to death.

Like I watched him.

In the hallway, I brush past Caleb, who has not been speaking to me anyway. There are no more words between us, each one has a charge on it, an ion that might attach to either him or to me and push us farther apart. In my bedroom, I kick off my shoes and crawl fully dressed under the covers. I pull them up over my head; breathe in the same cocoon. If you pass out, and there's still no air, what will happen?

I can't get warm. This is where I will stay, because now any of my decisions may be suspect. Better to do nothing at all, than to take another risk that might change the world.

It's an instinct, Patrick realizes – to want to hurt someone as badly as they've hurt you. There were moments in his career in the military police that his arrests became violent, blood running over his hands that felt like a balm at the time. Now, he understands that the theory can go one step further: It's an instinct to want to hurt someone as badly as they've hurt someone you care about. This is the only explanation he can offer for sitting on a 757 en route from Dallas-Fort Worth to New Orleans.

The question isn't what he would do for Nina. 'Anything,' Patrick would answer, without hesitation. She had expressly warned him away from hunting down Arthur Gwynne, and all of Patrick's actions up to this point could be classified as information-seeking, but even he could not couch the truth, now: He had no reason to fly to Louisiana, if not to meet this man face-to-face.

Even now, he cannot tell himself what is going to happen. He has spent his life guided by principle and rules – in the Navy, as a cop, as an unrequited lover. But rules only work when everyone plays by them. What happens when someone doesn't, and the fallout bleeds right into his life? What's stronger – the need to uphold the law, or the motive to turn one's back on it?

It has been shattering for Patrick to realize that the criminal mind is not all that far away from that of a rational man. It comes down, really, to the power of a craving. Addicts will sell their own bodies for another gram of coke. Arsonists will put their own lives in danger to feel something go up in flames around them. Patrick has always believed, as an officer of the law, he is above this driving need. But what if your obsession has nothing to do with drugs or thrills or money? What if what you want most in the world is to recapture the way life was a week, a month, a year ago – and you are willing to do whatever it takes?

This was Nina's error; she wrongly equated stopping time with turning it backward. And he couldn't even blame her, because he'd made the same mistake, every time he was in her company.

The question Patrick knew he should be asking was not what he would do for Nina . . . but what he *wouldn't*.

The flight attendant pushes the beverage cart like a baby carriage, braking beside Patrick's row. 'What can I get for you?' she asks. Her smile reminds him of Nathaniel's Halloween mask from last year.

'Tomato juice. No ice.'

The man sitting beside Patrick folds his newspaper. 'Tomato juice and vodka,' he says, grinning through his thick Texan drawl. 'Yes, ice.'

They both take a sip of their drinks as the flight attendant moves on. The man glances down at his newspaper and shakes his head. 'Ought to fry the sumbitch,' he mutters.

'Excuse me?'

'Oh, it's this murder case. Y'all must have heard about it . . . there's some fool who wants an eleventh hour pardon from death row because she's found Jesus. Truth is, the governor's afraid to give her the cocktail because she's a woman.'

Patrick has always been in favor of capital punishment. But he hears himself say, 'Seems reasonable.'

'Guess you're one of those Yankee left-wingers,' the man

scoffs. 'Me, I think it don't matter if you've got a pecker or not. You shoot someone in the back of the head at a convenience store, you pay the price. You know?' He shrugs, then finishes his drink. 'You flying out on business or pleasure?'

'Business.'

'Me, too. I'm in sales. Hav-A-Heart traps,' he confides, as if this is privileged information.

'I'm a lawyer with the ACLU,' Patrick lies. 'I'm flying down to plead that woman's case to the governor.'

The salesman goes red in the face. 'Well. I didn't mean no disrespect –'

'Like hell you didn't.'

He folds his newspaper again, and stuffs it into the seat pocket in front of him. 'Even you bleeding hearts can't save them all.'

'One,' Patrick answers. 'That's all I'm hoping for.'

There is a woman wearing my clothes and my skin and my smell but it isn't me. Sin is like ink, it bleeds into a person, coloring, making you someone other than you used to be. And it's indelible. Try as much as you want, you cannot get yourself back.

Words can't pull me back from the edge. Neither can daylight. This isn't something to get over, it is an atmosphere I need to learn to breathe. Grow gills for transgression, take it into my lungs with every gasp.

It is a startling thing. I wonder who this person is, going through the motions of my life. I want to take her hand.

And then I want to push her, hard, off a cliff.

Patrick finds himself peeling off layers of clothing as he walks through the streets of Belle Chasse, Louisiana, past wrought-iron gates and ivy-trellised courtyards. Christmas looks wrong in this climate; the decorations seem to be sweating in the humid heat. He wonders how a Louisiana boy like Glen Szyszynski ever survived so far north.

But he already knows the answer. Growing up among Cajuns and the Creoles wasn't all that far a stretch from tending to the Acadians in his parish. The proof of that rests in his breast pocket, public records copied by a clerk at the Louisiana Vital Records Registry in New Orleans. Arthur Gwynne, born 10/23/43 to Cecilia Marquette Gwynne and her husband, Alexander Gwynne. Four years later, the marriage of Cecelia Marquette Gwynne, widowed, to Teodor Szyszynski. And in 1951, the birth of Glen.

Half-brothers.

Szyszynski's will was last revised in 1994; it is entirely possible that Arthur Gwynne is no longer a member of the Belle Chasse community. But it is a starting point. Priests don't go unnoticed in a predominantly Catholic town; if Gwynne had any contact at all with his neighbors, Patrick knows he can pick up a paper trail and track his whereabouts from there. To this end, there is another clue in his pocket, one ripped from the rear of a phone book. Churches. The largest one is Our Lady of Mercy.

He doesn't let himself think what he will do with the information, once he gets it.

Patrick turns the corner, and the cathedral comes into view. He jogs up the stone steps and enters the nave. Immediately in front of him is a pool of Holy Water. Flickering candles cast waves on the walls, and the reflection from a stained-glass window bleeds a brilliant puddle on the mosaic floor. Above the altar, a cypress carving of Jesus on the cross looms like an omen.

It smells of Catholicism: beeswax and starch and darkness and peace, all of which bring Patrick back to his youth. He finds himself unconsciously making the sign of the cross as he slides into a pew at the rear of the building.

Four women nod their heads in prayer, their faith settling softly around them, like the skirts of Confederate belles. Another sobs quietly into her hands while a priest comforts her in whispers. Patrick waits patiently, running his hands along the bright, polished wood and whistling under his breath.

Suddenly the hair stands up on the back of his neck. Walking along the lip of the pew behind him is a cat. Its tail strokes Patrick on the nape again, and he lets out his breath in a rush. 'You scared the hell out of me,' he murmurs, and then glances at the carving of Jesus. 'The *heck*,' he amends.

The cat blinks at him, then leaps with grace into the arms of the priest who has come up beside Patrick. 'You know better,' the priest scolds.

It takes Patrick a moment to realize the cleric is speaking to his kitten. 'Excuse me. I'm trying to locate a Father Arthur Gwynne.'

'Well.' The man smiles. 'You found me.'

Every time Nathaniel tries to see his mother, she's sleeping. Even when it's light outside; even when it's time for *Franklin* on Nickelodeon. *Leave her alone,* his father says. *It's what she wants.* But Nathaniel doesn't think that's what his mother wants at all. He thinks about how sometimes in the middle of the night he wakes up dreaming of spiders under his skin and screams that don't go away, and the only thing that keeps him from running out of the room is how dark it is and how far it seems from his bed to the door.

'We have to do something,' Nathaniel tells his father, after it has been three days, and his mother is still asleep.

But his father's face squeezes up at the top, like it does when Nathaniel is yelling too loud while he's having his hair washed and the sound bounces around the bathroom. 'There's nothing we *can* do,' he tells Nathaniel.

It's not true. Nathaniel knows this. So when his father goes outside to put the trash cans at the end of the driveway *(Two minutes, Nathaniel . . . you can sit here and be good for two minutes, can't you?)* Nathaniel waits until he can no longer hear the scratch-drag on the gravel and then bolts upstairs to his bedroom. He overturns his garbage can to use as a stool and takes what he needs from his dresser. He twists the knob to his parents' room quietly, tiptoes inside as if the floor is made of cotton.

It takes two tries to turn on the reading lamp near his mother's side of the bed, and then Nathaniel crawls on top of the covers. His mother isn't there at all, just the great swollen shape under the blankets that doesn't even move when he calls her name. He pokes at it, frowns. Then he pulls away the sheet.

The Thing That Isn't His Mother moans and squints in the sudden light.

Her hair is wild and matted, like the brown sheep at the petting zoo. Her eyes look like they've fallen too deep in her face, and grooves run the length of her mouth. She smells of sadness. She blinks once at Nathaniel, as if he might be something she remembers but can't quite fish to the front of her mind. Then she pulls the blankets over her head again and rolls away from him.

'Mommy?' Nathaniel whispers, because this place cries for quiet. 'Mommy, I know what you need.'

Nathaniel has been thinking about it, and he remembers what it felt like to be stuck in a dark, dark place and not be able to explain it. And he also remembers what she did, back then, for him. So he takes the sign-language binder he got from Dr. Robichaud and slips it under the blankets, into his mother's hands.

He holds his breath while her hands trace the edges and rifle through the pages. There is a sound Nathaniel has never heard before – like the world opening up at the start of an earthquake, or maybe a heart breaking – and the binder slips from beneath the sheets, cracking open onto the floor. Suddenly the comforter rises like the hinged jaw of a white whale and he finds himself swallowed whole.

Then he is in the spot where he put the sign-language book, smack in the middle of her arms. She holds him so tight there is no room for words between them, spoken or signed. And it doesn't matter one bit, because Nathaniel understands exactly what his mother is telling him.

*Christ,* I think, wincing. *Turn off the lights.*

But Fisher starts laying out papers and briefs on the blankets, as if it is every day that he conducts meetings with a client too exhausted to leave her bedroom. Then again, what do I know? Maybe he does.

'Go away,' I moan.

'Bottom line: He had a bone marrow transplant,' Fisher says briskly. 'You shot the wrong priest. So we need to figure out how to use that to our best advantage and get you off.' Before he remembers to check himself, his eyes meet mine, and he cannot hide it: the shock and, yes, distaste of seeing me like this. Unwashed, undressed, uncaring.

*Yes, look, Fisher,* I think. *Now you don't have to* pretend *I'm crazy.*

I roll onto my side, and some of the papers flutter off the edge of the bed. 'You don't have to play this game with me, Nina,' Fisher sighs. 'You hired me so that you won't go to jail, and goddammit, you're not going to jail.' He pauses, as if he is about to tell me something important, but what he says doesn't matter at all. 'I've already filed the paperwork requesting a jury, but you know, we can waive it at the last minute.' His eyes take in my nightgown, my tangled hair. 'It might be easier to convince one person that . . . that you were insane.'

I pull the covers over my head.

'We got the report back from O'Brien. You did a nice job, Nina. I'll leave it for you to look over . . .'

In the dark under here, I begin to hum, so that I can't hear him.

'Well.'

I stick my fingers in my ears.

'I don't think there's anything else.' I feel a commotion to my left as he gathers his files. 'I'll be in touch after Christmas.' He begins to walk away from me, his expensive shoes striking the carpet like rumors.

I have killed a man; I have killed a man. This has become a part of me, like the color of my eyes or the birthmark on my right shoulder blade. I have killed a man, and nothing I do can take that away.

I pull the covers down from my face just as he reaches the door. 'Fisher,' I say, the first word I've spoken in days.

He turns, smiles.

'I'm taking the stand.'

That smile vanishes. 'No you're not.'

'I am.'

He approaches the bed again. 'If you take the stand, Brown is going to rip you to shreds. If you take the stand, even *I* can't help you.'

I stare at him, unblinking, for a lifetime. 'So?' I say.

'Someone wants to talk to you,' Caleb announces, and he drops the portable phone on the bed. When I don't bother to reach for it, Caleb seems to think twice. 'It's Patrick,' he adds.

Once, on a trip to the beach, I let Nathaniel bury me in the sand. It took so long that the hills enclosing my legs – the spot where he'd started – had dried and hardened. The weight of the beach pressed down on my chest, and I remember feeling claustrophobic as his small hands built a dune around me. When I finally *did* move, I was a Titan, rising from the earth with enough leashed power to topple gods.

Now, I watch my hand crawl across the covers toward the phone, and I cannot stop it. As it turns out, there is one thing strong enough to seduce me away from my careful paralysis and self-pity – the possibility of action. And even though I have looked the consequences right in their yellow-wolf eyes, it turns out I am still addicted. *Hello, my name is Nina, and I need to know where he is.*

'Patrick?' I press the receiver to my ear.

'I found him. Nina, he's in Louisiana. A town called Belle Chasse. He's a priest.'

All my breath leaves my lungs in a rush. 'You arrested him.'

There is a hesitation. 'No.'

As I sit up, the covers fall away. 'Did you . . .' I cannot finish. There is a part of me hoping so hard that he will tell me something horrible, something I desperately want to hear. And there is another part of me hoping that whatever I have turned into has not poisoned him too.

'I talked to the guy. But I couldn't let him know I was onto him, or that I was even from Maine. You remember going through this at the beginning, with Nathaniel – tip off a molester and he's going to run, and we'll never get a confession. Gwynne's even more cagey, because he knows his half-brother was killed due to an allegation of child sexual abuse that he committed himself.' Patrick hesitates. 'So instead I said I was getting married and looking for a church for the ceremony. It was the first thing that came to mind.'

Tears spring to my eyes. He was within Patrick's grasp, and still nothing has happened. 'Arrest him. For God's sake, Patrick, get off this phone and run back there –'

'Nina, stop. I'm not a cop in Louisiana. The crime didn't happen here. I need an arrest warrant in Maine before I can get a fugitive charge lodged against Gwynne in Louisiana, and even then, he might fight extradition.' He hesitates. 'And what do you imagine my boss will say when he finds out I'm using my shield to dig up information about a case that I haven't even been assigned to?'

'But Patrick . . . you *found* him.'

'I know. And he's going to be punished.' There is a silence. 'Just not today.'

He asks me if I am all right, and I lie to him. How can I be all right? I am back where I started. Except now, after I am tried for the murder of an innocent man, Nathaniel will be embroiled in another trial. While I sit in jail, he'll have to face his abuser, drag back the nightmare. Nathaniel will suffer; he will hurt.

Patrick says good-bye, and I hang up the phone. I stare at the receiver in my hand for a minute, rub the edge of the smooth plastic.

The first time, I had much more to lose.

'What are you doing?'

My head pops through the turtleneck to find Caleb standing in the bedroom. 'What does it look like I'm doing?' I button my jeans. Stuff my feet into my clogs.

'Patrick got you out of bed,' he says, and there is a note in his voice that strikes off-chord.

'Patrick gave me information that got me out of bed,' I correct. I try to move around Caleb, but he blocks my exit. 'Please. I have to go somewhere.'

'Nina, you're not going anywhere. The bracelet.'

I look at my husband's face. There are lines on his brow I cannot remember seeing; with no small shock I realize I have put them there.

I owe him this.

So I put my hand on his arm, lead him to the bed, have him sit beside me on the edge. 'Patrick found the name of the bone marrow donor. He's the priest that came to visit St. Anne's this October. The one with the cat. His name is Arthur Gwynne, and he works at a church in Belle Chasse, Louisiana.'

Caleb's face goes pale. 'Why . . . why are you telling me this?'

*Because the first time, I acted alone, when I should have at least told you my plans. Because when they ask you in court, you will not have to testify.* 'Because,' I say, 'it's not finished yet.'

He reels back. 'Nina. No.' I get up, but he catches my wrist, pulls me up close to his face. My arm, twisted, hurts. 'What are you gonna do? Break your house arrest to go kill another priest? One life sentence isn't enough for you?'

'They have the death penalty in Louisiana,' I shoot back.

My response is a guillotine, severing us. Caleb releases me so quickly I stumble and fall onto the floor. 'Is that what you want?' he asks quietly. 'Are you that selfish?'

'Selfish?' By now I am crying, hard. 'I'm doing this for our son.'

'You're doing this for *yourself*, Nina. If you were thinking of Nathaniel, even a little, you'd concentrate on being his mother. You'd get out of bed and get on with your life and let the legal system deal with Gwynne.'

'The legal system. You want me to wait for the courts to get around to charging this bastard? While he rapes ten, twenty other children? And then wait some more while the governors of our states fight over who gets the honor of holding his trial? And then wait again while Nathaniel testifies against the son of a bitch? And watch Gwynne get a sentence that ends before our son even stops having nightmares about what was done to him?' I draw in a long, shaky breath. 'There's your legal system, Caleb. Is it worth waiting for?'

When he doesn't answer, I get to my feet. 'I'm already going to prison for killing a man. I don't have a life anymore. But Nathaniel *can.*'

'You want your son to grow up without you?' Caleb's voice breaks. 'Let me save you the trouble.'

Standing abruptly, he leaves the bedroom, calling Nathaniel's name. 'Hey, buddy,' I hear him say. 'We're going on an adventure.'

My hands and feet go numb. But I manage to get to Nathaniel's bedroom, and find Caleb haphazardly stuffing clothes into a Batman knapsack. 'What . . . what are you doing?'

'What does it look like I'm doing?' Caleb replies, an echo of my own earlier words.

Nathaniel jumps up and down on his bed. His hair flies to the sides like silk. 'You can't take him away from me.'

Caleb zips shut the bag. 'Why not? You were willing to take yourself away from him.' He turns to Nathaniel, forces a smile. 'You ready?' he asks, and Nathaniel leaps into his outstretched arm.

'Bye, Mommy!' he crows. 'We're on an adventure!'

'I know.' Smiling is hard, with this knot in my throat. 'I heard.'

Caleb carries him past me. There is the thunder of footsteps on the stairs, and the definitive slam of a door. The engine of Caleb's truck, revving and reversing down the driveway. Then it is so quiet I can hear my own misgivings, small susurrations in the air around me.

I sink onto Nathaniel's bed, into sheets that smell of crayons and gingerbread. The fact of the matter is, I cannot leave this house. The moment I do, police cars will come screaming up behind me. I will be arrested before I ever board a plane.

Caleb has succeeded; he's stopped me from doing what I so badly want to.

Because he knows if I do walk out that door now, I won't go after Arthur Gwynne at all. I'll be searching for my son.

Three days later Caleb has not called me. I have tried every hotel and motel in the area, but if he is staying at one, it's not under his own name. It's Christmas Eve, though, and surely they will come back. Caleb is a big one for having holiday traditions, and to this end I have wrapped all of Nathaniel's Christmas presents – ones I've stored in the attic all year. From the dwindling supply of food in the refrigerator I have cooked a chicken and made celery soup; I have set the table with our fancy wedding china.

I have cleaned up, too, because I want Caleb to notice that the moment he walks through the door. Maybe if he sees a difference on the outside, he will understand that I'm different within, too. My hair is coiled into a French twist, and I'm wearing black velvet pants and a red blouse. In my ears are the present Nathaniel gave me last Christmas – little snowman earrings made from Sculpy clay.

And yet, this is all just a surface glaze. My eyes are ringed with circles – I have not slept since they left, as if this is some kind of cosmic punishment for dozing away the days when we were all together. I walk the halls at night, trying to find the spots in the carpet that have been worn down by Nathaniel's running feet. I stare at old photographs. I haunt my own home.

We have no tree, because I wasn't able to go out to chop one down. It's a tradition for us to walk our property the Saturday before Christmas and pick one out as a family. But then, we have not been much of a family this holiday season.

By four P.M. I've lit candles and put on a Christmas CD. I sit with my hands folded in my lap and wait.

It's something I'm working on.

At four-thirty, it begins to snow. I rearrange all of Nathaniel's presents in size order. I wonder if there will be enough of an accumulation for him to sled down the back hill on the Flexible Flyer that stands propped against the wall, festooned with a bow.

Ten minutes later, I hear the heavy chug of a truck coming down the driveway. I leap to my feet, take one last nervous look around, and throw open the door with a bright smile. The UPS man, weary and dusted with snowflakes, stands on my porch with a package. 'Nina Frost?' he asks in a monotone.

I take the parcel as he wishes me a Merry Christmas. Inside, on the couch, I tear it open. A leather-bound desk calendar for the year 2002, stamped on the inner cover with the name of Fisher's law office. HAPPY HOLIDAYS *from Carrington, Whitcomb, Horoby, and Platt, Esqs.* 'This will come in so handy,' I say aloud, 'after I'm sentenced.'

When the stars shyly push through the night sky, I turn off the stereo. I look out the window, watch the driveway get erased by snow.


Even before Patrick got his divorce, he'd sign up to work on Christmas. Sometimes, he even does double shifts. The calls most often bring him to the homes of the elderly, reporting a strange bump or a suspicious car that's disappeared by the time Patrick arrives. What these people want is the company on a night when no one else is alone.

'Merry Christmas,' he says, backing away from the home of Maisie Jenkins, eighty-two years old, a recent widow.

'God bless,' she calls back, and goes into a home as empty as the one that Patrick is about to return to.

He could go visit Nina, but surely Caleb has brought Nathaniel back for the night. No, Patrick wouldn't interrupt that. Instead he gets into his car and drives down the slick streets of Biddeford. Christmas lights glitter like jewels on porches, inside windows, as if the world has been strewn with an embarrassment of riches. Cruising slowly, he imagines children asleep. What the hell are sugar plums, anyway?

Suddenly, a bright blur barrels across the range of Patrick's headlights, and he brakes hard. He steers into the skid and avoids hitting the person who's run across the road. Getting out of the car, he rushes to the side of the fallen man. 'Sir,' Patrick asks, 'are you all right?'

The man rolls over. He is dressed in a Santa suit, and alcohol fumes rise from his phony cotton beard. 'St. Nick, to you, boyo. Get it straight.'

Patrick helps him sit up. 'Did you hurt anything?'

'Lay off.' Santa struggles away from him. 'I could sue you.'

'For *not* hitting you? I doubt it.'

'Reckless operation of a vehicle. You're probably drunk.'

At that, Patrick laughs. 'As opposed to you?'

'I haven't had a drop!'

'Okay, Santa.' Patrick hauls him to his feet. 'You got somewhere to call home?'

'I gotta get my sleigh.'

'Sure you do.' With a bracing arm, he steers the man toward his cruiser.

'The reindeer, they chew up the shingles if I leave them too long.'

'Of course.'

'I'm not getting in there. I'm not finished yet, you know.'

Patrick opens the rear door. 'I'll take the chance, Pop. Go on. I'll take you down to a nice warm bunk to sleep this off.'

Santa shakes his head. 'My old lady'll kill me.'

'Mrs. Claus will get over it.'

His smile fades as he looks at Patrick. 'C'mon, officer. Cut me a little slack. You know what it's like to go home to a woman you love, who just wishes you'd stay the hell away?'

Patrick ducks him into the car, with maybe a little too much force. No, he doesn't know what it's like. He can't get past the first part of that sentence: *You know what it's like to go home to a woman you love?*

By the time he gets to the station, Santa is unconscious, and has to be hauled into the building by Patrick and the desk officer. Patrick punches out on the clock, gets into his own truck. But instead of driving home, he heads in the opposite direction, past Nina's house. Just to make sure everything's all right. It is something he has not done with regularity since the year he returned to Biddeford, when Nina and Caleb were already married. He would drive by on the graveyard shift and see all the lights out, save the one in their bedroom. An extra dose of security, or so he told himself back then.

Years later, he still doesn't believe it.

It is supposed to be a big deal, Nathaniel knows. Not only does he get to stay up extra late on Christmas Eve, but he can open as many presents as he wants, which is all of them. And they're staying in a real live old castle, in a whole new country called Canada.

Their room at this castle-hotel has a fireplace in it, and a bird that looks real but is dead. Stuffed, that's what his father called it, and maybe it did look like it had eaten too much, although Nathaniel doesn't think you can die from that. There are two huge beds and the kinds of pillows that squinch when you lie on them, instead of popping right back.

Everyone talks a different language, one Nathaniel doesn't understand, and that makes him think of his mother.

He has opened a remote-control truck, a stuffed kangaroo, a helicopter. Matchbox cars in so many colors it makes him dizzy. Two computer games and a tiny pinball machine he can hold in his hand. The room is littered with wrapping paper, which his father is busy feeding into the mouth of the fire.

'That's some haul,' he muses, smiling at Nathaniel.

His father has been letting Nathaniel call the shots. To that end, they got to play at a fort the whole day, and ride up and down a cable car, the funsomething, Nathaniel forgets. They went to a restaurant with a big moose head mounted outside and Nathaniel got to order five desserts. They went back to the room and opened their presents, saving their stockings for tomorrow. They have done everything Nathaniel has asked, which never happens when he is at home.

'So,' his father says. 'What's next?'

But all Nathaniel wants to do is make it the way it used to be.

The doorbell rings at eleven, and it's a Christmas tree. Then Patrick's face pokes through the branches, from behind the enormous balsam. 'Hi,' he says.

My face feels rubbery, this smile strange upon it. 'Hi.'

'I brought you a tree.'

'I noticed.' Stepping back, I let him into the house. He props the tree against the wall, needles raining down around our feet. 'Caleb's truck isn't here.'

'Neither's Caleb. Or Nathaniel.'

Patrick's eyes darken. 'Oh, Nina. Christ, I'm sorry.'

'Don't be.' I give him my best grin. 'I have a tree now. And someone to help me eat Christmas Eve dinner.'

'Why, Miz Maurier, I'd be delighted.' At the same moment, we realize Patrick's mistake – calling me by my maiden name, the name by which he first knew me. But neither one of us bothers to make the correction.

'Come on in. I'll get the food out of the fridge.'

'In a second.' He runs out to his car, and returns with several Wal-Mart shopping bags. Some are tied with ribbons. 'Merry Christmas.' An afterthought, he leans forward and kisses me on the cheek.

'You smell like bourbon.'

'That would be Santa,' Patrick says. 'I had the unparalleled pleasure of sticking St. Nick in a cell to sleep off a good drunk.' As he talks, he starts unpacking the bags. Cracker Jacks, Cheetos, Chex Mix. Non-alcoholic champagne. 'There wasn't much open,' he apologizes.

Picking up the fake champagne, I turn it over in my hands. 'Not even gonna let me get trashed, huh?'

'Not if it gets you busted.' Patrick meets my gaze. 'You know the rules, Nina.'

And because he has always known what is right for me, I

follow him into the living room, where we set up the tree in the empty stand. We light a fire, and then hang ornaments from boxes I keep tucked in the attic. 'I remember this one,' Patrick says, pulling out a delicate glass teardrop with a figurine inside. 'There used to be two.'

'And then you sat on one.'

'I thought your mother was going to kill me.'

'I think she would have, but you were already bleeding –'

Patrick bursts out laughing. 'And you kept pointing at me, and saying, "He's cut on the butt."' He hangs the teardrop on the tree, at chest level. 'I'll have you know, there's still a scar.'

'Yeah, right.'

'Wanna see?'

He is joking, his eyes sparkling. But all the same, I have to pretend I am busy with something else.

When we are finished, we sit down on the couch and eat cold chicken and Chex Mix. Our shoulders brush, and I remember how we used to fall asleep on the floating dock in the town swimming pond, the sun beating down on our faces and chests and heating our skin to the same exact temperature. Patrick puts the other Wal-Mart bags beneath the tree. 'You have to promise me you'll wait till the morning to open them.'

It strikes me then; he is going.

'But the snow . . .'

He shrugs. 'Four-wheel drive. I'll be fine.'

I twirl my glass, so that the fake champagne swirls inside. 'Please,' I say, that's all. It was bad enough, before. Now that Patrick's been here, his voice filling the living room, his body spanning the space beside mine, it will seem that much emptier when he leaves.

'It's already tomorrow.' Patrick points to the clock: 12:14 A.M. 'Merry Christmas.' He pushes one of the plastic bags into my lap.

'But I haven't gotten you anything.' I do not say what I am thinking: that in all the years since Patrick has returned to

Biddeford, he has not given me a Christmas gift. He brings presents for Nathaniel, but there is an unspoken agreement between us – anything more would be tightrope-walking on a line of propriety.

'Just open it.'

Inside the first Wal-Mart bag is a pup tent. Inside the second, a flashlight and a brand-new game of Clue. A smile darts across Patrick's face. 'Now's your chance to beat me, not that you can.'

Delighted, I grin right back. 'I'm going to whip you.' We pull the tent out of its protective pouch and erect it in front of the Christmas tree. There is barely room enough for two, and yet we both crawl inside. 'Tents have gotten smaller, I think.'

'No, we've gotten bigger.' Patrick sets up the game board between our crossed legs. 'I'm even going to let you go first.'

'You're a prince among men,' I say, and we start to play. Each roll of the die reverses a year, until it is easy to imagine that the snow outside is a field of Queen Anne's lace; that this tournament is life-or-death; that the world is no larger than Patrick and me and a backyard campsite. Our knees bump hard and our laughter fills the tiny vinyl pyramid. The winking strand on the Christmas tree, out there, might be lightning bugs. The flames behind us, a bonfire. Patrick takes me back, and that is the best present I could ever receive.

He wins, by the way. It is Miss Scarlett, in the library, with the wrench.

'I demand a rematch,' I announce.

Patrick has to catch his breath; he's laughing that hard. 'How many years did you go to college?'

'Shut up, Patrick, and start over.'

'No way. I'm quitting while I'm ahead. By – what is it? – three hundred games?'

I grab for his game piece, but he holds it out of my reach. 'You're such a pain in the ass,' I say.

'And you're a sore loser.' He jerks his hand higher, and in

an effort to reach it, I knock the board sideways and overturn the tent as well. We go down in a tumble of vinyl and Clue cards and land on our sides, cramped and tangled. 'Next time I buy you a tent,' Patrick says, smiling, 'I'm springing for the next size up.'

My hand falls onto his cheek, and he goes absolutely still. His pale eyes fix on mine, a dare. 'Patrick,' I whisper. 'Merry Christmas.' And I kiss him.

Almost as quickly he jerks away from me. I can't even look at him, now. I cannot believe that I have done this. But then his hand curves around my jaw, and he kisses me back as if he is pouring his soul into me. We bump teeth and noses, we scratch and we scrape, and through this we do not break apart. The ASL sign for friends: two index fingers, locked at the first knuckles.

Somehow we fall out of the tent. The fire is hot on the right side of my face, and Patrick's fingers are wrapped in my hair. This is bad, I know this is bad, but there is a place in me for him. It feels like he was first, before anyone else. And I think, not for the first time, that what is immoral is not always wrong.

Drawing back on my elbows, I stare down at him. 'Why did you get divorced?'

'Why do you think?' he answers softly.

I unbutton my blouse and then, blushing, pull it together again. Patrick covers my hands with his own and slides the sheer sleeves down. Then he pulls off his shirt, and I touch my fingers lightly to his chest, traveling a landscape that is not Caleb.

'Don't let him in,' Patrick begs, because he has always been able to think my thoughts. I kiss across his nipples, down the arrow of black hair that disappears beneath his trousers. My hands work at the belt, until I am holding him in my hands. Shifting lower, I take him into my mouth.

In an instant he has yanked me up by the hair, crushed me to his chest. His heart is beating so fast, a summons. 'Sorry,' he breathes into my shoulder. 'Too much. All of you, it's too much.'

After a moment, he tastes his way down me. I try not to think of my soft belly, my stretch marks, my flaws. These are the things you do not have to worry about, in a marriage. 'I'm not . . . you know.'

'You're not what?' His words are a puff of breath between my legs.

'*Patrick.*' I yank at his hair. But his finger slides inside, and I am falling. He rises over me, holds me close, fits. We move as if we have been doing this forever. Then Patrick rears back, pulls out, and comes between us.

It binds us, skin to skin, a viscous guilt.

'I couldn't –'

'I know.' I touch my fingers to his lips.

'Nina.' His eyes drift shut. 'I love you.'

'I know that too.' That is all I can allow myself to say, now. I touch the slope of his shoulders, the line of his spine. I try to commit this to memory.

'Nina.' Patrick hides a grin in the hollow of my neck. 'I'm still better at Clue.'

He falls asleep in my embrace, and I watch him. That's when I tell him what I cannot manage to tell anyone else. I make a fist, the letter *S*, and move it in a circle over his heart. It is the truest way I know to say I'm sorry.

Patrick wakes up when the sun is a live wire at the line of the horizon. He touches his hand to Nina's shoulder, and then to his own chest, just to make sure this is real. He lies back, stares into the glowing coals of the fireplace, and tries to wish away morning.

But it will come, and with it, all the explanations. And in spite of the fact that he knows Nina better than she knows herself, he is not sure which excuse she will choose. She has made a living out of judging people's misdeeds. Yet no matter what argument she uses, it will all sound the same to him: *This should not have happened; this was a mistake.*

There is only one thing Patrick wants to hear on her lips, and that is his own name.

Anything else – well, it would just chip away at this, and Patrick wants to hold the night intact. So he gently slides his arm out from beneath the sweet weight of Nina's head. He kisses her temple, he breathes deeply of her. He lets go of her, before she has a chance to let go of him.

The tent, standing upright, is the first thing I see. The second is the absence of Patrick. Sometime during that incredible, deep sleep, he left me.

It is probably better this way.

By the time I've cleaned up our feast from the previous night and showered, I have nearly convinced myself that this is true. But I cannot imagine seeing Patrick again without picturing him leaning over me, his black hair brushing my face. And I don't think that the peace inside me, spread like honey in my blood, can be chalked up to Christmas.

*Forgive me Father, for I have sinned.*

But have I? Does Fate ever play by the rules? There is a gulf as wide as an ocean between *should* and *want*, and I am drowning in it.

The doorbell rings, and I jump up from the couch, hurriedly wiping my eyes. Patrick, maybe back with coffee, or bagels. If *he* makes the choice to return, I'm absolved of blame. Even if it was what I was wishing for all along.

But when I open the door, Caleb is standing on the porch, with Nathaniel in front of him. My son's smile is brighter than the dazzle of snow on the driveway, and for one panicked moment I peer over Caleb's shoulder to see whether the tracks made by Patrick's police cruiser have been covered over by the storm. Can you smell transgression, like a perfume deep in the skin? 'Mommy!' Nathaniel shouts.

I lift him high, revel in the straight weight of him. My heart beats like a hummingbird in my throat. 'Caleb.'

He will not look at me. 'I'm not staying.'

This is a mercy visit, then. In minutes, Nathaniel will be gone. I hug him closer.

'Merry Christmas, Nina,' Caleb says. 'I'll pick him up tomorrow.' He nods at me, then walks off the porch. Nathaniel chatters, his excitement wrapping us tighter as the truck pulls away. I study the footprints Caleb has left in the snowy driveway as if they are clues, the unlikely proof of a ghost that comes and goes.

# III

Our virtues are most frequently but vices disguised.

– François, Duc de La Rochefoucauld

*Today in school Miss Lydia gave us a special snack.*

*First, we had a piece of lettuce with a raisin on it. This was an egg.*

*Then we had a string cheese caterpillar.*

*Next came a chrysalis, a grape.*

*The last part was a piece of cinnamon bread, cookie-cuttered into the body of a butterfly.*

*After, we went outside and set free the monarchs that had been born in our classroom. One landed on my wrist. It looked different now, but I just knew this was the same caterpillar I found a week before and gave to Miss Lydia. Then it flew into the sun.*

*Sometimes things change so fast it makes my throat hurt from the inside out.*

# 7

When I was four I found a caterpillar on my bedroom windowsill and decided to save its life. I made my mother take me to the library so that I could look it up in a Field guide. I punched pinholes in the top of a jar; I gave it grass and leaves and a tiny thimbleful of water. My mother said that if I didn't let the caterpillar go, it would die, but I was convinced I knew better. Out in the world, it could be run over by a truck. It could be scorched by the sun. My protection would stack the odds.

I changed its food and water religiously. I sang to it when the sun went down. And on the third day, in spite of my best intentions, that caterpillar died.

Years later, it is happening all over again.

'No,' I tell Fisher. We have stopped walking; the cold January air is a cobra charmed up the folds of my coat. I thrust the paper back at him, as if holding my son's name out of sight might keep it from being on the witness list at all.

'Nina, it's not your decision,' he says gently. 'Nathaniel's going to have to testify.'

'Quentin Brown's just doing this to get to me. He wants me to watch Nathaniel have a relapse in court so maybe I'll snap again, this time in front of a judge *and* a jury.' Tears freeze on the tips of my eyelashes. I want it over, *now*. It was why I had murdered a man – because I thought that would stop this boulder from rolling on and on; because if the defendant was gone then my son would not have to sit on a witness stand and recount the worst thing that had ever happened to him. I wanted Nathaniel to be able to close this godawful chapter and so, ironically, I *didn't*.

But even this great sacrifice – of the priest's life, of my own future – has not done what it was supposed to.

Nathaniel and Caleb have kept their distance since Christmas, but every few days Caleb brings him to the house to spend a few hours with me. I don't know how Caleb has explained our living arrangements to Nathaniel. Maybe he says I am too sick to take care of a child, or too sad; and maybe either of these are true. One thing is certain – it is not in Nathaniel's best interests to watch me plan for my own punishment. There is already too much he's witnessed.

I know the name of the motel where they are staying, and sometimes, when I feel particularly courageous, I call. But Caleb always answers the phone, and either we have nothing to say to each other, or there are so many words clogging the wires between us that none of them fall forward.

Nathaniel, though, is doing well. When he comes to the house, he is smiling. He sings songs for me that Miss Lydia has taught the class. He no longer jumps when you come up behind him and touch his shoulder.

All of this progress, and it will be erased at a competency hearing.

In the park behind us, a toddler lies on his back making a snow angel. The problem with one of those is that you have to ruin it when you stand up. No matter what, there is always a footprint binding you to the ground. 'Fisher,' I say simply, 'I'm going to jail.'

'You don't –'

'Fisher. Please.' I touch his arm. 'I can handle that. I even believe that it's what I deserve, because of what I did. But I killed a man for one reason and one reason only – to keep Nathaniel from being hurt any more. I don't want him to think about what happened to him ever again. If Quentin wants to punish someone, he can punish me. But Nathaniel, he's off limits.'

He sighs. 'Nina, I'll do the best I can –'

'You don't understand,' I interrupt. 'That's not good enough.'

*            *            *

Because Judge Neal hails from Portland, he doesn't have chambers at the Alfred Superior Court, so he's been given another judge's lair to borrow for the duration of my trial. Judge McIntyre, however, spends his free time hunting. To this end, the small room is decorated with the heads of moose and ten-point bucks, prey that has lost the battle. *And me?* I think. *Will I be next?*

Fisher has filed a motion, and the resulting meeting is being held in private chambers to prevent the media from getting involved. 'Judge, this is so outrageous,' he says, 'that I can't begin to express my absolute chagrin. The state has Father Szyszynski's death on videotape. What possible need do they have for this child to testify to anything?'

'Mr. Brown?' the judge prompts.

'Your Honor, the alleged rationale for the murder was the boy's psychiatric condition at the time, and the fact that the defendant believed her son had been the victim of molestation at the hands of Father Szyszynski. The state has learned that, in fact, this is not the truth. It's important that the jury get to hear what Nathaniel actually told his mother before she went out and killed this man.'

The judge shakes his head. 'Mr. Carrington, it's going to be very difficult for me to quash a subpoena if the state alleges they can make it relevant. Now, once we're in trial, I may be able to rule that it's not relevant at all – but as it stands now, this witness's testimony goes to motive.'

Fisher tries once again. 'If the state will submit a written allegation of what they believe the child's testimony to be, maybe we can stipulate to it, so that Nathaniel doesn't have to take the stand.'

'Mr. Brown, that seems reasonable,' the judge says.

'I disagree. Having this witness, in the flesh, is critical to my case.'

There is a moment of surprised silence. 'Think twice, counselor,' Judge Neal urges.

'I have, Your Honor, believe me.'

Fisher looks at me, and I know exactly what he is about to do. His eyes are dark with sympathy, but he waits for me to nod before he turns to the judge again. 'Judge, if the state is going to be this inflexible, then we need a competency hearing. We're talking about a child who's been rendered mute twice in the past six weeks.'

The judge will leap at this compromise, I know. I also know that of all the defense attorneys I've seen in action, Fisher is one of the most compassionate toward children during competency hearings. But he won't be, not this time. Because the best-case scenario, now, is to get the judge to declare Nathaniel not competent, so that he will not have to suffer through a whole trial. And the only way Fisher can do that is to actively try to make Nathaniel fall to pieces.

Fisher has kept it to himself, but his personal opinion is that art is beginning to imitate life. That is, his insanity defense for Nina – a complete fabrication at first – is starting to hit quite close to the mark. To keep her from dissolving after the motions hearing this morning, he took her out to lunch in a swanky restaurant, a place where she was less likely to have a breakdown. He had her tell him all the questions the prosecutor would ask Nathaniel on the stand, questions she'd asked child witnesses a thousand times.

The courthouse is dark now, empty except for the custodial staff, Caleb, Nathaniel, and Fisher. They move down the hall quietly, Nathaniel clutched in his father's arms.

'He's a little nervous,' Caleb says, clearing his throat.

Fisher ignores the comment. He might as well be walking a tightrope ten thousand feet above the ground. The last thing he wants to do is deal harshly with the boy; but then again, if he's too solicitous, Nathaniel might feel comfortable enough at the hearing to be declared competent to stand trial. Either way, Nina will have his head.

Inside the court, Fisher switches on the overhead lights. They hiss, then flood the room with a garish brilliance. Nathaniel burrows closer to his father, his face pressed into the big man's shoulder. Where is a roll of Tums when you need it?

'Nathaniel,' Fisher says tersely, 'I need you to go sit in that chair. Your father is going to be in the back. He can't say anything to you, and you can't say anything to him. You just have to answer my questions. You understand?'

The boy's eyes are as wide as the night. He follows Fisher to the witness stand, then scrambles onto the stool that has been placed inside. 'Get down for a second.' Fisher reaches inside and takes out the stool, replacing it with a low chair. Now, Nathaniel's brow does not even clear the lip of the witness stand.

'I . . . I can't see anything,' Nathaniel whispers.

'You don't need to.'

Fisher is about to begin asking practice questions when a sound distracts him – Caleb, methodically gathering every high stool in the courtroom, corralling them near the double doors. 'I thought maybe these might be . . . better off somewhere else. So they're not around first thing in the morning.' He meets Fisher's gaze.

The attorney nods. 'The closet. One of the janitors can lock them up.'

When he turns back to the boy, he has to work to keep a smile off his face.

Now Nathaniel knows why Mason always tries to pull out of his collar – this thing called a tie that doesn't have a bow in it at all is choking his neck. He tugs at it again, only to have his father grab his hand. There are flutters in his stomach, and he'd rather be at school. Here, everyone is going to be staring at him. Here, everyone wants him to talk about things he doesn't like to say.

Nathaniel clutches Franklin, his stuffed turtle, more tightly. The closed doors of the courtroom sigh open, and a man who looks like a policeman but isn't one waves them inside. Nathaniel moves hesitantly down the rolled red tongue of carpet. The room is not as spooky as it was last night in the dark, but he still has the feeling that he is walking into the belly of a whale. His heart begins to tap as fast as rain on a windshield, and he holds his hand up to his chest to keep everyone else from hearing, too.

His mommy is sitting in the front row. Her eyes are puffy, and before she sees him standing there she wipes them with her fingers. It makes Nathaniel think of all the other times she's pretended she isn't crying, says it with a smile, even though there are tears right on her cheeks.

There is a big man in the front of the room too, with skin the color of chestnuts. It is the same man who was in the supermarket; who made his mother get taken away. His mouth looks like it has been sewn shut.

The Lawyer sitting next to his mother gets up and walks toward Nathaniel. He does not like the Lawyer. Every time the Lawyer comes to his house, his parents have yelled at each other. And last night, when Nathaniel had been brought here to practice, the Lawyer was downright mean.

Now, he puts his hand on Nathaniel's shoulder. 'Nathaniel, I know you're worried about your mommy. I am, too. I want her to be happy again, but there is someone here who doesn't like your mommy. His name is Mr. Brown. Do you see him over there? The tall man?' Nathaniel nods. 'He's going to ask you some questions. I can't stop him from doing that. But when you answer them, remember – I'm here to help your mommy. He isn't.'

Then he walks Nathaniel to the front of the courtroom. There are more people there than last night – a man wearing a black dress and holding a hammer; another person with hair that stands straight up on his head in little curls; a lady with a typewriter. His mom. And the big man who doesn't like her. They walk to the little fence-box where Nathaniel had to sit before. He crawls onto the chair that is too low, then folds his hands in his lap.

The man in the black dress speaks. 'Can we get a higher seat for this child?'

Everyone starts looking left and right. The almost-policeman says what everyone else can see: 'There don't seem to be any around.'

'What do you mean? We always have extra stools for child witnesses.'

'Well, I could go to Judge Shea's courtroom to see if he has any, but there won't be anybody here to watch the defendant, Your Honor.'

The man in the dress sighs, then hands Nathaniel a fat book. 'Why don't you sit on my Bible, Nathaniel?'

He does, wiggling a little, because his bum keeps sliding off. The curly man walks up to him with a smile. 'Hi, Nathaniel,' he says.

Nathaniel doesn't know if he is supposed to talk yet.

'I need you to put your hand on the Bible for me.'

'But I'm sitting on it.'

The man takes out another Bible, and holds it in front of Nathaniel like a table. 'Raise your right hand,' he says, and Nathaniel lifts one arm into the air. 'Your other right hand,' the man corrects. 'Do you swear to tell the truth, the whole truth, and nothing but the truth, so help you God?'

Nathaniel vehemently shakes his head.

'Is there a problem?' This from the man in the black dress.

'I'm not supposed to swear,' he whispers.

His mommy smiles, then, and hiccups out a laugh. Nathaniel thinks it is the prettiest sound he has ever heard.

'Nathaniel, I'm Judge Neal. I need you to answer some questions for me today. Do you think you can do that?'

He shrugs.

'Do you know what a promise is?' When Nathaniel nods, the judge points to the lady who is typing. 'I need you to speak out, because that woman is writing down everything we say, and she has to hear you. You think you can talk nice and loud for her?'

Nathaniel leans forward. And at the top of his lungs, yells, '*Yes!*'

'Do you know what a promise is?'

'*Yes!*'

'Do you think you can promise to answer some questions today?'

'*Yes!*'

The judge leans back, wincing a little. 'This is Mr. Brown, Nathaniel, and he's going to talk to you first.'

Nathaniel looks at the big man, who stands up and smiles. He has white, white teeth. Like a wolf. He is nearly as tall as the ceiling and Nathaniel takes one look at him coming closer and thinks of him hurting his mother and then turning around and biting Nathaniel himself in two.

He takes a deep breath, and bursts into tears.

The man stops in his tracks, like he's lost his balance. 'Go away!' Nathaniel shouts. He draws up his knees, and buries his face in them.

'Nathaniel.' Mr. Brown comes forward slowly, holding out his hand. 'I just need to ask you a couple of questions. Is that okay?'

Nathaniel shakes his head, but he won't look up. Maybe the big man has laser eyes too, like Cyclops from the X-Men. Maybe he can freeze them with one glance and with the next, make them burst into fire.

'What's your turtle's name?' the big man asks.

Nathaniel buries Franklin under his knees, so that he won't have to see the man either. He covers his face with his hands and peeks out, but the man has gotten even closer and this makes Nathaniel turn sideways in the chair, as if he might slip through the slats on the back side of it.

'Nathaniel,' the man tries again.

'No,' Nathaniel sobs. 'I don't want to!'

The man turns away. 'Judge. May we approach?'

Nathaniel peers over the lip of the box he is sitting in and sees his mother. She's crying too, but then that makes sense. The man wants to hurt her. She must be just as scared of him as Nathaniel is.

         ★         ★         ★

Fisher has told me not to cry, because I will get kicked out of the room. But I can't control myself – the tears come as naturally as a blush or a breath. Nathaniel burrows into the wooden chair, all but hidden by the frame of the witness stand. Fisher and Brown walk toward the bench, where the judge is angry enough to be spitting sparks. 'Mr. Brown,' he says. 'I can't believe you insisted on taking this so far. You know very well you didn't need this testimony, and I'm not going to allow psychological mind games to be played in my courtroom. Don't even think about making an argument to revisit this.'

'You're right, Judge,' answers that bastard. 'I asked to approach because clearly this child should not have to testify.'

The judge raps his gavel. 'This court rules that Nathaniel Frost is not competent to stand trial. The subpoena is quashed.' He turns to my son. 'Nathaniel, you can go on down to your dad.'

Nathaniel bolts out of the chair and down the steps. I think he is going to run to Caleb, in the back of the courtroom – but instead he rushes straight to me. The force of his body sends my chair scooting back a few inches. Nathaniel wraps his arms around my waist, squeezing free the breath I have not even noticed I am holding.

I wait until Nathaniel glances up, terrified by the faces in this foreign world – the clerk, the judge, the stenographer, and the prosecutor. 'Nathaniel,' I tell him fiercely, drawing his attention. 'You were the best witness I could have had.'

Over his head, I catch Quentin Brown's eye. And smile.

When Patrick met Nathaniel Frost, the child was six months old. Patrick's first thought was that he looked just like Nina. His second thought was that, right here, in his arms, was the reason they would never be together.

Patrick made an extra effort to get close to Nathaniel, even though sometimes it was painful enough to make him ache for days after a visit. He'd bring Weed little dolphins to float in the bathtub; Silly Putty; sparklers. For years Patrick had wanted to get under Nina's skin; Nathaniel, who'd grown below her heart, surely had something to teach him. So he tagged along on hikes, swapping off with Caleb to carry Nathaniel when his legs got tired. He let Nathaniel spin in his desk chair at the station. He even baby-sat for a whole weekend, when Caleb and Nina went away for a relative's wedding.

And somewhere along the way, Patrick – who'd loved Nina forever – fell just as hard for her son.

The clock hasn't moved in two hours, Patrick would swear to that. Right now, Nathaniel is undergoing his competency hearing – a procedure Patrick couldn't watch, even if he wanted to. And he doesn't. Because Nina will be there too, and he hasn't seen or spoken to her since Christmas Eve.

It's not that he doesn't want to. God, he can't seem to think of anything but Nina – the feel of her, the taste of her, the way her body relaxed against his in her sleep. But right now, the memory is crystallized for Patrick. Any words that come between them, aftershocks, are only going to take away from that. And it isn't what Nina would say to him that worries Patrick – it's what she *wouldn't* say. That she loves him, that she needs him, that this meant as much to her as it did to him.

He rests his head in his hands. Deep inside, there is a part of him that also knows this was a grave error. Patrick wants to get this off his chest, to confess his doubts to someone who would understand implicitly. But his confidante, his best friend, is Nina. If she cannot be that anymore . . . and she cannot be *his* . . . where does that leave them?

With a deep sigh he grabs the phone from his desk and dials an out-of-state number. He wants resolution, a present to give to Nina before he has to take the stand and testify against her. Farnsworth McGee, the police chief in Belle Chasse, Louisiana, answers on the third ring. 'Hello?' he drawls, extending the word an extra syllable.

'It's Detective-Lieutenant Ducharme, from Biddeford, Maine,' Patrick says. 'What's the latest on Gwynne?'

Patrick can easily envision the chief, with whom he'd met

before leaving Belle Chasse. Overweight by a good fifty pounds, with a shock of Elvis-black hair. A fishing rod propped up in the corner behind his desk; a bumper sticker tacked to the bulletin board: HELL, YES, MY NECK'S RED. 'Y'all got to understand that we move carefully in our jurisdiction. Don't want no hasty mishaps, if you understand my meaning.'

Patrick grits his teeth. 'Did you arrest him yet or not?'

'Your authorities are still talkin' to our authorities, Detective. Believe me, you'll be the first to know when something happens.'

He slams down the phone – angry at the idiot deputy, angry at Gwynne, angriest at himself for not taking matters into his own hands when he was in Louisiana. But he couldn't make himself forget that he was a law enforcement officer, that he was obligated to uphold certain rules. That Nina had said *no*, even if it was what she really wanted.

Patrick stares at the phone in its cradle. Then again, it is always possible to reinvent oneself. Particularly in the image of a hero.

He's seen Nina do it, after all.

After a moment, Patrick grabs his jacket and walks out of the station, intent on effecting change, rather than waiting for it to steamroll him.

It has turned out to be the best day of my life. First, Nathaniel was ruled not competent. Then Caleb asked me to watch Nathaniel after the hearing, and overnight, because he is scheduled to do a job up near the Canadian border. 'Do you mind?' he'd politely said, and I couldn't even form an answer, I was so delighted. I have visions of Nathaniel standing beside me in the kitchen while we cook his favorite dinner; I imagine watching his Shrek video twice in a row with a bowl of popcorn bridged between us.

But in the end, Nathaniel is exhausted from the events of the day. He falls asleep on the couch by six-thirty P.M. and doesn't wake when I carry him upstairs. In his bed, his hand unfurls on the pillow, as if he is offering me a hidden gift.

When Nathaniel was born, he waved tight fists in the air, as if he were angry at the world. They softened moment by moment, until I would nurse him and watch his fingers scrabble at my skin, clutching for purchase. I was mesmerized by that grasp, because of all its potential. Would Nathaniel grow up to wield a pencil or a gun? Would he heal with his touch? Create music? Would his palm be covered with calluses? Ink? Sometimes I would separate the tiny fingers and trace the lines of his palm, as if I could truly read his future.

If Nathaniel had been difficult to conceive in the wake of my cyst surgery, he'd been a positively horrendous delivery. Thirty-six hours of labor rendered me trancelike. Caleb sat on the edge of the bed watching a *Gilligan's Island* marathon on the hospital TV, something that seemed equally as painful as my contractions. 'We'll name her Ginger,' he vowed. 'MaryAnn.'

The vise inside me ratcheted tighter every hour, until agony became a black hole, each pain pulling in another. Over my head Gilligan voted for a chimp as beauty pageant queen, so that he wouldn't offend any of the stranded ladies. Caleb got behind me, propping up my back when I couldn't even find the energy to open my eyes. 'I can't,' I whispered. 'It's your turn.'

So he rubbed my spine and he sang. 'The weather started getting rough . . . the tiny ship was tossed . . . come *on*, Nina! If not for the courage of the fearless crew . . .'

'Remind me,' I said, 'to kill you later.'

But I forgot, because minutes afterward Nathaniel was born. Caleb held him up, a being so small he curled like an inchworm in my husband's hands. Not a Ginger or a MaryAnn, but a Little Buddy. In fact, that was what we called him for three days, before we decided on a name. Caleb wanted me to choose, since he refused to take credit for work that was nearly all mine. So I picked Nathaniel Patrick Frost, to honor my deceased father, and my oldest friend.

Now, it is hard to believe that the boy sleeping in front of me was ever so tiny. I touch my hand to his hair, feel it slip through my fingers like time. *I suffered once before,* I think. *And look at what I got in return.*

Quentin, who will cross a black cat's path without blinking and walk beneath ladders without breaking a sweat, is strangely superstitious about trials. On mornings that he's set to go to court, he gets fully dressed, eats breakfast, and then takes off his shirt and tie to shave. It's inefficient, of course, but it all goes back to his very first case, when he was so nervous he nearly walked out the door with a night's beard.

Would have, too, if Tanya hadn't called him back in.

He rubs the shaving lather on his cheeks and jaw, then drags the razor the length of his face. He's not nervous today. In spite of the deluge of media that's sure to flood the court, Quentin knows he has a strong case. Hell, he's got the defendant committing the crime on videotape. Nothing she or Fisher Carrington do will be able to erase that action from the eyes of the jury.

His first trial was a traffic ticket, which Quentin argued as if it were a capital murder. Tanya had brought Gideon; had been bouncing him on her hip in the back of the courtroom. Once he'd seen that, well, he had to put on a show.

'Damn!' Quentin jumps as he nicks his jaw. The shaving cream burns in the cut, and he scowls and presses a tissue to the spot. He has to hold it there for a couple of seconds until it clots, blood welling between his fingers. It makes him think of Nina Frost.

He wads up the tissue and sends it shooting across the bathroom, into the trash can. Quentin doesn't bother to watch his perfect shot. Quite simply, when you think you're incapable of missing, you don't.

This is what I have tried on so far: my black prosecutor's suit, the one that makes me look like Marcia Clark on a tear; the pale rose suit I wore to my cousin's wedding; the corduroy jumper Caleb got me one Christmas that still has the tags on it. I've tried slacks, but that's too mannish, and besides, I can't ever figure out whether you can wear loafers with slacks or if that comes off as too casual. I am angry at Fisher for not thinking of this – dressing me, the way defense attorneys dress prostitutes – in oversize clothes with ugly floral prints, garments handed down from the Salvation Army that never fail to make the women look slightly lost and impossibly young.

I know what to wear so that a jury believes I'm in control. I have no idea how to dress helpless.

The clock on the nightstand is suddenly fifteen minutes later than it should be.

I pull on the jumper. It's nearly two sizes too big – have I changed that much? Or did I never bother to try it on in the first place? I hike it up to my waist and pull on a pair of stockings, only to notice that they have a run in the left leg. I grab a second pair – but they are ripped too. 'Not today,' I say under my breath, yanking open my underwear drawer, where I keep a reserve pair of stockings for emergencies. Panties and bras spill like foam over the sides of the bureau and onto my bare feet while I search for the plastic packet.

But I used that spare pantyhose the day I killed Glen Szyszynski, and since I haven't been working since then, never thought to replace them.

'Goddammit!' I kick the leg of the dresser, but that only hurts my toes and brings tears to my eyes. I toss out the remaining contents of the drawer, yank the whole thing from its slot in the bureau and throw it across the room.

When my legs give out, I find myself sitting on the soft cloud of undergarments. I tuck my knees up under the skirt of my jumper, bury my face in my arms, and cry.


'Mommy was on TV last night,' Nathaniel says as they are driving to the courthouse in Caleb's truck. 'When you were in the shower.'

Lost in his own thoughts, Caleb nearly drives off the side of the road at this comment. 'You weren't supposed to be watching TV.'

Nathaniel hunches his shoulders, and immediately Caleb is sorry. So quickly, these days, he thinks he has done something wrong. 'It's all right,' Caleb says. He forces his attention to the road. In ten minutes, he'll be at the superior court. He can give Nathaniel to Monica in the children's playroom; maybe she'll have some better answers.

Nathaniel, however, isn't finished yet. He chews the words in his mouth for a bit, then spits them out in one great rush. 'How come Mommy yells at me when I pretend a stick is a gun but she was playing with one for real?'

Caleb turns to find his son staring up at him, expecting explanations. He puts on his signal and pulls the truck onto the shoulder of the road. 'Remember when you asked me why the sky was blue? And how we went to go look it up on the computer and there was so much science stuff there that neither of us could really understand it? Well, this is kind of the same thing. There's an answer, but it's really complicated.'

'The man on TV said what she did was wrong.' Nathaniel worries his bottom lip. 'That's why today she's gonna get yelled at, right?'

Oh, Christ, if only it could be that easy. Caleb smiles sadly. 'Yeah. That's why.'

He waits for Nathaniel to speak again, and when he doesn't, Caleb pulls the truck back into the line of traffic. He drives three miles, and then Nathaniel turns to him. 'Daddy? What's a *martyr?*'

'Where did you hear that?'

'The man, last night, on TV.'

Caleb takes a deep breath. 'It means your mother loves you, more than anything. And that's why she did what she did.'

Nathaniel fingers the seam of his seat belt, considering. 'Then why is it wrong?' he asks.

The parking lot is a sea of people: cameramen trying to get their reporters in their sights, producers adjusting the line feeds from their satellites, a group of militant Catholic women demanding Nina's judgment at the hands of the Lord. Patrick shoulders his way through the throngs, stunned to see national newscasters he recognizes by virtue of their celebrity.

An audible buzz sweeps the line of onlookers hovering around the courthouse steps. Then a car door slams, and suddenly Nina is hurrying up the stairs with Fisher's avuncular arm around her shoulders. A cheer goes up from the waiting crowd, along with an equally loud catcall of disapproval.

Patrick pushes closer to the steps. 'Nina!' he yells. 'Nina!'

He yanks his badge out, but brandishing it doesn't get him where he needs to be. 'Nina!' Patrick shouts again.

She seems to stumble, to look around. But Fisher grabs her arm and directs her into the courthouse before Patrick has the chance to make himself heard.

'Ladies and gentlemen, my name is Quentin Brown, and I'm an assistant attorney general for the state of Maine.' He smiles at the jury. 'The reason you're all here today is because on October thirtieth, 2001, this woman, Nina Frost, got up and drove with her husband to the Biddeford District Court to watch a man being arraigned. But she left her husband waiting there while she went to Moe's Gun Shop in Sanford, Maine – where she paid four hundred dollars cash for a Beretta nine-millimeter semiautomatic handgun and twelve rounds of ammunition. She tucked these in her purse, got back in her car, and returned to the courthouse.'

Quentin approaches the jury as if he has all the time in the world. 'Now, you all know, from coming in here today, that you had to pass through a security-screening device. But on October thirtieth, Nina Frost didn't. Why? Because she'd worked as a prosecutor for the past seven years. She knew the bailiff posted at the screening device. She walked by him without a backward glance, and she took that gun and the bullets she'd loaded into it, into a courtroom just like this one.'

He moves toward the defense table, coming up behind Nina

to point a finger at the base of her skull. 'A few minutes later she put that gun up to Father Glen Szyszynski's head and fired four rounds directly into his brain, killing him.'

Quentin surveys the jury; they are all staring at the defendant now, just like he wants. 'Ladies and gentlemen, the facts in this case are crystal clear. In fact, WCSH News, which was covering that morning's arraignment, caught Ms. Frost's actions on tape. So the question for you will not be *if* she committed this crime. We *know* that she did. The question will be: Why should she be allowed to get away with it?'

He stares into the eyes of each juror in sequence. 'She would like you to believe that the reason she should be held exempt from the law is because Father Szyszynski, her parish priest, had been charged with sexually molesting her five-year-old son. Yet she didn't even bother to make sure that this allegation was true. The state will show you scientifically, forensically, *conclusively*, that Father Szyszynski was not the man who abused her child . . . and still the defendant murdered him.'

Quentin turns his back on Nina Frost. 'In Maine, if a person unlawfully kills someone with premeditation, she is guilty of murder. During this trial, the state will prove to you beyond a reasonable doubt that this is exactly what Nina Frost did. It doesn't matter if the person who is murdered was accused of a crime. It doesn't matter if the person who was murdered was murdered by mistake. If the person was murdered, period, there needs to be punishment exacted.' He looks to the jury box. 'And that, ladies and gentlemen, is where you come in.'

Fisher only has eyes for that jury. He walks toward the box and meets each man's or woman's gaze, making a personal connection before he even speaks a word. It's what used to drive me crazy about him, when I faced him in a courtroom. He has this amazing ability to become everyone's confidante, no matter if the juror is a twenty-year-old single welfare mother or an e-commerce king with a million tucked into the stock market.

'What Mr. Brown just told you all is absolutely true. On the morning of October thirtieth, Nina Frost did buy a gun. She did drive to the courthouse. She did stand up and fire four bullets into the head of Father Szyszynski. What Mr. Brown would like you to believe is that there's nothing to this case beyond those facts . . . but we don't live in a world of facts. We live in a world of feelings. And what he's left out of his version of the story is what had been going on in Nina's head and heart that would lead her to such a moment.'

Fisher walks behind me, like Quentin did while he graphically showed the jury how to sneak up on a defendant and shoot him. He puts his hands on my shoulders, and it is comforting. 'For weeks, Nina Frost had been living a hell that no parent should have to live. She'd found out that her five-year-old son had been sexually abused. Worse, the police had identified the abuser as her own priest – a man she had confided in. Betrayed, heartbroken, and aching for her son, she began to lose her grasp on what was right and what was wrong. The only thing in her mind by the time she went to court that morning to see the priest arraigned was that she needed to protect her child.

'Nina Frost, of all people, knows how the system of justice works for – and fails – children. She, of all people, understands what the rules are in an American court of law, because for the past seven years she has measured up to them on a daily basis. But on October thirtieth, ladies and gentlemen, she wasn't a prosecutor. She was just Nathaniel's mother.' He comes to stand beside me. 'Please listen to everything. And when you make your decision, don't make it only with your head. Make it with your heart.'

Moe Baedeker, proprietor of Moe's Gun Shop, does not know what to do with his baseball cap. The bailiffs made him take it off, but his hair is matted and messy. He puts the cap on his lap and finger-combs his hair. In doing so, he catches sight of his nails, with grease and gun blueing caught beneath the cuticles, and he quickly sticks his hands beneath his thighs. 'Ayuh, I recognize her,' he says, nodding at me. 'She came into my store once. Walked right up to the counter and told me she wanted a semiautomatic handgun.'

'Had you ever seen her before?'

'Nope.'

'Did she look around the store at all?' Quentin asks.

'Nope. She was waiting in the parking lot when I opened, and then she came right up to the counter.' He shrugs. 'I did an instant background check on her, and when she came out clean, I sold her what she wanted.'

'Did she ask for any bullets?'

'Twelve rounds.'

'Did you show the defendant how to use the gun?'

Moe shakes his head. 'She told me she knew how.'

His testimony breaks over me like a wave. I can remember the smell of that little shop, the raw wood on the walls, and the pictures of Rugers and Glocks behind the counter. The way the cash register was old-fashioned and actually made a *ching* sound. He gave me my change in new twenty-dollar bills, holding each one up to the light and pointing out how you could tell whether they were counterfeit or not.

By the time I focus again, Fisher is doing the cross-exam. 'What did she do while you were running the background check?'

'She kept looking at her watch. Pacing, like.'

'Was there anyone else in the store?'

'Nope.'

'Did she tell you why she needed a gun?'

'Ain't my place to ask,' Moe says.

One of the twenties he'd given me had been written on, a man's signature. 'I did that once,' Moe told me that morning. 'And, swear to God, got the same bill back six years later.' He'd handed me my gun, hot in my hand. 'What goes around comes around,' he'd said, and at the time, I was too self-absorbed to heed this as the warning it was.

*    *    *

The cameraman had been filming for WCSH and was set up in the corner, according to Quentin Brown's diagram of the Biddeford courtroom. As the videotape is slipped into a TV/VCR, I keep my eyes on the jury. I want to watch them watching me.

Once, maybe, I saw this segment. But it was months ago, when I believed I had done the right thing. The familiar voice of the judge draws my attention, and then I cannot help but stare at this small screen.

My hands shake when I hold up the gun. My eyes are wide and wild. But my motion is smooth and beautiful, a ballet. As I press the gun to the priest's head my own tilts backward, and for one stunning moment my face is split into masques of comedy and tragedy – half grief, half relief.

The shot is so loud that even on tape, it makes me jump in my seat.

Shouts. A cry. The cameraman's voice, saying, 'Holy fucking shit!' Then the camera tilts on its axis and there are my feet, flying over the bar, and the thud of the bailiffs' bodies pinning me, and Patrick.

'Fisher,' I whisper. 'I'm going to be sick.'

The viewpoint shifts again, spinning to rest on its side on the floor. The priest's head lies in a spreading pool of blood. Half of it is missing, and the spots and flecks on the film suggest the spray of brain matter on the camera lens. One eye stares dully at me from the screen. *'Did I get him?'* My own voice. *'Is he dead?'*

'Fisher . . .' The room revolves.

I feel him stand up beside me. 'Your Honor, if I could request a short recess . . .'

But there isn't time for that. I jump out of my seat and stumble through the gate at the bar, flying down the aisle of the courtroom with two bailiffs in pursuit. I make it through the double doors, then fall to my knees and vomit repeatedly, until the only thing left in my stomach is guilt.

★          ★          ★

'Frost Heaves,' I say minutes later, when I have cleaned myself up and Fisher has whisked me to a private conference room away from the eyes of the press. 'That'll be tomorrow's headline.'

He steeples his fingers. 'You know, I've got to tell you, that was good. Amazing, really.'

I glance at him. 'You think I threw up on *purpose?*'

'Didn't you?'

'My God.' Turning away, I stare out the window. If anything, the crowd outside has grown. 'Fisher, did you *see* that tape? How could any juror acquit me after that?'

Fisher is quiet for a moment. 'Nina, what were you thinking when you were watching it?'

'Thinking? Who had time to think, with all the visual cues? I mean, that's an unbelievable amount of blood. And the brains –'

'What were you thinking about yourself?'

I shake my head, close my eyes, but there are no words for what I've done.

Fisher pats my arm. 'That,' he says, 'is why they'll acquit you.'

In the lobby, where he is sequestered as an upcoming witness, Patrick tries to keep his mind off Nina and her trial. He's done a crossword puzzle in a paper left on the seat beside him; he's had enough cups of coffee to raise his pulse a few notches; he's talked to other cops coming in and out. But it's all pointless; Nina runs through his blood.

When she staggered from the courtroom, her hand clapped over her mouth, Patrick had risen out of his chair. He was already halfway across the lobby, trying to make sure she was all right, when Caleb burst out of the double doors on the heels of the bailiffs.

So Patrick sat back down.

On his hip, his beeper begins to vibrate. Patrick pulls it off his belt and glances at the number on the screen. *Finally*, he thinks, and he goes to find a pay phone.

\*      \*      \*

When it is time for lunch, Caleb gets sandwiches from a nearby deli and brings them back to the conference room where I am ensconced. 'I can't eat,' I say, as he hands me one wrapped sub. I expect him to tell me that I have to, but instead Caleb just shrugs and lets the sandwich sit in front of me. From the corner of my eye I watch him chew his food in silence. He has already conceded this war; he no longer even cares enough to fight me.

There is a rattle of the locked door, followed by an insistent banging. Caleb scowls, then gets up to tell whoever it is to go away. But when he opens it a crack, Patrick is standing on the other side. The door falls open, and the two men stand uneasily facing each other, a seam of energy crackling between them that keeps them from getting too close.

I realize at that moment that although I have many photographs of Patrick and many photographs of Caleb, I haven't got a single one of all three of us – as if, in that combination, it is impossible to fit so much emotion in the frame of the camera.

'Nina,' he says, coming inside. 'I have to talk to you.'

*Not now*, I think, going cold. Surely Patrick has enough sense to not bring up what happened in front of my husband. Or maybe that is exactly what he wants to do.

'Father Gwynne's dead.' Patrick hands me a faxed Nexus article. 'I got a call from the Belle Chasse police chief. I got tired of working on Southern time a few days ago, and I put a little pressure on the authorities . . . anyway, it seems that by the time they went to arrest him, he'd died.'

My face is frozen. 'Who did it?' I whisper.

'No one. It was a stroke.'

Patrick keeps talking, his words falling like hailstones onto the paper I'm trying to read. '. . . took the damn chief two whole days to get around to calling me . . .'

*Father Gwynne, a beloved local chaplain, was found dead in his living quarters by his housekeeper.*

'. . . apparently, he had a family history of cardiovascular disease . . .'

*'He looked so peaceful, you know, in his easy chair,' said Margaret Mary Seurat, who had worked for the priest for the past five years. 'Like he'd just fallen asleep after finishing his cup of cocoa.'*

'. . . and get this: They said his cat died of a broken heart . . .'

*In a strange, connected twist, Gwynne's cherished pet, a cat well known to his parishioners, died shortly after authorities arrived. To those who knew the Father, this was no surprise: 'She loved him too much,' Seurat suggested. 'We all did.'*

'It's over, Nina.'

*Archbishop Schulte will lead a funeral Mass at Our Lady of Mercy, Wednesday morning at 9:00 A.M.*

'He's dead.' I test the truth on my tongue. 'He's *dead*.' Maybe there is a God, then; maybe there are cosmic wheels of justice. Maybe this is what retribution is supposed to feel like. 'Caleb,' I say, turning. Everything else passes between us without a single word: that Nathaniel is safe, now; that there will be no sexual abuse trial for him to testify at; that the villain in this drama will never hurt someone else's little boy; that after my verdict, this nightmare will truly be finished.

His face has gone just as white as mine. 'I heard.'

In the middle of this tiny conference room, with two hours of damning testimony behind me, I feel an unmitigated joy. And in that instant it does not matter what has been missing between Caleb and myself. Much more important is this triumph of news, and it's something to share. I throw my arms around my husband.

Who does not embrace me in return.

Heat floods my cheeks. When I manage to lift my gaze with some shred of dignity, Caleb is staring at Patrick, who has turned his back. 'Well,' Patrick says, without looking at me. 'I thought you'd want to know.'

Bailiffs are human fire hydrants: They're placed in the court in case of an emergency but fade into the landscape otherwise and are rarely put to practical use. Like most bailiffs of my acquaintance, Bobby Ianucci isn't too athletic or too bright.

And like most bailiffs, Bobby understands he is lower on the feeding chain than the attorneys in the courtroom – which accounts for his absolute intimidation at the hands of Quentin Brown.

'Who was in the courtroom when you brought Father Szyszynski in from the holding cell?' the prosecutor asks, a few minutes into the testimony.

Bobby has to think about this, and the effort is visible on his doughy face. 'Uh, well, the judge, yeah. On the bench. And there was a clerk, and a stenographer, and the dead guy's lawyer, whose name I don't remember. And a DA from Portland.'

'Where were Mr. and Mrs. Frost sitting?' Quentin asks.

'In the front row with Detective Ducharme.'

'What happened next?'

Bobby straightens his shoulders. 'Me and Roanoke, that's the other bailiff, we walked the Father across the room to his lawyer. Then, you know, I stepped back, because he had to sit down, so I stood behind him.' He takes a deep breath. 'And then . . .'

'Yes, Mr. Ianucci?'

'Well, I don't know where she came from. I don't know how she did it. But the next thing, there's gunshots being fired and blood all over the place, and Father Szyszynski's falling out of his chair.'

'What happened after that?'

'I tackled her. And so did Roanoke, and a couple of other guys posted at the back of the courtroom, and Detective Ducharme, too. She dropped the gun and I grabbed it, and then Detective Ducharme, he hauled her up and took her off to the holding cell in cuffs.'

'Did you get shot, Mr. Ianucci?'

Bobby shakes his head, lost in his memories. 'No. But if I'd been, like, five inches to the right, she could have hit me.'

'So would you say the defendant was very careful with how she aimed that weapon at Father Szyszynski?'

Fisher stands beside me. 'Objection.'

'Sustained,' Judge Neal rules.

The prosecutor shrugs. 'Withdrawn. Your witness.'

As he returns to his seat, Fisher approaches the bailiff. 'Did you talk to Nina Frost the morning before the shooting?'

'No.'

'In fact, you were busy doing your job – maintaining the security of the courthouse, and dealing with prisoners – so you had no need to watch Mrs. Frost, did you?'

'No.'

'Did you see her pull the gun out?'

'No.'

'You said several bailiffs immediately jumped on her. Did you have to fight Mrs. Frost for the gun?'

'No.'

'And she didn't struggle with any of you when you tried to sub-due her?'

'She was trying to see around us. She kept asking if he was dead.'

Fisher dismisses this with a shrug. 'But she wasn't trying to get away from you. She wasn't trying to hurt you.'

'Oh, no.'

Fisher lets that answer hang for a moment. 'You knew Mrs. Frost before this, didn't you, Mr. Ianucci?'

'Sure.'

'What was your relationship with her like?'

Bobby glances at me; then his eyes skitter away. 'Well, she's a DA. She comes in all the time.' He pauses, then adds. 'She's one of the nice ones.'

'Had you ever considered her to be violent before?'

'No.'

'In fact, on that morning, she seemed nothing like the Nina Frost you knew, isn't that right?'

'Well, you know, she looked the same.'

'But her *actions*, Mr. Ianucci . . . had you ever seen Mrs. Frost act like this before?'

The bailiff shakes his head. 'I never saw her shoot nobody, if that's what you mean.'

'It is,' Fisher says, sitting down. 'Nothing further.'

That afternoon when court is adjourned, I don't go directly home. Risking an extra fifteen minutes' grace before my electronic bracelet is reactivated, I drive to St. Anne's and enter the church where this all began.

The nave is open to the public, although I don't think they've found a replacement chaplain yet. Inside, it's dark. My shoes strike the tile, announce my presence.

To my right is a table where white votives burn in tiers. Taking a stick, I light one for Glen Szyszynski. I light a second one for Arthur Gwynne.

Then I slip into a pew and get down on the kneeler. 'Hail Mary, full of grace,' I whisper, praying to a woman who stood by her son, too.

The lights in the motel room go out at eight, Nathaniel's bedtime. Beside his son, on a matching twin bed, Caleb lies with his hands folded behind his head, waiting for Nathaniel to fall asleep. Then, sometimes, Caleb will watch TV. Turn on one lamp and read the day's paper.

Today he wants to do neither. He is in no mood to hear local pundits guessing Nina's fate based on the first day of testimony. Hell, he doesn't want to guess, himself.

One thing is clear: The woman all those witnesses saw; the woman on that videotape – she isn't the woman Caleb married. And when your wife is not the same person you fell in love with eight years ago, where exactly does that leave you? Do you try to get to know who she has become, and hope for the best? Or do you keep deceiving yourself in the hope that she might wake up one morning and have gone back to the woman she used to be?

Maybe, Caleb thinks with a small shock, *he* isn't the same person he once was, either.

That brings him directly to the topic he didn't want to remember, especially not now in the dark with nothing to distract him. This afternoon, when Patrick had come to the conference room to bring them the news of Gwynne's death . . . well, Caleb must be reading into things. After all, Nina and Patrick have known each other a lifetime. And although the guy is something of an albatross, his relationship with Nina has never really bothered Caleb, because when push came to shove *he* was the one sleeping with Nina every night.

But Caleb has not been sleeping with Nina.

He squeezes his eyes shut, as if this might block out the memory of Patrick turning away abruptly when Nina put her arms around Caleb. That, in and of itself, wasn't disturbing – Caleb could list a hundred times that Nina touched him or smiled at him in the other man's presence that unsettled Patrick in some way . . . even if Nina never seemed to see. In fact, there have been times Caleb's even felt sorry for Patrick, for the blatant jealousy on his face the moment before he masks it.

Today, though, it wasn't envy in Patrick's eyes. It was grief. And that is why Caleb cannot pull away from the incident; cannot stop picking the moment apart like a carrion vulture going for the bone. Envy, after all, comes from wanting something that isn't yours.

But grief comes from losing something you've already had.

Nathaniel hates this stupid playroom with its stupid book corner and its stupid bald dolls and its stupid crayon box that doesn't even have a yellow. He hates the way the tables smell like a hospital and the floor is cold under his socks. He hates Monica, whose smile reminds Nathaniel of the time he took an orange wedge at the Chinese restaurant and stuffed it into his mouth, rind out, in a silly, fake grin. Most of all he hates knowing that his mom and dad are just twenty-two stairs up but Nathaniel isn't allowed to join them.

'Nathaniel,' Monica says, 'why don't we finish this tower?'

It is made of blocks; they built it all afternoon yesterday and put a special sign on overnight, asking the janitors to leave it until this morning.

'How high do you think we can go?'

It is already taller than Nathaniel; Monica has brought over a chair so that he can keep building. She has a small stack of blocks ready to go.

'Be careful,' she warns as he climbs onto the chair.

He places the first block at the top, and the whole structure wobbles. The second time, it seems certain to fall over – and then doesn't. 'That was close,' Monica says.

He imagines that this is New York City, and he is a giant. A *Tyrannosaurus rex*. Or King Kong. He eats buildings this big like they are carrot sticks. With a great swipe of his enormous paw, Nathaniel swings at the top of the tower.

It falls in a great, clattering heap.

Monica looks so sad that for just the slightest moment, Nathaniel feels awful. 'Oh,' she sighs. 'Why'd you do that?'

Satisfaction curls the corners of his mouth, blooming from a root inside. But Nathaniel doesn't tell her what he's thinking: *Because I could.*

Joseph Toro looks nervous to be in a courtroom, and I can't blame him. The last time I saw the man he was cowering beside the bench, covered with his own client's blood and brain matter.

'Had you met with Glen Szyszynski before you came to court that day?' Quentin asks.

'Yes,' the attorney says timidly. 'In jail, pending the arraignment.'

'What did he say about the alleged crime?'

'He categorically denied it.'

'Objection,' Fisher calls out. 'Relevance?'

'Sustained.'

Quentin reconsiders. 'What was Father Szyszynski's demeanor the morning of October thirtieth?'

'Objection.' Fisher stands this time. 'Same grounds.'

Judge Neal looks at the witness. 'I'd like to hear this.'

'He was scared to death,' Toro murmurs. 'He was resigned. Praying. He read to me aloud, from the book of Matthew. The part where Christ keeps saying '*My God, why hast thou forsaken me?*''

'What happened when they brought your client in?' Quentin asks.

'They walked him to the defense table where I was sitting.'

'And where was Mrs. Frost at the time?'

'Sitting behind us, and to the left.'

'Had you spoken with Mrs. Frost that morning?'

'No,' Toro answers. 'I'd never even met her.'

'Did you notice anything unusual about her?'

'Objection,' Fisher says. 'He didn't know her, so how could he judge what was and wasn't customary?'

'Overruled,' the judge answers.

Toro looks at me, a bird gathering courage to dart a glance at the cat sitting a few feet away. 'There *was* something unusual. I was waiting for her to come in . . . because she was the mother of the alleged victim, of course . . . but she was late. Her husband was there, waiting . . . but Mrs. Frost almost missed the beginning of the arraignment. I thought of all days, it seemed very strange that on this one, she wouldn't be on time.'

I listen to his testimony, but I am watching Quentin Brown. To a prosecutor, a defendant is nothing but a victory or a loss. They are not real people; they do not have lives that interest you beyond the crime that brought them into court. As I stare at him, Brown suddenly turns. His expression is cool, dispassionate – one I have cultivated in my repertoire as well. In fact I have had all the same training as him, but there is a gulf between us. This case is only his job, after all. But it is my future.

The Alfred courthouse is old, and the bathrooms are no exception. Caleb finishes up at the long trough of the urinal just as someone comes to stand beside him. He averts his eyes as the other man unzips, then steps back to wash his hands, and realizes it is Patrick.

When Patrick turns, he does a double-take. 'Caleb?'

The bathroom is empty, save the two of them. Caleb folds his arms, waits for Patrick to soap his hands and dry them with a paper towel. He is waiting, and he doesn't know why. He just understands that at this moment, he can't leave yet, either.

'How is she today?' Patrick asks.

Caleb finds that he cannot answer, cannot force a single word out.

'It must be hell for her, sitting in there.'

'I know.' Caleb forces himself to look directly at Patrick, to make him understand this is not a casual reply, is not even a sequitur. 'I *know*,' he repeats.

Patrick looks away, swallows. 'Did she . . . did she tell you?'

'She didn't have to.'

The only sound is the rush of water in the long urinal. 'You want to hit me?' Patrick says after a moment. He splays his arms wide. 'Go ahead. Hit me.'

Slowly, Caleb shakes his head. 'I want to. I don't think I've ever wanted anything as much. But I'm not going to, because it's too fucking sad.' He takes a step toward Patrick, pointing his finger at the other man's chest. 'You moved back here to be near Nina. You've lived your whole life for a woman who doesn't live hers for you. You waited until she was skating over a weak spot, and then you made sure you were the first thing she could grab onto.' He turns away. 'I don't have to hit you, Patrick. You're already pathetic.'

Caleb walks toward the bathroom door but is stopped by Patrick's voice. 'Nina used to write me every other day. I was overseas, in the service, and that was the only thing I looked forward to.' He smiles faintly. 'She told me when she met you. Told me where you took her on dates. But the time she told me that she'd climbed some mountain with you . . . that was when I knew I'd lost her.'

'Mount Katahdin? Nothing happened that day.'

'No. You just climbed it, and came down,' Patrick says. 'Thing is, Nina's terrified of heights. She gets so sick, sometimes, that she faints. But she loved you so much, she was willing to follow you anywhere. Even three thousand feet up.' He pushes away from the wall, approaching Caleb. 'You know what's pathetic? That you get to live with this . . . this goddess. That out of all the guys in the world, she picked *you*. You were handed this incredible gift, and you don't even know it's in front of you.'

Then Patrick pushes past Caleb, knocking him against the wall. He needs to get out of that bathroom, before he is foolish enough to reveal the whole of his heart.

Frankie Martine is a prosecutor's witness – that is to say, she answers questions clearly and concisely, making science accessible to even the high school dropout on a jury. Quentin spends nearly an hour walking her through the mechanics of bone marrow transplants, and she manages to keep the jury's interest. Then she segues into the mechanics of her day job – spinning out DNA. I once spent three days at the state lab with Frankie, in fact, getting her to show me how she does it. I wanted to know, so that I'd fully grasp the results that were sent to me.

Apparently, I didn't learn enough.

'Your DNA is the same in every cell in your body,' Frankie explains. 'That means if you take a blood sample from someone, the DNA in those blood cells will match the DNA in their skin cells, tissue cells, and bodily fluids like saliva and semen. That's why Mr. Brown asked me to take DNA from Father Szyszynski's blood sample and use it to see if it matched the DNA found in the semen on the underpants.'

'And did you do that?' Quentin asks.

'Yes, I did.'

He hands Frankie the lab report – the original one, which was left anonymously in my mailbox. 'What were your findings?'

Unlike some of the other witnesses the prosecutor's put on the stand, Frankie meets my eye. I don't read sympathy there, but I don't read disgust either. Then again, this is a woman who is faced daily with the forensic proof of what people are capable of doing to others in the name of love. 'I determined that the chance of randomly selecting an unrelated individual from the population other than the suspect, whose DNA matched the semen DNA at all the locations we tested, was one in six billion.'

Quentin looks at the jury. 'Six billion? Isn't that the approximate population of the whole earth?'

'I believe so.'

'Well, what does all this have to do with bone marrow?'

Frankie shifts on her seat. 'After I'd issued these results, the attorney general's office asked me to research the findings in light of Father Szyszynski's medical records. Seven years ago, he'd had a bone marrow transplant, which means, basically, that his blood was on long-term loan . . . borrowed from a donor. It also means that the DNA we got from that blood – the DNA that was typed to match the semen in the underwear – was not Father Szyszynski's DNA, but rather his donor's.' She looks at the jury, making sure they are nodding before she continues. 'If we'd taken saliva from Father Szyszynski, or semen, or even skin – anything but his blood – it would have excluded him as a donor to the semen stain in the child's underwear.'

Quentin lets this sink in. 'Wait a second. You're telling me that if someone has a bone marrow transplant, they've got two different types of DNA in their body?'

'Exactly. It's extremely rare, which is why it's the exception and not the rule, and why DNA testing is still the most accurate kind of evidentiary proof.' Frankie takes out another lab report, an updated one. 'As you can see here, it's possible to test someone who's had a bone marrow transplant to prove that they've got two different profiles of DNA. We extract tooth pulp, which contains both tissue and blood cells. If someone's had a bone marrow transplant, those tissue cells should show one profile of DNA, and the blood cells should show another.'

'Is that what you found when you extracted tooth pulp from Father Szyszynski?'

'Yes.'

Quentin shakes his head, feigning amazement. 'So I guess Father Szyszynski was the one person in six billion whose DNA might match the DNA found in the underwear . . . but who wouldn't have been the one to leave it there?'

Frankie folds the report and slips it into her case file. 'That's right,' she says.

'You've worked with Nina Frost on a few cases, haven't you?' Fisher asks moments later.

'Yes,' Frankie replies. 'I have.'

'She's pretty thorough, isn't she?'

'Yes. She's one of the DAs who calls all the time, checking up on the results we fax in. She's even come to the lab. A lot of the prosecutors don't bother, but Nina really wanted to make sure she understood. She likes to follow through from beginning to end.'

Fisher slants a look my way. *Tell me about it.* But he says, 'It's very important for her to make sure that she has the facts straight, isn't it?'

'Yes.'

'She isn't someone who'd jump to a conclusion, or rely on something she was told without double-checking it?'

'Not that I've seen,' Frankie admits.

'When you issue your lab reports, Ms. Martine, you expect them to be accurate, don't you?'

'Of course.'

'You issued a report, in fact, that said the chances of somebody other than Father Szyszynski contributing this semen to Nathaniel Frost's underwear were less than one in the population of the whole earth?'

'Yes.'

'You never put anything in that report qualifying your results in the case that the suspect was a bone marrow transplant recipient, did you? Because that's such a rare event that even you, as a scientist, would never assume it?'

'Statistics are statistics . . . an estimation.'

'But when you handed that initial report to the DA's office, you were prepared to ask the prosecutor to rely on it?'

'Yes.'

'You were prepared to ask a jury of twelve people to rely on it as evidence to convict Father Szyszynski?'

'Yes,' Frankie says.

'You were prepared to ask the judge to rely on it when he sentenced Father Szyszynski?'

'Yes.'

'And you were prepared to ask Nina Frost, the child's mother, to rely on it for closure and peace of mind?'

'Yes.'

Fisher turns to the witness. 'Then is it any wonder in your mind, Ms. Martine, that she *did?*'

'Of course Quentin objected,' Fisher says, his mouth full of pepperoni pizza. 'That's not the point. The point is that I didn't withdraw the question before I dismissed the witness. The jury's going to notice that nuance.'

'You are giving far too much credit to a jury,' I argue. 'I'm not saying the cross wasn't fantastic, Fisher, it was. But . . . watch it, you're going to get sauce on your tie.'

He looks down, then flips the tie over his shoulder and laughs. 'You're a riot, Nina. At what point during this trial do you think you might actually start to root for the defense?'

*Never,* I think. Maybe it is easier for Fisher, a defense attorney, to come up with rationalizations for why people do the things they do. After all, when you have to stand up next to felons on a daily basis and fight for their freedom, you either convince yourself they had some excuse for committing a crime . . . or you tell yourself this is nothing but a job, and if you lie on their behalf it's all in the name of billable hours. After seven years as a prosecutor, the world looks very black and white. Granted, it was easy enough to persuade myself that I was morally right-eous when I believed I'd killed a child molester. But to be absolved of murdering a man who was blameless – well, even Johnnie Cochran must have nightmares every now and then.

'Fisher?' I ask quietly. 'Do you think I ought to be punished?'

He wipes his hands on a napkin. 'Would I be here if I did?'

'For what you're making, you'd probably stand in the middle of a gladiator's ring.'

Smiling, he meets my eye. 'Nina, relax. I *will* get you acquitted.'

*But I shouldn't be.* The truth lies at the base of my stomach, even though I can't say it aloud. What good is the legal process if people can decide their motives are bigger than the law? If you remove one brick from the foundation, how long before the whole system tumbles down?

Maybe I can be pardoned for wanting to protect my child, but there are plenty of parents who shelter their children without committing felonies. I can tell myself that I was only thinking of my son that day; that I was only acting like a good mother . . . but the truth is, I wasn't. I was acting like a pros-ecutor, one who didn't trust the court process when it became personally relevant. One who knew better than to do what I did. Which is exactly why I deserve to be convicted.

'If I can't even forgive myself,' I say finally, 'how are twelve other people going to do it?'

The door opens and Caleb enters. Suddenly the atmosphere is plucked tight as a bowstring. Fisher glances at me – he knows that Caleb and I have been estranged, lately – and then balls his napkin up and tosses it into the box. 'Caleb! There's a couple slices left.' He stands up. 'I'm going to go take care . . . of that thing we were talking about,' Fisher says vacuously, and he gets out of the room while he can.

Caleb sits across from me. The clock on the wall, fast by five minutes, ticks as loud as my heart. 'Hungry?' I ask.

He traces the sharp corner of the pizza box. 'I'm starving,' Caleb answers.

But he makes no move to take one of the slices. Instead, we both watch as his fingers creep forward, as he clasps my hand between both of his. He scoots his chair closer and bows his head until it touches our joined fists. 'Let's start over,' he murmurs.

If I have gained anything over these months, it is the knowledge there is no starting over – only living with the mistakes you've made. But then, Caleb taught me long ago you can't build anything without some sort of foundation. Maybe we learn to live our lives by understanding, firsthand, how *not* to live them.

'Let's just pick up where we left off,' I reply, and I rest my cheek on the crown of Caleb's head.


How far can a person go . . . and still live with himself?

It's something that's been haunting Patrick. There are certain acts for which you easily make excuses – killing during wartime; stealing food if you're starving; lying to save your own life. But narrow the circumstances, bring them closer to home – and suddenly, the faith of a man who's dedicated his life to morality gets seriously shaken. Patrick doesn't blame Nina for shooting Glen Szyszynski, because at that moment she truly believed it was her only option. Likewise, he doesn't consider making love with her on Christmas Eve to be wrong. He'd waited for Nina for years; when she finally was his – even for a night – the fact of her marriage to another man was inconsequential. Who was to say that the bond between Patrick and Nina was any less strong because there was no piece of paper sanctifying it?

Justification is a remarkable thing – takes all those solid lines and blurs them, so that honor becomes as supple as a willow, and ethics burst like soap bubbles.

If Nina chose to leave Caleb, Patrick would be at her side in an instant, and he could come up with a multitude of reasons to defend his behavior. Truth be told, it's something he's let himself consider in the soft gray moments before sleep comes. Hope is his balm for reality; if Patrick spreads it thick enough, sometimes he can even envision a life with her.

But then, there's Nathaniel.

And that's the point Patrick cannot get past. He can rationalize falling in love with Nina; he can even rationalize her falling in love with him. There's nothing he would like more than to see Caleb gone from her life. But Caleb is not just Nina's husband . . . he is also the father of her son. And Patrick could not bear knowing that he was responsible for ruining Nathaniel's childhood. If Patrick did that after all that has happened, well . . . how could she ever love him?

Compared to a transgression of that size, what he is about to do seems insignificant.

He watches Quentin Brown from the witness box. The prosecutor is expecting this to go easily – just as easily as it did during the practice session. After all, Patrick is a law enforcement official, used to testifying. As far as Brown knows, despite his friendship with Nina, he's on the side of the prosecution. 'Were you assigned to work the Nathaniel Frost case?' Quentin asks.

'Yes.'

'How did the defendant react to your investigation of the case?'

Patrick can't look at Nina, not yet. He doesn't want to give himself away. 'She was an incredibly concerned parent.'

This is not the answer they have rehearsed. Patrick watches Quentin do a double-take, then feed him the response he was *supposed* to give. 'Did you ever see her lose her temper during the case?'

'At times she'd become distraught. Her child wasn't speaking. She didn't know what to do.' Patrick shrugs. 'Who wouldn't get frustrated in a situation like that?'

Quentin sends him a quelling glance. Commentary on the stand is not necessary, or desired. 'Who was your first suspect in the molestation case?'

'We didn't have a suspect until Glen Szyszynski.'

By now, Quentin looks ready to throttle him. 'Did you bring in another man for questioning?'

'Yes. Caleb Frost.'

'Why did you bring him in?'

Patrick shakes his head. 'The child was using sign language to communicate, and he ID'd his abuser with the sign for *father*. At the time, we didn't understand he meant *priest*, rather than *daddy*.' He looks directly at Caleb, in the front row behind Nina. 'That was my mistake,' Patrick says.

'What was the defendant's reaction to her son signing *father?*'

Fisher rises from his seat, poised to object, but Patrick speaks quickly. 'She took it very seriously. Her primary concern was always, *always*, protecting her child.' Confused, the attorney sits back down beside Nina.

'Detective Ducharme –' the prosecutor interrupts.

'I'm not quite done yet, Mr. Brown. I was going to say that I'm sure it tore her up inside, but she got a restraining order against her husband, because she thought it was the best way to keep Nathaniel safe.'

Quentin walks closer to Patrick, hisses through his teeth so that only his witness will hear. *'What the hell are you doing?'* Then he faces the jury. 'Detective, at what point did you make the decision to arrest Father Szyszynski?'

'After Nathaniel gave a verbal disclosure, I went down to talk to him.'

'Did you arrest him at that moment?'

'No. I was hoping he'd confess first. We always hope for that in molestation cases.'

'Did Father Szyszynski ever admit to sexually abusing Nathaniel Frost?'

Patrick has been a witness at enough trials to know that the question is blatantly unacceptable, because it calls for hearsay. The judge and the prosecutor both stare at Fisher Carrington, waiting for him to object. But by now, Nina's lawyer has caught on. He sits at the defense table with his hands steepled, watching this unfold. 'Child molesters almost never admit they've hurt a child,' Patrick says, filling the silence. 'They know jail's not going to be a pleasant place for them. And frankly, without a confession, a molestation trial is a roll of the dice. Nearly half the time, these guys get off because of insufficient evidence or because the child is too terrified to testify, or because they *do* testify and the jury doesn't believe the word of a kid . . .'

Quentin breaks in before Patrick can do any further damage. 'Your Honor, may we have a recess?'

The judge looks over his bifocals at him. 'We *are* in the middle of the direct.'

'Yes, Judge, I'm aware of that.'

Shrugging, Neal turns to Fisher. 'Does the defense object to stopping at this point?'

'I don't believe so, Your Honor. But I would ask the Court to remind all counsel that the witnesses have been sequestered and can't be approached during the break.'

'Fine,' Quentin grits out. He storms from the courtroom so quickly he doesn't see Patrick finally make eye contact with Nina, smile gently at her, and wink.

'Why is this cop working for us?' Fisher demands, as soon as he's bustled me into a private conference room upstairs.

'Because he's my friend. He's always been there for me.' At least, that is the only explanation I can give. I knew, of course, that Patrick would have to testify against me, and I didn't take it to heart. Part of what makes Patrick Patrick is his absolute devotion to the clear line dividing right and wrong. It is why he would not let me talk to him about the murder; it is why he has wrestled so hard to stand by my side while I was awaiting trial. It is why his offer to find Father Gwynne on my behalf meant so very much to me, and was so difficult for him.

It is why, when I think back to Christmas Eve, I cannot believe it ever happened.

Fisher seems to be considering this odd gift that has dropped into his lap. 'Is there anything I should watch out for? Anything he *won't* do to protect you?'

The reason we slept together isn't because Patrick tossed

morality to the wind that night. It's because he was too damn honest to convince himself the feelings weren't there.

'He won't lie,' I answer.

Quentin returns on the attack. Whatever game this detective's playing, it's going to stop right now. 'Why were you in court the morning of October thirtieth?'

'It was my case,' Ducharme answers coolly.

'Did you speak to the defendant that morning?'

'Yes. I spoke with both Mr. and Mrs. Frost. They were both very nervous. We discussed who they could leave Nathaniel with during the proceedings, because naturally, they were very wary of putting him into anyone's care at that point.'

'What did you do when the defendant shot Father Szyszynski?'

Ducharme meets the prosecutor's gaze head on. 'I saw a gun, and I went for it.'

'Did you know Mrs. Frost had a gun before that point?'

'No.'

'How many officers did it take to wrestle her to the ground?'

'She dropped to the ground,' the detective corrects. 'Four bailiffs dropped on top of her.'

'Then what did you do?'

'I asked for cuffs. Deputy Ianucci gave me a pair. I secured Mrs. Frost's hands behind her back and took her into the holding cell.'

'How long were you in there with her?'

'Four hours.'

'Did she say anything to you?'

In the practice session, Ducharme had told Quentin that the defendant confessed to him that she'd committed a crime. But now, he puts on a choirboy's expression and looks at the jury. 'She kept repeating over and over, "I did everything I could; I can't do any more." She sounded crazy.'

*Crazy?* 'Objection,' Quentin roars.

'Your Honor, it's his own witness!' Fisher says.

'Overruled, Mr. Brown.'

'Approach!' Quentin storms up to the bench. 'Judge, I'm going to ask to have this witness declared hostile, so that I can ask leading questions.'

Judge Neal looks at Ducharme, then back at the prosecutor. 'Counselor, he *is* answering your questions.'

'Not the way he's supposed to be!'

'I'm sorry, Mr. Brown. But that's your problem.'

Quentin takes a deep breath, turning away. The real issue here isn't that Patrick Ducharme is single-handedly destroying this case. The issue is *why*.

Either Ducharme is holding a grudge against Quentin, whom he does not even really know . . . or he's trying to help Nina Frost for some reason. He glances up, and notices the detective and the defendant staring at each other, a bond so charged that Quentin imagines walking through it might give him a shock.

*Well.*

'How long have you known the defendant?' he asks evenly.

'Thirty years.'

'That long?'

'Yes.'

'Can you describe your relationship with her?'

'We work together.'

*My ass,* Quentin thinks. *I'd bet my retirement pension you play together, too.* 'Do you ever see her outside the office in a nonprofessional capacity?'

It might not be noticeable to someone watching less closely than Quentin . . . but Patrick Ducharme's jaw tightens. 'I know her family. We have lunch together every now and then.'

'How did you feel when you heard this had happened to Nathaniel?'

'Objection,' Carrington calls out.

The judge rubs a finger over his upper lip. 'I'll allow it.'

'I was concerned for the boy,' the detective answers.

'How about Nina Frost? Were you concerned for her?'

'Of course. She's a colleague.'

'Is that all?' Quentin accuses.

He is prepared for Ducharme's reaction – a face bleached completely of color. An added bonus: the way Nina Frost looks as if she's been molded of stone. *Bingo,* Quentin thinks.

'Objection!'

'Overruled,' the judge says, narrowing his eyes at the detective.

'We've been friends for a long time.' Ducharme picks through a minefield of words. 'I knew Nina was upset, and I did what I could to make it easier.'

'Such as . . . help her kill the priest?'

Nina Frost shoots out of her seat at the defense table. *'Objection!'*

Her attorney shoves her back down. Patrick Ducharme looks ready to kill Quentin, which is fine by him, now that the jury thinks it's possible the detective could have been an accessory to one murder already. 'How long have you been a policeman?'

'Three years.'

'And before that, you were a detective in the military police?'

'Yes, for five years.'

Quentin nods. 'As an investigator and a detective and a police officer in both the United States military and the Biddeford Police Department, how often have you testified?'

'Dozens of times.'

'You are aware that as a witness, you're under oath, Detective.'

'Of course.'

'You've told the court today that during the four hours you spent in a holding cell with the defendant, she sounded crazy.'

'That's right.'

Quentin looks at him. 'The day after Father Szyszynski was murdered, you and Detective Chao came in to talk to me at the district attorney's office. Do you remember what you told me then about the defendant's state of mind?'

There is a long stalemate. Finally Ducharme turns away. 'I said she knew exactly what she was doing, and that if it was my son, I'd have done the same thing.'

'So . . . your opinion the day after the shooting was that Nina Frost was perfectly sane. And your opinion today is that she was crazy. Which one is it, Detective . . . and what on earth did she do between then and now to make you change your mind?' Quentin asks, and he sinks into his chair and smiles.

Fisher is playing the insider with the jury, but I can barely even follow his words. Watching Patrick on the stand has turned me inside out. 'You know,' Fisher begins, 'I think Mr. Brown was trying to imply something about your relationship with Mrs. Frost that isn't accurate, and I'd like to have a chance to make clear to the jury what *is* true. You and Nina were close friends as children, isn't that right?'

'Yes.'

'And like all children, you probably told a fib every now and then?'

'I suppose so,' Patrick says.

'But that's a far cry from perjury, isn't it?'

'Yes.'

'Like all children, you two hatched plots and schemes and maybe even carried through with them?'

'Sure.'

Fisher spreads his hands. 'But that's a far cry from planning a murder, right?'

'Absolutely.'

'And as children, you two were particularly close. Even now, you're particularly close. But that's all you two are – *friends*. Correct?'

Patrick looks directly at me. 'Of course,' he says.

The state rests. Me, I'm too keyed up for that. I pace the confines of the small conference room where I have been left alone – Caleb is checking on Nathaniel, and Fisher has left to call his office. I am standing by the window – something Fisher's told me not to do, because photographers down there have some super telephoto lenses they're using – when the door cracks and the sound from the hallway oozes inside. 'How is he?' I ask without turning around, assuming Caleb has returned.

'Tired,' Patrick answers, 'but I figure I'll bounce back.'

I whirl around and walk to him, but now there is a wall between us, one only he and I can see. Patrick's eyes, that beautiful blue, are swimming with shadows.

I state the obvious. 'You lied about us. On the stand.'

'Did I?' He comes closer, and it hurts. To have so little space between us, and to know I cannot erase it entirely.

We *are* only friends. It's all we're ever going to be. We can wonder, we can pretend otherwise for a single evening, but that is not the measure of a life together. There is no way to know what might have happened if I hadn't met Caleb; if Patrick hadn't gone overseas. But I've made a world with Caleb. I can't cut out that piece of myself, any more than I can carve away the part of my heart that belongs to Patrick.

I love them both; I always will. But this isn't about me.

'I didn't lie, Nina. I did the right thing.' Patrick's hand comes up to my face, and I turn my cheek into his palm.

I will be leaving him. I will be leaving everyone.

'The right thing,' I repeat, 'is thinking before I act, so that I stop hurting the people I love.'

'Your family,' he murmurs.

I shake my head. 'No,' I say, my good-bye. 'I meant you.'

After court is dismissed, Quentin goes to a bar. But he doesn't particularly feel like drinking, so he gets into his car and drives aimlessly. He goes to a Wal-Mart and buys $104.35 of items he does not need; he stops at a McDonald's for dinner. It isn't until two hours later that he realizes he has somewhere he needs to be.

It is dark by the time he pulls up to Tanya's house, and he has trouble getting the passenger out of the car. It wasn't as difficult as you'd imagine to find a plastic skeleton; the Halloween merchandise at the costume store was discounted sixty percent, heaped into an untidy corner.

He hauls the skeleton up the driveway like a buddy who's drunk too much, phalanges dragging on the gravel, and he uses one long bony finger to push in the doorbell. A few moments later, Tanya answers the door.

She's still wearing her scrubs, and her braids are pulled back into a ponytail. 'Okay,' she says, looking at Quentin and the skeleton. 'I've got to hear this.'

He shifts position, so that he can hold the skull and let the rest dangle, freeing up one hand. Quentin points to the shoulder. 'Scapula,' he recites. 'Ischium, ilium. Maxilla, mandible, fibula, cuboid.' He has labeled each of these on the appropriate bone, with a black permanent marker.

Tanya starts to close the door. 'You've lost it, Quentin.'

'No!' He wedges the wrist of the skeleton inside. 'Don't.' Taking a deep breath, Quentin says, 'I bought this for you. I wanted to show you . . . that I didn't forget what you taught me.'

She tilts her head. God, he used to love the way she did that. And how she'd massage her own neck when the muscles got sore. He looks at this woman, who he does not know at all any longer, and thinks she looks just the way *home* should.

Tanya's fingers slip over the bones he could not recall, wide white ribs and parts of the knee and ankle. Then she reaches for Quentin's arm, and smiles. 'You got a lot left to learn,' she replies, and she tugs him inside.

That night I dream that I am in court, sitting next to Fisher, when the hair stands up on the back of my neck. The air gets heavier, harder to breathe, and behind me whispers run like mice on the hardscrabble floor. 'All rise,' the clerk says, and I'm about to, but then there is the cold click of a gun against my scalp, the surge and stream of a bullet in my brain, and I am falling; I am falling.

The sound wakes me. Unmistakable, a celebration of clangs and clatter in ringing tin. Raccoons, but in January?

In my flannel pajamas I tiptoe downstairs. Stuff my bare feet into boots, my arms into a parka. Just in case, I grab the fireplace poker, and then I slip outside.

The cover of snow masks my footsteps as I walk the few feet to the garage. As I get closer, the huddled black shape is too large to be a raccoon. The head is bent into the trash. It isn't until I smack the poker against the can like a gong that the man even lifts his head, dizzy and ringing.

He is dressed like a cat burglar, and my first, too-charitable thought is that he must be freezing. His hands, covered in rubber gloves, are slick with the contents of my refuse. Like condoms, I think – he does not want to catch any dread disease, and who knows what you can contract by looking at the detritus of someone's life?

'What the hell are you doing?' I ask.

A war plays across his face. Then he takes a tape recorder out of his pocket. 'Would you be willing to give me a statement?'

'You're a *reporter?* You're going through my trash, and you're a reporter?' I advance on him. 'What did you think you would find? What else could you possibly need to say about my life?'

Now I notice how young he is: Nathaniel, give or take fifteen years. He is shaking, and I don't know if it is the temperature out here, or the fact that he has come face-to-face with someone as evil as me. 'Do your readers want to know that I had my period last week? That I finished a box of Honey Nut Cheerios? That I get too much junk mail?'

I grab the tape recorder and punch the record button. 'You want a statement? I'll give you a statement. You ask your readers if they can account for every minute of their lives, every thought in their heads, and be proud of it. You ask them if they've never jaywalked . . . never gone thirty-one miles per hour in a thirty-mile zone . . . if they've never sped up when they saw that yellow light. And when you find that single, sorry person who hasn't taken a misstep, that one person with the right to judge me, you tell him he's just as human as I am. That tomorrow, his world could turn upside down and he might find himself capable of actions he'd never believed possible.' I turn away, my voice breaking. 'You tell him . . . he could have been me.'

Then I take the tape recorder and throw it as hard and far as I can, into a high drift of snow. I walk inside and lock the door behind me, lean against it, and catch my breath.

Nothing I do will bring back Father Szyszynski. But nothing I do will ever wipe from my mind the error I've made. No jail sentence can punish me more than I will punish myself, or turn back time, or keep me from thinking that Arthur Gwynne deserved to die as much as his half-brother didn't.

I have been moving in slow motion, waiting for an inevitable ax to fall, listening to testimony as if these witnesses are discussing the destiny of a stranger. But now, I feel myself waking. The future may unfold in indelible strokes, but it doesn't mean we have to read the same line over and over. That's exactly the fate I *didn't* want for Nathaniel . . . so why should I want it for *me?*

Snow starts to fall, like a blessing.

I want my life back.

*The bird looked like a tiny dinosaur, too small to have feathers or know how to open its eyes. It was on the ground next to a stick shaped like a V, and a yellow-hatted acorn. Its mouth folded back, a hinge, and one stub of a wing flopped. I could see the outline of its heart.*

*'It's okay.' I got down on the ground so I wouldn't be so scary. But it just lay there on its side, its belly swelled like a balloon.*

*When I looked up, I could see its brothers and sisters in the nest. With one finger I pushed it onto my hand. 'Mom!'*

*'What's the matter? Oh, Nathaniel!' She made that click with her tongue and grabbed my wrist, pushing it back to the ground. 'Don't pick it up!'*

*'But . . . but . . .' Anyone could see how sick it was. You were supposed to help people who were too sick or sad to take care of themselves; Father Glen said so all the time. So why not birds, too?*

*'Once a human touches the baby, its mother doesn't want it anymore.' And just like she said, the big robin came out of the sky and hopped right past the baby. 'Now you know better,' she said.*

*I kept staring at the bird. I wondered if it would stay there next to the V stick and the acorn until it died. I covered it with a big leaf, so that it would stay warm. 'If I was a bird and someone touched me, would I die?'*

*'If you were a bird,' she said, 'I never would have let you fall out of the nest.'*

# 8

These are the things he takes: his Yomega Brain yo-yo; the starfish arm he found on a beach. His Bravest Boy ribbon, a flashlight, a Batman trading card. Seventy-six pennies, two dimes, and a Canadian quarter. A granola bar and a bag of jellybeans left over from Easter. They are treasures he brought with him when he moved to the motel with his father; he cannot leave them behind now. Everything fits in the white pillowcase and thumps lightly against Nathaniel's stomach when he zips it up inside his coat.

'You all set?' his father asks, the words lobbed like a stick into a field and forgotten. Nathaniel wonders why he's even bothered to try to keep this a secret, when his dad is too busy to notice him anyway. He climbs into the passenger seat of the truck and fastens the seat belt – then on second thought, unlatches it.

If he's going to be really bad, he might as well start now.

Once, the man at the cleaner's offered to take Nathaniel to see where the big moving millipede of pressed clothes began. His dad had lifted him over the counter and he'd followed Mr. Sarni into the way back, where the clothes were being cleaned. The air was so heavy and wet that Nathaniel wheezed as he pushed the big red button; started the conveyor of hangers chugging in its loop again. The air in the courthouse, it reminds Nathaniel of that. Maybe it's not as hot here, or as sticky, but it is hard to breathe all the same.

When his dad brings him to the playroom downstairs with Monica, they speak in marshmallow bites of words that they think Nathaniel cannot hear. He does not know what a hostile witness is, or juror bias. But when his father talks the lines on his face appear on Monica's, like it is a mirror.

'Nathaniel,' she says, fake-bright, as soon as his dad goes upstairs. 'Let's take off that coat.'

'I'm cold,' he lies, and he hugs his pack against his middle.

She is careful to never touch Nathaniel, and he wonders if that's because Monica has the X-ray vision to see how dirty he is on the inside. She looks at him when she thinks he doesn't see, and her eyes are as deep as a pond. His mom stares at him with the same expression. It is all because of Father Gwynne; Nathaniel wishes just once someone would come up to him and think of him as some kid, instead of The One This Happened To.

What Father Gwynne did was wrong – Nathaniel knew it then, from the way his skin shivered; and he knows it now, from talking to Dr. Robichaud and Monica. They have said over and over that it isn't Nathaniel's fault. But that doesn't keep him from turning around sometimes, really fast, sure that he's felt someone's breath on his neck. And it doesn't keep him from wondering if he cut himself open at the belly, like his father does when he catches a trout, would he find that black knot that hurts all the time?

'So, how are we doing this morning?' Fisher asks, as soon as I sit down beside him.

'Shouldn't *you* know that?' I watch the clerk set a stack of files on the judge's bench. The jury box, without its members, looks cavernous.

Fisher pats my shoulder. 'It's our turn,' he assures me. 'I'm going to spend the whole day making the jurors forget what Brown told them.'

I turn to him. 'The witnesses –'

'– will do a good job. Trust me, Nina. By lunchtime, everyone in this court is going to think you were crazy.'

As the side door opens and the jury files in, I look away and wonder how to tell Fisher that's not what I want, after all.

★          ★          ★

'I have to pee,' Nathaniel announces.

'Okay.' Monica puts down the book she has been reading to him and stands up, waiting for Nathaniel to follow her to the door. They walk down the hall together to the restrooms. Nathaniel's mother doesn't let him in the boy's room by himself, but it's okay here, because there's only one potty and Monica can check before he goes inside. 'Wash your hands,' she reminds him, and she pushes open the door so Nathaniel can go inside.

Nathaniel sits on the cold seat of the toilet to muddle it all out. He let Father Gwynne do all those things – and it was bad. *He* was bad; but he didn't get punished. In fact, ever since he was so bad, everyone's been paying extra attention to Nathaniel, and being extra nice.

His mother did something really bad, too – because, she said, it was the best way to fix what happened.

Nathaniel tries to make sense of all this, but the truths are too tangled in his head. All he knows is that for whatever reason, the world is upside-down. People are breaking rules like crazy – and instead of getting into trouble, it's the only way to make things right again.

He pulls up his pants, cinches the bottom of his jacket, and flushes. Then he closes the lid and climbs from the tank to the toilet tissue holder to the little ledge up high. The window there is tiny, only for fancy, because this is a basement floor. But Nathaniel can open it and he's small enough to slip through.

He finds himself behind the courthouse, in one of the window wells. Nobody notices a kid his size. Nathaniel skirts the trucks and vans in the parking lot, crosses the frozen lawn. He starts walking aimlessly down the highway, not holding an adult's hand, intent on running away. *Three bad things*, he thinks, *all at once*.

'Dr. O'Brien,' Fisher asks, 'when did Mrs. Frost first come to your office?'

'On December twelfth.' At ease on the stand – as he should be, for all the testimony he's given in his career – the psychiatrist relaxes in the witness chair. With the silver hair at his temples and his casual pose, he looks like he could be Fisher's brother.

'What materials had you received before you met with her?'

'An introductory letter from you, a copy of the police report, the videotape taken by WCSH-TV, and the psychiatric report prepared by Dr. Storrow, the state's psychiatrist, who had examined her two weeks earlier.'

'How long did you meet with Mrs. Frost that first day?'

'An hour.'

'What was her state of mind when you met?'

'The focus of the conversation was on her son. She was very concerned about his safety,' O'Brien says. 'Her child had been rendered mute; she was frantic with worry; she was feeling guilt as a working mother who hadn't been around enough to see what had been going on. Moreover, her specialized knowledge of the court system made her aware of the effects of molestation on children . . . and more anxious about her son's ability to survive the legal process without significant trauma. After considering the circumstances that led Mrs. Frost to my office, as well as meeting with her in person, I concluded that she was a classic example of someone suffering from post-traumatic stress disorder.'

'How might that have affected her mental stability on the morning of October thirtieth?'

O'Brien leans forward to address the jury. 'Mrs. Frost knew she was heading to court to face her son's abuser. She believed wholeheartedly that her son was permanently scarred by the event. She believed that testifying – as a witness, or even at a competency hearing – would be devastating to the child. Finally, she believed that the abuser would eventually be acquitted. All this was going through her mind, and as she drove to the courthouse, she became more and more agitated – and less and less herself – until she finally snapped. By the moment she put the gun to Father Szyszynski's head, she could not consciously stop herself from shooting him – it was an involuntary reflex.'

The jury was listening, at least; some of them were brave

enough to sneak glances at me. I tried for an expression that fell somewhere between Contrite and Shattered.

'Doctor, when was the last time you saw Mrs. Frost?'

'A week ago.' O'Brien smiles kindly at me. 'She feels more capable of protecting her son now, and she understands that her means of doing it was not right. In fact, she is filled with remorse for her previous actions.'

'Does Mrs. Frost still suffer from post-traumatic stress disorder?'

'PTSD isn't like chicken pox, which can be cured forever. In my opinion, however, Mrs. Frost is at a point where she understands her own feelings and thoughts and can keep herself from letting them overwhelm her. With subsequent outpatient therapy, I believe she will function quite normally.'

This lie cost Fisher, and therefore me, two thousand dollars. But it is worth it: Several members of the jury are nodding. Maybe honesty is overvalued. What's truly priceless is picking out from a stream of falsehoods the ones you most need to hear.

Nathaniel's feet hurt, and his toes are frozen in his boots. His mittens are in the playroom, so the tips of his fingers have turned pink, even buried in the pockets of his jacket. When he counts out loud, just to have something to do, the numbers hang in front of him, curled in the cold.

Because he knows better, he climbs over the guardrail and runs into the middle of the highway. A bus zooms by, its horn flaring as it swerves into the distance.

Nathaniel spreads his arms for balance, and begins to walk the tight-rope of the dotted line.

'Dr. O'Brien,' Quentin Brown says. 'You believe Mrs. Frost feels capable of protecting her son now?'

'Yes, I do.'

'So who's she going to pull a gun on next?'

The psychiatrist shifts in the chair. 'I don't believe she'll go to that extreme.'

The prosecutor purses his lips, considering. 'Maybe not now. But what about in two months . . . two years? Some kid on the playground threatens her son. Or a teacher looks at him the wrong way. Is she going to spend the rest of her life playing Dirty Harry?'

O'Brien raises a brow. 'Mr. Brown, this wasn't a situation where someone looked at her son the wrong way. He had been sexually molested. She believed that she knew beyond a reasonable doubt who'd done it. I also understand that the individual who was eventually identified as the real perpetrator has since died of natural causes, so she certainly no longer has an alleged vendetta to fulfill.'

'Doctor, you reviewed the state psychiatrist's report. Isn't it true that you reached the exact opposite conclusion that he did, regarding Mrs. Frost's mental state? That he not only deemed her competent to stand trial but also believed she was sane at the time of the offense?'

'Yes, Dr. Storrow did indicate that. But this is the first evaluation he's done for a court. On the other hand, I've been a forensic psychiatrist for over forty years.'

'And you don't come cheap, do you?' Brown says. 'Isn't the defense paying you for your testimony today?'

'My fee is two thousand dollars per day, plus expenses,' O'Brien answers, shrugging.

There is a stir in the back of the courtroom. 'Doctor, I believe you used the words "she finally snapped." Is that correct?'

'That's not the clinical term, of course, but it's the way I would describe it in conversation.'

'Did she snap before or after she drove to the gun store?' Brown asks.

'Clearly, that was part of her continuing mental decline . . .'

'Did she snap before or after she loaded six rounds into a nine millimeter semiautomatic handgun?'

'As I said earlier, that would be part –'

'Did she snap before or after she slipped past the metal detector, knowing the bailiff wouldn't stop her?'

'Mr. Brown –'

'And, Doctor, did she snap before or after she very carefully aimed at one person and only one person's head in a crowded courtroom?'

O'Brien's mouth flattens. 'As I told the court before, at that point Mrs. Frost had no control over her actions. She could no more stop herself from shooting the priest than she could stop herself from breathing.'

'She sure managed to stop someone else from breathing, though, didn't she?' Brown crosses toward the jury box. 'You're an expert on post-traumatic stress disorder, aren't you?'

'I'm considered to be rather knowledgeable in the field, yes.'

'And PTSD is triggered by a traumatic event?'

'That's correct.'

'You first met Mrs. Frost after Father Szyszynski's death?'

'Yes.'

'And,' Brown says, 'you believe that it was the molestation of Mrs. Frost's son that triggered her PTSD?'

'Yes.'

'How do you know it wasn't shooting the priest?'

'It's possible,' O'Brien concedes. 'It's just that the other trauma came first.'

'Isn't it true that Vietnam veterans can be plagued by PTSD their whole lives? That thirty years later these men still wake up with nightmares?'

'Yes.'

'Then you can't, with any degree of scientific certainty, tell this jury that the defendant is over the illness that – in your words – caused her to snap?'

More raised voices from the rear of the courtroom. I focus my attention forward.

'I doubt that Mrs. Frost will ever completely forget the events of the past few months,' O'Brien says diplomatically. 'However, in my personal opinion, she is not dangerous now . . . nor will she be dangerous in the future.'

'Then again, Doctor,' Brown says, 'you're not wearing a white collar.'

'Please,' a familiar voice shouts, and then Monica shoves

away from the bailiff restraining her and runs up the central aisle of the courtroom. Alone. She crouches down beside Caleb. 'It's Nathaniel,' she sobs. 'He's gone missing.'

The judge grants a recess, and the bailiffs in the courtroom are sent to look for Nathaniel. Patrick calls in the county sheriff and the state police. Fisher volunteers to appease the frenzy of media that's caught wind of a new problem.

I can't go, because I am still wearing that fucking electronic bracelet.

I think of Nathaniel, kidnapped. Of him wandering into the boxcar of an old train and freezing to death. Of the ship where he might stow away when no one is looking. He could travel the world, and I would still be imprisoned by these four walls.

'He told me he had to go to the bathroom,' Monica says tearfully. We wait in the lobby, which has been emptied of reporters. I know she wants absolution, but I'll be damned if I am going to give it to her. 'I thought maybe he was feeling sick, because it was taking so long. But when I went in, that window was open.' She grabs my sleeve. 'I don't think he was taken by anyone, Nina. I think he just did this for the attention.'

'Monica.' I am holding onto the thinnest filament of control. I remind myself that she could not have known what Nathaniel would do. That nobody is perfect; and that I had not protected him any better, apparently, than she could. But still.

Irony: I will be acquitted, and my son will be gone.

Out of a crowd of cries, I have always been able to hear Nathaniel's. As an infant; on a playground full of children; even with my eyes closed, playing Marco Polo in the shallow end of a pool. Maybe if I cry loud enough, now, Nathaniel will be able to hear me.

Two bright circles of color have appeared on Monica's cheeks. 'What can I do?' she whispers.

'Bring him back.' Then I walk away, because guilt is not only contagious but also deadly.

*               *               *

Caleb watches the police speed away in their cruisers, the lights flashing. Maybe they'll attract Nathaniel; maybe not. He knows one thing – these officers have forgotten what it is like to be five. To this end, he puts his back up against the window that leads into the basement bathroom. He kneels, until he is Nathaniel's height. Then he squints, taking into account everything that might capture his attention.

A clump of matted bushes, bare and shaking. An umbrella, turned inside out by the wind and discarded. A handicapped ramp painted with yellow zigzagged lines.

'Mr. Frost.' The deep voice startles Caleb. He gets to his feet and turns to find the prosecutor standing there, shoulders hunched against the cold.

When Monica ran into the courtroom to deliver the bad news, Fisher Carrington took one look at Nina's face and requested a recess. Brown, on the other hand, stood up and asked the judge if this might not be a ploy for sympathy. 'For all we know,' he said, 'the boy is safe and sound in a conference room upstairs.'

It didn't take him long to realize his tactical error, as the jury watched Nina become hysterical. But all the same, he is the last person Caleb expects to see out here.

'I just wanted to tell you,' Brown says now, 'if there's anything I can do . . .'

He lets his sentence trail off. 'You can do something, all right,' Caleb replies. Both men know what it is; know it has nothing to do with Nathaniel.

The prosecutor nods and walks inside. Caleb gets down on his knees again. He begins to move in a spiral around the court building, like the way he lays stone in a round patio – widening his circles so that he leaves out no space and maintains the arc of the ring. He does this as he does everything – slowly and tenaciously – until he is certain that he's seeing the world through the eyes of his son.

On the other side of the highway is a steep hill that Nathaniel slides down on his bottom. His pants snag on a branch and rip and it doesn't matter, because *no one will punish him*. He steps in melting puddles of icy water and through the ragged seam of the treeline, where he walks until he stumbles over a piece of the forest that has been left out by mistake.

It is the size of his bed at home and has been flattened by the tracks of animals. Nathaniel sits down on a log at the edge and pulls his pillowcase out from inside his coat. He takes out his granola bar and eats halfway, then decides to save the rest. He turns on his flashlight and holds it up to his palm so that the back of his hand glows red.

When the deer come, Nathaniel holds his breath. He remembers what his father told him – they are more afraid of us than we are afraid of them. The big one, a doe, has a coat the color of caramels and tiny high-heeled hoofs. Her baby looks the same, with white spots on her back, as if she has not been colored in the whole way. They bend their long throats to the ground, pushing through the snow with their noses.

It is the mother deer who finds the grass. Just a tuft, hardly a bite. But instead of eating it she shoves the fawn closer. She watches the baby eat, although it means she herself will get nothing.

It makes Nathaniel want to give her the other half of his granola bar.

But the minute he reaches into his pillowcase the heads of the deer jerk up, and they leap from all four feet, their tails white sails as they disappear farther into the woods.

Nathaniel examines the rip on the back of his pants; the muddy tops of his boots. He places the half of the granola bar on the log, in case the deer come back. Then he gets up and slowly heads back toward the road.

Patrick has canvassed a one-mile square around the courthouse, certain that Nathaniel left of his own free will, and even more certain that the kid couldn't have gotten much farther. He picks up his radio to place a call to the Alfred dispatch, asking if anyone's found anything yet, when a movement at the side of the road strikes his eye. As he watches, a quarter mile up the road, Nathaniel crawls over the iron horse of the guardrail and starts walking along the shoulder of the highway.

'I'll be damned,' Patrick breathes, pulling his truck forward slightly. It looks like Nathaniel knows exactly where he is going; from this spot, even someone as small as Weed would be able to see the high roof of the courthouse. But the boy can't see what Patrick can, from the high cab of his truck – Caleb, coming closer on the opposite side of the road.

He watches Nathaniel look right and then left, and Patrick realizes what he is planning to do. Sticking his flashing magnetic light on the roof of the truck, Patrick hurriedly swerves to block traffic. He gets out and clears the way, so that by the time Nathaniel sees his father waiting, he can run across the highway and into Caleb's arms safely.

'Don't do that again,' I say into Nathaniel's soft neck, holding him close to me. 'Ever. Do you hear me?'

He pulls back, puts his palms on my cheeks. 'Are you mad at me?'

'No. Yes. I will be, anyway, when I'm done being so happy.' I hug him tighter. 'What were you thinking?'

'That I'm bad,' he says flatly.

Over Nathaniel's head, I meet Caleb's eyes. 'No you're not, sweetheart. Running away, that wasn't good. You could have been hurt; and you worried me and Daddy like you can't believe.' I hesitate, picking my words. 'But you can do a bad thing and not be a bad person.'

'Like Father Gwynne?'

I freeze. 'Actually, no. He did a bad thing, and he *was* a bad person.'

Nathaniel looks up at me. 'What about you?'

Shortly after Dr. Robichaud, Nathaniel's psychiatrist, takes the stand, Quentin Brown is on his feet to object. 'Your Honor, what does this witness have to offer?'

'Judge, this goes to my client's state of mind,' Fisher argues. 'The information she received from Dr. Robichaud regarding her son's declining condition was highly relevant to her mental status on October thirtieth.'

'I'll allow it,' Judge Neal rules.

'Doctor, have you treated other children who were rendered mute after sexual abuse?' Fisher asks.

'Yes, unfortunately.'

'In some of these cases, do children never regain their voices?'

'It can take years.'

'Did you have any way of knowing whether this would be a long-term condition for Nathaniel Frost?'

'No,' Dr. Robichaud says. 'In fact, that was why I began to teach him rudimentary sign language. He was becoming frustrated with his inability to communicate.'

'Did it help?'

'For a while,' the psychiatrist admits. 'Then he began talking again.'

'Was the progress steady?'

'No. It broke down when Nathaniel lost contact with Mrs. Frost for a week.'

'Do you know why?'

'I understood she was charged with violating her bail conditions and was imprisoned.'

'Did you see Nathaniel during the week that his mother was in jail?'

'Yes, I did. Mr. Frost brought him in, quite upset that the child was no longer speaking. He'd regressed to the point where all he would sign for was his mother.'

'In your opinion, what caused that regression?'

'Clearly, it was the sudden and prolonged separation from Mrs. Frost,' Dr. Robichaud says.

'How did Nathaniel's condition change when his mother was released again?'

'He cried out for her.' The psychiatrist smiles. 'A joyful noise.'

'And, Doctor, were he to undergo a sudden and prolonged separation from his mother again . . . what do you think the likely outcome would be for Nathaniel?'

'Objection!' Quentin calls.

'Withdrawn.'

Moments later, the prosecutor stands up to cross-examine. 'In dealing with five-year-olds, Doctor, don't you find that they often become confused about events?'

'Absolutely. That's why courts have competency hearings, Mr. Brown.'

At the very mention, Judge Neal gives him a warning glance. 'Dr. Robichaud, in your experience, court cases of this type take several months to several years to come to trial, don't they?'

'Yes.'

'And the developmental difference between a five-year-old and a seven-year-old is significant, isn't it?'

'Definitely.'

'In fact, haven't you treated children who seemed like they might have trouble testifying when they first came to you . . . yet a year or two later – after therapy and time had healed them a bit – they were able to take the stand without a setback?'

'Yes.'

'Isn't it true that you have no way of predicting whether Nathaniel would have been able to testify a few years from now without it causing significant psychological harm?'

'No, there's no way to say what might have happened in the future.'

Quentin turns toward me. 'As a prosecutor, Mrs. Frost would certainly be aware of this time lag for court appearances, don't you think?'

'Yes.'

'And as the mother of a child this age, she would be aware of the development changes possible over the next few years?'

'Yes. In fact, I tried to tell Mrs. Frost that in a year or so, Nathaniel might be doing far better than she expected. That he might even be capable of testifying on his own behalf.'

The prosecutor nods. 'Unfortunately, though, the defendant killed Father Szyszynski before we could find out.'

Quentin withdraws the statement before Fisher can even object. I tug on the edge of his jacket. 'I have to talk to you.' He stares at me as if I have lost my mind. 'Yes,' I say. 'Now.'

I know what Quentin Brown is thinking, because I have seen a case through his eyes. *I proved she murdered him. I did my job.* And maybe I have learned not to interfere in the lives of others, but surely it's my responsibility to save myself. 'It's up to me,' I tell Fisher in the conference room. 'I need to give them a reason to say it doesn't matter.'

Fisher shakes his head. 'You know what happens when defense attorneys overtry a case. The prosecution has the burden of proof, and all I can do is pick holes in it. But if I pick too hard, the whole thing deflates. Put on one too many witnesses, and the defense loses.'

'I understand what you're saying. But Fisher, the prosecution *did* prove that I murdered Szyszynski. And I'm not your average witness.' I take a deep breath. 'Sure, there are cases where the defense loses because they put on one witness too many. But there are other cases where the prosecution loses because the jury hears from the defendant. They know horrible things have been done – and they want to hear why, right from the horse's mouth.'

'Nina, you can barely sit still when I'm doing cross-exams, you want to object so badly. I can't put you on the stand as a witness when you're such a goddamned prosecutor.' Fisher sits down across from me, splaying his hands on the table. 'You think in facts. But just because you're telling the jury something doesn't mean they're going to accept it as reality. After all the groundwork I've laid, they like me; they believe me. If I tell them you were so overcome with emotion you were beyond rational thought, they'll buy it. On the other hand, no matter *what* you say to them, they're predisposed to think you're a liar.'

'Not if I tell them the truth.'

'That you really meant to shoot the other guy?'

'That I wasn't crazy.'

'Nina,' Fisher says softly, 'that'll undo your whole defense. You can't tell them that.'

'Why not, Fisher? Why can't I make twelve lousy people understand that somewhere between a good deed and a bad deed are a thousand shades of gray? Right now, Quentin's got me convicted, because he's told them what I was thinking that day. If I take the stand, I can give them an alternative version. I can explain what I did, why it was wrong, and why I couldn't see that, then. Either they'll send me to jail . . . or they'll send me home with my son. How can I not take that chance?'

Fisher stares down at the table. 'You keep this up,' he says after a moment, 'and I may have to hire you when we're through.' He holds out a hand, counting off on his fingers. 'You answer only the questions I ask. The minute you start trying to educate the jury I'm yanking you off. If I mention temporary insanity, you damn well find a way to support it without perjuring yourself. And if you show any temper what-soever, get ready for a nice long stay in prison.'

'Okay.' I leap to my feet, ready to go.

But Fisher doesn't move. 'Nina. Just so you know . . . even if you can't convince that jury, you've convinced me.'

Three months ago, if I'd heard that from a defense attorney, I'd have laughed. But now I smile at Fisher, wait for him to come up beside me at the door. We walk into that courtroom as a team.

My office, for the past seven years, has been a courtroom. It's a space that is intimidating for many people, but not for me. I know what the rules are there: when to approach the clerk, when to talk to the jury, how to lean back and whisper to someone in the gallery without calling attention to myself. But now I am sitting in a part of that office I've never been in before. I am not allowed to move. I am not allowed to do the work I usually do.

I'm starting to see why so many people fear this.

The witness box is so small my knees bump up against the front. The stares of a couple hundred people poke at me, tiny needles. I think of what I have told thousands of witnesses during my career: *Your job is to do three things: Listen to the question, answer the question, and stop talking.* I remember something my boss used to say all the time – that the best witnesses were truck drivers and assembly line workers because they were far less likely to run off at the mouth than, for example, overeducated lawyers.

Fisher hands me the restraining order I took out against Caleb. 'Why did you procure this, Nina?'

'I thought at the time that Nathaniel had identified my husband as the person who'd sexually abused him.'

'What did your husband do to make you believe this?'

I find Caleb in the gallery, shake my head. 'Absolutely nothing.'

'Yet you took the extraordinary step of getting a restraining order to prevent him from seeing his own child?'

'I was focused on protecting my son. If Nathaniel said this was the person who hurt him . . . well, I did the only thing I could to keep him safe.'

'When did you decide to terminate the restraining order?' Fisher asks.

'When I realized that my son had been signing the word *father* not to identify Caleb, but to identify a priest.'

'Is that the point where you believed Father Szyszynski was the abuser?'

'It was a lot of things. First, a doctor told me that anal penetration had occurred. Then came Nathaniel's hand sign. Then he whispered a name to Detective Ducharme that sounded like "Father Glen." And finally, Detective Ducharme told me he'd found my son's underwear at St. Anne's.' I swallow hard. 'I've spent seven years putting together pieces to make cases that will stand up in court. I was just doing what seemed absolutely logical to me.'

Fisher glares at me. *Absolutely logical.* Oh, damn.

'Nina, *listen carefully* to my next question, please,' Fisher warns. 'When you started to believe that Father Szyszynski was your son's abuser, how did you feel?'

'I was a mess. This was a man I'd trusted with my own beliefs and my family's beliefs. With my son. I was angry with myself because I'd been working so hard – if I'd been home more, I might have seen this coming. And I was frustrated because now that Nathaniel had identified a suspect, I knew the next step would be –'

'Nina,' Fisher interrupts. *Answer the question,* I remind myself with a mental kick. *Then shut up.*

Brown smiles. 'Your Honor, let her finish answering.'

'Yes, Mr. Carrington,' the judge agrees. 'I don't believe Mrs. Frost is done.'

'Actually I am,' I say quickly.

'Did you discuss the best plan of action for your son with his psychiatrist?'

I shake my head. 'There was no best plan of action. I've tried hundreds of cases involving child victims. Even if Nathaniel started speaking normally again, and got stronger . . . even if there were a year or two before the case went to trial . . . well, the priest never admitted to what he did. That means it all hinged on my son.'

'What do you mean?'

'Without a confession, the only thing a prosecutor's got against the defendant is the child's testimony. That means Nathaniel would have had to go through a competency hearing. He'd get up, in a room full of people like this, and say what that man had done to him. That man, of course, would be sitting six feet away, watching – and you can be sure that he's told the child, more than once, not to tell. But no one would be sitting next to Nathaniel and nobody would be holding him, nobody would be telling him it's okay to talk now.

'Either Nathaniel would be terrified and fall apart during this hearing, and the judge would rule him not competent to stand trial – which means that the abuser would never get punished . . . or Nathaniel would be told he was able to stand trial – which means he'd have to go through it all over again in court, with the stakes cranked up a notch and a whole new set of people watching. Including twelve jurors predisposed to not believe him, because he's only a child.' I turn to the jury. 'I'm not all too comfortable here, now, and I've been in a court-room every day for the past seven years. It's scary to be trapped in this box. It's scarring for any witness. But we were not talking about *any* witness. We were talking about Nathaniel.'

'What about the best-case scenario?' Fisher asks gently. 'What if, after all that, the abuser was put in jail?'

'The priest would have been in prison for ten years, only ten years, because that's what people with no criminal record get for destroying a child's life. He would have most likely been paroled before Nathaniel even hit puberty.' I shake my head. 'How can anyone consider that a best-case scenario? How can any court say that would protect my son?'

Fisher takes one last look at me and requests a recess.

In the conference room upstairs, Fisher crouches down in front of my chair. 'Repeat after me,' he says.

'Oh, come on.'

'Repeat after me: *I am a witness. I am not an attorney.*'

Rolling my eyes, I recite, 'I am a witness. I am not an attorney.'

'*I will listen to the question, answer the question, and shut up,*' Fisher continues.

If I were in Fisher's shoes, I would want the same promise from my witness. But I am not in Fisher's shoes. And by the same token, he isn't in mine. 'Fisher. Look at me. I am the woman who crossed the line. The one who actually did what any parent would want to do in this horrible situation. Every single person on that jury is looking at me and trying to figure out whether that makes me a monster or a hero.' I look down, feeling the sudden prick of tears. 'It's something *I'm* still trying to figure out. I can't tell them why I did it. But I *can* explain that when Nathaniel's life changes, mine changes. That if Nathaniel never gets over this, then neither will I. And when you look at it that way, sticking to the testimony doesn't seem quite as important, does it?' When Fisher doesn't answer, I reach as far down inside me as I can for whatever confidence has been left behind. 'I know what I'm doing,' I tell Fisher. 'I'm completely in control.'

He shakes his head. 'Nina,' he sighs, 'why do you think I'm so worried?'

'What were you thinking when you woke up the morning of October thirtieth?' Fisher asks me, minutes later.

'That this would be the worst day of my life.'

Fisher turns, surprised. After all, we have not rehearsed this. 'Why? Father Szyszynski was about to be arraigned.'

'Yes. But once he was charged, that speedy trial clock would start ticking. Either they'd bring him to trial or let him go. And that meant Nathaniel would have to get involved again.'

'When you arrived at the courthouse, what happened?'

'Thomas LaCroix, the prosecutor, said they were going to try to clear the courtroom because this was such a high-profile case. It meant the arraignment would be delayed.'

'What did you do?'

'I told my husband I had to go to the office.'

'Did you?'

I shake my head. 'I wound up at a gun shop, in the parking lot. I didn't really know how I'd gotten there, but I knew it was a place I was supposed to be.'

'What did you do?'

'I went in when the store opened, and I bought a gun.'

'And then?'

'I put the gun in my purse and went back to court for the arraignment.'

'Did you plan what you were going to do with the gun during the drive?' Fisher asks.

'No. The only thing on my mind was Nathaniel.'

Fisher lets this lie for a moment. 'What did you do when you arrived at the courthouse?'

'I walked in.'

'Did you think about the metal detectors?'

'No, I never do. I just walk around them because I'm a prosecutor. I do it twenty times a day.'

'Did you purposefully go around the metal detectors because you were carrying a gun in your purse?'

'At that moment,' I answer, 'I was not thinking at all.'

*I am watching the door, just watching the door, and the priest is going to come out of it at any moment. My head, it's pounding past the words that Caleb says. I have to see him. I can't hear anything but my blood, that buzzing. He will come through that door.*

*When the knob turns, I hold my breath. When the door swings open, and the bailiff appears first, time stops. And then the whole room falls away and it is me and him, with Nathaniel bound between us like glue. I cannot look at him, and then I cannot look away.*

*The priest turns his head and, unerringly, his eyes find mine.*

*Without saying a word, he speaks:* I forgive you.

*It is the thought of* him *pardoning me* that *breaks something loose inside. My hand slides into my purse and with almost casual indifference I let it happen.*

*Do you know how sometimes you know you are dreaming, even while it occurs? The gun is tugged forward like a magnet, until it comes within inches of his head. At the moment I pull the trigger I am not thinking of Szyszynski; I am not thinking of Nathaniel; I am not even thinking of revenge.*

*Just one word, clamped between the vise of my teeth:*

No.

'Nina!' Fisher hisses, close to my face. 'Are you all right?'

I blink at him, then at the jury staring at me. 'Yes. I'm . . . sorry.'

But in my head I'm still there. I hadn't expected the recoil of the gun. For every action, there is an equal and opposite reaction. Kill a man, and you will be punished.

'Did you struggle when the guards fell on top of you?'

'No,' I murmur. 'I just wanted to know he was dead.'

'Is that when Detective Ducharme took you into the holding cell?'

'Yes.'

'Did you say anything to him back there?'

'That I didn't have any choice. I had to do it.'

Which, it turns out, was true. I had said it, at the time, to deliberately sound crazy. But what those psychiatrists have testified to is technically accurate – I had no conscious control of my actions. They are only wrong in thinking that this means I was insane. What I did was no mental illness, no psychotic break. It was instinct.

Fisher pauses. 'You found out some time later that, in fact, Father Szyszynski was not the man who sexually abused your son. How did that make you feel?'

'I wanted to be put in jail.'

'Do you still feel that way?' Fisher asks.

'No.'

'Why not?'

In that instant, my eye falls on the defense table, where neither Fisher nor I are sitting. It is already a ghost town, I think. 'I did what I did to keep my son safe. But how can I keep him safe when I'm not with him?'

Fisher catches my eye meaningfully. 'Will you ever take the law into your own hands again?'

Oh, I know what he wants me to say. I know, because it is what I would try to draw from a witness at this moment too. But I have told myself enough lies. I'm not going to hand-feed them to this jury, too.

'I wish I could tell you I never would . . . but that wouldn't be true. I thought I knew this world. I thought I could control it. But just when you think you've got your life by the reins, that's when it's most likely to run away with you.

'I killed someone.' The words burn on my tongue. 'No, not just someone, but a wonderful man. An *innocent* man. That's something I'm going to carry with me, forever. And like any burden, it is going to get heavier and heavier . . . except I'll never be able to put it down, because now it's a part of who I am.' Turning to the jury, I repeat, 'I would like to tell you that I'd never do anything like this again, but then, I never thought I was capable of doing anything like this in the first place. And as it turned out, I was wrong.'

Fisher, I think, is going to kill me. It is hard to see him through the tears. But my heart isn't hammering, and my soul is still. *An equal and opposite reaction.* After all this time, it turns out that the best way to atone for doing something blatantly wrong is to do something else blatantly right.

But for the grace of God, Quentin thinks, and it could be him sitting in that box. After all, there is not that much difference between himself and Nina Frost. Maybe he wouldn't have killed for his son, but he certainly greased wheels to make Gideon's conviction for drug possession go down much easier than it might have. Quentin can even remember that visceral pang that came when he found out about Gideon – not because he'd broken the law, like Tanya thought, but because his boy must have been scared shitless by the system. Yes, under different circumstances, Quentin might have liked Nina; might even have had something to talk to her about over a beer. Still, you make a bed, you've got to lie in it . . . which has landed Nina on the other side of the witness box, and Quentin six feet away and determined to take her down.

He raises one eyebrow. 'You're telling us that in spite of everything you know about the court system and child abuse cases, on the morning of October thirtieth you woke up with no intention of killing Father Szyszynski?'

'That's right.'

'And that as you drove to the courthouse for this man's arraignment, which – as you said – would start the clock ticking . . . at that point, you had no plans to kill Father Szyszynski?'

'No, I didn't.'

'Ah.' Quentin paces past the front of the witness stand. 'I guess it came to you in a flash of inspiration when you were driving to the gun store.'

'Actually, no.'

'Was it when you asked Moe to load the semiautomatic weapon for you?'

'No.'

'So I suppose when you skirted the metal detector, back at the courthouse, killing Father Szyszynski was still not part of your plan?'

'It wasn't.'

'When you walked into the courtroom, Mrs. Frost, and took up a position that would give you the best vantage point to kill Glen Szyszynski without harming anyone else in the room . . . even that, at that moment, you had no plans to kill the man?'

Her nostrils flare. 'No, Mr. Brown, I didn't.'

'What about at the moment you pulled the gun out of your pocketbook and shoved it up to Glen Szyszynski's temple? Did you still have no plans to kill him then?'

Nina's lips draw tight as a purse. 'You need to give an answer,' Judge Neal says.

'I told the court earlier I wasn't thinking at all at that moment.'

Quentin's drawn first blood, he knows it. 'Mrs. Frost, isn't it true that you've handled over two hundred child molestation cases in your seven years with the district attorney's office?'

'Yes.'

'Of those two hundred cases, twenty went to trial?'

'Yes.'

'And of those, twelve were convictions.'

'That's true.'

'In those twelve cases,' Quentin asks, 'were the children able to testify?'

'Yes.'

'In fact, in several of those cases, there was no corroborating physical evidence, as there was in the case of your son, isn't that right?'

'Yes.'

'As a prosecutor, as someone with access to child psychiatrists and social workers and an intimate knowledge of the legal process, don't you think you would have been able to prepare Nathaniel to come to court better than just about any other mother?'

She narrows her eyes. 'You can have every resource in the world at your fingertips, and still never be able to prepare a child for that. The reality, as you know, is that the rules in court are not written to protect children, but to protect defendants.'

'How fortunate for you, Mrs. Frost,' Quentin says dryly. 'Would you say you were a dedicated prosecutor?'

She hesitates. 'I would say . . . I was *too* dedicated a prosecutor.'

'Would you say you worked hard with the children you put on the stand to testify?'

'Yes.'

'In light of those twelve convictions, wouldn't you consider the work you did with those children to be successful?'

'No, I wouldn't,' she bluntly replies.

'But didn't all those perpetrators go to jail?'

'Not long enough.'

'Still, Mrs. Frost,' Quentin presses. 'You made the justice system work for those twelve children.'

'You don't understand,' she says, her eyes blazing. 'This was *my* child. As a prosecutor, my responsibility was completely different. I was supposed to take justice as far as I could for each of them, and I did. Anything else that happened outside the bounds of that courtroom was up to the parents, not me. If a mother decided to go into hiding to keep an abusive father away from her child – that was *her* decision to make. If a mother walked away from a verdict and shot an abuser, it had nothing to do with me. But then one day I wasn't just the prosecutor anymore. I was the parent. And it was up to me to take every step to make sure my son was safe, no matter what.'

It is the moment Quentin's waited for. Finely tuned to her anger, he steps closer to her. 'Are you saying that your child is entitled to more justice than another child?'

'Those kids were my job. Nathaniel is my *life*.'

Immediately, Fisher Carrington bobs out of his seat. 'Your Honor, may we take a short break –'

'No,' Quentin and the judge say simultaneously. 'That child was your life?' Quentin repeats.

'Yes.'

'Were you willing to exchange your freedom, then, to save Nathaniel?'

'Absolutely.'

'Were you thinking about that when you held the gun up to Father Szyszynski's head?'

'Of course I was,' she answers fiercely.

'Were you thinking that the only way to protect your son was to empty those bullets into Father Szyszynski's head –'

'Yes!'

'– and to make sure he never left that courtroom alive?'

'*Yes.*'

Quentin falls back. 'But you told us you weren't thinking at all at that moment, Mrs. Frost,' he says, and stares at her until she has to turn away.

When Fisher stands up to redirect, I am still shaking. How could I, who knew better, let that get away from me? I frantically scan the faces of the jury, but I can't tell a thing; you can never tell a thing. One woman looks near tears. Another is doing a crossword puzzle in the corner.

'Nina,' Fisher says, 'when you were in the courtroom that morning, were you thinking that you would be willing to exchange your freedom to save Nathaniel?'

'Yes,' I whisper.

'When you were in the courtroom that morning, were you thinking that the only way to stop that clock from ticking was to stop Father Szyszynski?'

'Yes.'

He meets my gaze. 'When you were in the courtroom that morning, were you planning to kill him?'

'Of course not,' I reply.

'Your Honor,' Fisher announces, 'the defense rests.'

Quentin lies on the godawful bed in the efficiency suite, wondering why the heat hasn't kicked in, when he's cranked it up to eighty degrees. He yanks the covers over himself, then flips through the channels on the television again. An entertainment program, *Wheel of Fortune,* and an infomercial for balding men. With a small grin, Quentin touches his shaved head.

He gets up and pads to the refrigerator, but the only thing inside it is a six-pack of Pepsi and a rotting mango he cannot recall buying. If he's going to eat dinner, he's going to have to get dinner. With a sigh, he sinks down on the bed to put on his boots and accidentally sits on the remote.

The channel switches again, this time to CNN. A woman with a smooth space helmet of red hair is speaking in front of a small graphic of Nina Frost's face. 'Testimony in the DA Murder Trial finished this afternoon,' the anchor says. 'Closing arguments are scheduled for tomorrow morning.'

Quentin turns off the TV. He ties his boots and then his gaze falls on the telephone beside the bed.

After three rings, he starts debating with himself about whether or not to leave a message. Then suddenly music explodes into his ear, a deafening backfire of rap. 'Yeah?' a voice says, and then the sound is turned down.

'Gideon,' Quentin says. 'It's me.'

There is a pause. 'Me who?' the boy replies, and it makes Quentin smile; he knows damn well who this is. 'If you're looking for my mom, she's not here. Maybe I'll tell her to call you back and then again maybe I'll just forget to give her the message.'

'Gideon, wait!' Quentin can almost hear the phone, halfway to its cradle, being brought back to his son's ear.

*'What.'*

'I didn't call to talk to Tanya. I called to talk to you.'

For a long moment, neither of them speaks. Then Gideon says, 'If you called to talk, you're doing a lousy job of it.'

'You're right.' Quentin rubs his temples. 'I just wanted to say I'm sorry. About the whole rehabilitation sentence, all of it. At the time I really believed that I was doing what was best for you.' He takes a deep breath. 'I had no right to start telling you how to live your life when I voluntarily walked out of it years before.' When his son stays silent, Quentin begins to get nervous. Did he get disconnected, without knowing it? 'Gideon?'

'Is that what you wanted to talk to me about?' he says finally.

'No. I called to see if you wanted to meet me for some pizza.' Quentin tosses the remote control on the bed, watches it bounce. The moment he waits for Gideon's response stretches to an eternity.

'Where?' Gideon asks.

Funny thing about a jury: no matter how scattered they seem during testimony; no matter who falls asleep in the back row and who paints their nails right during your cross-examinations, the minute it's time to get down to business, they suddenly rise to the challenge. The jurors stare at Quentin now, their attention focused on his closing argument. 'Ladies and gentlemen,' he begins, 'this is a very difficult case for me. Even though I do not know the defendant personally, I would have called her my colleague. But Nina Frost is not on the side of the law anymore. You all saw with your own eyes what she did on the morning of October thirtieth, 2001. She walked into a courtroom, put a gun up to an innocent man's head, and she shot him four times.

'The ironic thing is that Nina Frost claims she committed this crime in order to protect her son. Yet as she found out later . . . as we all would have found out later, had the court system been allowed to work the way it is supposed to work in a civilized society . . . that in killing Father Szyszynski, she did not protect her son at all.' Quentin looks soberly at the jury. 'There are reasons we have courts – because it's very easy to accuse a man. Courts hold up the facts, so that a rational judgment can be made. But Mrs. Frost acted without facts. Mrs. Frost not only accused this man, she tried him, convicted him, and executed him all by herself on that morning.'

He walks toward the jury box, trailing his hand along the railing. 'Mr. Carrington will tell you that the reason the defendant committed this crime is because she knew the justice system, and she truly believed it would not protect her son. Yes, Nina Frost knew the justice system. But she used it to stack the odds. She knew what her rights would be as a defendant. She knew how to act to make a jury believe she was temporarily insane. She knew exactly what she was doing the moment she stood up and shot Father Szyszynski in cold blood.'

Quentin addresses each juror in turn. 'To find Mrs. Frost guilty, you must first believe that the state of Maine has proved beyond a reasonable doubt that Father Szyszynski was unlawfully killed.' He spreads his hands. 'Well, you all saw it happen on videotape. Second, you must believe that the defendant was the one who killed Father Szyszynski. Again, there's no doubt in this case that this is true. And finally, you must believe that Mrs. Frost killed Father Szyszynski with premeditation. It's a big word, a legal word, but you all know what it is.'

He hesitates. 'This morning, as you were driving to court, at least one of you came upon a four-way intersection with a traffic light that was turning yellow. You needed to make a decision about whether or not to take your foot off the gas and stop . . . or whether you should speed through it. I don't know what choice you made; I don't need to. All I need to know – all *you* need to know – is that the split second when you made the decision to stop or to go was premeditation. That's all it takes. And when Mrs. Frost told you yesterday that at the moment she held the gun to Father Szyszynski's head, she was thinking that she needed to keep him from leaving the courtroom alive in order to protect her son – that, too, was premeditation.'

Quentin walks back toward the defense table and points at Nina. 'This is not a case about emotions; this is a case about facts. And the facts in this case are that an innocent man is dead, that this woman killed him, and that she believed her son deserved special treatment that only she could give.' He turns toward the jury one last time. 'Don't give her any special treatment for breaking the law.'

'I have two daughters,' Fisher says, standing up beside me. 'One's a high school junior; the other goes to Dartmouth.' He smiles at the jury. 'I'm crazy about them. I'm sure many of you feel the same about your kids. And that's the way Nina Frost feels about her son, Nathaniel.' He puts his hand on my shoulder. 'However, one completely ordinary morning, Nina found herself facing a horrible truth no parent ever wants to face: Someone had anally raped her little boy. And Nina had to face a second horrible truth – she knew what a molestation trial would do to her son's fragile emotional balance.'

He walks toward the jury. 'How did she know? Because she'd made other parents' children go through it. Because she had witnessed, time after time, children coming to court and dissolving into tears on the witness stand. Because she had seen abusers walk free even as these children were trying to fathom why they had to relive this nightmare all over again in front of a room full of strangers.' Fisher shakes his head. 'This was a tragedy. Adding to it is the fact that Father Szyszynski was not the man who had hurt this little boy, after all. But on October thirtieth, the police believed that he was the abuser. The prosecutor's office believed it. Nina Frost believed it. And on that morning, she also believed that she had run out of options. What happened in court that morning was not a premeditated, malicious act but a desperate one. The woman you saw shooting that man might have looked like Nina Frost, might have moved like Nina Frost – but ladies and gentlemen, that woman on the videotape was someone different. Someone not mentally capable of stopping herself at that moment.'

As Fisher takes another breath to launch into the definition of not guilty by reason of insanity, I get to my feet. 'Excuse me, but I'd like to finish.'

He turns around, the wind gone from his sails. 'You *what?*'

I wait until he is close enough for me to speak privately. 'Fisher, I think I can handle a closing argument.'

'You are not representing yourself!'

'Well, I'm not misrepresenting myself either.' I glance at the judge, and at Quentin Brown, who is absolutely gaping. 'May I approach, Your Honor?'

'Oh, by all means, go right ahead,' Judge Neal says.

We all go up to the bench, Fisher and Quentin sandwiching me. 'Your Honor, I don't believe this is the wisest course of action for my client,' Fisher says.

'Seems to me that's an issue she needs to work on,' Quentin murmurs.

The judge rubs his brow. 'I think Mrs. Frost knows the risks here better than other defendants. You may proceed.'

Fisher and I do-si-do for an awkward moment. 'It's your funeral,' he mutters, and then he steps around me and sits down. I walk up to the jury, finding my footing again, like a long-ago sailor stepping back on the deck of a clipper. 'Hello,' I begin softly. 'I think you all know who I am by now. You've certainly heard a lot of explanations for what brought me here. But what you haven't heard, straight out, is the truth.'

I gesture toward Quentin. 'I know this, because like Mr. Brown, I was a prosecutor. And truth isn't something that makes its way into a trial very often. You've got the state, tossing facts at you. And the defense, lobbing feelings. Nobody likes the truth because it's subject to personal interpretation, and both Mr. Brown and Mr. Carrington are afraid you might read it the wrong way. But today, I want to tell it to you.

'The truth is, I made a horrible mistake. The truth is, on that morning, I was not the vigilante Mr. Brown wants you to believe I was, and I wasn't a woman having a nervous breakdown, like Mr. Carrington wants you to believe. The truth is I was Nathaniel's mother, and that took precedence over everything else.'

I walk up to one juror, a young kid wearing a backward baseball cap. 'What if your best friend was being held at gunpoint, and you had a revolver in your own hand? What would you do?' Turning to an older gentleman, I ask, 'What if you came home and found your wife being raped?' I step back. 'Where is the line? We're taught to stand up for ourselves; we're taught to stand up for others we care about. But all of a sudden, there's a new line drawn by the law. *You sit back,* it says, *and let us deal with this.* And you know that the law won't even do a very good job – it will traumatize your child, it will set free a convict in only a few years. In the eyes of this law that's *dealing* with your problem, what's morally right is considered wrong . . . and what's morally wrong, you can get away with.'

I level my gaze at the jury. 'Maybe I knew that the judicial system would not work for my son. Maybe I even knew, on some level, that I could convince a jury I looked crazy even though I wasn't. I wish I could tell you for sure – but if I've learned anything, it's that we don't know half of what we think we do. And we know ourselves least of all.'

I turn toward the gallery and look, in turn, at Caleb and Patrick. 'For each of you sitting there, condemning me for my actions: How can you know that you wouldn't have done the same thing, if put to the test? Every day, we do little things to keep the people we love from being hurt – tell a white lie, buckle a seat belt, take away car keys from a buddy who's had one drink too many. But I've also heard of mothers who find the strength to lift cars off trapped toddlers; I've read of men who jump in front of bullets to save women they can't live without. Does that make them insane . . . or is that the moment when they are painfully, 100 percent lucid?' I raise my brows. 'It's not for me to say. But in that courtroom, the morning I shot Father Szyszynski, I knew exactly what I was doing. And at the same time, I was crazy.' I spread my hands, a supplicant. 'Love will do that to you.'

Quentin stands up to rebut. 'Unfortunately for Mrs. Frost, there are not two systems of justice in this country – one for people who think they know everything, and one for everyone else.' He glances at the jury. 'You heard her – she's not sorry that she killed a man . . . she's sorry she killed the *wrong* man.

'Enough mistakes have been made lately,' the prosecutor says wearily. 'Please don't make another one.'

When the doorbell rings, I think it might be Fisher. He hasn't spoken to me since we left court, and the three hours the jury deliberated after closing arguments does tend to support his belief that I shouldn't have gotten up to speak my mind. But when I open it, ready to defend myself – *again* – Nathaniel pitches into me. 'Mom!' he yells, squeezing me so tightly I stumble back. 'Mom, we checkered out!'

'Did you?' I say, and then repeat it over his head to Caleb. 'Did you?'

He sets down his small duffel bag, and Nathaniel's. 'I thought it might be a good time to come home,' he says quietly. 'If that's okay?'

By now Nathaniel has his arms around the barrel of our golden retriever's stomach; while Mason, wriggling, licks every spare inch of skin he can find. His thick tail thumps on the tile, a joyous tattoo. I know how that dog feels. Only now – in the presence of company – do I realize how lonely I have been.

So I lean against Caleb, my head tucked beneath his chin, where I cannot fail to listen to his heart. 'Perfect,' I reply.

The dog was a pillow breathing underneath me. 'What happened to Mason's mom?'

My mother looked up from the couch, where she was reading papers with big words printed so tiny it made my head hurt just thinking about them. 'She's . . . somewhere.'

'How come she doesn't live with us?'

'Mason's mother belonged to a breeder in Massachusetts. She had twelve puppies, and Mason was the one we took home.'

'Do you think he misses her?'

'I guess he used to, at first,' she answered. 'But it's been a long time, and he's happy with us. I bet he doesn't remember her anymore.'

I slid my finger past Mason's licorice gums, over his teeth. He blinked at me.

I bet she was wrong.

# 9

'Did you want the milk?' Nathaniel's mother asks.

'I already had a bowl of cereal,' his father replies.

'Oh.' She starts to put it back in the refrigerator, but his father takes it out of her hand. 'Maybe I'll have a little more.'

They look at each other, and then his mother steps back with a funny too-tight smile. 'All right,' she says.

Nathaniel watches this the way he would watch a cartoon – knowing in the back of his head that something is not quite real or right, but attracted to the show all the same.

Last summer when he was outside with his father he'd chased an electric green dragonfly all the way across the garden and the pumpkin patch and into the birdbath. There it found a bright blue dragonfly, and for a while they'd watched the two of them nip and thrust at each other, their bodies swords. 'Are they fighting?' Nathaniel had asked.

'No, they're mating.' Before Nathaniel could even ask, his father explained: It was the way animals and bugs and things made babies.

'But it looks like they're trying to kill each other,' Nathaniel pointed out.

Almost as soon as he said it, the two dragonflies hitched together like a shimmering space station, their wings beating like a quartet of hearts and their long tails quivering.

'Sometimes it's like that,' his father had answered.

Quentin had spent the night tossing on that godawful mattress, wondering what the hell was keeping the jury. No case was a sure thing, but for God's sake, they had this murder on tape.

It should have been pretty simple. Yet the jury had been deliberating since yesterday afternoon; and here it was nearly twenty-
four hours later with no verdict.

He has walked past the jury room at least twenty times,
trying ESP to will them toward a conviction. The bailiff posted
outside the door is an older man with the ability to sleep on
his feet. He snorts his way back to a deadpan position of
authority as the prosecutor passes. 'Anything?' Quentin asks.

'Lot of yelling. They just ordered lunch. Eleven turkey sandwiches and one roast beef.'

Frustrated, Quentin turns on his heel and heads down the
hall again, only to crash into his son coming around the corner.
'Gideon?'

'What's up.'

Gideon, in court. For a moment Quentin's heart stops, like
it did a year ago. 'What are you doing here?'

The boy shrugs, as if he can't figure it out himself. 'I didn't
have basketball practice today, and I figured I'd just come over
and chill out.' He drags his sneaker on the floor to make it
squeak. 'See what it looks like from the other side, and all.'

A slow smile itches its way across Quentin's face as he claps
his son on the shoulder. And for the first time in the ten years
that Quentin Brown has been in a courthouse, he is rendered
speechless.

Twenty-six hours; 1,560 minutes; 93,600 seconds. Call it what
you like; waiting in any denomination takes a lifetime. I have
memorized every inch of this conference room. I have counted
the linoleum tiles on the floor, marked the scars on the ceiling,
measured off the width of the windows. What are they doing
in there?

When the door opens, I realize that the only thing worse
than waiting is the moment that you realize a decision has been
made.

A white handkerchief appears in the doorway, followed by
Fisher.

'The verdict.' The words cut up my tongue. 'It's in?'

'Not yet.'

Boneless, I sink back in the chair as Fisher tosses the handkerchief at me. 'Is this in preparation for their finding?'

'No, it's me, surrendering. I'm sorry about yesterday.' He glances at me. 'Although a little advance notice that you wanted to do the closing would have been nice.'

'I know.' I look up at him. 'Do you think that's why the jury didn't come back fast with an acquittal?'

Fisher shrugs. 'Maybe it's why they didn't come back fast with a conviction.'

'Yeah, well. I've always been best at closings.'

He smiles at me. 'I'm a cross-examination man, myself.'

We look at each other for a moment, in complete accord. 'What's the part you hate most about a trial?'

'Now. Waiting for the jury to come back.' Fisher exhales deeply. 'I always have to calm down the client, who only wants a prediction about the outcome, and no one can predict that. You prosecutors are lucky; you just win or lose, and you don't have to reassure someone that he's not going to go to prison for the rest of his life when you know perfectly well that he . . .' He breaks off, because all the color has drained from my face. 'Well. Anyway. You know that no one can guess a jury's outcome.'

When I don't look particularly encouraged, he asks, 'What's the hardest part for you?'

'Right before the state rests, because that's the last chance I have to make sure I got all the evidence in and that I did it right. Once I say those three words . . . I know I'm going to find out whether or not I screwed up.'

Fisher meets my eye. 'Nina,' he says gently, 'the state rests.'

I lay on my side on an alphabet rug on the playroom floor, jamming the foot of a penguin into its wooden slot. 'If I do this penguin puzzle one more time,' I say, 'I will save the jury some trouble and hang myself.'

Caleb looks up from where he is sitting with Nathaniel, sorting multicolored plastic teddy bears. 'I want to go outside,' Nathaniel whines.

'We can't, buddy. We're waiting for some important news for Mommy.'

'But I want to!' Nathaniel kicks the table, hard.

'Maybe in a little while.' Caleb hands him a batch of bears. 'Here, take some more.'

'*No!*' With one arm, Nathaniel swipes the entire tray off the table. The sorting containers bounce and roll into the block area; the plastic bears scatter to all four corners of the room. The resulting clatter rings inside my head, in the empty spot where I am trying so hard to think of absolutely nothing.

I get to my feet, grab my son by the shoulders, and shake him. 'You do *not* throw toys! You will pick up every last one of these, Nathaniel, and I mean it!'

Nathaniel, now, is sobbing at the top of his lungs. Caleb, tight-faced, turns on me too. 'Just because you're at the end of your rope, Nina, doesn't mean that you –'

'*'Scuse me.*'

The voice at the door makes all three of us turn. A bailiff leans in, nods at us. 'The jury's coming in,' he says.

'It's not a verdict,' Fisher whispers to me minutes later.

'How do you know?'

'Because the bailiff would have said so . . . not just that the jury was back.'

I draw back, dubious. 'Bailiffs never tell *me* anything.'

'Trust me.'

I wet my lips. 'Then why are we here?'

'I don't know,' Fisher admits, and we both turn our attention to the judge.

He sits at the bench, looking overjoyed to have finally reached the end of this debacle. 'Mr. Foreperson,' Judge Neal asks, 'has the jury reached a verdict?'

A man in the front row of the jury box stands up. He takes

off his baseball cap and tucks it under his arm, then clears his throat. 'Your Honor, we've been trying, but we can't seem to get together on this. There's some of us that –'

'Hold on, Mr. Foreperson, don't say any more. Have you deliberated about this case and have you taken a vote to see what every juror's position is on the issue of guilt or innocence?'

'We've done it a bunch of times, but it keeps coming back to a few that won't change their minds.'

The judge looks at Fisher, and then at Quentin. 'Counsel, approach.'

I stand up, too, and the judge sighs. 'All right, Mrs. Frost, you too.' At the bench, he murmurs, 'I'm going to give them an Allen charge. Any objections?'

'No objection,' Quentin says, and Fisher agrees. As we walk back to the defense table, I meet Caleb's eye, and silently mouth, 'They're hung.'

The judge begins to speak. 'Ladies and gentlemen, you've heard all the facts, and you've heard all the evidence. I am aware it's been a long haul, and that you have a difficult decision to make. But I also know that you *can* reach closure . . . and that you're the best jury to do it. If the case has to be tried again, another group of jurors will not necessarily do a better job than you are doing.' He glances soberly at the group. 'I urge you to go back to the jury room, to respectfully consider each other's opinions, and to see if some progress can't be made. At the end of the afternoon, I'm going to ask you to come back and let me know how you're doing.'

'Now what?' Caleb whispers, from behind me.

I watch the newly energized jury file out again. Now we wait.

Watching someone tie themselves in a knot makes you squirm in your own seat, or so Caleb discovers after spending two and a half more hours with Nina while the jury is deliberating. She sits hunched forward on a tiny chair in the playroom, completely ignorant of Nathaniel making airplane sounds as he zooms around with his arms extended. Her eyes stare intensely at absolutely nothing; her chin rests on her fist.

'Hey,' Caleb says softly.

She blinks, comes back to him. 'Oh . . . hey.'

'You okay?'

'Yes.' A smile stretches her lips thin. *'Yes!'* she repeats.

It reminds Caleb of the time years ago that he attempted to teach her to water-ski: She is trying too hard, instead of just letting it happen. 'Why don't we all go down to the vending machines?' he suggests. 'Nathaniel can get some hot chocolate, and I'll treat you to the dishwater that passes for soup.'

'Sounds great.'

Caleb turns to Nathaniel and tells him they are going to get a snack. He runs to the door, and Caleb walks up behind him. 'Come on,' he says to Nina. 'We're ready.'

She stares at him as if they have never had a conversation, much less one thirty seconds ago. 'To do what?' she asks.

Patrick sits on a bench behind the courthouse, freezing his ass off, and watching Nathaniel whoop his way across a field. Why this child has so much energy at four-thirty in the afternoon is beyond him, but then he can remember back to when he and Nina used to spend entire days playing pond hockey without tiring or getting frostbite. Maybe time is only something you notice when you get old and have less of it at your disposal.

The boy collapses beside Patrick, his cheeks a fiery red, his nose running. 'Got a tissue, Patrick?'

He shakes his head. 'Sorry, Weed. Use your sleeve.'

Nathaniel laughs, and then does just that. He ducks his head beneath Patrick's arm, and it makes Patrick want to shout. If only Nina could see this, her son seeking out someone's touch – oh, God, what it would do for her morale right now. He hugs Nathaniel close, drops a kiss on the top of his head.

'I like playing with you,' Nathaniel says.

'Well, I like playing with you too.'

'You don't yell.'

Patrick glances down at him. 'Your mom been doing that?'

Nathaniel shrugs, then nods. 'It's like she got stolen and they left someone mean in her place who looks just like her. Someone who can't sit still and who doesn't hear me when I talk and when I do talk it's always giving her a headache.' He looks into his lap. 'I want my old mom back.'

'She wants that too, Weed.' Patrick looks to the west, where the sun has begun to draw blood from the horizon. 'Truth is, she's pretty nervous right now. She isn't sure what kind of news she's going to hear.' When Nathaniel shrugs, he adds, 'You know she loves you.'

'Well,' the boy says defensively. 'I love her too.'

Patrick nods. *You're not the only one,* he thinks.

'A mistrial?' I say, shaking my head. 'No. Fisher, I can't go through this again. You know trials don't get any better with age.'

'You're thinking like a prosecutor,' Fisher admonishes, 'except this time, you're right.' He turns around from the window where he is standing. 'I want you to chew on something tonight.'

'What?'

'Waiving the jury. I'll talk to Quentin in the morning, if you agree, and see if he's willing to let the judge decide the verdict.'

I stare at him. 'You know that we were trying this case on the emotion, not the law. A jury *might* acquit based on emotion. But a judge is *always* going to rule based on the law. Are you crazy?'

'No, Nina,' Fisher answers soberly. 'But neither were you.'

We lie in bed that night with the weight of a full moon pressing down on us. I have told Caleb about my conversation with Fisher, and now we both stare at the ceiling, as if the answer might appear, skywritten with stars. I want Caleb to take my hand across the great expanse of this bed. I need that, to believe we are not miles apart.

'What do you think?' he asks.

I turn to him. In the moonlight his profile is edged in gold, the color of courage. 'I'm not making decisions by myself anymore,' I answer.

He comes up on an elbow, turning to me. 'What would happen?'

I swallow, and try to keep my voice from shaking. 'Well, a judge is going to convict me, because legally, I committed murder. But the upside is . . . I probably won't be sentenced as long as I would have been with a jury verdict.'

Suddenly Caleb's face looms over mine. 'Nina . . . you can't go to jail.'

I turn away, so that the tear slips down the side of my face he cannot see. 'I knew I was taking this chance when I did it.'

His hands tighten on my shoulders. 'You can't. You just can't.'

'I'll be back.'

'When?'

'I don't know.'

Caleb buries his face in my neck, drawing in great draughts of air. And then suddenly I am clutching at him, too, as if there cannot be any distance between us today, because tomorrow there will be so much. I feel the rough pads of his hands mark my back; and the heat of his grief is searing. When he comes inside me I dig my nails into his shoulders, trying to leave behind a trace of myself. We make love with near violence, with so much emotion that the atmosphere around us hums. And then, like all things, it is over.

'But I love you,' Caleb says, his voice breaking, because in a perfect world, this should be all the excuse one needs.

That night I dream I am walking into an ocean, the waves soaking the hem of my cotton nightgown. The water is cold, but not nearly as cold as it usually is in Maine, and the beach beneath is a smooth lip of sand. I keep walking, even when the water reaches my knees, even when it brushes my hips and my nightgown sticks to my body like a second skin. I keep walking, and the water comes up to my neck, my chin. By the time I go under I realize I am going to drown.

At first I fight, trying to ration the air I have in my lungs. Then they start to burn, a circle of fire beneath my ribs. My wide eyes burst black, and my feet start to thrash, but I am getting nowhere. *This is it,* I think. *Finally.*

With that realization I let my arms go still, and my legs go limp. I feel my body sinking and the water filling me, until I am curled on the sand at the base of the sea.

The sun is a quivering yellow eye. I get to my feet, and to my great surprise, begin to walk with ease on the bottom of the ocean floor.

Nathaniel doesn't move the hour I sit on his bed, watching him sleep. But when I touch his hair, unable to hold back any longer, he rolls over and blinks at me. 'It's still dark,' he whispers.

'I know. It's not morning.'

I watch him trying to puzzle this out: What could have brought me, then, to wake him in the middle of the night? How am I supposed to explain to him that the next time I have the opportunity to do this, his body might reach the whole length of the bed? That by the time I come back, the boy I left behind will no longer exist?

'Nathaniel,' I say, with a shuddering breath, 'I might be going away.'

He sits up. 'You can't, Mommy.' Smiling, he even finds a reason. 'We just got back.'

'I know . . . but this isn't my choice.'

Nathaniel pulls the covers up to his chest, suddenly looking very small. 'What did I do this time?'

With a sob I pull him onto my lap and bury my face against his hair. He rubs his nose against my neck, and it reminds me so much of him as an infant that I cannot breathe. I would trade everything, now, to have those minutes back, tucked into a miser's lockbox. Even the ordinary moments – driving in the car, cleaning up the playroom, cooking dinner with Nathaniel. They are no less miraculous simply because they are something we did as a matter of routine. It is not *what* you do with a child that brings you together . . . it is the fact that you are lucky enough to do it at *all*.

I draw away to look at his face. That bow of a mouth, the slope of his nose. His eyes, preserving memories like the amber they resemble. *Keep them,* I think. *Watch over them for me.*

By now, I am crying hard. 'I promise, it won't be forever. I promise that you can come see me. And I want you to know every minute of every day that I'm away from you . . . I'm thinking of how long it'll be before I come back.'

Nathaniel wraps his arms around my neck and holds on for dear life. 'I don't want you to go.'

'I know.' I draw back, holding his wrists loosely.

'I'll come with you.'

'I wish you could. But I need someone here to take care of your father.'

Nathaniel shakes his head. 'But I'll miss you.'

'And I'll miss you,' I say softly. 'Hey, how about if we make a pact?'

'What's that?'

'A decision two people make together.' I try for a smile. 'Let's agree *not* to miss each other. Is that a deal?'

Nathaniel looks at me for a long moment. 'I don't think I can do it,' he confesses.

I pull him close again. 'Oh, Nathaniel,' I whisper. 'Me neither.'

Nathaniel is glued to my side the next morning when we walk into the courthouse. The reporters that I have almost become accustomed to seem like a cruel torture, their questions and their blinding video cameras a modern gauntlet I have to survive. These will be my Before and After pictures; DA-cum-convict. *Print your headlines now,* I think, *since I am going to jail.*

As soon as I reach the barrier of the double doors, I hand Nathaniel to Caleb and make a dead run for the restroom, where I dry heave into a toilet and splash water on my face and wrists. 'You can get through this,' I say to the mirror. 'You can at least end it with dignity.'

Taking a deep breath I push my way out the swinging door to where my family is waiting, and see Adrienne, the trans-sexual, wearing a red dress two sizes too small and a grin as large as Texas. 'Nina!' she cries, and comes running to hug me. 'Last place I ever thought I'd want to be is in a courtroom again, but honey, I'm here for you.'

'You're out?'

'Since yesterday. Didn't know if I'd make it in time, but that jury deliberation's taking longer than my sex change operation.'

Suddenly Nathaniel has wormed his way between us, and is doing his best to climb me like a tree. I heft him into my arms. 'Nathaniel, this is Adrienne.'

Her eyes light up. 'I have heard so much about you.'

It is a toss-up as to who is more stunned by Adrienne's presence – Nathaniel or Caleb. But before I can offer any explanations, Fisher hurries toward us.

I meet his gaze. 'Do it,' I say.

Quentin finds Fisher waiting for him in the courtroom. 'We have to speak to Judge Neal,' he says quietly.

'I'm not offering her a plea,' Quentin answers.

'And I'm not asking for one.' He turns, heading for the judge's chambers without waiting to see if the prosecutor will follow.

Ten minutes later, they are standing in front of Judge Neal, the angry heads of safari animals bearing witness. 'Your Honor,' Fisher begins, 'we've been here so long; it's clear that the jury is going to hang. I've talked to my client . . . and if Mr. Brown is willing, we'd like to submit this case to Your Honor and have you decide the facts and the verdict.'

Well, if Quentin was expecting anything it wasn't this. He looks at the defense attorney as if the man has lost his mind. Granted, nobody likes a mistrial, but to let the judge rule is to adhere, strictly, to the letter of the law – something far more beneficial to the prosecution, in this case, than the defense. Fisher Carrington has just handed Quentin a conviction on a silver platter.

The judge stares at him. 'Mr. Brown? What would the state like to do?'

He clears his throat. 'The state finds this perfectly acceptable, Your Honor.'

'Fine. I'm going to let the jury go then. I need an hour to review the evidence, and then I'll make my ruling.' With a nod, the judge dismisses the two lawyers, and begins the process of deciding Nina Frost's future.

Adrienne, it turns out, is a godsend. She gets Nathaniel out of my arms by making herself into a jungle gym when Caleb and I are wrung too dry to play. Nathaniel crawls over her back and then down the long slide of her shins. 'If he's tiring you out,' Caleb says, 'just tell him to stop.'

'Oh, honey, I've been waiting my whole life for this.' She flips Nathaniel upside down, so that he giggles.

I am torn between watching them and joining in. My biggest fear is that if I let myself touch my son again, nothing they will do will be able to drag me away.

When there is a knock at the playroom door, we all turn. Patrick stands uncomfortably at the threshold. I know what he wants, and I also know that he will not ask for it with my family here.

To my surprise, Caleb takes the decision out of everyone's hands. He nods toward Patrick, and then to me. 'Go on,' he says.

So Patrick and I find ourselves walking down twisted basement corridors, a foot of space separating us. We travel so far in silence that I realize I have no idea where we now are. 'How could you?' he finally bursts out. 'If you'd gone with another jury trial, at least, you'd have a shot at an acquittal.'

'And I would have dragged Nathaniel and Caleb and you and everyone else along through it again. Patrick, this has to stop. It has to be over. No matter what.'

He stops walking, leans against a heating duct. 'I never really thought you'd go to jail.'

'There are a lot of places,' I reply, 'that I thought I'd never go.' I smile faintly. 'Will you bring me Chinese food every now and then?'

'No.' Patrick looks down at the floor between his shoes. 'I won't be here, Nina.'

'You . . . what?'

'I'm moving. There are some job openings out in the Pacific Northwest I might take a look at.' He takes a deep breath. 'I always wanted to see what it was like out there. I just didn't want to do it without you.'

'Patrick –'

With great tenderness, he kisses my forehead. 'You will be fine,' he murmurs. 'You've done it before.' He offers me a crooked smile to slip into my breast pocket. And then he walks down the hall, leaving me to find my own way back.

The bathroom door at the base of the staircase flies open, and suddenly Quentin Brown is no more than four feet away from me. 'Mrs. Frost,' he sputters.

'After all this, I would think you could call me Nina.' It is an ethical violation for him to speak to me without Fisher present, and we both know it. Yet somehow, bending that rule doesn't seem quite so horrific, after all this. When he doesn't respond, I realize he doesn't feel the same way and I try to step around him. 'If you'll excuse me, my family's waiting in the playroom.'

'I have to admit,' Quentin says as I am walking away, 'I was surprised by your decision.'

I turn. 'To let the judge rule?'

'Yes. I don't know if I'd do the same thing, if I were a defendant.'

I shake my head. 'Somehow, Quentin, I can't picture you as a defendant.'

'Could you picture me as a parent?'

It surprises me. 'No. I never heard that you had a family.'

'A boy. Sixteen.' He stuffs his hands in his pockets. 'I know, I know. You've done such a good job imagining me as a ruthless villain that it's hard to give me a vein of compassion.'

'Well.' I shrug. 'Maybe not a ruthless villain.'

'An asshole then?'

'Your words, counselor,' I reply, and we both grin.

'Then again, people can surprise you all the time,' he muses. 'For example, a district attorney who commits murder. Or an assistant attorney general that drives past a defendant's home at night just to make sure she's okay.'

I snort. 'If you drove by at all, it was to make sure I was still *there*.'

'Nina, didn't you ever wonder who in your office left you the lab report from the underwear?'

My jaw drops open. 'My son's name,' Quentin says. 'It's Gideon.'

Whistling, he nods to me, and jogs up the staircase.

The courtroom is so quiet that I can hear Caleb breathing behind me. What he said the moment before we walked in to hear the judge's verdict echoes too, in the silence: *I am proud of you.*

Judge Neal clears his throat and begins to speak. 'The evidence in this case clearly shows that on October thirtieth, 2001, the defendant Nina Frost went out, purchased a handgun, concealed it, and brought it into a Biddeford district courtroom. The evidence also shows that she positioned herself near Father Szyszynski, and intentionally and knowingly shot him four times in the head, thereby causing his death. The evidence is also clear that at the time she did these things, Nina Frost was under the mistaken impression that Father Szyszynski had sexually molested her five-year-old son.'

I bow my head, each word a blow. 'So what does the evidence not support?' the judge asks rhetorically. 'Specifically, the defendant's contention that she was legally insane at the time of the shooting. Witnesses testified that she acted deliberately and methodically to exterminate the man who she thought had harmed her child. And at the time, the defendant was a trained, practicing assistant district attorney who knew very well that every person charged with a crime – Father Szyszynski included – was innocent until proven guilty in a court of law. Basically, this court believes Nina Frost to be a prosecutor through and through . . . so much so, that to break a law, she would have had to give the act careful consideration.'

He raises his head and pushes his glasses up on his nose. 'And so I reject the defendant's insanity defense.'

A shuffling to my left, from Quentin Brown.

'However –'

Quentin stills.

'– in this state there is another reason to justify the act of murder – namely, if a defendant was under the influence of a reasonable fear or anger brought about by reasonable provocation. As a prosecutor, Nina Frost didn't have reason to be fearful or angry the morning of October thirtieth . . . yet as Nathaniel's mother, she did. Her son's attempt to identify the victim, the wild card of the DNA evidence, and the defendant's intimate knowledge of the treatment of a witness in the criminal justice system all add up, in this court's opinion, to reasonable provocation under the law.'

I have stopped breathing. This cannot be true.

'Will the defendant please rise?'

It is not until Fisher grabs my arm and hauls me to my feet that I remember the judge means me. 'Nina Frost, I find you Not Guilty of Murder. I do find you Guilty of Manslaughter pursuant to 17-A M.R.S.A. Section 203 (1)(B). Does the defendant wish to waive a presentence report and be sentenced today?'

'Yes, Your Honor,' Fisher murmurs.

The judge looks at me for the first time this morning. 'I sentence you to twenty years in the Maine State Prison, with credit for the time you have already served.' He pauses. 'The remainder of the twenty years will be suspended, and you'll be on probation for that time. You need to check in with your probation officer before you leave court today, and then, Mrs. Frost, you are free to go.'

The courtroom erupts in a frenzy of flashbulbs and confusion. Fisher embraces me as I burst into tears, and Caleb leaps over the bar. 'Nina?' he demands. 'In English?'

'It's . . . good.' I laugh up at him. 'It's *great*, Caleb.' The judge, in essence, has absolved me. I will never have to serve out my prison term, as long as I manage not to kill anyone again. Caleb grabs me and swings me around; over his shoulder I see Adrienne pump her fist in the air. Behind her is Patrick. He sits with his eyes closed, smiling. Even as I watch, they blink open to focus on me. *Only you,* Patrick mouths silently; words I will wonder about for years.

When the reporters run off to call their affiliates with the verdict and the crowd in the gallery thins, I notice one other man. Quentin Brown has gathered his files and his briefcase. He walks to the gate between our tables, stops, and turns to me. He inclines his head, and I nod back. Suddenly my arm is wrenched behind me, and I instinctively pull away, certain that someone who has not understood the judge's verdict is about to put handcuffs on me again. 'No,' I say, turning. 'You don't understand . . .' But then the bailiff unlocks the electronic bracelet on my wrist. It falls to the floor, ringing out my release.

When I look up again, Quentin is gone.

After a few weeks, the interviews stop. The eagle eye of the news refocuses on some other sordid story. A caravan of media vehicles snakes its way south, and we go back to what we used to be.

Well, most of us do.

Nathaniel is stronger every day; and Caleb has picked up a few new jobs. Patrick called me from Chicago, his halfway point to the West Coast. So far, he is the only one who has been brave enough to ask me how I will fill my days now that I am not a prosecutor.

It has been such a big part of me for so long that there's no easy answer. Maybe I'll write the book everyone seems to want me to write. Maybe I'll give free legal advice to senior citizens at the town recreation hall. Maybe I will just stay at home and watch my son grow up.

I tap the envelope in my hand. It is from the Bar Disciplinary Committee, and it has been on the kitchen counter, unopened, for nearly two months. There's no point in opening it now, either. I know what it will say.

Sitting down at the computer, I type a very concise note. *I am voluntarily turning in my license; I no longer wish to practice law. Sincerely, Nina Frost.*

I print it, and an envelope to match. Fold, lick, seal, stamp. Then I put on my boots and walk down the driveway to the mailbox.

'Okay,' I say out loud, after I put it inside and raise the red flag. 'Okay,' I repeat, when what I really mean is, *What do I do now?*

There's always one week in January that's a thaw. Without warning, the temperature climbs to fifty degrees; the snow melts in puddles wide as a lake; people take to sitting on Adirondack chairs in their shorts, watching it all happen.

This year, however, the thaw's gone on for a record number of days. It started the day of Nina's release. That very afternoon, the town skating pond was closed due to spotty ice; by the end of the week teenagers were skateboarding down sidewalks; there was even word of a few crocuses pushing their way up through the inevitable mud. It has been good for business, that's for sure – construction that couldn't get done in the dead of winter has suddenly been given a reprieve. And it has also, for the first time Caleb can recall, made the sap run in the maple trees this early in the year.

Yesterday Caleb set up his taps and buckets; today, he is walking the perimeter of his property, collecting the sap. The sky seems crisp as a lancet, and Caleb has his shirtsleeves rolled up to the elbow. The mud is a succubus, grabbing for his boots, but even that can't slow him. Days like this, they just don't come around often enough.

He pours the sap into huge vats. Forty gallons of this sweet juice will boil down to a single gallon of maple syrup. Caleb makes it right on the kitchen stove, in a spaghetti pot, straining each batch through a sieve before it thickens. For Nina and Nathaniel, it's all about the end product – pouring it on pancakes and waffles. But to Caleb, the beauty is in the way you get there. The blood of a tree, a spout, and a bucket. Steam rising, the scent filling every corner of the house. There is nothing quite like it: knowing every breath you take is bound to be sweet.

Nathaniel is building a bridge, although it might turn out to be a tunnel. The cool thing about Legos is that you can change them right in the middle. Sometimes when he builds he pretends he is his father, and he does it with the same careful planning. And sometimes when he builds he pretends he is his mother, and takes a tower as high as it can go before it falls to the ground.

He has to work around the dog's tail, because Mason happens to be sleeping right on the middle of his bedroom floor, but that's all right too, because this could be a village with a monstrous beast. In fact, he might be creating the wicked awesome getaway boat.

But where will they all go? Nathaniel thinks for a minute, then lays down four greens and four reds, begins to build. He makes sturdy walls and wide windows. A level of a house, his father has told him, is called a *story*.

Nathaniel likes that. It makes him feel like maybe he is living between the covers of a book himself. Like maybe everyone in every home is sure to get a happy ending.

Laundry is always a good, mindless start. Ours seems to reproduce at the dank bottom of its bin, so that regardless of how careful we are with our clothes, there is always a full basket every other day. I fold the clean wash and carry it upstairs, putting Nathaniel's items away before I tackle my own.

It is when I go to fold a pair of my jeans over a hanger that I see the duffel bag. Has it really been sitting here, shoved into the back of the closet, for two weeks? Caleb probably never even noticed; he has enough clothes in his drawers to have overlooked unpacking the bag he took with him to the motel. But seeing it is an eyesore; it reminds me of the moment he moved out.

I pull out a few long-sleeved shirts, some boxers. It is not until I toss them into the laundry bin that I realize my hand is sticky. I rub my fingers together, frown, pick up one shirt again and shake it out.

There is a big, green stain on one corner.

There are stains on some socks too. It looks as if something has spilled all over, but when I look in the bag, there's no open bottle of shampoo.

Then, it doesn't smell like shampoo either. It is a scent I cannot place, exactly. Something industrial.

The last item in the bag is a pair of jeans. Out of habit, I reach into the pockets to make sure Caleb hasn't left money or receipts inside.

In the left rear pocket is a five-dollar bill. And in the right rear pocket are boarding passes for two US Air flights: one from Boston to New Orleans, one from New Orleans to Boston, both dated January 3, 2002. The day after Nathaniel's competency hearing.

Caleb's voice comes from a few feet behind me. 'I did what I had to do.'

*Caleb is yelling at Nathaniel to stop playing with the antifreeze.*

'*How many times do I have to tell you . . . It's poison.*' Mason, lapping at the puddle because it tastes so sweet; he does not know any better.

'The cat,' I whisper, turning to him. 'The cat died too.'

'I know. I figure it got at the rest of the cocoa. Ethylene glycol is toxic . . . but it's sweet enough.' He reaches for me, but I back away. 'You told me his name. You said it wasn't over yet. All I did,' Caleb says softly, 'is finish what you started.'

'Don't.' I hold up my hand. 'Caleb, don't tell me this.'

'You're the only one I *can* tell.'

He is right, of course. As his wife, I am not obligated to testify against him. Not even if Gwynne is autopsied, and there are traces of poison in the tissues. Not even if evidence leads right to Caleb.

But then, I have spent three months learning the repercussions of taking the law into one's own hands. I have watched my husband walk out the door – not because he was judging me, it turns out, but because he was trying himself. I have come so close to losing everything I ever wanted – a life I was too foolish to value until it was nearly taken away.

I stare at Caleb, waiting for an explanation.

Yet there are some feelings so far-flung and wide that words cannot cover them. As language fails Caleb, his eyes lock onto mine, and he spells out what he cannot speak. His hands come up to clasp each other tightly. To someone who does not know how to listen in a different way, it looks like he is praying for the best. But me, I know the sign for *marriage*.

It is all he needs to say to make me understand.

Suddenly Nathaniel bursts into our bedroom. 'Mom, Dad!' he yells. 'I made the coolest castle in the world. You have to see it.' He spins before he has even come to a complete stop, and runs back, expecting us to follow.

Caleb watches me. He cannot take the first step. After all, the only way to communicate is to find someone who can comprehend; the only way to be forgiven is to find someone who is willing to forgive. So I start for the door, turning back at the threshold. 'Come on,' I say to Caleb. 'He needs us.'

*It happens when I am trying to come down the stairs superfast, my feet ahead of the rest of me. One of the steps just isn't where it is supposed to be, and I fall really hard onto the railing where hands go. I hit the part of my arm that makes a corner, the part with the name that sounds just like what it is. L-bow.*

*The hurt feels like a shot, a needle going in right there and spreading out like fire under the rest of my arm. I can't feel my fingers, and my hand goes wide. It hurts more than when I fell on the ice last year and my ankle got as fat as the rest of my leg. It hurts more than when I went over the handlebars of my bike and scraped up the whole front of my face and needed two stitches. It hurts so much that I have to get past the ouch of it before I can remember to cry.*

*'Moooooooooooom!'*

*When I yell like that, she can come quick as a ghost, the air empty one minute and full of her the next. 'What hurts?' she cries. She touches all the places I am holding close to myself.*

*'I think I broke my funny bone,' I say.*

*'Hmm.' She moves that arm up and down. Again. Then she puts her hands on my shoulders and looks up at me. 'Tell a joke.'*

*'Mom!'*

*'How else are we going to know for sure if it's broken?'*

*I shake my head. 'It doesn't work that way.'*

*She picks me up and carries me into the kitchen. 'Says who?' She laughs, and before I know it I am laughing back, which must mean I'm going to be okay after all.*

# A CONVERSATION WITH JODI PICOULT

**Q:** Your ability to tell a story from so many varying points of view in an engaging and believable manner is impressive. How do you crawl into the minds of so many different characters, with different motivations, insecurities, views on life, etc.? Are there exercises you do to help yourself understand where your characters are coming from?

**A:** Crawling into the minds of characters is actually one of the best parts of writing for me. After all, I'm never going to get to be a five-year-old boy, so it's a challenge to be able to pull it off. It's a little like trying on a costume – and getting to shrug it off my shoulders when I'm finished. When I write in multiple points of view, I'm very careful to make sure they all sound different, even to me – so that Patrick, for example, doesn't think like Nina, who doesn't think like Caleb. I will even deliberately change the syntax of their sentences, sometimes, to keep everyone separate and equal. As for exercises – the closest I come to this is knowing my characters all very well before I ever start writing for them. For example, we may never see Nina eat breakfast, but I can tell you that she grabs coffee and whatever's left on Nathaniel's plate. Patrick, however, has the same cereal – something healthy – every morning. And so on. If I don't know my characters well enough to provide details like this in a snap, I'm not ready to write in their minds yet.

**Q:** The scenes where Nathaniel is abused are striking and disturbing. Was it difficult for you, especially as a mother, to imagine yourself into that scenario? Did you know that you were going to include these scenes from the beginning? Were you dreading writing them?

**A:** You have NO idea! Most of my other books are totally

unrelated to my real life, but while writing this one I would go to the breakfast table every morning and talk to my kids, and take their comments and filter them through Nathaniel's sad affect and into his narrative. In addition, many of Nathaniel's ways of looking at the world – poetically, and somehow startling and focused – came from actual experiences I had with my middle son, Jake. You know that 'slice of sky' Nathaniel describes lying on the ground in the first interchapter? Jake said that to me. Putting any piece of my children into Nathaniel was painful – but it also allowed for me to write Nina with heart. Because the more uncomfortable and upset I felt even marginally imagining my children as Nathaniel, she would be feeling a thousand times worse.

I knew that I would put the scenes of abuse in, because I really wanted to explain how and why a child might wind up in that situation – and how a child might feel responsible afterward. So much of the writing that's been done on child sexual abuse focuses on the perpetrators that we sometimes forget to listen to the voices of the victims. So yes, those segments were intentional and necessary and awful and revelatory all at once.

**Q:** It is interesting, and a bit shocking, that Nina gets away with the murder of Father Szyszynski. Why did you choose to let her go free? Did you have any alternate endings at any point in the process?

**A:** Actually, the DA I've worked with as a research consultant for several books was the reason I tipped the verdict the way I did. For years now, she's been complaining because I never convict anyone . . . so finally I decided I'd convict a DA. Naturally, she balked. I thought about it some more and realized that on a purely emotional level, the last thing I wanted was for Nathaniel to suffer any more trauma. I wanted the Frosts intact at the end of the book – not left with Mom in jail. So, legally, I chose to go with that freaky clause on the Maine books – the one that says, basically, if you have just cause to be angry enough to kill someone, it's okay. There is never any question that Nina has committed a crime – the question is really whether it's permissible, in certain circumstances to commit a crime. (And no, I'm not gonna answer that!) In my opinion, her verdict is an honest one for much the same reason that I felt it was okay to let Chris Harte free at the end of *The Pact:* I don't think Nina is going to go around blowing away people who upset her son. I think this is a one-time act she was driven to, and I think that at the end of the book she has acquired the forethought to reason through the consequences of her actions in a way she isn't capable of doing at the beginning of the book.

**Q:** The attention to detail regarding DNA analysis, police and court procedures, and medical matters in your novels is flawless. How do you get all your information? For instance, how did you come up with the idea that the priest's semen would match the semen found on Nathaniel's shorts, but would not actually be his?

**A:** I'm so glad you noticed! I love doing research, and research often drives story ideas for me. When necessary, I will go down to State Forensics labs to work with detectives, I will ride with policemen, I will visit labs. In fact, the reason I wrote this book, in part, came from DNA research I did while writing *Salem Falls:* the researcher mentioned that DNA is damning evidence, because it is accurate in 99.9% of the cases. And being me, I asked, 'What's the other one percent?' Well, the answer lies in the science that I included in *Perfect Match:* a bone marrow recipient doesn't have his own blood anymore. Hence, his bodily fluids will have a DNA different from that of a blood sample taken from his arm . . . which of course would render inaccurate any semen evidence that's left behind and matched up via a traditional blood stick.

**Q:** You must have written this manuscript long before the recent priest scandal broke, but was there a particular news story that inspired this novel?

**A:** No. However, when I decided to make it a priest who was the perp, I interviewed four priests – all of whom said they knew someone who had been accused or transferred on allegations of sexual abuse. That told me I wasn't pulling this problem out of thin air . . . and that I had a legitimate reason to write the book with that particular plot twist. But then, when real life began to imitate my fiction, it was a little bizarre. I had one interviewer ask me if for my next book I could write about Mideast peace!

**Q:** Is there some over-arching message that you would like readers to take from this novel?

**A:** That we never know anyone as well as we think we do – least of all ourselves. And that we shouldn't rush to judgment until we've walked a mile in someone else's shoes. I can't tell you I would do what Nina did in her situation . . . but I can't tell you I wouldn't, either.

**Q:** What kind of unique challenges did writing *Perfect Match* present to you?

**A:** One of the most difficult things about *Perfect Match* was that it required me to write with a first-person narrator who was very hard to like! Nina is opinionated, single-minded, and thinks she knows all the right answers, even when she doesn't – there were times I wanted to knock her head against a wall, and I was the AUTHOR! But I had such fun trying on her voice, because she may be wrong, but she's impassioned, and it's very entertaining to write a character who fights you every step of the way. My other first-person narrator – Nathaniel – was equally difficult. I needed him to sound like a five-year-old, which limited my vocabulary and choice of phrase – and yet Nathaniel is much wiser than normal kids his age, because of what happened. That was a fine literary line to walk, too. And yet, I felt both first-person narratives were crucial, because to me, this is really a story about a mother and her child, and I wanted the reader to hear them both.

Q: The following quote near the end of the novel is quite striking: 'Remembering that although the future may unfold in indelible strokes, it doesn't mean we have to read the same line over and over.' Is this line a plea for self-efficacy, or just hope for the future? Do you believe that people can easily shake off the past and start fresh?

A: I'm laughing, because I think I keep changing my mind on this one with every subsequent book! In *Perfect Match*, I definitely come down on the side of free will rather than fate. But in other books, like *Salem Falls*, I've gone the other way. I guess I'm still deciding for myself! I will admit, though, that people who think they can shake off the past are usually wrong. You can build on your past, you can even whitewash over it, but it doesn't ever really go away.

Q: You have been quoted as saying, 'I'm a better mother because I have my writing and I'm a better writer because of the experiences of motherhood that have shaped me.' Discuss your experience of writing this book as a mother. Were there moments when you had to step back from the characters and observe them, not as a mother, but objectively, as an author? If so, was that difficult?

A: This is a hard read for parents of young children. I do believe that sometimes when you're a mother or father, it's just too painful to 'go' somewhere fictionally that you're terrified of in real life.

Me, I zoom off in the other direction. I pretend that if I attack a topic that scares me to death, fictionally, it's like a good-luck charm – and I've got immunity from it in real life. (Which means, if you've read my other books, you realize that clearly my children are well protected from all sorts of horrors!) So yes, I had to definitely step back and think of the book from an overseer's perspective . . . but only sometimes. When I started thinking like a mom, I became too sympathetic to Nina. When I stopped thinking like a mom, I wanted to lock her up for life. I think readers will veer between the two extremes, and book clubs will come to blows over them. But actually, that's okay with me. Because the question I am asking is not an easy question, and it shouldn't have an easy answer.

## Book Club Discussion Questions
### for *Perfect Match*

1) Disguises figure prominently in *Perfect Match*, and what you seem to be is not always what you are. Discuss.

2) What is the metaphorical significance of Caleb's job?

3) Immediately after shooting and killing Father Szyszynski, Nina says repeatedly, 'I did what I had to do'. Do you think she really felt she had no other choice but to do it, to protect her son as well as for the greater good, as she claimed? Or was it just to aid in her defense?

4) Was Nina justified in her actions, or was she 'simply a reckless woman who thought she knew better than anyone else'? Was she morally right to do what she did? Is there a difference?

5) Do you feel Nina's sentence is a fair one, or do you think the judge was too lenient? Why?

6) In what ways do some of Caleb's and Nina's domestic moments foreshadow the bigger differences between them?

7) Compromised trust appears to be an issue at play for some of the characters in *Perfect Match*. Discuss each of the characters affected. Who will have the most difficult time learning to trust again?

8)  During the course of the story, did you feel Caleb was supportive enough of Nina? Was his anger justified?

9)  In your opinion, which person involved in the case has the most selfless motives? Discuss.

10) What has Quentin Brown learned from his involvement in Nina's prosecution? Explain.

11) What is the metaphorical significance of Nathaniel's silence?

12) How far would you be willing to go if you discovered that someone you trusted molested your own child, or a child you love deeply, knowing that the justice system does not often work in favour of the child? Would you be capable of murder? Can a person really know oneself enough to be sure, if it's never happened to them?

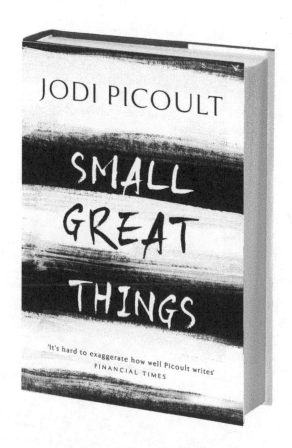

# *Ruth*

The miracle happened on West 74th Street, in the home where Mama worked. It was a big brownstone encircled by a wrought-iron fence, and overlooking either side of the ornate door were gargoyles, their granite faces carved from my nightmares. They terrified me, so I didn't mind the fact that we always entered through the less-impressive side door, whose keys Mama kept on a ribbon in her purse.

Mama had been working for Sam Hallowell and his family since before my sister and I were born. You may not have recognized his name, but you would have known him the minute he said hello. He had been the unmistakable voice in the mid-1960s who announced before every show: *The following program is brought to you in living color on NBC!* In 1976, when the miracle happened, he was the network's head of programming. The doorbell beneath those gargoyles was the famously pitched three-note chime everyone associates with NBC. Sometimes, when I came to work with my mother, I'd sneak outside and push the button and hum along.

The reason we were with Mama was because it was a snow day. School was canceled, but we were too little to stay alone in our apartment while Mama went to work – which she did, through snow and sleet and probably also earthquakes and Armageddon. She muttered, stuffing us into our snowsuits and boots, that it didn't matter if she had to cross a blizzard to do it, but God forbid Ms Mina had to spread the peanut butter on her own sandwich bread. In fact the only time I remember my mother taking time off work was 25 years later, when she had a double hip replacement, generously paid for by the Hallowells. She stayed home for a week, and even after that, when it didn't quite heal right and she insisted on returning to work, Mina found her tasks to do that kept her off her feet. But when I was little, during school vacations and bouts of fever and snow days like this one, Mama would take us with her on the B train downtown.

Mr Hallowell was away in California that week, which happened often, and which meant that Ms Mina and Christina needed Mama even more. So did Rachel and I, but we were better at taking care of ourselves, I suppose, than Ms Mina was.

When we finally emerged at 72nd Street, the world was white. It was not just that Central Park was caught in a snow globe. The faces of the men and women shuddering through the storm to get to work looked nothing like mine, or like my cousins' or neighbors'.

I had not been into any Manhattan homes except for the Hallowells,' so I didn't know how extraordinary it was for one family to live, alone, in this huge building. But I remember thinking it made no sense that Rachel and I had to put our snowsuits and boots into the tiny cramped closet in the kitchen, when there were plenty of empty hooks and open spaces in the main entry, where Christina's and Ms Mina's coats were hanging. Mama tucked away her coat, too, and her lucky scarf – the soft one that smelled like her, and that Rachel and I fought to wear around our house because it felt like petting a guinea pig or a bunny under your fingers. I waited for Mama to move through the dark rooms like Tinker Bell, alighting on a switch or a handle or a knob so that the sleeping beast of a house was gradually brought to life.

'You two be quiet,' Mama told us, 'and I'll make you some of Ms Mina's hot chocolate.'

It was imported from Paris, and it tasted like heaven. So as Mama tied on her white apron, I took a piece of paper from a kitchen drawer and a packet of crayons I'd brought from home and silently started to sketch. I made a house as big as this one. I put a family inside: me, Mama, Rachel. I tried to draw snow, but I couldn't. The flakes I'd made with the white crayon were invisible on the paper. The only way to see them was to tilt the paper sideways toward the chandelier light, so I could make out the shimmer where the crayon had been.

'Can we play with Christina?' Rachel asked. Christina was six, falling neatly between the ages of Rachel and me. Christina had the biggest bedroom I had ever seen and more toys than anyone I knew. When she was home and we came to work with our mother, we played school with her and her teddy bears, drank water out of real miniature china teacups, and braided the corn-silk hair of her dolls. Unless she had a friend over, in which case we stayed in the kitchen and colored.

But before Mama could answer, there was a scream so piercing and so ragged that it stabbed me in the chest. I knew it did the same to Mama, because she nearly dropped the pot of water she was carrying to the sink. 'Stay here,' she said, her voice already trailing behind her as she ran upstairs.

Rachel was the first one out of her chair; she wasn't one to follow instructions. I was drawn in her wake, a balloon tied to her wrist. My hand skimmed over the bannister of the curved staircase, not touching.

3

Ms Mina's bedroom door was wide open, and she was twisting on the bed in a sinkhole of satin sheets. The round of her belly rose like a moon; the shining whites of her eyes made me think of merry-go-round horses, frozen in flight. 'It's too early, Lou,' she gasped.

'Tell that to this baby,' Mama replied. She was holding the telephone receiver. Ms Mina held her other hand in a death grip. 'You stop pushing, now,' she said. 'The ambulance'll be here any minute.'

I wondered how fast an ambulance could get here in all that snow.

'Mommy?'

It wasn't until I heard Christina's voice that I realized the noise had woken her up. She stood between Rachel and me. 'You three, go to Miss Christina's room,' Mama ordered with steel in her voice. '*Now.*'

But we remained rooted to the spot as Mama quickly forgot about us, lost in a world made of Ms Mina's pain and fear, trying to be the map that she could follow out of it. I watched the cords stand out on Ms Mina's neck as she groaned; I saw Mama kneel on the bed between her legs and push her gown over her knees. I watched the pink lips between Ms Mina's legs purse and swell and part. There was the round knob of a head, a knot of shoulder, a gush of blood and fluid, and suddenly, a baby was cradled in Mama's palms.

'Look at you,' she said, with love written over her face. 'Weren't you in a hurry to get into this world?'

Two things happened at once: the doorbell rang, and Christina started to cry. 'Oh, honey,' Ms Mina crooned, not scary anymore but still sweaty and red-faced. She held out her hand, but Christina was too terrified by what she had seen, and instead she burrowed closer to me. Rachel, ever

4

practical, went to answer the front door. She returned with two paramedics, who swooped in and took over, so that what Mama had done for Ms Mina became like everything else she did for the Hallowells: seamless and invisible.

The Hallowells named the baby Louis, after Mama. He was fine, even though he was almost a full month early, a casualty of the barometric pressure dropping with the storm, which caused a PROM – a premature rupture of membranes. Of course, I didn't know that back then. I only knew that on a snowy day in Manhattan I had seen the very start of someone. I'd been with that baby before anyone or anything in this world had a chance to disappoint him.

The experience of watching Louis being born affected us all differently. Christina had her baby via surrogate. Rachel had five. Me, I became a labor and delivery nurse.

When I tell people this story, they assume the miracle I am referring to during that long-ago blizzard was the birth of a baby. True, that was astonishing. But that day I witnessed a greater wonder. As Christina held my hand and Ms Mina held Mama's, there was a moment – one heartbeat, one breath – where all the differences in schooling and money and skin color evaporated like mirages in a desert. Where everyone was equal, and it was just one woman, helping another.

*That* miracle, I've spent thirty-nine years waiting to see again.

# Here's what I know about me as a writer: I would write no matter what – even if there was no one out there to read what I'd written.

But the fact that you are there? That's amazing.

I love to hear from you. If you want to let me know what you thought about the questions I raise in this novel, or find out more about what I'm doing next, here are some easy ways to stay in touch:

- Follow me on twitter @jodipicoult
- Like my Facebook page
  www.facebook.com/JodiPicoultUK
- Visit my website www.jodipicoult.co.uk, and sign up to my newsletter.

Thank you for reading!

The best books live on in your head long after they are finished. As you read, you are turning the pages faster and faster to find out what happens next, only to feel bereft when you reach the end.

If that is how you feel now, you might like to join us at www.hodder.co.uk, or follow us on Twitter @hodderbooks, and be part of our community of people who love the very best of books and reading.

Whether you want to find out more about this book, or a particular author, watch trailers and interviews, have the chance to win early limited editions, or simply browse our expert readers' selection of the very best books, we think you'll find what you're looking for.

And if you don't, that's the place to tell us what's missing.

**We love what we do, and we'd love you to be part of it.**

www.hodder.co.uk

@hodderbooks

HodderBooks

HodderBooks